A Connection is Forged

SOMETHING PERSONAL WE *can use against her.*

"Something that will drive her insane."

He closed his eyes and delved into the places of Stephania's mind she kept hidden, even from herself.

A horrible laugh bubbled up from his throat. *This place is riddled with Corrupt Magic. Someone's been a bad little dragon.*

He followed the corruption as it led him to the heart of New-Fars, to one fateful day when the Magic had taken over her, spilled out from her, and turned her into a murderer.

Though Stephania had left New-Fars, she had left a piece of herself there—a form of the Corrupt Magic. It was just enough to prepare an attack so horrible and twisted, it would haunt her for the rest of her life.

Thaddeus drew a hand down one of the spines that grew from Kyrell's tail as it curled around him. "Tomorrow, they march for Trans-Falls while I pay New-Fars a special visit for a bit of unfinished business. Then our little game will finally begin."

Dragon Bone Publishing titles by Effie Joe Stock

The Shadows of Light Series

Child of the Dragon Prophecy

Heir of Two Kingdoms

Anthologies
(as editor)

Aphotic Love: An Anthology on the Depths of Romance

Other Publications

What Darkness Fears Anthology (Twenty Hills Publishing)

Fool's Honor Anthology (Twenty Hills Publishing)

A Sky of Tragic Moons (Nathaniel Luscombe & SJ Blasko)

Here Lies Wanderland (Alex Silvius & SJ Blasko)

HEIR OF
TWO
KINGDOMS

EFFIE JOE STOCK

Second Installment of <u>The Legends of Rasa</u>

©Copyright 2023 Effie Joe Stock

Heir of Two Kingdoms

Book 2 of The Shadows of Light

ISBN:

979-8-9860641-6-1 (paperback)

979-8-9860641-7-8 (ebook)

979-8-9860641-8-5 (hardback)

Published in Hackett, Arkansas USA by Dragon Bone Publishing 2023.

Cover and illustrations are created by and copyright of Effie Joe Stock.

Edited by H.A. Pruitt.

Publisher's Note: This novel is a work of fiction. Names, characters, places, and incidents are either products of the author's imagination, or used fictitiously. All characters are fictional, and any similarity to people living or dead is purely coincidental.

To Tron,

The Trojan to my Stephania, my greatest friend who taught me to run with the wolves.

And to anyone else who forged an unbreakable bond, only to find that nothing is invincible.

"While you remember the light, and while the Light is still in this world, believe in the light, so that you might then become *The Shadows of Light.*"

—A Long Forgotten Teacher

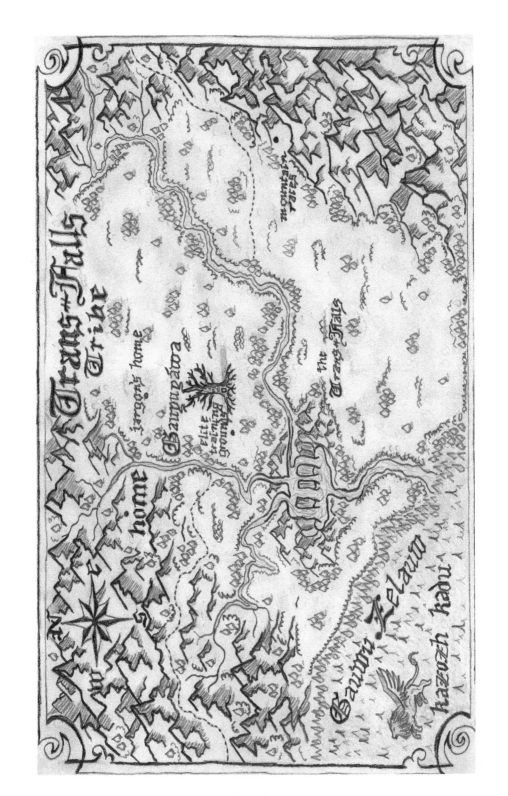

Trebuli Galli

the Trei'a

Banupátoa

fargois home

Iei temoíne

the
Crang-Fals

home

Paunud
Bemelen
a'i'a

Gawm Felaru

kazuzh kadu

Pronunciation Guide & Glossary on pages I-VIII in back of book.

Bonus Content on Pages 403-409

BOOK 2

THE SHADOWS OF LIGHT

HEIR OF
TWO KINGDOMS

EFFIE JOE STOCK

MEMORIES THAT ELUDE

Eta Stronghold in North Ventronovia

Sometime after Stephania left New-Fars

DARKNESS SWIRLED, SILENCE the only answer to hundreds of questions he wanted answered. If only he had something to hold on to in this abyss, something he could latch on to, to draw her to him.

A shooting stab of bright red pain pierced the darkness, but he pushed past it, focusing only on the color of the pain. *Red.* A faint vision of a mother, father, friend, and child came into view. It was a family, but not his family. It was *her* family.

Red drew his attention to the child. Red curly hair moved gently by a soft breeze. Bright red eyes staring, staring into his soul, burning his soul. He remembered the first day he laid eyes on her—the perfect Duvarharian. But he had failed her and himself.

He pushed back the pain of that day, refusing to bear it yet again, and reached instead to a different memory.

Laughter filled the darkness, and the family came back into focus. The smell of roasting mountain goat filled his mind and made his mouth water. Their conversation—dark, elusive, distant—was barely audible. Some of it was easy to comprehend, like when dragons were mentioned or the setting suns behind them. But some of it wasn't, like when new laws or impending attacks were discussed. It was as if a veil was between him and them making it all hard to grasp, as if he had the mind of a lesser creature.

Gritting his teeth, he forced himself further into the vision. An explosion of pain tore through his mind, but he pressed on until he was surrounded by darkness again.

He opened the eyes of the body he'd entered.

Everything was much different from his new perspective. His eyes glanced across the patio and into the mountainous room. Distantly, he felt as the body his consciousness was in shifted its wings, a single black feather falling to his feet. The four-winged crow moved forward into the doorway, its keen eyes taking in the scene, though none of the room's occupants seemed to notice its presence.

A child with flaming red hair sat in a raised chair at the table, waving her chubby arms as she laughed at something the young man sitting across from her was saying.

Stephania. The deep voice of his dragon penetrated the memory and into his mind.

Yes, it is her. A hunger welled up inside Thaddeus as he fixated on the little girl. So much raw power was stored in that small body, and here she was, food across her cheeks and gripped tightly between her fingers. *And her family.* He hardly cast a glance at the mother and father—two riders he knew better than any others. *But who is the man?*

He wanted to slink into the room, blend into the shadows or into the rocky cracks of the cave home, but the crow whose body and memories he was still inhabiting, did no more than bounce from one foot to the other and eye the breadcrumbs on the floor with hunger.

Frustration bubbled up inside him until the young man stood, bringing his face into sight. As soon as he spotted the man's golden eyes, his black hair, and the scar under his jaw, hatred boiled inside him. He tried to thrash out at the man, wishing nothing more than to separate his head from his shoulders, but the four-winged crow's body did not respond.

Instead, he poured all his hate into every curse he could think of. If he had been in his own body, he would've spit acid in the young man's face. *Syrus Vespucci.*

Thaddeus's dragon wasn't nearly as bitter as he. *The rider of the Sun-Flash Dragon, the military commander, dining and playing with the child of the Dragon Prophecy. How ... intriguing.* The deep drawl of Kyrell's thoughts calmed Thaddeus.

Indeed. He resisted the sardonic laugh welling up inside him.

Intriguing, yes, but it was nothing of special interest to him. He was tired of exploiting the meaningless memories of the degenerate, mindless creatures that subjugated themselves to him. He wanted more. He wanted Stephania's memories.

Taking a deep breath, he released his hold on the crow's memory, and in only a moment, the abyss of nothingness surrounded him. He sensed nothing to reach out onto—no memories, thoughts, or emotions. Holding back a curse, he concentrated on the words to go into *Dasejuba*—the path between all realms, time, space, and matter— and focused on one memory, the only memory he shared with Stephania.

The screams and battle cries of Centaurs exploded around him. The smell of a damp forest flooded his senses, and he reeled, trying to grasp on to the familiarity of his own body, of his axe and magic.

He could sense none of it.

Instead, he felt only the flailing incompetence of a young child. Then, through the screaming, thrashing bodies, and the splattering blood, all was still, and he found himself looking up into his own purple eyes through Stephania's.

A sense of awe filled him as he sensed the young Stephania's fear and hatred turn into curiosity as his own voice from those many, many years ago drifted down to her.

"Do not worry, sweet child ... I will never harm you ... You have nothing to fear."

A strange emotion welled up in him. He had nearly forgotten how he had felt when he held the young girl in his arms. Now, as her curiosity turned to trust, he felt it again.

That boiling desire filled him, and he held on to the memory tighter. It was just a memory, but he longed to change its outcome. He knew what was coming next, and everything in him revolted against it.

The memory of him looked up, rage pouring from every inch of him. "You are too late, Igentis. Stephania is mine."

Fool. I was a fool. I should've taken her right then. Siv, he cursed inwardly, gritting his teeth.

The memory played out just as he remembered it.

Magic exploded, tearing through everything, before darkness consumed it. All he felt was excruciating pain. But, in that moment, in that space of time when his hands had still clung to the young girl, defying all attempts of her being taken away, he felt a door open. It was small, like the door a mouse might use if it could.

Without wasting another moment, he thrust himself back into his own memory and forced his magic through the door to block it open. Looking back, he spotted crack of red shining through the door, and could feel the presence of the young girl on the other side.

A ripple of victory surged through him. The door, he knew, was a rip between their consciousnesses—an opening between space, mater, beings, and time. It was like a sliver of *Dasejuba* between him and Stephania—a pathway of memories.

Extending his hand, he tried reaching through the cack. A force pushed him back, but he persevered. Reaching further, he felt an orb touch his hand. Without thinking or hesitating, he grasped onto it and felt as his consciousness was once more raked into a nothingness.

Again, he was in a child's body—Stephania's. The memory was tainted, broken somehow. Shatters and muted colors clouded the images instead of being crisp and clear. From her mind, no one was familiar, but from his own consciousness, he easily recognized a few of them: Artigal, Frawnden, and Aeron. A younger Centaur was there too, and another older one. However, he didn't recognize them, and so left them to drift away. A great congregation of Centaurs stood before them, and vaguely he heard Artigal pronounce Stephania adopted into the Centaur tribe. Then the memory shattered, and he was thrown back into the darkness once again.

So, she went with the Centaurs. But why? Why didn't they immediately contact Syrus or Dalton?

I don't know, Kyrell, he answered. *But with this connection, with these memories, I can find out.*

Again, he forced his hand through the door, but this time, an explosion of immense pain coursed through his body, throwing him away from the door and out of that dark nothingness.

Gasping, he opened his eyes and clutched his chest. It took him a moment to grasp his bearings. He was back in his throne room in the Eta stronghold. It was night, and the moons' light poured through the window behind him, casting eerie shadows around the dark granite hall. The stone throne beneath him dug into the sore spots in his back and legs.

Cursing, he looked down at the wound on his chest. The white veins under his skin glowed brightly. The light burned his skin, his soul, his mind. The wound was nearly identical, he was sure, to the one his spies had seen on Artigal.

"Curse the gods of Wyriders and Men. So this also prevents me from accessing the magic I need to travel across the very path it made."

Or rather the path Stephania made. I do not think it was just Shushequmok—Pure Magic—that made such a path. For there to be room for creation, there must first be destruction.

"Then I shall try again, and again, and again until I regain control over my magic find what is keeping her hidden from me." He closed his eyes and whispered the spells under his breath, but a low growl interrupted him.

Thaddeus ... do not be rash. You cannot try again so soon. You are not strong enough. Additionally, the borders grow weak. Our people need your leadership.

Thaddeus gritted his teeth and dragged his eyes back open. Slow movement in the dark shadows behind the throne room's many pillars caught his eye, and he watched with pride as his soulmate moved into the moonlight.

The glinting eyes of the Acid Dragon blinked slowly once then twice before his rumble shook the walls.

You've been wandering the dream realm for over four days. There is more to conquering a world than what can be done inside the mind.

Thaddeus laughed but winced as the movement brought throbbing pain to his chest. "Perhaps. But you know as well as I do that, between dragons and riders, we riders were made to control the mind and you dragons the body."

Kyrell's tail slid across the floor as he dragged himself to his feet. *Mayhap, but we are still a team. When you have made an appearance to the Human Domain and gathered more supplies for our own kingdom, then I will let you succumb to the mind once again. But you cannot now. Do not think I don't feel the pain your body gives you.*

Thaddeus's eyes darkened as he caught sight of the shadowy white wound on his dragon's chest—the ghost of his own.

Pulling himself from his throne, his hand brushing over the annoyingly long stubble that had grown across his chin, he limped down the steps and over to the dragon. Staring into the swirling purple eyes of the great beast and feeling the immeasurable bond between them, he slid his hand down the length of Kyrell's jaw he could reach. A sly smile curved his lips.

It is as if the gods finally graced us. We finally have what we need to find her, after sixteen years of being captive to pain and failure. Now, if we can just find a way to heal ourselves from this Pure Magic, we won't have to bother with the drivel of humans and petty Etas.

It was hard to tell which was speaking—the dragon or the rider—since their minds were almost as one.

Perhaps we will find that too through the door that just opened.

Perhaps.

And until then, we wait.

Patiently, as we have been for the last eight hundred years.

What is another one hundred years? Only mortals fear time.

Thaddeus stared into the moons, wondering if across Ventronovia, Stephania was looking up into their light as well.

"I'm coming for you, Stephania," he hissed through his dark smile. He extended his hand to the moons as if reaching out to grab them and her. "No matter where you are, I will find you. You are *mine*."

PART ONE
Remember Me

CHAPTER 1

Just outside of Trans-Falls, Centaur Territory

Year: Rumi 6,113 Q.RJ.M.

Present Day

WHAT'S WRONG? *If you said my name, surely you must remember, despite the spell ... Sister ..."*

Stephania clenched her eyes against the words that repeated themselves over and over in her mind, mocking her. *Gods of all, why didn't I just say I didn't know him? Why did I have to say his name? Of course he would think I remembered if I had said his name. And why did it have to be him? Why not any other commander?*

Her shoulders sagged, and she gripped Braken's reins tighter. They were slowly making their way to Trans-Falls. The Centaur battalion Trojan had been leading demanded they escort her and Dalton back to the tribe. Many Warriors and Centaurs they passed on the journey had bowed low before her, muttering "Farloon" under their breath, but she had done her best to ignore them. The last thing she wanted was to be the center of attention right now.

Even so, despite the sickening feeling of regret and dread that refused to leave her, she couldn't help but feel a certain amount of awe at what was going on.

She was with *Centaurs*—half man, half horse creatures. They were real. They were walking with her. Talking, laughing, *existing* almost carefree all around her. Like Duvarharians, they weren't just some stories in a book anymore. The sound of their hooves on the soft forest floor, the long, curved ears, and the horse-like snorts and grunts that sometimes came from them were almost impossible to believe. Every chance she got, she tried to sneak glances. A few caught her staring at them, but even more, she caught them staring at her. She was sure they were just as enraptured by her own physic as she was theirs, which only made the whole experience stranger.

Dalton was riding just ahead of her and conversing in low tones with a Centaur commander by the name of Landen. Apparently, he had traveled with Aeron many years ago when Stephania was being taken to New-Fars. Everything they were discussing and all the many names they mentioned sounded fascinating, though a bit too complicated to understand. Despite how hard she tried, none of it sounded familiar. She busied herself with braiding a few strands of Braken's mane.

Vulnerable.

She shuddered at the word whispering itself to her from the dark corners of her mind. *I cannot be vulnerable.* And yet, without her memories and surrounded by those who *did* remember her, she was very much vulnerable ... and helpless. It seemed some of these creatures knew her better than she knew herself. Once again the spiraling feeling of losing control washed over her, and her breath caught in her throat. She struggled back the rising lump in her throat and forced herself to look at the scenery they were passing.

The trees had begun to grow larger and stranger. They reminded her much of the trees in the cursed forest back at New-Fars, giving the unnerving impression that, if you stared at them long enough, they would grow faces, open their eyes, and speak.

The flora began to look more exotic as well. Each flower seemed to glow with its own light, and with a bit of magical prodding, Stephania realized they each contained nearly 100 times more energy than the average flower possessed.

A shining blue creature shot from the bushes on her right and disappeared deeper into the forest. She jumped at the sound, her heart racing with more than just momentary fright. The creature had looked like a rabbit, but something about it had been much different. Quickly, she glanced around to see if anyone had been as surprised as her.

No one batted an eyelid.

So it was a common creature, then. She settled back in the saddle in awe. Part of her temporarily forgot about what she had been dreading as she thought of all the wonderful new things she would find in Trans-Falls.

"Stephania!" Dalton's yell snapped her back to the present. She blinked her eyes in surprise as he laughed. "I don't mean to yell, child. I just couldn't get your attention."

She blushed as the Centaurs accompanying them laughed. "I'm sorry," She fiddled with the reins.

"It's fine of course. I was just saying that creature is a *Ñáfagaræy*. They're usually nocturnal and actually have four eyes to see better in dim lighting. Obviously, we scared it out of its nest."

She nodded, her eyes wide. *Four eyes! How absurd!* She tried to think of anything else she knew of that had four eyes but couldn't come up with anything.

"So, you really are Stephania—Aeron and Frawnden's daughter." A new voice grabbed her attention, and she looked around for the speaker, her eyes resting on Landen as he glanced back at her, his face emotionless.

"Um. Yes," she drawled uncertainly. "I am."

He narrowed his eyes at her, and his tail swished twice before staying still. "So you are the child who Aeron was so eager to return to that he traversed through crowded woods and mountains for months on end. Alone."

Heat rose into her face as she shifted uncomfortably. Her eyes met Dalton's, and he frowned. She quickly looked away. "I guess so."

"And you really don't remember him? Or Frawnden? Or Trojan?"

He had obviously been a close witness to the spectacle between her and Trojan and wanted to see if she was truthful or if she had pranked him. He was clearly very protective of Trojan, despite the young Centaur being his senior commander. She wondered just how many Centaurs she was going to offend for something she couldn't even control.

"No. I do not. I have no recollection of any of them, or of this place."

His face remained stony as he turned back to lead them, saying nothing more.

A knot twisted itself in her gut, and what little reprieve she had felt watching the woods fled from her. She could feel Dalton's eyes staring at her, willing her to look up, but she ignored his gaze.

As they continued, the trees started thinning ever so slightly until they broke out of the woods at a fork in the road. Just to their right, the edge of a cliff jutted out before them. Her breath caught in her throat.

The cliff streaked down below them, tumbling and turning as it leveled out into small ledges before diving back down toward the grassy plains below. Until this point, the massive, ancient trees had obscured any view of the horizon, but now, Stephania could see for miles over the vast valley stretching out before them, protected on either side by rolling hills and small mountains.

From here, she could partially observe the large tribal city of Trans-Falls. A few little dotted houses and working tents were visible through the dense trees, each in a strategic and artistic order. Some ruins alluded to what might have been a larger city at one time, but even so, the city was still expansive.

"Standing here, you can see that the roads, buildings, and trees were designed to spell out the Sházuk words for 'One ruler'. Many of the buildings making it up are gone, but the trees remember."

Dalton laughed and shook his head in amazement. "And I thought Duvarharians were the only ones who liked trimming their bushes and buildings to mean strange things."

Stephania chuckled, and he turned back to wink at her. "Things are a little different here than in New-Fars, aren't they?"

Her smiled flickered to a frown as she nodded. Things were certainly different, but when it came to her, she felt she would remain the same: outcast.

She pushed the thoughts from her mind and once again focused on the land. Winter had begun to release its cold hand, the snow had already melted and the buds of plants yearning to wake from their freezing slumber, had sprung to life. The valley blooming with life and beauty filled Stephania with overwhelming wonder. New-Fars had never looked this full of splendor. It was as if everything here was *more* than back in New-Fars: the sky a little bluer, the clouds a little softer, the trees a little taller and greener. Even the new grass waved in the wind like a softly rolling sea.

"It's magnificent," she whispered, trying to see it all at once.

She was surprised when Landen answered her. "Truly, it is." He crossed his hands behind his back and stamped his hoof. His eyes surveyed the land, and she didn't think she had ever seen someone look at a place with so much love. She wondered if her parents had once looked at Duvarharia that way or if she herself had ever looked down on Trans-Falls that way.

"You have an incredible home here, Landen."

He turned to her, the sparkle in his eyes fading. "As do you, Farloon."

A shiver ran down her back, and she nodded quickly, suddenly eager to be moving again.

Dalton, picking up on her uneasiness, broke the still silence. "Well, shall we continue on?" He spurred Austin on, riding slightly ahead until Landen broke his gaze from her and followed.

Gritting her teeth against the churning in her stomach, she clicked to Braken and urged him forward.

"It'll be nice to sleep in a bed once again and eat good food again, right, Stephania? Perhaps Aeron and Frawnden will let you try their *uafañoshigo* wine." Dalton twisted in the saddle to look back at her, and she shrugged before nodding eagerly. It would be. It had been ... six ... no, seven months? How many had gone by since they had left New-Fars? How long had it been since she had called a place home?

Too long.

At least they had been able to take the most direct route to New-Fars. She remembered Dalton telling her how other roads from New-Fars to Trans-Falls could take a year or more. She felt a certain amount of sympathy for the Centaurs who were forced to take the longer routes to stay hidden from humans and other magic hating travelers. *I wonder which route the Centaurs took when bringing me to Dalton.* It was an interesting question to ponder until she remembered she had supposedly lived in Trans-Falls at one time.

Landen's words rang in her mind again. *"As do you, Farloon."* Perhaps she had once called this place home, but it didn't feel right to now. Not after she had crushed Trojan, her Centaur brother's, hopes that she still remembered him. If only Artigal hadn't taken away her memories all those years ago. If only she could've met Trojan differently, when she hadn't been so nervous or tired. Perhaps, if she had just been given time to talk to him first, or even, perhaps, if they had seen Artigal and he had given her memories back as soon as she got here, then all this would've been different. But none of that had happened. Instead, she was stuck in this horrific, numb reality.

Curse fate, destiny, and all the gods.

As they traveled, she tried to focus on the scenery, memorizing the twists and turns of the road, though she knew it would take many days of traveling through the forest for her to remember even a small portion of it. The trees, though so different and unique, were all so strange and twisted, it was hard to tell them apart after a while.

She could hear Landen and Dalton conversing ahead of her, exchanging news on recent battles, trading routes, and whatever piqued Dalton's interest regarding the history of the land around them.

The road turned to a decline as they zig-zagged down the mountainous cliffside. Sometimes they were traveling among trees, and other times they were out in the open air. Sometimes they were treading upon sticks and leaves, and other times lush green grass or rocky, pebbled paths.

The path was quite steep and treacherous in some places. Braken's footing rarely faltered, but, when it did, or they came to a particularly narrow path, Stephania and Dalton would dismount and lead the horses until they came to another place where they could ride alongside the Centaurs again.

After a while, she began to realize that the majority of the Centaurs who had been escorting them were gone. Now, only a few remained, and most of them were older.

She looked around to see if she could spot any of them off the path, but they were traversing a narrow walkway, and she couldn't see more than a dozen Centaurs.

"Where did they go?"

"Who?" Dalton asked, only half listening, his concentration on the last stretch of difficult path ahead of them.

"The younger Centaurs who were with us."

Landen laughed for the first time that she had heard. "They have gone to the races."

"The races?"

13

He nodded. "The mountain races. Probably to impress a certain young Duvarharian."

A raging blush decorated her cheeks, but before Dalton or Landen could further her embarrassment by their jests, a horn resounded from one of the cliffs behind them and echoed throughout the valley.

"Ah. And so they begin." Landen struggled and failed to hide the humor that sparkled in his eyes.

Stephania followed his gaze. Nearly thirty or forty young Centaurs were positioned at the edge of a steep cliff, lined up as if to run their race—Stephania realized with horror—straight over the edge.

She pulled back on her horse's reins, turning the buckskin around to face the cliff. "What are they doing?" Her mouth hung open in horror. It looked like mass suicide.

"Running a race, Dragon Child, apparently in your honor."

Her heart slammed in her chest. "No, no, no. How do you know that?" She turned her wide eyes to him, but he looked so inexplicably calm, as if this kind of thing happened regularly.

"Listen to their chant. It is for you."

Sure enough, they were chanting something and stomping their hooves on the rocks. The beat echoed louder than the horn, and a strange wildness coursed through her veins at the sound.

Landen was translating the chant, but she hardly heard him other than the words, "... for the Dragon Child, the Farloon, to prove our worth ..."

A second horn rent the air, and the Centaurs were silent, crouched, and ready to launch themselves off the cliff.

The hot blood in her turned cold. "They can't do that! They'll kill themselves. It's insane!"

"Yes, it does seem a little foolish." Landen's face was solemn as ever, but she didn't miss the glint of vicious pride in his eyes. Realization dawned on her; this occurred regularly, and most likely wasn't as dangerous as it seemed. The realization did nothing to ease her fears, however. She most certainly didn't want them risking their lives for some ridiculous race in her honor.

But with no power over the circumstances, she merely turned her awestruck face to the cliff as a Centaur shouted the countdown in their language. A nervous chuckle bubbled in her lips when he stalled his counting, causing a few of the Centaurs to lurch forward, their hooves sliding dangerously close to the edge. A few rocks tumbled down the steep slope as if taunting them with the danger of the trek.

Then, with one last shout, the Centaurs leapt in a majestic cascade of hooves, bodies, manes, and tails.

It was breathtaking, the agility of the Centaurs and the strength and disciplined control with which they galloped down the treacherous cliff. All fear left her as she watched the dust fly and the rocks tumble down the hill before and after the Centaurs. As the racers neared the end, she found herself almost wishing it would never end. It was too beautiful to watch but too beautiful to stop as well. In that moment she truly realized she was in a different world. No longer was she in New-Fars where magic and mythical creatures were naught but bedtime stories. It was real, and she was real along with it. Subconsciously, she was aware that her life had just been turned upside down.

She quickly found herself cheering on a gold and black appaloosa Centaur, her heart racing with them as if she too were pitting herself against them and the mountain.

Just as it seemed the appaloosa Centaur would finish last, he leapt high over a ledge all the others had galloped around and soared over the majority of his opponents. He nearly fell but caught himself in time before putting on an extra burst of speed. He crossed the finish line in a close second with only a dark brown Centaur in front of him.

With roaring cheers, the others crossed as well. Shouts and battle cries along with their congratulations for each other filled the air.

Stephania's blood coursed through her veins, a strange knot in her stomach. She wanted to run over to them, congratulate them herself, and smack a few for doing something so dangerous in her honor. She wanted, she realized with surprise, to be a part of them.

"Go."

Red curls bounced around her face as she turned her head, her eyes wide and staring into Dalton's soft gaze.

"Go to them. Make some friends. You do belong here, after all. This is your new life. Don't let it slip through your fingers."

Her attention fell back on the sweaty, gleaming bodies of the warriors, and her heart raced as she caught a few of them staring at her with wide, awestruck eyes. "Is it really okay? Do you think they'll make fun of me?"

He followed her gaze, and she could feel worry radiating from him but also anticipation.

"No. They won't. I'm sure of it. Instead of a monster, you are a dream come true to them. And you are no more unusual to them than they are to you. That, at least, is something you will have in common. Go, my child."

A Centaur waving her over caught her attention. She distantly felt Dalton's warm hand on her arm, but she couldn't tear her eyes away from the stamping hooves, swishing tails, and the hand beckoning her, pleading her to come over.

Swallowing, her heart slamming in her chest, she nudged Braken forward into a slow walk. Everything in her screamed to run away, to disappear into the forest and never let her face be seen again. The bullying, hateful remarks from the humans all through her childhood rang in her mind, tying knots of hesitation in her stomach. She fought the overwhelming urge to turn back. But something Dalton had promised her a long time ago echoed in her mind.

"Friends. Will I have friends, Uncle Dalton?"

A frown tugged down his lips. "Yes, I'm sure you will, Stephania. I'm sure you will."

Despite everything that had happened to her in New-Fars, she had always held out for it. For a long time, she resented him for saying those words, thinking he had been lying, but now she knew he had only meant eventually. Eventually, she would have a place to belong and friends with it. That time was here—now—and she was terrified. To make friends would mean to take off the mask of hardened apathy she had worked so hard to build in New-Fars. Without it, did she even know who she was? Would she even be able to remove it long enough to make friends? Was it even worth it?

As Braken's hooves dug into the soft dirt and grass, bringing her closer and closer to the Centaurs, they quieted, their gazes turning to her.

She felt their eyes burning holes into her as she let Braken slow to a stop. She didn't look up from the bit of mane entwined with her fingers. For a long, awkward, anxious moment, only silence could be heard. Finally, she lifted her eyes and smiled nervously, shoving aside the instinct to stare them down with practiced hate. "Hello."

No answer.

The mask instantly snapped back into place, and she felt her heart go cold. *Gods of all, why did I come over? Surely, they don't care about me. They probably think I'm a freak, a monster, a mutant with only two legs. In a moment, they'll all burst out laughing and jeering, and everything I ever believed about myself being an outcast will still be true. Curse them.*

"Dragon Child." A quiet, meek voice spoke up, startling Stephania from her spiraling thoughts. She frantically searched for the speaker. A female Centaur who looked about Stephania's age, pushed to the front of the group. Stephania instantly recognized her as the Centaur who had beckoned to her. "Welcome." With a fist over her heart, she bowed low, extending one of her front legs forward.

Instantly, the other Centaurs followed suit until they were all bowing before her, utterly still and utterly silent.

Stephania's mouth went dry, and she felt her cheeks burn. "Stand up," she whispered, but not loud enough. Had this not been the very thing she had begun to thirst for from the New-Fars villagers—fear and respect? It was here in front of her, but it twisted uncomfortable emotions in her gut. This was wrong. She didn't deserve this.

16

She cleared her throat, and Braken shifted nervously under her. "Please," She pleaded before sucking in a deep breath. "Please stand up."

One by one, they stood, their eyes shining and a few of them whispering amongst themselves.

The female extended her hand, and Stephania found herself reaching out to grip her forearm. Their eyes met, and Stephania saw nothing but peace, comfort, and awe in the female's eyes. There was no hate, no fear, no malice. "Welcome to Trans-Falls, Dragon Child."

CHAPTER 2

A SMILE OF DISBELIEF BLOOMED hesitantly across her face as Stephania's stomach filled with a new nervousness. "Thank you. May the suns smile upon your presence." Her voice sounded much more confident than she felt. However, as soon as the words left her mouth, she instantly regretted using the saying. *What if they don't say that here? What if they think I'm too foreign and strange? What if–*

But her fears were unfounded as the Centaur beamed and responded eagerly. "As do the stars sing upon yours!" She didn't let go of Stephania's arm, though, and only gripped harder. "My name is Lamora."

Stephania grinned. "Stephania."

The Centaurs whispered amongst themselves at her name, but she sensed no mockery in their tones, only wonder.

"Lamora, if you don't let go of her arm, she's going to lose feeling in it." A sturdy-built male moved to Lamora's side, his eyes sparkling humorously.

A blush raged on Lamora's cheeks, and she quickly let go, muttering her apologizes as she tucked a lock of dark hair behind her ear.

Stephania recognized the Centaur as the appaloosa she had secretly rooted for, and her heart beat wilder. "You're the Centaur who won!"

He chuckled and modestly shook his head. "Second, actually. Lamora here won."

Stephania's eyes widened. She hadn't been paying close attention, but now that he mentioned it, she easily recognized Lamora as the first place Centaur.

The female warrior smirked and elbowed him in the side. "Finally beat you, *gume-wa.*"

"Only until next time."

A look passed between them that caused Stephania to blush, but she didn't inquire after it since the two of them didn't seem to notice and she was sure it wasn't her business.

"Are you going to introduce yourself or are you just going to drool over her legs?"

Lamora stuck her hands on her waist and jutted out a back leg, swatting him with her tail.

A fiery blush painted his cheeks as he snapped his eyes away from Stephania's legs and tripped over his words trying to assure Lamora he wasn't staring.

"Ravillian. My apologies, Dragon Child. You are the first Duvarharian I have laid eyes on." He quickly stuck his hand out, and Stephania gripped his forearm, equally as embarrassed as him, but much more amused.

"Don't worry about it. You all are the first Centaurs I have seen, and I know I've already done my fair share of staring, though I don't think I'm any less amazed. And please, just call me Stephania."

Ravillian's dark eyebrows shot up. "But I thought you used to live—"

Lamora shook her head and quickly interrupted, completely brushing aside Ravillian's comment. "Stephania is fine. Beautiful name, really. Very Duvarharian."

Stephania breathed a sigh of relief, and Lamora winked at her.

Is this how friends act? Is this how you make friends? Do I even have a right to have friends?

Ravillian coughed and nodded before laughing. "Stephania it is, then." He tipped his head at her, and her heart skipped a beat.

Then, in a whirlwind of excited introductions and foreign names, she was introduced to every other Centaur present. A few quickly grew quite attached to her and, as she steered Braken back to where Dalton and Landen were waiting, they followed, excitedly telling her everything they could about their beloved Tribe. Despite how difficult it was to keep up with nearly three Centaurs talking to her at once, she was grateful for the knowledge.

"You've picked the perfect time to arrive here. The *Luyuk-daiw* is positively the most incredible Centaur festival of all, even if the land spirits don't wake anymore. It's not something you would want to miss for anything. The music, dancing, lights ..." After the Centaur finished an especially descriptive explanation of the spring equinox feast *Luyuk-daiw,* which was fast approaching, Stephania laughed with the other Centaurs as he blushed. He was obviously very passionate about their festivals.

"Listening to you all makes me feel as if I already know Trans-Falls so well." She instantly regretted the words as they left her lips.

Ravillian's smile faded into a confused frown. Again, he tried to broach the subject. "What about when you were—" But again, he was interrupted by Lamora as she quickly shouted for everyone to look up.

Stephania, thinking it was just a convenient distraction from their conversation, was awed to see hundreds of small hummingbird-like creatures buzzing in the giant trees above them. Only these weren't regular birds; these *glowed*.

Red, blue, green, yellow, and orange birds populated the treetops above them, their light so bright, it was easy to see even in the midmorning. The Centaurs whooped and hollered in excitement, and Stephania had to yell to be heard. "What are they all so excited about?"

Ravillian didn't turn his face away from the birds as he answered. "They're the *Leño-kofolu*—the spring singers. They only come out after the last snowfall before Spring. Their arrival marks an important time in the Centaurs' lives. It used to be that after they appeared, the land spirits would begin awaking as well and the whole forest would be awake and alive with them. Usually, they would collectively choose the *Luyuk-daiw* festival to do so since the Centaur's traditions revolve a lot around the forest's magic."

"Land spirits?" Stephania laughed as a bird swooped down and buzzed all around Braken's face.

"The tree and water spirits."

"Oh, the Forest Children? Aren't they supposed to be extinct or something?"

Ravillian and Lamora stopped dead in their tracks, their eyes wide as they faced her.

Something like horror shadowed Ravillian's face. "Yes, the Forest Children. But by the stars, they aren't extinct!"

Lamora frowned. "They might as well be."

He scowled at her. "But they aren't."

"What happened, then?"

"Long, long ago, a creature used a dark magic against them. Since the forest spirits are almost entirely soul and magic, the dark magic forced them to near death in something we call the Sleeping. They haven't been seen since."

The memory of a Faun's ethereal yellow eyes flashed before her; a chill ran down her spine. In the cursed forest back in New-Fars, that Faun had given her what Dalton had called the *Zelauwgugey*—the Forest Essence. *The Lyre*. The weight of the instrument now strapped to her horse was suddenly monumental. "Is there anything that can break the curse?"

Lamora stamped her hoof. "If there even *is* a curse. I think it's just a forest tale told to keep little foals from cutting down trees or building dams against the rivers."

"You doubter. Your parents clearly didn't believe in the Great Emperor."

Lamora shrugged and looked away from him. "Maybe not. All I'm saying is, I'm not convinced."

Ravillian frowned but didn't pursue the debate. "According to the legends, there was a Lyre, the one called *Zelauwgugey*, or translated to the common tongue, the Forest

Essence. Apparently, it was some sort of Sházuk relic that held power over the forest. From what I've read, it was used as a weapon once, and after that, its power was twisted and used to enforce the Sleeping. Supposedly, it is the only thing that can reverse the curse, but no one knows what happened to it. Many assume it fell under its own curse and now only exists in the spirt realm, unable to be used. Some think it passes through this realm, only partially existing in the spirit realm and partially here."

Stephania felt as if everything around her had slowed. *A weapon. It had been used as a weapon. And now it only partially exists.* Her hand subconsciously strayed to where it rested in the saddle. A low humming filled her senses, dulling everything else, drawing her in. Dalton had said that while she would be able to see it regularly, the Lyre would remain invisible to others unless she was touching it. Since that was true ... *Am I the only one who can use it? As a weapon and to waken the forest? The Luyuk-daiw is a festival that once surrounded the awakening of the forest. Is it destiny or coincidence that it's only a few weeks away, if even less–almost the same time I've arrived in Trans-Falls?*

"Stephania? Dragon Child!"

Stephania snapped out of the trance to see both Ravillian and Lamora's worried gazes fixed on her. "Sorry, what?"

"You blanked out for a moment. We had to yell to get your attention." Lamora moved her hand from Stephania's arm.

"Are you well?"

Stephania rubbed the back of her neck and forced her mind from the Lyre. "Yes, I think so. Let's just talk about something else. Talking about the curse is making the forest look a little grim." She forced a chuckle, but it didn't sound very convincing.

Lamora shot Ravillian a look that clearly showed how much she didn't appreciate his talk of dark lore, and he just as clearly tried to ignore it.

Looking ahead and wishing the atmosphere wasn't suddenly awkward, she caught Dalton looking back at her. When their eyes met, a broad grin swept his face and he cocked his head to the side, asking how she was.

Meeting his grin with her own, she nodded and mouthed, "Thank you."

Smiling tenderly, he turned back to his conversation with Landen before Stephania was quickly assaulted by the questions Lamora and Ravillian poured on her about Dalton.

All too soon, her emotional encounter with Trojan and the dark talk of the Lyre slipped from her mind. But the darkness of dread always hung in the back of her mind, much the same way her hardened mask waited, ready to be used in the event that these new friends turned against her.

Landen's voice rang out over the excited whispers of the Centaurs around them. "Behold, Dragon Riders, the greatest Centaur tribe in Ravenwood—Trans-Falls!"

CHAPTER 3

STEPHANIA'S BREATH CAUGHT in her throat as they peaked over the crest of a small hill and Trans-Falls stretched out before her. It was even more beautiful here than it had appeared on the cliff.

Most of the buildings were artful log cabins with sprawling gardens and intricately carved signs displaying the name of the residents or the building's use. Numerous tents of all different shapes, sizes, and styles filled the land; some were permanent and others temporary; some were colorful and others a simple earthy color. With the mixture of styles and decoration every way she turned, Stephania didn't think she could ever have imagined a place more full of culture and diversity.

"It's beautiful, isn't it?" Lamora sighed dreamily as she followed Stephania's gaze over her tribe.

"Yes." Stephania pulled gently on the reins so she could take in the full view for as long as possible. "It's so ... diverse!"

Ravillian laughed, his eyes sparkling. "I suppose it is, especially compared to the human cities. Trans-Falls has long been the center of Centaur culture, going back thousands of years. It's only right that so many lifestyles have come to rest here."

"How do they not blend into one culture?" It seemed impossible that so many different creatures could exist in one space and not mix into one societal structure.

"Stubbornness and pride."

"Two traits of which Ravillian has inherited full shares of." Lamora dodged his playful swipe, and they all fell into fits of laughter.

But amongst their joy, a darker thought stirred in Stephania's heart. *Is it okay to be enjoying myself like this? Do I have a right to this kind of happiness? Or friends like this? Can I really be friends with them? Are they even my friends? How would I even know?* But she wasn't given more time to let it fester before Dalton called out to them from farther down the road, hurrying them along.

As they made their way down onto the main road through the industrial area, Stephania's eyes swept from Centaur, to building, to flower, to sky, and then to the treetops where hundreds of little *Leño-kofolu* sang and flew. A feeling of wonder and awe welled up inside her. With vines stretching from the tall trees down to the ground and the rooftops, glowing lizards running up and down the vines, and the trilling birds flitting through the trees, it seemed like a place found only in a faraway dream.

When Ravillian and Lamora got into a lighthearted argument about the lizards, Dalton slowed his pace to ride alongside Stephania.

"How are you?" His deep brown eyes searched hers and she was somewhat surprised to see so much worry behind them.

"What? Oh, I'm ... fine, actually." Her answer stunned her, but it was true. Ravillian and Lamora, though a tad overwhelming at times, were pleasant to walk with and she found their insincere arguments comical.

"Are you sure? Are they treating you alright?" Skeptically, he glanced over to the two Centaurs as they dissolved into laughter.

A small smile spread across Stephania's face as she chuckled at the Centaur friends. "Yes. They are. I like them a lot."

Dalton grunted and nodded curtly. "Good. If they say anything that even remotely makes you uncomfortable though, you let me know, alright?"

"I will, Uncle Dalton. Thank you."

A broad smile decorated his face. "You never have to thank me, child. It's my pleasure and my duty." With a gentle nudge to Austin, he quickened his pace to ride beside Landen once more.

A warm feeling of safety bloomed in her. *Despite our differences these last few months, I'm glad he's here with me.* She urged Braken over to the friends and laughed with them as they explained their petty debate while continuing to journey farther into Trans-Falls.

The deeper they traveled into the tribal city, the more the residents took notice of her. The crowds around them had become increasingly thick, forcing them to slow their travels. Landen called something out in their native tongue, and instantly, a path parted for them.

Through the path and the bodies gathering around her, Stephania spotted a large clearing where a huge tree had once grown, its dead, hollow, refurbished trunk still towering majestically in the center of the city.

"The *Gauyuyáwa*. The heart of Trans-Falls," Dalton breathed out in awe. The name struck something in her, something close to familiarity, but it quickly fled her. She tried to think nothing of it, but it disturbed her.

As their small procession continued, Stephania realized with unease that the crowds had gone silent. Even Lamora and Ravillian's pleasant chatter had ceased, their faces solemn and reserved.

Only one word was whispered on the tribe's lips now: Farloon.

Someone shouted it as loud as they could, and for a single, still moment, no creature in the forest moved. Then, with the kicking of dirt and the sound of hundreds of moving bodies, each and every Centaur, male or female, young or old, big or small, bowed, even Lamora and Ravillian. It took her a moment to stop looking around for some great leader and realize they were bowing to *her*.

Her face, ears, and neck burned, and she couldn't help but wonder if she was as red as her hair. Quickly, she bowed her head, trying to hide her face, desperately wishing she was wearing her cloak with the hood.

With confusion, she watched as Dalton halted his horse, dismounted, and knelt as well. Though he wasn't kneeling to her. The other Centaurs around them rose and then bowed once again, but this time in the direction of the *Gauyuyáwa*.

Not wanting to look ignorant or out of place but also not wanting to bow to someone or something she had no knowledge of, she quickly dismounted Braken and whispered for him to stay put before making her way through the bowed Centaurs around her.

How do they stay so still? she wondered with unease but shoved the thought aside. Only after she had picked her way past Landen and Dalton and was standing at the base of low stairs did she realize why they were bowing.

It was Artigal: as beautiful, sparkling white, wise, and strong as the legends had described him.

She sucked in a sharp breath but refused to bow. Something deep in her told her she was not obligated to. A mix between anger, depression, relief, and joy nauseated her.

Her feet moved with a mind of their own, she confidently took the steps two at a time until she was on the platform with him. She was faintly aware that all the Centaurs of Trans-Falls were watching her with piercing gazes. A sense of fear washed over her, but she realized it wasn't her own. It was the fear of the Centaurs because she stood before their highest leader without respect.

But she did not fear.

Though she remembered nothing of the Igentis, she felt a special significance in her at the sight of him. With a growing sense of unease, she realized, at this point, he knew more about her than she did herself. This realization made her want to run as far away from here as she could. But something made her stay. Something familiar dragged her to this place, to Artigal.

Awe settled inside of her, for though she knew she had once lived alongside him, this was her first time to really meet him—Artigal, the thousand-year-old Centaur, the

Igentis of the United Centaur Tribes, and the Centaur who had saved her from Thaddeus. This was the Centaur who had given her a family and then saw fit to take it all away. She had no room for fear. Clenching her teeth, her hands in fists, she forced her eyes to meet his.

A mixture of all the colors of the spectrum converged into a blinding white light in his gaze and burned her eyes. She cried out and covered them but couldn't shut out the images flashing before her. She felt the wooden platform against her knees as she fell.

"Me yuwuk fezh, Stephania."

"I'll give them back to you some day. I promise."

"I love you, Stephania! I will always be waiting here for you! Please don't forget me!"

When the visions and pain had subsided, she chanced to look up at him.

Her eyes met his, and she saw something that totally contradicted her expectations of indifference and anger: fear and hope.

A burning rage filled her as she stared up into his eyes. Hastily, she pulled herself to her feet, her hands clenched into fists. *How dare he stand there and refuse to apologize for what he did, after all the pain he has caused. How dare he say nothing! How dare he be fearful!* A strength coursed through her as anger welled up inside her. "Get away from me, traitor." The words jumped from her lips before she could stop them.

Artigal's face hardened, but not in his own anger—in hurt.

His obvious pain stabbed her like a cold knife. *Why am I angry at him? He did what he thought was right. Even Uncle Dalton had agreed. So why do I feel this rage when I think of him? Why have I always?* She took deep breaths to calm herself, but her mind refused to lie still. The rage riled up, trying to consume her, and a strength grew in her—the same strength that had powered her in New-Fars. This anger, this rage, it wasn't hers; it was something else. Everything went hot, cold, and then quiet as she panicked. The faces of the dead villagers flashed before her eyes; bile rose in her throat as she thought of all the Centaurs who could be hurt if she let that demonic power feed off her resentment and overpower her again. *Not again,* she whimpered to herself, but the anger would not leave now that it had taken root.

Abruptly, a voice pierced through her thoughts. The words from a distant memory repeated in her mind. *"I'll give them back to you some day. I promise."* Somehow, she knew it was Artigal's voice. She was sure of it.

His multicolored eyes pleaded with her to listen. A strange gentleness reached out and touched her mind. Wildly, she recoiled from it and stumbled away, but the peace emitting from Artigal surrounded her, and as soon as she let it touch her mind, the anger dissipated, along with the demonic power.

She was left feeling drained, dizzy, and embarrassed, but she didn't have time to recollect her thoughts. A strong hand grabbed hers and raised it above her head. Difficult as it was, she forced herself to listen to the words being projected out over the stunned and confused tribe. She could only imagine how strange her and Artigal's encounter must have appeared to the onlookers, but she couldn't worry about it; at least, she tried not to.

"Trans-Falls! Farloon Stephania Lavoisier, adopted child of Aeron, your Chief, and Frawnden, Second High Medic, has returned!"

With a deafening and chaotic roar, the crowd erupted into cheers and celebration as the word spread.

Struggling to find solid footing despite Artigal's firm grip on her hand, she blushed, her hands shaking nervously as her eyes wandered to anywhere but the Centaurs around her.

Artigal released her hand and placed his on her shoulder, as if wary she would lash out at him again.

Turning her attention to him, though unwilling to meet his gaze after her violent display of uncontrolled rage, she smiled meekly.

"Welcome home, child." His smile faltered for a moment as he searched her face before he suddenly turned away.

Her heart and shoulders sank. She didn't know what she had been hoping to see in his gaze, but instead, she had seen the same search for familiarity Trojan had looked at her with. Both had found her eyes void of it. Whatever Artigal had done to her memory, he had done it well. Besides her waking nightmares, and despite being in the very place full of the memories she had lost, she had no recollection of anything from her past.

She wanted to call after him, to apologize like she should have to Trojan, but to what end? It wasn't her fault. It was his. Who would she be apologizing for?

"Stephania!" A musical, ecstatic female voice split through the crowd, and the young Dragon Rider's head snapped around from watching Artigal disappear into the forest to face where the new voice had come from.

"My little dragon! By the stars, you've come home." A buckskin Centaur, one who bore an uncanny resemblance to Trojan, broke out from the crowd, a dappled grey male only paces behind her. She took the stairs nearly four at a time in her haste. Her arms reached out when she mounted the last step, and with a cry of joy, she embraced Stephania. Her tears dampened the young woman's cheeks, and her foreign words of praise and welcoming tickled her ears. She smelled strongly of herbs and spices, and for just a fleeting moment, Stephania remembered something like this years and years ago. But it faded into unfamiliarity, and the claustrophobia of being in a stranger's arms gripped her mind.

Stephania resisted the urge to shrink away. When the female Centaur finally pulled away, Stephania clearly saw the hurt and mourning.

"Forgive me," she quickly muttered and stepped back, her tail swishing anxiously. "I am out of place. My name is Frawnden." She held out her hand in formal greeting, and Stephania hesitantly gripped her arm. "I am your mother."

The words caused Stephania to freeze. *Mother. She is my mother. My mother.* Over and over and over again, the words pounded in her mind. She had never heard someone call herself her mother before, at least, not that she could remember. A mix of emotion flooded her—one she couldn't begin to decipher.

"And this is Aeron, your father." Frawnden quickly stepped aside, pulling her arm from Stephania's, who merely stood in a daze.

The dappled grey Centaur stepped forward, and this time, Stephania had to crane her neck to look into his eyes. He seemed taller than the other Centaurs, but, as her eyes quickly darted to the crowd, she realized he only seemed that way compared to the Centaurs she had meet thus far. A surprising amount of difference in height and body types ranged amongst them, and she wondered if it was due to their mixed culture.

"Stephania?" Dalton's soft voice and touch jerked her back to reality, and she stuttered trying to find out what she had missed. "Aeron was introducing himself to you. Did you hear him?"

Awkwardly, she shook her head and stuck her hand out to grip his. "No. No, I'm sorry, I was thinking about ... something else." Her cheeks burned as she met Aeron's eyes and was disappointed in herself when she saw the betrayal in his eyes. It was clear her first impression had been one of apathy toward him. Her heart sank deeper within her.

"It's nice to meet you, Aeron," she mumbled and then added under her breath, "again."

His brows furrowed, but he only nodded solemnly. "You as well, Stephania." He made sure to step away from her, and she felt the distance between them like a chasm.

However, she could feel Dalton close behind her, and she reached her hand back to him, relieved when he gripped it in his and gave an encouraging squeeze.

"Stephania, I am fully aware you do not remember us." Frawnden's voice quivered, but she pushed past it, holding her head proudly. "And it is a tragedy, but years and years ago, from the time you were about one and a half years old until we gave you to Dalton, we were your adopted parents. I suppose, by all law, we still are. At least, until you turn eighteen years."

Stephania found herself unable to meet their eyes and instead fiddled with a loose string on her shirt. She could feel her face burning, and she wanted more than anything else to just run away and hide.

"Now, I know this is a lot for you to take in, but Aeron and I would like you to come stay again with us in our home, at least until you or Dalton make other plans."

Everything in her was frozen. She couldn't make herself move, speak, or even think. The words *"We were your adopted parents ... and still are,"* rang in her head like New-Fars' noonday bells.

"We would love that." Dalton put his arm around her and gave her a little shake. "Wouldn't we?"

"Huh? Oh, yes. Of course," she muttered, barely aware of what she had just agreed to.

Gently, he guided her to Braken and held the horse's reins still as she mounted.

"See you later, Stephania!" Ravillian and Lamora called after her, and she subconsciously waved back before they quickly disappeared into the crowd. *Will I see them again, or were they only being nice since I am Farloon and the Chief's daughter?*

"Do you want me to ride beside you?" Dalton's hand on her thigh snapped her back.

"Um ..." A frown dipped down her lips. *What do I want?* She wanted to be alone but didn't at the same time. It was too new and unpredictable of a place to be alone, but she also didn't feel like having to speak or explain her feelings right now. "No, I'm fine."

His eyes searched her face. "Are you sure?"

Before she could change her mind, she nodded choppily. He nodded before quickly mounting Austin and nudging the horse on ahead. Frawnden and Aeron were already waiting on the other side of the platform.

"Wait, Uncle Dalton?" She was surprised when he heard her whisper and turned back.

"Yes?"

Just as she was opening her mouth to ask him to ride with her, something stopped her. *Don't be vulnerable. Be strong. Don't be anyone's problem. Don't attract attention or pity.* The habits she had formed in New-Fars raised their ugly heads, and she blanched. "Never mind." She forced a smile onto her face and tried not to notice the unconvinced look in his eyes. "I'm fine."

His eyes darkened, but he didn't press her and instead continued on.

She hated herself for misleading him and wished she could ignore the sudden emptiness settling in her, but as she watched Dalton strike up a conversation with her Centaur parents, she knew the less anyone had to deal with her and her memory loss, the better.

Though she herself didn't feel better about it at all, she clicked her tongue and heeled Braken into a slow walk, just fast enough to keep the others in sight. As the forest closed in around them, she had the unnerving sensation she was being watched, but when she scanned the brush and trees around her, she saw no one.

CHAPTER 4

Gauyuyáwa

Trans-Falls, Centaur Territory, Ravenwood

Present Day

I GENTIS, ARTIGAL." THE SEASONED Warrior knelt before his leader, doing his best to stave off the fury that had risen within him after Stephania's welcoming ceremony. His fists clenched and teeth ground against the venomous words he longed to let free. That wretched look of unfamiliarity, of *fear* Stephania had given him festered with his anger and ate at his heart like rot, but he shoved it further down inside him. His duty as a Synoliki Warrior came first.

"Yes, Trojan?" Artigal didn't move to face him, and Trojan didn't blame him.

The air between them burned hot with tension.

"I sense the forest moving in its slumber. Something it desires has moved into it." He paused to look at his markings. They were once more burning a bright glowing blue, just as they had months previously.

"Yes, the *Zelauwgugey*. It is here in Trans-Falls." Artigal finally turned from the decorated walls of the *Gauyuyáwa* to face Trojan, and though his face was stony and unreadable, his flashing, colorful eyes betrayed the hurt inside him. Trojan had no pity. It was his sister who had been lost, not Artigal's.

"The forest is calling to the *Zelauwgugey's* holder. It demands to be played."

"Indeed, it does. And do you know who it was given to?" Artigal's eyes pierced his, and he swallowed.

A confusing turmoil of emotions and realizations crashed over him. He doubted any creature of the forest would entrust the faithless Dalton to carry such an important relic, and the only other creature who had arrived in Trans-Falls recently was Stephania. A part of him rejoiced. She could play the Lyre and awaken the forest. But that spark of hope quickly darkened. She didn't remember anything of the forest or the dangerous magic surrounding it. In her hands the Lyre wasn't just an instrument of salvation, it was also one of extreme destruction. His face paled.

"I see you understand the gravity of this situation."

Trojan nodded numbly.

"Now, I cannot take the *Zelauwgugey* from her. She must come to its power in her own time. However, I sense a darkness about her—"

Trojan wasn't listening. The emotion he had tried so desperately to lock deep down welled to the surface. "This is all your fault. She would have her memories if it weren't for you. She wouldn't be a danger to the forest if it weren't for you." His voice went quiet as his eyes met Artigal's.

He sighed as if too tired to want to think about this. "Yes."

Anger sparked in Trojan at Artigal's seeming indifference. His hands shook and bile rose in his throat. "She didn't remember me, Artigal." His voice trembled with fury before quieting with horror. "I called her my sister, thinking that if she had said my name, that she remembered me. But she cringed from my touch." He looked at his hands as if they were stained with blood. "She was scared of me, uncomfortable with me. I was nothing more than a stranger. Everything we had been through was just ... gone." His hands clenched into fists. "Do you even understand that?"

"Yes, I do."

Trojan's sword materialized in his hand, the blue blade burning with energy. "How could you?" He leapt to his feet. "How could you possibly understand? You are nothing but an unfeeling statue. You know nothing of feelings, pain, grief. You have lived for thousands of years, watching creatures die, many of whom you sent to their deaths without second thought. Everyone and everything is just a pawn to you, just a number on a war sheet. How could you understand what I, what my whole family, is having to go through? You lost nothing!"

"*Zuru zhor*, Trojan!" Artigal's calm pretense exploded, and his eyes burned a fiery orange. "Don't assume what I know or do not know of. *You* know nothing about *me*. I have loved and lost more deeply than the trenches of the ocean and the pits of Susahu."

His words stung but Trojan didn't flinch.

"Just leave, Trojan. This isn't helping anything."

"No."

Their eyes locked and neither moved. Artigal's hands trembled with suppressed emotion as Trojan's eyes blurred with tears.

"I won't. Not until you give her back to me. If I have to stand here a thousand years until you bring her back, I will." He raised his sword in front of him. "This is all your fault. All of it. I should have never trusted her to you. That day the Susahu Viper attacked her, I swore to protect her, no matter what, and I failed. But I swear now, I won't fail again."

Artigal's face contorted in an array of emotion as his mouth opened then closed. When he spoke, his voice trembled. "No, Trojan. You did not fail her. *I* failed her. But it needed to be done. You must understand that. The only way she has been safe these past long years has been because of this. You must know that. Your sacrifices through this, all our sacrifices through this, have kept her safe."

Trojan lowered his weapon, and his shoulders sank. Artigal stepped forward slowly and placed a hesitant hand on the Warrior's shoulder.

"I know. I know." Trojan gazed at the Centaur who had trained him and raised him when his father hadn't been able to; his heart softened. Quiet tears trickled down his cheeks. "Then bring her back. You have to promise me you'll bring her back to me. Please."

Artigal clenched his jaw and quickly turned away, shaking his head. "I cannot promise bringing her memories back will bring back the girl you remember. She may still reject you."

"Please, Artigal. You have to."

Artigal covered his face with his hands. "I don't know if I can. But I will try. I promise I will try."

CHAPTER 5

"STEPHANIA, ARE YOU COMING IN?" Frawnden's guarded voice pulled Stephania from the trance she had settled in at the bottom of the steps ahead of her.

"Huh? Oh. Yes. Of course." It took too much effort to push the words out of her mouth and drag her eyes up the steps to meet Frawnden's.

The Centaur woman frowned before nodding and forcing a smile on her kindly face. "Alright, then. Come in whenever you're ready."

Stephania nodded once and watched as her Centaur mother slipped into the cabin, the door clicking shut behind her.

"If I'll ever be ready," she whispered but then instantly regretted her negative attitude. This was supposed to be an adventure. It was supposed to be new and exciting, a journey where she could find out who she was.

It was nothing like that.

She let Braken's reins fall from her hands, and he wandered a few paces before hungrily tearing up the grass around the porch.

Slowly, almost guiltily because she knew she should be inside with the others, she sat down on the bottom step and propped her head up on her hands. Her gaze wandered mindlessly over the treetops and across the valley.

When she had found out she was a Dragon Rider, she had expected to be able to start a new life, to be someone else. However, coming to Trans-Falls and having to face her missing past head on showed her that would not be the case. Instead, she had to deal with filling the shoes of a little dragon girl she never remembered being.

She groaned and let her head drop to her knees as she hugged her legs to her chest.

Braken snorted, blowing a few strands of her hair into her face, and nibbled her arm.

A smile reluctantly curved the edges of her lips, and she scratched his chin just where he liked it.

"Well, shall I go in?"

He shook his mane, but she wasn't sure what he was trying to tell her.

"Aeron said he'd come to get you after you grazed for a while." With deft fingers, she slid his bridle off and hung it on the end of the stair railing. "Good boy," she murmured as he shook his head and wandered off to eat the grass again.

As she stared up the long steps, she couldn't help but feel their size and shape, designed to be easy for Centaurs to climb up, only made them more intimidating.

Even so, she was at the top before she wanted to be, the large doors looming ahead of her. Voices from an open window drifted out to her, and she caught her name.

Deciding against going inside just yet, she slipped over to the window and leaned her ear close, careful to not be seen.

A vaguely familiar male voice was speaking in quiet tones and, if she didn't know better, she would've thought he was crying.

"... please. You don't understand ... I can't. No ... Please not tonight."

Frawnden was urgently pleading with the male, but he was adamant.

Hoofbeats echoed through the room, coming closer to the door, and Stephania panicked. She neither wanted to be caught eavesdropping nor seem like she was avoiding anyone any more than she already was, so she did the only other thing she could think of and opened the door.

Blue eyes stared down into hers, and her mouth opened, but no words came out. She clutched the open door's handle tighter.

The room went silent. The air was thick with tension.

"Trojan," she managed to choke out.

Emotions flashed over his face faster than lighting as he stared down at her. His mouth opened, then closed, then opened again, but he didn't speak. His fists tightened, and his tail swished from side to side.

"I'm sorry." She quickly sidestepped him, giving him room to move past her.

He didn't make any effort to step through, and she felt heat rising into her face. From the corner of her eye, she watched his jaw clench before his shoulders sagged and he quickly stepped outside, shutting the door rather loudly behind him.

She swallowed painfully and looked up, meeting the staring eyes of the others in the room.

Her throat suddenly dry and her eyes rather watery, she decided to let them speak first.

Frawnden, who looked as if she were going to cry, simply covered her mouth with her hands, muttered something about dinner, and trotted to the kitchen.

"He won't be joining us for dinner tonight," Aeron forced out with a smile. "Something about needing to take care of some Synoliki business or something." The look on his face told her he knew it was obvious he was lying, but no one said anything more before he too disappeared to the kitchen.

Only Dalton was left.

"I'm glad you decided to come in, Stephania." His smile was warm and sympathetic, and it melted her heart.

"Thanks." Her answer was pathetic and she knew it.

He closed the space between them, wrapped his arm around her, and steered her through the large living room, past the doors to the kitchen, and toward the dining room.

"I know you don't remember it, but Aeron and Frawnden assured me that everything here is almost the exact same way it was last time you were here."

A stab of pain riddled her. She should be feeling a wave of comforting familiarity about being *home*. Instead, she had been denied it. Now she only felt disquieted.

"Really? Do they never change anything?" She turned back to the living room, eyes roaming, taking in the rich wood tones, lanterns, tasteful Centaur furniture, and animal skins from fierce creatures like the *Zelauw-fafu* and *Raffudafaf* Dalton used to tell her stories about. A spiral staircase to her right led up to a balcony. Just beyond the staircase was a hallway leading into the mountain. The doors they had entered through were on the opposite wall of the hallway—the east facing wall; just to the right of the doors were massive windows, then a fireplace, then more windows. It was open, yet secluded, giving a feeling of fresh warmth and comfort. A strange sense of disassociation settled over her as if she were looking at this room through eyes not her own.

"Did you hear me?"

"Huh?"

Dalton's warm eyes were worried, and she realized they had stopped walking so he could turn to look at her.

"I said, they're not home often because Aeron has to lead the wars and Frawnden is a front-line medic."

"Oh." For some reason, the topic no longer seemed as interesting, and she was glad when they reached the dining table. The feast before them offered a distraction she was grateful for, small as it was.

"Why is there so much food?"

"To celebrate!" Frawnden walked into the room in time to answer her, her arms laden with even more dishes. Aeron quickly helped her set them down.

"What? How did you know Uncle Dalton and I would be arriving today?"

The smile faltered on Frawnden's face. "Well, actually, we were planning on celebrating Trojan's return."

"He just got back from the Human Domain today," Aeron finished for her.

Stephania's heart plummeted, and her blood ran cold. *Of course. How could I be so stupid?* Her fingers twirled the loose string on her shirt, pulling the stitching out even more. "I'm sorry."

"No, no, no." Frawnden shook her head. "It's not something to bother the *Ñáfagaræy* with. Trojan was just too tired to eat with us tonight is all. Nothing to be sorry about."

Aeron turned his face away, and Stephania found it hard to meet either of her Centaur parents' faces. The hurt behind their eyes was unbearable, and she wished more than anything to plead fatigue and run away as well.

As if he could read her mind, Dalton squeezed her shoulders and gave her a little shake. "His loss. His feast looks fit for a Duvarharian Lord."

Aeron seemed to catch Dalton's attempt to save the rest of the evening and forced a smile on his face. "Well, I am High Chief of the Centaurs after all. Which is similar enough."

Frawnden laughed and smacked her mate with one of the napkins. "And you let it go to your head far too often."

Stephania couldn't help but smile ever so slightly and graciously took her seat, bowing her head as Aeron praised their Great Emperor.

Though the air was tense as everyone did their best to avoid delicate topics, it was a relatively lively meeting. Stephania had never tasted so many different types of food and found Centaur cuisine much more to her liking since it utilized more herbs and spices than she had been accustomed to back in New-Fars. Frawnden and Aeron had also pulled out an aged case of tart *uafañoshigo* wine, which Stephania found also suited her palate just fine.

While Dalton, Aeron, and Frawnden had a lot to talk about concerning Centaur politics, Human Domain issues, weather, and some rumored sightings of wild dragons in the Cavos Desert, Stephania had been more than content to simply fall into the background and listen.

Eventually, the candles burned low as the suns set outside, and Stephania found herself nodding and yawning more than eating and talking.

"Oh, excuse me. Let me show you to your room, little dragon." Frawnden helped Stephania up from the table, her touch warm and motherly, and, though unfamiliar, Stephania found it somewhat comforting.

She didn't remember much after that except Dalton leaving to bring in her packs and Aeron telling her Braken was taken care of and wishing her good night. Then

Frawnden helped her into bed, covered her with a soft fur, and kissed her forehead. It wasn't long before she slipped into a dark, disturbing sleep.

§

"KILL HER."

His dragon roared as he watched the Lord struggle to keep his wife from running blindly into death. Her screams filled the air when the cries of her dragon fell silent. He could feel the blood running down his dragon's throat—his throat. He felt as his dragon grappled with the now silent Combustion Dragon.

Then something hit him, almost knocking him to the ground. He screamed with pain as he felt sharp nails dig into his skin, poison dripping across his body, flowing in his veins.

He gritted his teeth against the burning in his back. He was holding back her hand from his neck, her knife inches away from his skin, green poison dripping from its blade.

With a groan of exertion, he commanded his magic to overcome her poison and bend reality. The rocks moved and shifted around them, the ground below them mirroring the sky, making it seem as if they were floating upside-down with the earth above their heads. Four hazy images of himself shimmered to life as he struggled to pull her off him.

Her eyes widened in fear at the clones of him. Her hand around his neck slipped, terror filling her as the images drew their axes.

But they faltered, one by one. He could feel the poison wreaking havoc on his concentration.

His reality confusion failed, and she wrenched her hand out of his, managing to drive her knife into his arm.

He blanched, tried not to scream, tried not to give her the satisfaction of his pain.

But he knew she wouldn't win. Time was on his side. He could feel the death creeping in her, especially the death of her dragon. He could hear the screams ringing through his mind, could still taste her blood in his dragon's mouth. He felt the hole inside the woman and the hole inside the magic realm. The death of a dragon was no small thing. It was dragging him down, pulling him in.

He threw her to the ground and staggered away, but her knife caught his leg. He cried out before aiming a kick at her. She dodged and lunged at him again. Her eyes were dull, lifeless. She was dead inside. Only half of her lived. The other half lay dead with her dragon.

It hurt too much to hold her gaze.

With a resounding ring, his axe met her knife, but she was hard to predict. She fought like a wild animal. He knew he couldn't win—not alone.

His mind dragged. He took another cut to his shoulder. The world spun around him. Everything slowed down. The hole where the dragon once stood in the magic realm continued to pull him in. He was too deep into the essence of magic itself to escape it. He had torn open too many holes in that realm, and now they were beginning to catch up to him. Soon, he wouldn't be able to escape.

His pain he let fill him. His anger he let consume him. The power rose within him. The evil grew, spread, possessed.

His eyes snapped open. The poison fled from his mind as something else stepped in– something stronger–someone stronger. Evil seeped into his being, empowering him.

With a flick of his hand, he sent the woman flying against a rock, her body cracking against the solid mountain, her motionless figure sinking to the ground.

The Lord struggled after her.

Another quick motion of his hand left the man screaming, frothing at the mouth, withering on the ground. The man's devastating aguish filled him with power as the evil fed on it. With a cruel laugh, he approached the riders, ready to watch them die.

§

STEPHANIA WOKE WITH a muffled scream and bolted upright; her sheets were soaked from a cold sweat. Her hand covered her mouth as she struggled back a sob. The images from the nightmare replayed over and over in her mind—all the blood, poison, screaming dragons, dying people, and deep chasms opening to swallow her whole.

Tears streamed down her face as she drew her knees to her chest, her shoulders shaking.

She had been the murderer in the dream. *Or was it a memory?* It had been her magic lashing out against them and her dragon who killed the other. And yet, it hadn't been her; she was sure it had been someone else. But it had been so vivid for a dream. *Too vivid.*

Her nails dug into her skin. Her head throbbed, her magic raging against her control. It felt as if she were standing at the edge of a powerful whirlpool that threatened to drag her down into the pits of Susahu. It was the same feeling she had felt in the nightmare when the dragon had died, and even though the dream had ended, the feeling hadn't left her, as if the chasm were real and it desired her as a sacrifice.

The shadows in her room caused her to jump, and she quickly decided she didn't want to be there anymore.

Carefully feeling around her while peeling the sheets off her clammy body, she touched the edge of a nightstand and used it to steady her as she stood.

A sharp pain shot through her hand, and she recoiled with a yelp, flashes of violent knives and swords from her nightmare taunting her as she forced herself to take deep breaths, fighting against the impending panic.

The moonlight from the window caught the splinter in her hand; little purple light rays danced across the room as she studied it. Her stomach did a somersault as stabbing anguish tore through her chest. She gasped, dragging her nails across her hand, trying to scratch the splinter out as quickly as she could. *Gods, no, no, no.* Sobs racked her body as she slid down her bed to the ground, struggling to take a breath.

Purple eyes flashed before her. A purple axe streaked through the air. They tore into her body, her mind, her soul, stabbing, seeking, searching for something.

The pain was unbearable, and nothing she did lessened it. Finally, she slumped to the ground, cradling her head in her hands, choking on her tears and muted cries for help until the visions finally faded and exhaustion dragged her back into sleep.

§

"STEPHANIA. IT'S TIME TO WAKE UP." Dalton's hands gently shook her awake, and she groaned against the morning light as it shone gratingly through the window. "Why are you on the floor?"

She sat up and whined when her head throbbed, choosing to not answer his question.

A chill ran down her spine as the events of last night came flooding back to her. Tears collected in her eyes, and at once Dalton knelt beside her, his arms around her.

"Shhh. It's okay, Stephania. It's okay, my child. You're safe now. You're safe."

She nodded against his chest, desperately trying to bite back the tears. A part of her raged against this—against being comforted, against being a burden. But she was too tired, too scared to pull any strength from her quivering heart. *Tomorrow,* she thought miserably. *Tomorrow, I'll be stronger.*

"Was it a nightmare?"

She didn't want to answer, lest it all come rushing back to her, so she only nodded.

He groaned and held her closer. "I'm sorry," he murmured into her hair. "I'm sorry."

Again, she only nodded, but this time, she moved away from him. He shifted his weight as she wrapped her arms around herself and refused to meet his gaze.

She could feel him searching her face, but neither said a word. She didn't want to talk about it, and she could only hope he would respect that.

In the long silence that stretched between them, her heart stopped racing and her breath evened. Somewhere in the silent seconds that slipped by, she found a sliver of peace, along with overwhelming gratitude for Dalton.

Finally, he spoke. "Artigal wants to see you today."

Her brows furrowed. "Why?"

Dalton stood and held his hand out to her. She hesitated before taking it and letting him help her to her feet.

"I think he wants to talk to you about your memories."

Her stomach plummeted and her ears rang. *My memories.* Her arms tightened around herself. She didn't feel ready for that, but she needed answers to the thousands of questions racing through her mind, chief of which was, *Will I get them back?*

She nodded. "Okay. When?"

"Around noon, I believe, but I don't think you need to rush. Take your time. Go for a walk or a ride or something. Clear your head first, and make sure you have breakfast please."

A ghost of a smile lifted her lips. "Okay." She turned to leave, but his hand on her elbow stopped her. She didn't want him to ask anything, so she gave him a question of her own. "Are you coming?"

He shook his head slowly. "I wish I could, to make sure Artigal treats you right and he follows through with his promise, but—" His shoulders slumped. "He requested it be only you. Even Frawnden and Aeron aren't allowed to go. Something to do with family emotions complicating things." He looked as distressed about the stipulation as she felt.

Alone. I'll be all alone. Fresh tears collected in her eyes.

"Are you alright?"

She froze and opened her mouth, wanting to answer, but too many confusing questions, rants, terrors, and hopes filled her mind, so she only said what she had trained herself to say for so many years. "Of course. I'm just tired. It was just a bad dream." She stepped away, his hand falling from her arm. She tried not to look back, but when she got to the door, she couldn't help it. When she turned, she saw him shake his head and gently brush the broken purple crystal shards into his hand before stuffing them into his pocket.

Icy blood spread through her veins from the top of her head as a bit of embarrassment opened in her gut. He knew her weakness, of how purple triggered her debilitating nightmares. She'd tried so hard to fool him into thinking she was better, that she wasn't suffering as much anymore, but she had failed. He must see her as a weak child still.

Biting her lip, she quickly slipped out of the room into the long hallway.

The house was quiet, and she wondered how late she had slept in. The suns' light was harsh against her eyes, and judging by the angle it streamed through the windows, it was almost noonday.

It felt somewhat intrusive to meander through someone else's house, and even stranger since it was supposed to be hers as well. The kitchen was cold, the fires having been put out earlier that morning. A loaf of herb bread sat regally on the counter, a testament to the oven and chef's diligent work.

Despite Dalton instructing her to get breakfast and her stomach grumbling discomfortingly, she wasn't sure she was allowed to simply eat whatever she wanted.

"You can have the bread if you want." Dalton's voice startled her, and she turned to see him shouldering his satchel. It looked heavy with tomes and scrolls.

"Where are you going?" she asked, ignoring what he had said and hoping he would forget about her needing to eat.

"Hm?" He looked up from adjusting the satchel's straps.

"Where are you going?" She pointed to the books.

"Oh. Aeron was telling me about a particularly old library in Trans-Falls that dates back to the cold war between the Centaurs and Duvarharians, and I was interested in taking a look at it. The librarians have some weathered manuscripts they might need help restoring. He also said they might have some tomes on covering magic traces I thought you could use."

A small smile bloomed on her face. She hadn't seen him so excited for something in a long time. The library was always where he was meant to be—among words, and stories, and secrets, just like the ones he kept locked away in his own heart. "Have fun."

He grinned boyishly. "I will. Thank you, child." Just as he made his way to the door, he called over his shoulder, "And please don't forget to eat something."

She groaned but couldn't displace the warmth that lingered in her chest. "I will," she laughed before the door closed behind him. Then, once again, she was left alone in the quiet house.

The joy she had felt from seeing Dalton so happy faded when she realized everyone here had a place but her.

Her mood suddenly sour, she dug a knife into the bread and spread honey across it before wolfing it down, hardly appreciating how rich and flavorful it was. She found a cup of still warm *muluk* sitting over the cooling oven and downed it, hoping to feel its energizing effects sooner rather than later.

After wandering through the cabin's halls for a few more minutes and begrudgingly pulling on her clothes, which she realized with surprise had been washed and mended, she stepped outside into the warm noon suns.

Braken was already saddled and grazing in the yard. He pranced over to her, shaking his mane proudly as if showing off, and she couldn't help but laugh when she realized why. All the knots and tangles had been brushed out of his mane and tail and every mud spot and bur smoothed out of his coat. His hooves had been cleaned and shined, and even his tack had been cleaned. She had never seen such remarkable skill in horse grooming before, and she couldn't help but wonder if that came naturally to all Centaurs. The thought put a smile on her face as she mounted and pointed him down the road, the trees swallowing her and Braken into their dark, leafy embrace.

Though she knew Artigal had wanted to see her around noon, which was very soon upon them, she didn't feel any need to hurry. Though she wanted answers, she wasn't sure if she really wanted to talk about her memories. Just the thought of the night terrors and half remembered visions quickened her pace and made her stomach churn.

Thankfully, she was rescued from her spiraling thoughts by a little cabin sitting in the middle of a vast, sprawling garden. It was a little oasis of flowers, light, and warmth in the middle of the dark, seemingly never-ending forest.

Braken sensed her awe and walked up to the gate, nibbling at the latch as if he were trying to open it. An old, weathered, wood-burned sign hung on the gate. It read *Uwarñoe,* obviously something in the Centaurs' language, Sházuk, but she couldn't even begin to translate it. Perhaps it was the resident's name?

Voices drifted to her on the still air, and she could almost hear a little girl and a little boy laughing. She closed her eyes. The sound of the breeze through the trees and the grasshoppers singing buzzed in her ears. She heard the thud of an arrow in a target, and she could almost hear ...

"I thought I might find you here."

Stephania yelped as Braken jumped, knocking into the gate with a clatter. She steadied him with a small burst of magic and quickly sought after who had startled her.

A black Centaur stood just down the road, his hands behind his back, and a strange twinkle in his dark eyes. "I'm sorry I startled you, Stephania."

Her eyes narrowed. "Apology accepted. Who are you?"

He spread his hands out as if a gesturing he meant no harm. "Walk with me and guess. You knew me once, perhaps you'll know me again."

It was hard not to simply kick Braken into a gallop and leave this teasing Centaur behind, but a spark of curiosity lit inside her. "You speak in riddles."

"Not really. Would you at least like me to show you the way to Trans-Falls? I think you're rather lost."

A blush raged on her cheeks. "I'm not."

Deep laughter rang through the trees. "And I have two legs. I know you do not remember this place, Stephania. And I know you do not remember the way, just as you do not remember me."

"Then tell me." A challenging edge clung to her voice. Seeing how much she didn't remember and how others expected her to be was beginning to wear thin.

"This is my house, Trans-Falls is over yonder," he pointed first to the cabin and then in a general southern direction. "And I am a good friend of your mother's and was once a fairly often companion of yours. If you would like, I can tell you much about what you do not know so you are not so frightened to face what lies before you."

Their eyes locked, and she tried to find any malice in him.

"So. Will you walk with me?"

Her mind fell blank as her emotions raged and fought each other. Was it worth it to extend her friendship? She remembered all too easily how the other girls in New-Fars had accepted her into their circle, only to brutally reject and humiliate her. Would this be the same? *But this isn't the same,* she tried to tell herself. *Surely, Trans-Falls is different. They accept magic and Dragon Riders here. Let the mask fall, even if just a little. Maybe it is worth it.* Stars dotted her vision as she squeezed her eyes shut, her hands forming fists. Taking a deep breath and opening her eyes to the treetops above, she tried to relax to take off the mask once more, though she wasn't sure if she truly knew how. With a skeptical gaze, she nodded curtly and made her decision. "Okay. I will."

He winked jovially as she nudged Braken forward to walk side by side with him. However, before they had even made it ten feet down the road, Jargon stepped off the path, and trotted into the trees.

"What in Rasa ..." She shook her head in bafflement, but before she could question his decision, Braken happily followed him and within seconds, the forest swallowed them in its leafy embrace.

"Shouldn't we be following the road?"

Jargon shot her a strange, mischievous look over his shoulder. "We are. Or at least, something like a road. It's the quickest path to the tribe's center from my house. At least, that's what I've been told."

"But how do you know which way we're going?" She thought about conjuring a compass from magic like Dalton had taught her, but Jargon rolled his eyes in such a way she felt it would be rude.

"Where's your sense of adventure?"

She didn't have an answer for that, but some of her concerns faded when she caught sight of his hand running over old grooves in the trees they walked by. Maybe it was a sort of path after all.

"You have changed."

She scowled. "So I've noticed."

"But not a lot."

Their eyes met, and he chuckled. "Even when you were younger, you were always skeptical of everything and a little on the quiet side as well. You were a bit more trusting, however, but trust is something most creatures deal out less easily as they get older, so I'm not surprised."

"You don't seem to be surprised by much," she laughed a bit more sourly than she had intended.

"Ah, now *that* is something that *has* changed. You've gained a bit of an attitude, haven't you?" He didn't wait for an answer before he continued. "Perhaps you were bullied as a child? So now you tend to hurt others before they hurt you?"

Her mouth dropped open, and she felt her face burn again.

"You don't have to answer that, of course. It's just an observation. To answer your sarcasm, I'm not surprised by much, though both you and Artigal have always given me much to be shocked about."

"Like what?" She couldn't be more relived he had changed the subject, but she also couldn't help but feel disappointed. She hadn't talked much about being bullied and how it had made her feel, and something about this Centaur did feel especially comforting. But perhaps it was for the best. She didn't need everyone knowing everything about her. Especially those who already knew more than she did.

"Things mostly related to magic, actually. You and Artigal each have an affinity for getting into trouble with Ancient Magic of the kind that is especially hard to control and heal, even for me."

"You are a medic?"

He nodded. "An astute observation for sure. I am Trans-Fall's Chief Medic."

"Something I should probably already know, right?"

"There's that attitude again." He clicked his tongue and stroked his dark beard. "It is something you once knew, not something you *should* know. It's important to make that distinction. And even if you *should* know it, it is much more fun to learn it all again, don't you think?"

Her brows furrowed, and she tightened her fists around Braken's reins. She wasn't sure how to respond or act with this Centaur; he was much too disarming and hard to predict. He made her want to completely shut herself off from him while at the same time want to be completely vulnerable. "I suppose it is."

"Good. Then what else do you want to know? I don't like to keep many secrets. They get all dusty in my mind and don't make very good gossip."

Before she could stop herself, she burst out laughing, suddenly feeling much more relaxed. "Tell me about the birds."

He nodded, seemingly pleased with her menial question, and dove into everything he could tell her about the strange birds of Trans-Falls.

Time passed by much too quickly, and Stephania found herself extremely disappointed when they left the forest and stepped onto the bustling streets of Trans-Falls.

"Are you glad you walked with me?"

Stephania brushed tears of laughter from her eyes and nodded. "Very much so. Thank you for showing me the way. I'm not sure I would've made it if you hadn't found me."

He winked. "Then it was a good thing I was looking."

Again, she found herself at a loss for words, but this time, it didn't make her uncomfortable. It was a sort of speechlessness she thought she could almost get used to.

As he motioned for her to follow, she realized she still didn't have his name, and so she asked him.

He smiled broadly, shining white teeth against black skin. "Jargon, though it won't mean much to you now. But don't forget it again, alright?" With a flick of his tail, he trotted into the crowd, expecting her to follow.

Not knowing whether to feel endeared that he had told her his name or offended because he had made a joke of her memory loss, she shrugged her shoulders and nudged Braken forward.

It wasn't hard for them to make their way through the crowded streets when the Centaurs realized who was among them. A path formed for her to ride through, and the Centaurs standing to the side bowed low, murmuring "Farloon" or "Dragon Child". What little comfort she had gained from talking to Jargon was laid low under their wide stares and reverent poses.

"Please stop," she whispered under her breath, wishing she had the courage to speak louder. It felt so wrong to be worshiped when she wasn't the Dragon Rider or protector they believed her to be.

After what seemed like an eternity, they were once again at the base of the *Gauyuyáwa*.

"I remember this."

"Thank the stars," he snickered.

She stared at him in offense.

"You just saw it yesterday. I'd be really worried about you if you didn't remember it."

Shifting her weight uncomfortably and laughing with him, she shrugged. *He's right of course. I'm the fool.*

47

"This isn't where you're meeting him, though." Jargon bypassed the steps up to the platform at the base of the tree, and she quizzically followed.

"Why not?"

"Despite its security, things talked about in the *Gauyuyáwa* often travel quickly through the *zhego-leláfa*."

"The what?"

He chuckled. "The *zhego-leláfa*. It means blossomvine. It's the same as what the humans say: grapevine."

She nodded but didn't attempt to say the foreign word lest she sound ridiculous. "So where are we going, then?"

"To the elite training grounds."

Jargon skirted into the forest, masterfully weaving his way around buildings and private property. Stephania followed as closely as possible, her mind swept away in wonder at the city built flawlessly into the forest.

Soon, they were on the other side of the large tree after passing through a magic barrier that sent shivers down her spine.

"This is the strictly prohibited section of the forest reserved for Artigal and the warriors he keeps close to himself." Jargon's voice was low, almost revered. "Very few creatures ever set foot in here."

She nodded, taking a deep breath, trying to feel the reverence for the Igentis everyone else seemed to feel.

Their pace had slowed considerably, and she felt Jargon was giving her time to take it all in. She dismounted and proceeded on foot, leading Braken absentmindedly.

It was a much different place than the rest of Trans-Falls, being much more rugged than the shop-lined streets she had just walked on. This strange place, which seemed a world of its own, was filled with targets and obstacle courses that were perfectly hidden in the trees and brush.

Goose bumps prickling on her skin, Stephania wondered if she had been here a long time ago.

"Artigal himself trained you and Trojan on these grounds once or twice long ago," Jargon said, as if he could hear her thoughts.

"By the gods." She shook her head. An obviously old target caught her eye.

It was burned.

Whatever wood hadn't been burned had been rotted by time. She wondered why it hadn't been torn down, as it was useless now. An eerie feeling settled inside her.

Her eyes darted to the other targets around her.

They were all kept in pristine condition.

Though Jargon was leading her down a path to her right, she continued to walk straight toward the target.

"Stephania?" Jargon turned to call her back, but it wasn't his voice she heard.

"How far do you usually shoot away from the target, Stephania?"

"About fifteen paces, sir."

"Then shoot twenty paces away."

The glade faded around her. She felt a bow in her hand, felt as she pulled back the string, felt as she aimed at the target, felt as she released the string. The target in front of her burst into flames, and she stumbled backward, gasping in shock. The target morphed into a black cloaked figure with a gaping mouth dripping with blood. Screams filled the air. The creature lunged for her and sank its claws into her ...

"Stephania!"

Stephania gasped, her eyes flying open. She gripped Jargon's arms as he roughly shook her awake. Sweat dripped off her face and saturated her shirt. Her mind was clouded; her breath evaded her.

"Stephania, are you okay?"

Her eyes traveled beyond Jargon to the old, burned target. It was still there. The vines were still growing on it. The wood was still rotten.

"Yes, I think so." She held her throbbing head, her eyes never straying from that mutilated target. "What happened?"

Jargon helped her to her feet and steadied her when she swayed. His gaze followed hers to the target, a frown creasing his forehead.

"I think you had a *sukunhale.*"

She frowned in confusion, her eyes seeking his for answers.

His face was full of worry but also wonder. "A *sukunhale* is the Duvarharian word for a curse lift. It means something inside of you is trying to lift the curse Artigal put on your memories."

Her frown only deepened. "Is that even possible?"

He shrugged, his eyes wide. "Sometimes, yes, but only for minor spells. The kind of spell Artigal put on you is not only very complicated, but it was also made from very strong magic. A curse can only be lifted by magic which is stronger than that which put it there."

Stephania didn't know what to say, her mind having gone blank a while ago.

"How long have you had these hallucinations?"

"All my life."

"All your life?"

She nodded. "I'd have them about really weird things too. For instance, I couldn't

49

look at my piano without a man appearing and playing it. Then he would turn into this faceless creature, and everything would get really cold and ... terrifying." She shuddered subconsciously.

Jargon's eyes darkened and narrowed. "Those would be the gaps in the wall Artigal built where the memory is only barely able to surface. What other things have you seen?"

Tears clouded her vision. "I keep seeing—" She found herself unable to continue, and Jargon held her hand tightly. "I keep seeing a man and woman being killed, but ..." She choked past emotion, the image bright in her mind, "But *I'm* the murderer. And there's a purple lizard, or, no—" She shook her head. "It's a dragon. And I have a scar. Down my face." Absentmindedly, her fingers trailed down her cheek.

Jargon muttered something like a curse and a name under his breath.

"It's only bits and pieces, but I feel everything *he* feels." Tears spilled down her cheeks, and she stifled back a sob. Her eyes closed. Sometimes, like now, she could see all the blood and death when she closed her eyes. It never left her. It was always lurking in the back of her mind, waiting to torment her in a dream or a vision. "It's awful."

He wrapped her in his embrace, and she sagged against him. She wished she didn't feel as vulnerable as she did, wished she could just stop talking, put her mask back on, and act as if nothing was wrong. She hated when the crushing need to tell someone, *anyone,* these horrors and visions overcame her.

She sniffed before pulling away. "But then, sometimes, it's just little things. There's this room I keep seeing in my dreams. And a mountain. It's always the same. And sometimes, that man and woman are there, but I don't know what they're doing or who they are."

"These definitely sound like memories."

Her eyes pierced into his. "Then, who are they?"

He opened his mouth then closed it, avoiding her gaze. "I can't say." He forced a realistic smile onto his face and only met her eyes for an instant. "They aren't *my* memories, you know."

A small smile shone momentarily on her face. "I know."

He was just about to hurry her along to their destination when she frowned. "But sometimes, I don't think they *are* memories."

He cocked his head, a strange glint of intrigue in his eyes. "What do you mean?"

"Well, there's this man, and he looks a lot like the man who plays at my piano, but he's more clear somehow. He almost even has a face. But he stands there a lot, in the mountain."

"In the mountain?"

"Mm-hm." Her eyes slid out of focus. "And he talks a lot. He's looking for some-one he's lost. He's desperate, hurt, broken."

Jargon followed her dazed gaze, but nothing stood in front of her. "Trojan, per-haps?"

"No." She quickly shook her head. "No. He's a rider, and he's lost so much more." Her fingers trailed the air in front of her.

"I don't know what to say, Stephania. This is beyond my control. Artigal knows much more about this and will have the answers you search for. I know you are upset with him, as you should be, but you need to put aside your persistent anger and see your options. He can help you. He *wants* to help you."

She grumbled but decided not to argue. Jargon was right. She needed to start act-ing like a Duvarharian leader and the Farloon, not some pathetic, whining human.

"But perhaps what you are experiencing is also a *sukunhale*, even if it takes a shape different from the others whatever the cause. Something inside of you is trying to get your memories back, but it isn't quite able to. Again, Artigal will know what to do."

She shook her head and brushed the red curls from her face. "But that doesn't make any sense. I mean, I can't control magic very well, and Artigal has the most pow-erful magic of anyone I know." She focused back on him. "How could I possibly have the magic to bring back my own memories? It just doesn't make any sense."

Jargon smiled softly. "I know. It *doesn't* make sense, but somehow, it's happening, that much we know. But Artigal knows more, which is exactly why we're here—to talk to him about your memoires."

Finally, she nodded and let him lead her to a strange, well hidden, earthy hut.

"Stephania, Jargon, welcome. May the suns smile upon your presence," beckoned Artigal's unmistakably deep, milky voice from inside.

Jargon nodded and opened the door. With a moment's hesitation, they stepped inside.

She took in the room. It was rather crude hut with only a table inside, no chairs, and no windows. The light came from little holes in the ceiling, which was made from gathered and bound tough straw and grass. The ground was dirt, and the walls looked almost like a log cabin. It was large, though, and had space enough for nearly ten fully grown Centaurs.

"Thank you for coming, Stephania. I have called you here in hopes we can assess the obvious issue concerning your memories."

Her face flushed and hands tightened to fists, but it seemed she was the only per-son in the room who was uncomfortable. Not knowing what to say, she decided against speaking at all, even if the silence felt awkward.

Her eyes strayed from Artigal to behind him. Two other Centaurs were present, both dressed in full armor and armed to the teeth. One was completely black, and the other had darkly tanned skin and a roan body. Both of their heads were bowed, concealing their faces. They were wearing a type of armor she hadn't seen before, but some of the markings on them matched markings she had seen only Artigal wear. She assumed they were some of his elite guard.

Artigal ignored her silence and swung a pack off his back, setting it on the table.

Jargon and Stephania moved closer as the Igentis began to carefully unpack bottles of many different shapes and sizes. From where she stood, Stephania could see that each contained something entirely unique from the others. Some of the liquid contents were beautiful greens and blues or dark, mysterious reds. Others had bubbling purples or rancid looking yellows and browns. A few even had solid contents, but she couldn't begin to decipher what they were.

"It's all here." Jargon's eyes shone brightly, but Artigal shook his head.

"Not quite." Artigal then pulled out one more bottle. It contained one large, red, poisonous looking berry, which seemed to leap and crack with its own energy.

Jargon took in a sharp breath. "Only one left." His voice was barely audible.

Stephania could feel the tension build.

Artigal nodded solemnly before placing the bottle on the table next to the rest. "Yes. Only one. I'm afraid Frawnden used the other on me nearly twelve years ago. A necessary sacrifice I'm sure, but a setback nonetheless."

Silence swelled in the room before Stephania frowned and butted in.

"I'm sorry, but what is this all for? And why couldn't Dalton come?" She didn't mean to sound as demanding or uninformed as she had, and a blush quickly decorated her cheeks.

"It is for you, Dragon Child." Artigal's eyes were cold and sharp. "It is for your memories, and it is the only thing to get them back. As for Dalton, it's better for you to understand these things on your own. Your family would only bring complicated emotions into an already delicate situation."

She paled slightly. "What do you mean?"

Artigal walked around the table, and for a moment his muted hoofbeats were the only sound in the room. "The spell I placed on you was made with the *Shushequmok*— the Pure Magic. I never took your memories away from you, I simply built a wall around them, one to keep you, or anything else, from accessing them. To reverse that, I'll need the Pure Magic to make a bridge or door through the wall."

"You didn't take them away?" Cold shock poured over her like water. Everyone had kept saying he had taken them from her, as if he had stolen them or destroyed them, but he hadn't. He had only protected them. Even so, if the only way to let her remember them was by the *Shushequmok*, then why couldn't Artigal just tear down the wall the same way he built it? And how was she somehow getting the memories back on her own?

"No." Artigal's voice was quiet, but it sounded like thunder in the room. Even Jargon looked surprised. "But I did the next worst thing. Even if I am able to make a door into your memories, you will never be able to experience them like you should. It will be a difficult journey to harness the control needed to use that door, and even then, the memories will be hazy and unclear, as if time had corrupted them."

Her heart dropped into her stomach. "Is there any other way to experience memories?"

Artigal's eyes turned from a dark brown to a sad blue. "Duvarharians should be able to access their memories as if they were happening in the present. Unless you stored them elsewhere before the wall was made, you won't be able to do that with the memories of your parents nor of your family here in Trans-Falls."

Stephania staggered back. It was all too much to bear. She would've been happy to get even a small portion of her memories back, but now that she knew she was losing so much more—even to the point of losing a Duvarharian trait—her head throbbed, and tears rose into her eyes.

Steady hands rubbed her shoulders, and she faintly heard Jargon comforting her.

"Why don't you just make the door, then? What's stopping you?" Her voice rang with bitterness as she turned from Jargon, her blurry eyes locking with Artigal's,

His shoulders sagged. "I can no longer channel the *Shushequmok* like I used to. I don't have the strength needed to fashion a door. Thus what you see before you." He gestured to the bottles on the table, and her eyes followed.

Now the bottles seemed much more important than they had previously. A flash of fear filled her. *If Artigal can't channel the magic he used to, then what does that mean for the rest of us?*

"So am I going to get my memories back today?" A pit of dread opened inside her. This was all happening so fast, and she didn't feel prepared.

"I wish, but we're missing just one more thing."

"What?"

"Four more *Negluu* berries."

Jargon took in a sharp breath, and the air in the room tensed. Stephania instantly got the impression obtaining the berry was a far more difficult task than any of them had wanted to attempt.

"Are they difficult to get?" she asked. She felt it appropriate to ask even though the answer was obvious. She turned to Jargon when he cleared his throat.

"*Negluu* berries only grow on the top of a certain volcano, which lies to the south-west of us, just before it is about to erupt. However, that volcano isn't scheduled to erupt for another five years."

"How do you know that?"

"The stars," Artigal answered, as if that were any explanation to her. "Even so, I am sending two of my elites to find these berries if by some miracle the Great Emperor decides to bless us."

"So we're just putting all of this in the hands of some god?" Stephania couldn't help but scoff. This was ridiculous. Not only would she have to possibly wait five years for the berries, but she wouldn't even get her memories back completely. On top of that, they were just going to hand it over to some impersonal deity? Helpless rage burned inside her as her fists closed and a lump rose in her throat. *Will I ever have control in my life?*

"No."

"What?"

"He's not just 'some god'. He is the maker of the Ancient Magic, and it is only through him any Ancient Magic flows. The *Negluu* berries are grown out of Pure Magic. There are no greater hands to put this in than the Great Emperor's."

Her brows creased. "I don't believe in Him or trust Him."

A smile almost flickered on Artigal's face before it was covered with his stoic mask. "He doesn't need to you believe in Him for Him to be real or in control."

Artigal seemed so confident in, so sure of this Great Emperor, but Stephania was not convinced. There had to be another way. Her thoughts wandered back to what Jargon had told her earlier at the target. She was having *sukunhales*. Somehow, she was finding a way through the wall Artigal had built around her memories.

"I've been having *sukunhales*." Her eyes locked with Artigal's, and she could feel the shock ripple through the room. "Jargon told me so. Somehow, I'm accessing something of my memories despite the wall you made."

If Artigal's face could get any more white, it did. His eyes changed many different colors as he stamped his hoofs. "Jargon, is this true?"

"It is," the medic answered almost hesitantly, as if he wished it weren't.

Artigal paced the room, his tail swishing anxiously. No one said a word. He was mumbling something, but she couldn't hear much of it, and what she did hear, she didn't understand. "The *Kijaqumok*," he whispered. His eyes landed on Stephania, a darkness glinting in their depths.

"No, surely that's not possible," Jargon pushed past Stephania as if he were trying to shield her from something.

A wild glint danced in Artigal's eyes. "Nothing is ever impossible with Ancient Magic."

"But what does that mean? What happens if she—"

"Can I use that to get my memories back?"

Jargon and Artigal turned to her, horror stamped on their faces. She suddenly felt even more small than she already did staring up at them.

"The *Kijaqumok*," she tried to mimic the name. "Can't we use that instead, since it's already working—"

"No!"

She stumbled back, her heart racing. Both Artigal and Jargon had yelled at her, and she felt the tears forcing their way down her cheeks. "I'm sorry, I just—"

In only a few seconds, Artigal crossed the room and grabbed her by the shoulders. She tried to push away, but his grip was an iron vise, his eyes commanding her to listen and be still. "Do not ever speak that name again as long as you live. You cannot even think of it. You must never try to use it to get your memories back or it will destroy you and everything around you, do you understand?"

She choked back a sob and nodded, but he only shook her shoulders more, his eyes turning a vicious red.

"Promise me, Stephania."

"I promise," she pleaded before he suddenly let her go.

Between her sobs, she heard Jargon murmuring condolences to her while Artigal ordered the elites to the mountain to bring back the berries. The door opened, then closed. Only her, Jargon, and Artigal remained.

Panic churned her gut when she reached for Dalton but remembered he wasn't here. She was surrounded by strangers she wasn't sure she could trust; strangers who confused her, scared her, and enraged her. When Jargon put a hand of comfort on her shoulder, she snapped. "Just leave me alone!" An angry sob escaped her throat. "I don't even know you! Either of you! And for you to presume to tell me what I can and cannot do, or what I can or cannot think. I'm sick of everyone shoving themselves down my throat." Her hands trembled as she balled them into fists, biting back her tears.

Jargon stepped closer, opening his mouth to say something, but she had already heard enough.

"Just leave. Both of you."

The look of pain that flashed through Jargon's eyes twisted her heart, but she shoved the feeling deep behind her mask. Artigal's eyes met hers and for a moment, she thought she saw something like regret.

She waited for him to apologize, but the only other words he spoke to them before he left as well were, "In a few weeks, my Centaurs *will* be back, and they *will* have the berries. You will get your memories back. The Great Emperor *will* provide." Then he was gone.

She wanted to lash out, to tear all the bottles off the table and smash them into pieces, to scream to the world that she would rather live without her memories than deal with this, but the faces of all those who loved her, those she didn't remember, flashed before her, and her rage was quenched in grief. "I hate this," she growled against her tears.

Jargon nodded before turning away. He held the door open for a moment behind him before he whispered, "I know, little dragon. I know. We all do." Then he was gone, and she was alone.

CHAPTER 6

A Couple Weeks After Arriving in Trans-Falls
Present Day

COME ON, EVERYONE! Gather your things, it's time to go!" Frawnden cantered past Stephania with an armful of medicinal herbs and flowers, almost knocking her over. "Sorry, little dragon! We need to go!"

Stephania caught her footing and shook her head, grumbling. "Curse this festival," she hissed under her breath, trying to ignore the look of helplessness Frawnden bestowed upon her. Even with the disproving and disappointed gaze of her adoptive mother on her, Stephania didn't regret her words or attitude. Ever since her meeting with Artigal in the hut, she hadn't been able to shake off a chasing feeling of dread. Half of her wanted the berries to be found, but the other half didn't. She wanted to be able to control what did or did not happen to her, even getting her memories back; but if she did get them back, days like this wouldn't be so horrifically awkward.

Frawnden's anxious voice brought Stephania back to the present. "Aeron, could you please grab the door?"

At a much slower pace, Aeron followed his mate, his own arms full of what she hadn't been able to carry. His eyes met Stephania's, and he winked before dropping a crown of newly bloomed *Leño-zhego* onto her head. "I'll be lucky if I even make it to the festival," he whispered in her ear.

Frawnden called to him again, her impatient hooves dancing on the floors.

"Coming, *da me koyuwuk*!" He heaved the basket over his shoulder and rolled his eyes. "Trans-Falls's true Chief calls me. Emperor, help me."

Grudgingly, a smile lifted just the corner of Stephania's mouth. At least she wasn't the only one annoyed with Frawnden's anxiousness, though she was sure Aeron was only trying to cheer her up.

As he trotted off to help his mate, Stephania could see the love in his eyes and didn't sense a breath of resentment from him. He planted a kiss to Frawnden's forehead and somehow managed to open the door while still taking one of the three baskets she held.

The sight almost warmed her. When Aeron's back was turned, she quickly pulled the flower crown from her head and tossed it onto the table. Even seeing the blossoms that symbolized a new beginning caused resentment to boil within her. *How is it so easy for everyone to be so frivolous and carefree? Why does it seem I am the only one burdened with more than my share?*

The doors shut behind her Centaur parents, cutting off Frawnden's rapid list of instructions and things they needed to do. Before Stephania even took another breath, the doors opened again, and Trojan stepped inside. Stephania caught the tail end of Frawnden asking Trojan to bring the *uafañoshigo* wine. Their eyes met for only a brief second before he quickly turned into the kitchen, and she ducked behind the spiral staircase.

She paused a moment, waiting for her heart to stop racing. Every time she ran into Trojan, she vowed she would say something, *anything,* to try to gain back some sort of connection between them, but each encounter only seemed to drive the wounds deeper. She clenched her eyes shut against the salty tears rising in them and swallowed around the lump that had formed in her throat. Though her initial target had been the kitchen to find a snack to eat, she suddenly found herself wondering if she needed to brush her hair, if only to avoid Trojan.

The front door slammed open once more, and a clatter of hooves filled the room. "Stephania! Stephania, are you still here?"

Just a few minutes. I just want a few minutes to rest ... to find some sort of control again. Clenching her hands in frustration, she stepped out from under the spiral stairs and wiped the hurt and confusion Trojan always left her feeling off her face. Even with her irritability, her words came out much colder than she meant. "I'm right here, Frawnden."

She nearly ran into Dalton as he stepped out from the hall.

"Sorry, my child. I didn't see you there." His warm smile untied one of the knots in her stomach.

He turned his attention to Frawnden, while trying to adjust a decorative scarf around his neck, having a little trouble with the intricate knot. "I thought you and Aeron already left."

"Oh, I did, but I forgot I promised Stephania I would help with her hair."

Stephania's stomach rolled, and she felt as if someone had poured ice water down her back. A few days ago, while she had sat at another awkward meal listening to how excited everyone was for the *Luyuk-daiw,* Frawnden had insisted on helping Dalton and

Stephania look their best for the festival. While trying to blend into her chair, her mind replaying the events with Jargon and Artigal at the hut over and over again, Stephania had absentmindedly agreed to let Frawnden brush her hair. She had forgotten about it until now. "Oh, you don't have to—"

Frawnden waved her hands, her dark eyes smiling happily. "I want to, little dragon. That's what a mother's for."

Stephania was opening her mouth to protest but felt Dalton's hand on her shoulder.

"Please, Stephania. Give them a chance," he whispered. "Remember, they're not the villagers. They're nothing like them."

She clamped her mouth shut. He was right. Frawnden and Aeron didn't deserve her hate. They at least deserved the same mask she had always put up for Dalton—fake joy.

Forcing a smile on her face, even if it was small and rather pathetic, Stephania nodded. "Sounds like fun."

Frawnden beamed. "Wonderful. Oh! Here, let me do that." The Centaur woman quickly pushed past Stephania and held her hands out to Dalton. "May I?"

A flush rose to Dalton's cheeks, but he nodded. "It's just been so long since I've tied a Duvarharian scarf like this. You'd think it'd be something you wouldn't forget ..." His eyes stared wistfully before he cleared his throat. "Stephania, if Frawnden is going to tackle your tangles and curls, you'd best go get the oil and brushes."

She barely heard him as she watched Frawnden bend down to tie his Duvarharian scarf. But suddenly, she wasn't seeing Frawnden, she was seeing a random Centaur warrior, and she wasn't in their cabin, she was in the middle of the wilderness, hiding behind a bush. A young Centaur was by her side.

"Hey, don't laugh." A young and familiar voice reached her ears from her companion. "I do that too."

She tried to hold back her laughter. "I know, and it's funny too."

Distantly, she heard another familiar voice calling them. "Stephania! Trojan! Come on. We're leaving!"

"Stephania! Stephania!"

Stephania snapped back into the present. She wasn't in the wilderness; she was in the cabin. Trojan was most likely still in the kitchen, not by her side, and it was Frawnden standing in front of her, bent down to Dalton, and not a Centaur warrior stretching as he rose from his post.

"Did you hear me? About the brushes and oils?" Dalton waved a hand in front of her face, and she shook her head, trying to grasp onto the last trails of the memory before it faded away completely.

"What? Yes, yes, I did." Tears choked her words, but before either one of them noticed, she dodged into the hall, grateful for the excuse to leave.

"Daughter?" Frawnden's voice, laced with worry, called her back. "Look through the top drawer of my chest. There's a key that goes to one of the upstairs closets. You should be able to find some old Duvarharian ceremony clothes."

Stephania stopped, took a deep breath, and wiped away the tears from her eyes. *Real Duvarharian clothes?* It was almost something she could be excited about if her heart wasn't in such shambles. "Are you sure?"

"Of course, Stephania. This is the *Luyuk-daiw* festival after all, and one of the first you've spent in Trans-Falls. I want this to be nothing but the best experience for you."

Unable to do anything other than nod, Stephania turned and ran through the tunnels, first finding the key and then the door it belonged to. When she opened the closet, the first thing she did was step inside, shut the door, lean against it, and let herself slide to the floor. Weaving her fingers through her hair, she buried her face between her knees. Moments ago, she had felt like screaming, chasing after the memory, cursing whatever god teased her with it, before begging them to bring it back. But now that she was alone, she was greeted only with the emptiness of her lifeless emotions. *How embarrassing.* She dug her nails into the palm of her hands. *I have gone from the terror of New-Fars to a sniveling girl in a closet who can hardly keep from crying, who can't keep the nightmares away. I'm worthless, helpless.* She dried her eyes on her sleeve and dragged herself to her feet. *I can do better than this. I have to do better than this. They'll never stop coddling me if I keep acting like a child.*

Taking a few deep breaths, she focused only on her surroundings in the here and now, not the trails of memory teasing her from the back of her mind.

Once her eyes adjusted to the dim lighting, she could hardly believe what she was seeing. Every size and color she could imagine of Duvarharian ceremony wear was present in this closet. She had never seen so many beautiful fabrics and colors in all her life. When her fingers brushed over the fabrics, she got the strangest feeling they had all been fashioned with magic.

The closet was organized, and so it wasn't hard to find the section in her size. Some were more flamboyant than others, so she picked something that wouldn't stand out too much: a tight, forest green cropped blouse that extended up her neck from a low gap between her breasts. It came with matching green leggings, embroidered with silver vines and designs that only came to life when the light struck them just right. Fitted on top of the blouse and leggings was a wispy, light green, almost grey dress that dipped low around her shoulders, tightened fashionably at her waist, and then spilled down around her arms and legs. A slit cut dress from the waist down, and she wondered if it was designed for riding a dragon.

"That's one of my favorites."

Stephania startled then turned to see Frawnden gazing at the clothes in her hands. She hadn't even heard Frawnden open the door. Her face flushed at being caught hiding in the closet. "I can see why," she muttered in embarrassment, but Frawnden didn't dwell on it.

"Would you like me to show you how to put it on?"

A moment of hesitation passed before Stephania took a deep breath. "Yes, I would love that." The flash of excitement she saw in Frawnden's eyes untied another small knot in her stomach.

After a whirlwind of clothes, skin oils, and a bottle of sparkle Stephania was sure was pure magic, she finally found herself standing before Frawnden's crystal mirror.

She hardly recognized herself. She looked ... amazing—so different from how she felt on the inside. It almost made her feel as if, maybe, she could forget about the press of her memories, of destiny, of the Lyre, and how, even now, she found her mind wandering to the instrument, feeling an insatiable need to have it close to her.

"With Aeron as Trans-Falls's High Chief, and I Second High Medic, we used to get a lot of visits from the Duvarharians back before you were born. As Centaur custom, we housed them here with us."

"That's why you have so many rooms and all the Duvarharian commodities."

Frawnden hummed as she surveyed her handiwork. "I've seen many a Dragon Woman wear this, but none with the regal beauty you have."

Stephania blushed. A knock on the door rang through the room.

"Come in!"

The door flung open. "Gods of all, child." Dalton's eyes shone with pride as he strode into the room and twirled Stephania around. She couldn't help but laugh as he shook his head in disbelief.

"It's a good thing you didn't have Duvarharian clothes in New-Fars, otherwise I would've had to beat the young men off you."

A small smile lifted her lips, and she pushed back a scoff. "Probably so." They both knew he was wrong. New-Fars wouldn't have wanted her, even looking like a queen.

"Now for the hair." Frawnden pulled a lock of the messy curls from Stephania's face as Dalton held up the brushes and oils.

"Let me help."

Frawnden frowned and waved him off. "No, no, no—"

"Please."

Neither woman failed to see the plea in his eyes, and Frawnden couldn't help but relent.

"Of course, Dalton. It'll be better with the two of us anyhow. I still have to get back to Trans-Falls for the opening ceremony." At the remembrance of her other duties, Frawnden's productivity increased once more, and her grunts of frustration over detangling Stephania's curls were almost comical.

"By the stars. I don't remember this being so hard when you were younger. Maybe the humidity is making it worse." Frawnden was twisting a lock of Stephania's hair into a braid, threading little rings and silver leaves throughout it. She had only finished a fourth of her section of hair while Dalton was almost done.

Frawnden paused her work and sighed when she saw how far Dalton had gotten. "You certainly have more practice than I."

"Oh, you pick up a few tricks along the way." He winked at Stephania through the mirror as a twist of his brown magic weaved its way through her hair, loosening the curls and threading little braids throughout. She tried to disguise her mischievous smirk as a wince when Frawnden pulled a tad too hard.

"Have you ever thought of dreadlocks?" Frawnden tied off the braid she was working on, taking a few steps back to stretch her cramped arms.

"No, I've never had trouble with my hair before."

Frawnden huffed before laughing. "I supposed dreads are more of a Centaur thing, not sure I've ever seen a Duvarharian with them."

"They don't need them." Dalton laughed before holding his hand out to Frawnden, brown magic dancing around his Shalnoa.

Her eyes widened before she sputtered awkwardly and then laughed. "I should have known! Dragon Riders and their tricks. What time is it?"

Dalton nodded to Stephania. "Why don't you try to see. Do you remember the spell?"

Stephania had to think for a moment. He had taught it to her during their miserably long trek from New-Fars to Trans-Falls, but she hadn't used it since arriving in Trans-Falls. In fact, she had hardly used any magic since arriving. The increase in her night terrors since arriving in Trans-Falls had made it harder to push back and ignore the memories of killing the villagers back in New-Fars. Before the memory could pull her back into its horrors again, she shook herself awake and did her best to remember the words. Dalton whispered the first few and once she heard them, she remembered the rest. Calling the magic to her, she directed her words and power toward the little stream of sunlight from the window. After a moment of concentration, she gathered the light into a little ball, which hung over her hand approximately where the suns hung in the sky in relation to the land.

"Suns and stars! I'm almost late!" Without even a goodbye, Frawnden cantered out of the room, the front door shutting loudly behind her. The house was suddenly very quiet.

"Are you alright?"

Stephania's eyes met his, and she frowned. The simple magic had left her feeling a little weaker and heavier now that the presence of the Lyre weighed on her mind. In fact, it was almost all she could think of. Her eyes darted to the door. She needed to retrieve it from her room before they left.

"Stephania?"

Her attention snapped back to Dalton. "Yes. I think I am. At least, I'm better than I was when I first arrived." It wasn't exactly a lie, but neither was it the truth.

He planted a kiss to the top of her head and gathered more hair. "I am so glad to hear it. What about making friends?"

A pit opened in her stomach. "What about friends?"

"Well, is there anyone you're hoping to spend the festival with?"

Her mind instantly went to Lamora and Ravillian. She had been avoiding them since they met, unsure they truly wanted to be her friends or if they had just been enamored with her newness; she wasn't even positive she was ready for friends yet. She certainly wasn't sure they were good enough of friends for them to want to spend this festival with her. "Well ... I found a strange bird that mimics what you say. I think it's smart enough to learn an actual language."

Dalton chuckled. "You've always had a way with animals. If it's smart enough to learn, I'm sure you'll be able to teach it."

A small smile lifted her lips. "Thank you, Uncle Dalton."

He nodded. "You know, when I was young ..."

But his words faded into the background as a thought wormed its way into her mind. *The Lyre. Where's the Lyre? I have to get the Lyre.* An empty, churning pit opened in her stomach. "You don't have to finish the rest," she sputtered. "It's fine the way it is. We shouldn't be late either." She went to stand from the chair, but Dalton gently pushed her back down.

"Frawnden isn't the only parent who wants their daughter to look and feel their best. Let me finish this for you, child. Besides, no Duvarharian is anything without their fashionably late entrance."

She relented, and it wasn't long before he was finished. Despite her irritability and impatience, she couldn't help but be extremely pleased with the finished result. She looked like a queen of the stars and dragons with the way her hair glittered and the light glinted off the metal jewelry. Even if she didn't feel at peace or in control, at least no one else would be able to tell.

As soon as Dalton let her, she rushed to her room and pulled the wrapped Lyre out from under her bed. With hesitant hands, she pulled back a corner of the cloak. Without even her touching it, the Lyre was glowing green. A stab of fear caused her hand to jerk back the fold of fabric. With heavy breaths, she wrapped it up tighter. She tried to push the instrument back under the bed but found she couldn't. Instead, she tucked it under her arm and stood.

"Stephania?"

She jumped at Dalton's voice and flung around. "Yes?"

"Are you alright?" His eyes strayed to the shape under her arm, and she knew he was aware of what it was. His gaze moved back to hers.

Though the Lyre felt like the very weight of the world in her arms, she couldn't deny the peace she suddenly felt now that it was with her. As long as she held it near, she could breathe easy. At least, for now. "Yes. Yes. I am. I'm ready."

Without another word, they gathered the rest of the flower crowns, food, medicine baskets, and packs of seeds, strapped them to the horses, and set out for Trans-Falls.

§

STEPHANIA HAD NEVER seen such a festival. Every Centaur in Trans-Falls and the surrounding valley was present. The thunder of hooves and laughter rang through the valley and hummed through the earth. Every home and store was open, and no one had to pay for anything, for all was given freely. Each household had something to share: knives they fashioned, cooking utensils, armor or clothes, food, tapestries, instruments, or, like Frawnden and Jargon, medicine.

Aeron, Trojan, Artigal, Frawnden, and Jargon were all dressed in different tribal ceremonial garb, accentuated with furs, flowers, feathers, or gems and metal. Fierce and beautiful paint decorated almost every inch of their bare skin, and each design was a token to an age of Trans-Falls and the Centaurs gone past. Each gave a short but powerful speech about the significance of the spring festival, giving thanks to the Great Emperor for His blessings.

Troupes performed dance and song numbers; some made Stephania want to cry; others made her want to sing and dance with them. If anyone had told her Centaurs danced before today, she would've laughed, but now she was sure she had never seen something so ethereally beautiful.

More than a few ceremonial duels were fought with all number of weapons. Frawnden led the archery competition and Aeron the broadsword.

"Stephania! Stephania!" The voice calling her sounded so familiar, but with the crowd pressing in around her and the sound of war horns ringing through the air, it was hard to recognize the voice, let alone find its owner.

"There you are!" A hand landed on her shoulder, and she startled, whirling around.

A blush rose onto her face. It was Ravillian and Lamora. *They've been looking for me. Why? Do they really want to spend time with me?* She started to mutter an apology for not coming to find them, but before she could do so, Lamora grabbed her hand and pulled her alongside them.

"Not so fast, please!" Stephania was almost being dragged along as the exuberant Centaur began to trot.

"Oh, stars!" Lamora came to a quick halt before dancing away, her face red with embarrassment. "I'm sorry, I forgot ... you only have two legs ... oh, how embarrassing." She was hiding her face in her hands, standing just behind Ravillian, who was roaring with laughter.

"What a fool you've made of yourself, Lamora."

Lamora playfully punched him.

Stephania laughed nervously, her hands straying to touch the edges of the Lyre's wrappings from where she had strapped it to her back. Silently, she prayed they wouldn't question her about it. "Um, if you just wait, I can go find Dalton. He should have my horse—"

"Oh, no, that won't do." Ravillian shook his head, ignoring Lamora so he wouldn't start laughing again. "You can't take a horse with you where we want to go."

Confusion muddled Stephania's mind. *How can I not take a horse somewhere in a tribe made of half-horse creatures?*

"Look, no, you've confused her." Lamora pushed past Ravillian, seemingly over her embarrassment.

"How ... That doesn't make any sense." Stephania fiddled with the long wispy sleeve on her dress. She wasn't sure she really wanted to go with them. What if when they got together with all the other Centaurs, they simply left her out or made fun of her? She tried to push the thought away. She already had enough on her mind with the Lyre and whether or not the *Negluu* would be found. "Where are we going?"

Lamora placed her hands on Stephania's shoulders and then pointed past her head, up into the trees.

"Up there."

"Gods of all." Stephania felt as if someone had stolen the breath from her lungs. The treetops were alive with life. Hundreds of *Leño-kofolu* filled the branches, their different hues of light shining and glowing brightly in the leafy canopies. But even more astonishing was the great suspended platform that hung high above the *Gauyuyáwa* and teemed with Centaurs.

Centaurs in trees. I never would've believed it.

"They build it into the rest of the canopy dwellings every *Luyuk-daiw*." Lamora proudly stepped away as Stephania struggled to find words.

"Incredible."

"It's more than incredible," Ravillian added. "It's *kaogouya*. It's where all of us young Centaurs go during the festival. Gives the best view of the games, fights, and performances. Plus, they have all you can drink *uafañoshigo* wine!"

"We were just about to go. Do you want to come with us?"

Stephania had to bite back her reply, *"Do you really want me to go?"* What if they just want me to come so they can brag about being with the Farloon? Should I be with my family as one of the leaders since I am Farloon and the Duvarharian heir? Or does it matter because I don't remember? The war raged within her. It was hard to think with all the music, dancing, bodies, lights, and chaos around her. If only everything could just be quiet, just for a moment, just so she could collect herself again.

"Please?"

"Come with us, Stephania. Please." Lamora took her hand in hers. Stephania's skin crawled with the contact, and visions of the New-Fars villagers grabbing and clawing at her flashed in her mind. But when her eyes met Lamora's, she neither saw nor sensed any malicious intent in her.

"Well, alright, but you're going to have to slow down a little."

Ravillian waved his hands and turned to Lamora. "Would you mind if she rode upon you?"

Lamora beamed and offered her hand. "Not at all."

Stephania took a step back. "I didn't think Centaurs let things be put on their backs? Isn't that rude?" She was less worried about the Centaur culture and more about how awkward it might be to ride someone else, and someone she barely knew for that matter.

Both Centaurs laughed. Lamora took Stephania's hand in hers and gave it a reassuring squeeze. "Oh it is, but only if it's something like a saddle or a cart. Besides, it's only the older Centaurs who really worry about things like that. Plus, you're no lowly human. You're Farloon for star's sake!"

Still not fully sure she was comfortable with the situation, but not wanting to offend them by refusing not only their solution to her slow pace but also to spend the holiday with them, she quickly mounted Lamora's back.

Lamora and Ravillian high-fived before they started off.

"Wait, I just need to go tell Uncle Dalton—"

Ravillian smiled and patted her boot. "No need. It's *Luyuk-daiw!* The one day of the year where we are all as free as the stars above us. It's a time when Winter releases its hold on the land, on our spirits, and we are no longer confined by anything. It's a time of new beginnings, purpose, and meaning. The life of the forest surges forward which coaxes our own souls awake. Then we and the forest become one, free spirit beneath the stars. We answer to no one but the life within us and the waking forest."

Stephania opened her mouth to protest but then stopped herself. *All my life I have hid behind a mask, listening to what the hate and mockery of others has told me I am and who I should be. One day to be as free as the stars. To be and do whatever I want. Surely, it won't hurt me or anyone else to simply be whoever I want.*

So when Lamora cantered toward the dizzyingly long winding stairs, she said nothing, only drank the small bottle of tart *uafañoshigo* wine Ravillian passed on to her, and ever so slightly let her mask slip.

Just as they were nearing the steps, she thought she heard someone call out her name.

She turned to look but didn't see anyone she knew.

Blue.

A flash of familiarity filled her, and her eyes locked with a Centaur's bright blue gaze. Trojan.

He broke out of the crowd only paces from them. Time seemed to slow.

His mouth was open as if he were going to ask her a question, but before he did, his eyes traveled to Ravillian and Lamora. Something like pain filled his eyes, and he stopped coming closer.

She wanted to reach out to him, to invite him along, to try and mend what she had broken, but she couldn't begin to find the words, and "I'm sorry" just didn't seem like enough. Before she could ask Lamora to stop, before she could even attempt to do something, they were climbing the stairs, and she lost Trojan's face in the crowd below.

With difficulty, she dragged her searching gaze from the crowd and focused her attention on the long stairs ahead of her, thinking of what awaited her at the top, thinking she was free to let down her mask, to let down her walls. She was free tonight: untied to her destiny, memories, and past families or enemies.

The air on top of the platform was light and jovial, the music throbbing and intoxicating. Ravillian was right. The platform did provide the best view of all the speeches, myth and legend reenactments, and entertainment. The Centaurs all tried to teach her their dances, but she quickly found she couldn't keep up with only two legs.

The day flew by in a jumble of laughter and song. She was introduced to more Centaurs than she would ever remember and more foods than she was able to eat.

Long after the suns dipped under the horizon, thousands of candles were lit under little paper lanterns and set off into the sky, one for each creature, each soul that hoped to be reunited with Hanluurasa someday.

Stephania wrapped her hands around a half empty bottle of *uafañoshigo* and yawned, watching the little lights fill the sky and listening to the music of a pan flute and lyre from down below. Her legs dangled from the edge of the platform, as close as she could come to the branches where the glowing *Leño-kofolu* roosted. Many of the young Centaurs had left the platform to strike out into the woods, though some had fallen asleep long before that. From her vantage point, Stephania could see almost all the Centaurs who were sleepy, would simply lay down where they were and doze off. *Truly free. Free from fear, want, greed. Free.*

Her own lids drooped, and she yawned again.

"Stephania?" Lamora's voice snapped her back awake.

She looked up to see Lamora's shining face, her cheeks flushed from the wine. "Ravillian and I are going with some others to the falls. Do you want to come with us? The *Leño-kofolu's* light is really beautiful reflected off the water."

It sounded beautiful. Stephania yawned and let out a heavy sigh. "I'd love to." But instead of standing, she simply lay down and curled her arm under her head.

Lamora giggled before draping a nearby blanket over her. "Good night, Stephania Dragon Child. May the suns smile upon your presence."

Before sleep overtook her, Stephania was almost positive she saw the unmistakable form of a Faun skipping through the trees below.

§

CENTAURS BREATHED QUIETLY around her as they stirred in their sleep. Nocturnal birds trilled almost inaudibly. Crickets chirped with the cicadas.

Stephania's eyes fluttered open. Darkness surrounded her, broken up only by little floating lights, most from the stars above, and a few from Trans-Falls's nocturnal creatures.

"Protector of the Lyre." A soft voice drifted to her on the cool night air.

She rolled over, groaning against the throbbing headache that suddenly made itself known.

Her breath caught in her throat, and she froze.

A Centaur woman was standing over her—one she didn't recognize. Her skin was the soft white-blue of starlight, and her hair an impossibly light pink tinged with age and silver. Her body was dark and covered in strange markings along with huge, horrible scars. A knotted staff was clutched between slender pale fingers tipped with what looked like black blood. But most strange and disturbing were her milky white unseeing eyes, and the way black blood seemed to leak from their lids.

Stephania opened her mouth to call for help, feeling suddenly very unsafe, but her muddled state of mind twisted her words into a helpless croak, and the world around her swam.

The Centaur none too gently prodded Stephania with her staff and scowled. "Protector of the Lyre. What a lie." She spat on the ground next to Stephania. "You are weak. It was foolish for him to entrust this to you. We need the forest *now*, do you understand? But you know nothing of its soul or its ways."

"I don't ..." Stephania groaned as she pushed herself upright, feeling nauseous and dizzy. She searched to see if anyone else was seeing this unsettling creature, but none of the other Centaurs moved. In fact, it seemed they weren't even breathing, everything was so still. In fact, the more she thought about it, she suddenly realized she couldn't hear the crickets or cicadas anymore. It was as if everything were frozen in time.

The Lyre slipped from the straps on her back and fell next to her. As soon as her eyes rested on it, her mind cleared. The glowing green of the instrument consumed her.

"See how it glows?" The Centaur woman reached down and traced her fingers across the Lyre as if she were caressing an old friend. A softness replaced the harsh disappointment in her whispered words. "It's beautiful."

"You can see it?" Stephania pulled the Lyre closer, feeling the need to protect it.

The Centaur straightened, her eyes piercing Stephania's soul in a way eerily similar to Artigal's stare, even though this Centaur was clearly blind. "Yes. I can see *everything*."

Before Stephania could move, the Centaur reached down and pressed one of her long black nails against her forehead.

Splitting pain raced through Stephania's body, and she groaned before opening her eyes. She was still in Trans-Falls, but everything looked both saturated and dead simultaneously. Anything not alive was black and white and faded into the background unimportant. However, anything alive, including all the sleeping Centaurs around her, the trees, and the animals, *shone*. She could see their souls, every single one of them. Thousands of lights lit up the forest where the land and tree spirits and Fauns lay curled in their trees or under bushes, sleeping.

"This is what is at stake, Dragon Child. It is time for them to awaken. I will wait no longer. Whether you are ready or not, they will wake. I will make sure of it."

The Centaur woman pulled her finger away from Stephania's head, and a bright light consumed her.

Stephania sat up gasping for air, sweat saturating her clothes. Her head throbbed horribly, and her body ached from how she had been sleeping. Everything was dark save for the small stars and a few dying fires below. Centaurs slept on around her, oblivious to her panic.

She searched desperately for the blind Centaur woman, wondering how any one of them could have missed her. The Lyre was still strapped to her back and no longer glowed like it had earlier that day. Everything was quiet and still.

Feeling something between her hands, she looked down to an empty bottle. Suddenly embarrassed, she pushed the bottle away and lay back down. She had drunk too much *uafañoshigo*. The Lyre had been heavy on her mind all day; it was only natural she had a strange dream about it. Additionally, the more she mulled it over, the strange Centaur woman from the dream had looked strangely like one of the actors who had played the part of a star in one of the festival's performances.

Though she repeated these things to herself over and over as sleep dragged her back down, she couldn't shake the feeling that just like the Faun who had given her the Lyre hadn't been a dream, neither had this. However, as soon the quiet darkness of sleep overtook her, the vision faded away into the depths of her mind, and she forgot all about it.

§

"STEPHANIA, IT'S TIME TO WAKE UP." A familiar voice accompanied by gentle shaking stirred her from sleep.

When her eyes blinked open, it was still dark out. "... not time to wake ..." she groaned and curled up tighter before hearing quiet laughter.

"Someone had a few too many bottles."

Only half aware of her embarrassment, she rolled over and recognized Dalton's form crouched next to her. "Mmm," was all she was able to grumble out.

"Did you have fun? Did Ravillian and Lamora teach you everything you needed to know about Centaur festivals?" Looping his strong arm under and around her, he helped her sit up, letting her dizziness fade for a moment.

Flashes of memories from earlier than night flitted through her sleepy mind: dancing with the Centaurs, playing a lyre and singing with them, and more than a few empty *uafañoshigo* bottles. A giggle parted her lips, interrupted by a loud hiccup. She nodded quickly. "I did. And they did. It was ... magical."

"I'm glad to hear it." A smile in his voice, he chuckled as he helped stand her on wobbly feet, letting her lean against him. "Maybe next time, though, go easy on the wine?"

Stephania giggled again, resting her head against his warm chest as he led her to the horses. "Alright. Maybe so."

He helped her onto Braken and after a slow decent from the platform, then a long walk through the forest, she only vaguely remembered him walking into the house, tucking her into bed, whispering into her ear how happy he was for her and her new-found friends.

CHAPTER 7

Gauyuyáwa, Trans-Falls

Present Day

T HE HUMAN DOMAIN IS almost completely under Thaddeus's control. It won't be long before their armies march into Ravenwood." A stern
Centaur commander slammed his fist on the table before him, his eyes boring holes into the other officers' around him. Most held his challenging gaze, but a few
of the younger leaders looked away, fiddling with their fingers, belts, manes, or knives.

"Synoliki, what is your take on this?" Artigal shifted his gaze toward the spiral
staircase of the *Gauyuyáwa*.

His arms crossed, his face nearly emotionless save for a piercing gaze, Trojan
stepped out from the shadows. His presence caused a solemn silence to sweep the
room; none of the Centaurs, whether they were nearly one hundred years old or just
thirty, were able to meet his gaze. They had seen him fight—as if he were twenty Centaurs instead of one—with a bloodlust that rocked even the most courageous. Nearly all
of them had been under his command in countless battles against Thaddeus's forces
and had experienced his incredible leadership abilities along with his utter lack of fear
for death. None had seen him waver in his decisions or his ability to keep a calm head.
Many were strongly reminded of Artigal by this young Centaur who seemed to never
show emotion besides his demand for authority and respect.

Today, his demeanor was even more cold, an undercurrent of quiet rage emitting
from him.

"I agree with Jorden."

The old Centaur nodded in appreciation and muttered, "Thank you."

"Please explain why." Artigal motioned to the table, and Trojan nodded.

Jorden excused himself as Trojan took his place in front of the officers, commanders, and advisors.

"Though many here believe Thaddeus is not the current ruler of the Human
Domain, I have plenty of evidence to the contrary. The Domain is now controlled by

a powerful man who parades under the name Lord Kosuke. He preaches the renewal of the Humans and calls himself their 'redeemer'."

Though many of the younger Centaurs didn't want to hear what Trojan had to say, they were enraptured by his commanding authority, and no one spoke a word out against him.

"Reclusive, Lord Kosuke prefers to maneuver within only the Domain's most populated cities, especially the capital Odessa, which are out of reach to our spies." Trojan slowly paced around the table, his arms still folded across his bare chest. His Synoliki markings glowed brightly, matching his eyes—a constant reminder to anyone who might challenge him that he was of an entirely different league. "However, according to what we have gathered, Kosuke is famous for his shocking purple eyes and his skills with a battle axe. Along with this information, we know he is unusually strong and boasts of mid length, blond hair."

He planted his fists on the table, his eyes searching every one of the leaders'. "Now, brethren, if that doesn't sound like a spot-on description of Thaddeus, then we mustn't know Thaddeus from our own ranks. Questions?"

The room exploded with questions and contradictions until Trojan nodded at one of the female leaders. "Yes, Gloria?"

"If Thaddeus really does have control over the Human Domain and is calling himself Kosuke, then how is he able to do that from the Eta stronghold so far north?"

"Good question." He made his way to one of the large maps of Ventronovia hanging on the wall and pointed to the Eta's territory in the north. "As we all know, Thaddeus has lived in the Eta castle, his main stronghold, for as long as he has been terrorizing the land. However, from what we have gathered from a few rebel humans, an unusual amount of building materials has been ordered—by Lord Kosuke—to be shipped up north around here." He pointed just east of the Cavos desert and the Zankie Sea to the extremely fertile land between the Zankie Sea and the Forgotten Sea. "Large work forces are being recruited and sent to this general location.

"Are you implying that Thaddeus is building his own fortress?" a Centaur quietly spoke up, his eyes darting everywhere but at Trojan.

Trojan recognized him as one of their scholars. "Yes, Lron. I am."

Once again, the room erupted into chaos until Trojan held up his hand, commanding silence. "Thaddeus has lived long enough in the Eta castle. King Veltrix is no longer strong enough to keep up with the castle; it is old, decrepit, and almost impossible for Thaddeus to repair with magic because of the Etas' presence. If he were to move to this new location, he would be well protected by the Cavos desert and mountains, along with both the Zankie and Forgotten Sea. This would also give him plenty of fertile lands to work, along with an abundance of open waterways for easy travel around his domain. From his greatest enemies—the Centaur tribes and the Duvarharians—he would have ample protection while he ruled the Human Domain with ease as Lord Kosuke.

"And what of the Wyriders?" a voice called from the back of the council room.

Mild annoyance flashed across Trojan's face. "What of them?"

"Are there not rumors that Thaddeus has begun to recruit them as well?" someone else interjected.

He nodded slowly, considering his words. "Yes, there are."

"Do you believe them?"

"I do." He quickly stared down three Centaurs who were just opening their mouths to slander his opinion. "Now, whether these rumors are true or not, the Wyriders have already proved they will not help the Centaurs, Duvarharians, or Humans against Thaddeus, and they weren't there to protect Chioni from him either. There is no reason to believe they might be on our side, or that they would rally to us against Thaddeus. That is ample enough reason to assume Thaddeus has convinced them to join his cause in wiping out the Duvarharians once and for all. That would make this location"—he once more tapped the projected area of Thaddeus's new fortress—"a prime spot for his new domain."

"And why now?"

He turned to a sly looking Centaur who stared back with contempt.

"Explain yourself, Colten."

Colten stood, his eyes fixed on Trojan. He was a relatively new officer and a constant thorn in Trojan's side. He had a few strong opinions of his own, most of which clashed loudly with the Synoliki's, including the adoption of Stephania into the tribe.

"Alright then, Trojan." Colten sneered as he stepped forward, purposefully using Trojan's personal name out of disrespect instead of addressing him as Synoliki.

Trojan's jaw ground against itself, but he didn't give the brash Centaur any satisfaction of seeing his frustration.

"Why would Thaddeus, after nearly eight hundred years of running around Ventronovia and Chioni destroying countries, suddenly build a new castle? Why not seven hundred years ago? Or even a hundred years ago?"

Murmurs of agreement rippled through some of the crowd while others stared at Colten with disgust as he continued.

"Also, why hasn't Thaddeus simply just killed off the rest of the Duvarharians? He's had eight hundred years to do it, and he's certainly possessed the power to do so for a long time. If he simply wanted the Duvarharians dead, wouldn't he have done it by now? The only other thing I could think of is that the Duvarharians are actually working with him in order to regain control over Ventronovia."

Trojan couldn't even be frustrated; what Colten was proposing was too ridiculous. Withholding his mocking laugher, Trojan scoffed instead. "Colten, I'm sorry thinking isn't so much of a strength for you as fighting is, but sometimes it really is okay to stay silent. I know we'd all understand."

Stung by the words, and obviously deeply offended, Colten's face reddened as he opened his mouth angrily, but Trojan calmly held up his hand, silencing him instantly.

"But, I digress. I will answer your question and do my best to make it comprehendible to you."

Stuttering in offense, Colten stumbled backward, his face growing more red as the other leaders tittered with mocking laughter. Centaur meetings, while they were extremely rigid with tradition and respect, could often turn into some of the most personally scathing discussions.

"As any good warrior knows, Thaddeus has, indeed, held the power and strength to completely take over all of Ventronovia, save Wyerland, for nearly five hundred years since he conquered Chioni. Obviously, he must have a different plan."

"I know, that's why I said the Duvarharians are—"

Trojan turned up his head at Colten, completely ignoring him. "Sisters and brothers, whether you believe the humans need to be protected or not, there is one thing we must all come to terms with. The end of Rasa is nearing."

A solemn, ill silence spread across the room, and Artigal narrowed his eyes at Trojan, a strange sparkle of what might have been pride shining in his eyes.

"How do we know this?"

Trojan latched his gaze on the older Centaur who had spoken up. "You know as well as the rest of us, the stars have sung of the end of the world for nearly one thousand years now, starting on the day of the Dragon Prophecy. Along with this, the *Zelauwgugey* has been found."

Titters and gasps of amazement rippled through the room as Trojan nodded slowly.

"Artigal and I have confirmed that the *Zelauwgugey* is in Trans-Falls and is in the possession of the Farloon."

Some cheered, some roared in anger.

Colten's voice could be heard over all the others. "The *wozauñouk!*" he cursed and spat on the ground.

Trojan's head snapped in his direction, and what little warmth or patience he had felt earlier couldn't be bothered as his eyes darkened and his jaw set in hate. He drew himself to his full height and stepped over to the brash commander. Colten, though he tried, was unable to stop himself from cowering.

No one else moved a muscle.

Though he was a full head taller than his inferior, Trojan brought his face mere inches from Colten's, his words coming out nearly inaudible to the rest of the Centaurs. "I have permitted your revilements toward the Tribes of Centaurs, the Duvarharians, the humans, and even our own high leader, but I will not tolerate vituperation toward Stephania Lavoisier for any reason."

"S–she is a disgrace to our Kind!" Colten's eyes darted back and forth from Trojan to others in the room, seeking for help that no one wanted to give.

Trojan's breath hissed between his teeth before he pulled away from Colten, staring down at him as if he were no more than a beetle. "No, Colten. *You* are a disgrace."

He turned to address the assembly once again. "Stephania Lavoisier, in case anyone else has forgotten, is the only child of Drox and Andromeda Lavoisier, the deceased Lord and Lady of Duvarharia. By Ancient High Duvarharian law, Stephania is the next heir by blood to the throne of the Dragon Palace. She is also the adopted daughter of Aeron and Frawnden, your High Chief and Second High Medic." He took his time staring into the souls of those watching him. "By the Law of the Tribes of Centaurs, Stephania, after myself, is also heir to the Trans-Falls Chief position. I do believe, Colten—" he turned back to the younger Centaur—"that makes her your superior in every sense of the ranks and therefore your better." Nearly failing to hide the smirk that crept onto his face when all color drained from Colten's face as he sputtered angrily, Trojan paced the room once more. "In addition, Stephania is also the Farloon, and I pray to the stars I don't have to remind you of the honor and prestige of that position which is, in and of itself, equal to Igentis." He bowed respectfully to Artigal, who nodded his head.

The leaders in the room who weren't loyal to Artigal or Stephania shifted uncomfortably, and the sound of stamping hooves and swishing tails mixed with awkward coughs.

"No matter your personal opinion on the issue at hand in regard to Stephania, you are all sworn to stand behind the Law of the Tribes of Centaurs, which, I am afraid, may rebuke your personal opinions. If you cannot put them aside to fulfill your duty to your tribes, then you will be discharged from your commanding positions. I expect to hear nothing more against our leaders and protectors and now hope I'll not have to repeat our law in an effort to assure your complete cooperation in the betterment of our tribe. Any questions?"

The pregnant silence grew, and Colten slunk to a more discreet part of the room.

"Excellent. Now, if we can all be civil about this, I will continue with my report on Thaddeus." He looked to Artigal for permission to continue, and Artigal nodded. "Brethren, in legends told since the beginning of time, we have always heard of predictions of the end of the world. Many legends speak of different occurrences about this time, and myth must be weighed out of them. However, nearly all the accounts tell of a time when the ancient powers of Rasa, those which gave life to the great beasts of destruction and creation but also governed the sky realm of Hannlurassa, will once more flow freely in Rasa. The general term for these ancient powers is the Duvarharian word *Sleshqumok,* which roughly translates to 'Ancient Magic'.

"In the past, many have been blessed by the Great Emperor with the Pure Magic, *Shushequmok.*" His eyes lingered on Artigal as if he were testing whether Artigal would say something or betray that he could no longer channel the magic like he used to, but the Igentis' face remained like stone.

"Others were given *Kijaqumok,* the Corrupt Magic, by a Fallen Warrior known to have corrupted the destructive side of the Ancient Magic's balance, turning it evil. In the end times, however, legend states some will be born with the ability to channel all *Sleshqumok,* not just one or the other. For those creatures, both Corrupt and Pure Magic will be available to them, and it will be their choice as to which magic they decide to channel—good or evil."

The silence that now reigned in the room was one of awe and intrigue. Though a good number of the Centaurs didn't believe in Ancient Magic, the Sky Realm, or the Great Emperor, most did. Even so, all were enraptured by Trojan's words.

"It's hardly difficult to look through Ancient Duvarharian manuscripts and gather that all those who bear the mark of the Great Lord, or any sort of blessing from him, are able to channel some form of Ancient Magic. With Thaddeus's vast knowledge of Ancient Duvarharian culture and history, it would be child's play for him to assume that Stephania—and the promised helper of the Great Lord's prophecy—would be able to channel Ancient Magic, making them two of the most powerful creatures to walk this planet right now."

Questions buzzed through the room until Gloria met eyes with Trojan and he nodded, showing she was free to ask her question.

"Are you implying that Thaddeus is trying to control Stephania in order to gain her power? That maybe he didn't want to kill her at the battle of the Prophecy but, instead, wanted to kidnap her, and that is why he hasn't exterminated all the Duvarharians, because he was waiting for the savior child of the prophecy?"

A small smile spread across Trojan's face, and relief sparkled in his eyes. "Yes. That is exactly what I am implying, Gloria."

The room erupted once again into chaos, but Trojan merely let them argue amongst themselves for a few minutes until Jorden spoke up.

"What does this have to do with the humans?"

Trojan nodded. "Good question." He pointed once more to the map. "As you know, Drox and Andromeda were slain at the battle of the Prophecy." His finger rested on the mountain range in which the battle had taken place. "After exchanging full battle accounts with Syrus, the military leader of the Duvarharians, we know Drox and Andromeda were not murdered with weapons, Eta poison, or Thaddeus's signature Duvarharian magic."

The room hummed with disbelief.

"An elder at the Dragon Palace by the name of Quinlan, who had studied Ancient Magic and the Sky Realm as a child, was able to find traces of the magic clinging to Syrus from the Lord and Lady's bodies and recognized it as *Kijaqumok*, the Corrupt Magic."

Gasps of amazement and doubt were on all the leaders' lips as they conversed among themselves.

Another younger Centaur, who was almost as new to leadership as Colten, but who had wildly different beliefs, spoke up meekly. "Would this mean Thaddeus was channeling Corrupt Magic when he killed Drox and Andromeda, and could do so again?"

"Absolutely. Past evidence shows that those who are given Ancient Magic either must have strong faith in the Magic's origin, the Great Emperor or the Fallen Warrior, or must have been possessed by the origin. It is more likely to believe that Thaddeus was, in fact, under the influence of the Fallen Warrior—a spirit or demi-god known to the Duvarharian legends only as Raythuz. Even so, it would only take a few years for a powerful Dragon Rider like Thaddeus to learn how to control and perfect the use of Corrupt Magic."

"I still don't see how this pertains to us protecting the humans or not." Colten's loud voice rang from the back of the room, and it took most of Trojan's self-control to resist rolling his eyes in annoyance.

"Colten, if you would let me come to my conclusion, perhaps your breath wouldn't be wasted, and you wouldn't be so confused."

A few Centaurs laughed and poked fun at the younger Centaur but only for a second before they turned their undivided attention back to the Synoliki.

"Harrow, would you please stand and give report on the recent human attack on a border-lying Centaur tribe."

Harrow, a burly, middle aged, black skinned, golden bodied Centaur, stood up, his green eyes slowly sweeping the room. He was a well-respected, proven leader, and not many chose to go up against his judgment.

"It was a straightforward attack, Synoliki. The humans swept in a pincer-like fashion around the center of the tribe with a few skirmishes at the outposts. There were about five thousand human warriors. It shouldn't have taken long to defeat them." He paused for a moment, his eyes staring off into the distance as if he were remembering something unpleasant or confusing. "But they wouldn't die."

"Would you please expound on that statement, Harrow?" Artigal's eyes were fixed unfalteringly on Harrow.

Harrow shrugged, clearly struggling to find a way to explain. "They just wouldn't die, Igentis. You could cut their arm off, but they wouldn't fall. They just kept fighting until they either bled out or you took their head off. They were starved, but they fought like Centaurs. Their feet were torn to shreds, as if they hadn't stopped marching on their way to battle, but they never stumbled. They never ate, though the battle lasted days; they never stopped for water. When we drove them from the tribe, those who were missing limbs merely wrapped up their bleeding stumps and continued on fighting. A darkness hung about them, along with the stench of death. While we fought, a black fog hung over the land and hid the sun. The darkness crept into our hearts and weakened my men. It was ..." His voice trailed off into the fear-stained silence gripping the room.

Trojan's voice, though nearly a whisper, boomed through the room. "Brethren, this is *low* level Corrupt Magic—the ability to make one feel no pain save for the release of death. Creatures cursed with this feel nothing: not the knife in their flesh or the pains of hunger, not the brisk wind on their face or the warmth of a fire. Yearning for death but unable to die, these creatures wreak havoc on whatever they so desire until they themselves are cut to pieces or their own body eats itself for lack of nutrients."

A chill filled the room along with a creeping darkness that wrapped everyone in a strange, unwelcome dread.

"If Thaddeus really is Lord Kosuke in disguise, then he will have full control over the Human Domain in less than a year. With such a large expanse of land and such a powerful empire under his control, it would take him only a few short months to gather himself an army and, depending on his mastery of Corrupt Magic, would be able to make them nearly unstoppable. As neighbors of the Human Domain and strong allies of the Duvarharians, it would not be foolish to believe we would be first to be attacked. By protecting some of the Human lands and regaining them from Lord Kosuke's rule, it is possible that we could put off these undead human armies just long enough for Stephania to regain control of Duvarharia, find the *Kvaźajo*, and destroy Thaddeus once and for all."

A powerful silence gripped the commanders as Trojan's voice rang though the air, reverberating off the polished wood walls.

"That is all I have to say." Trojan bowed his head to Jorden and then Artigal before retreating once more behind the staircase to watch the rest of the meeting in silence.

Slowly, the room moved to life again, and for the next half hour, the Centaurs conversed quietly among themselves before Artigal stood up to address them.

"All in favor of taking an offensive stance against Lord Kosuke and in defense of the Humans, for the cause of delaying Thaddeus's reign, raise your hand."

Nearly every hand in the room slowly rose, some more confidently than others.

Artigal's eyes swept the room as he counted the vote. Three votes were missing, Trojan quickly noticed, and it didn't take him long to realize they were two of Colten's friends and Colten himself as they slunk to the exit. When the door clicked shut signaling their departure, it also spoke plainly of their decision to abandon their right to vote.

A darkness only Trojan and Artigal seemed to notice seeped into the room, a strange black fog swirling at their feet. The room hummed with unease, and Trojan looked up to see Artigal desperately trying to hide the pain that was clearly racing through his chest.

Everything in Trojan revolted against the darkness, and he could feel the Synoliki magic surging through him, preparing to fight.

He knew he had to follow Colten and his friends. He was sure they were the bearers of this sudden darkness. As he was slipping out the door, he heard Artigal announce that the Tribes would be taking action to protect the humans.

A small spark of relief flooded him as he shut the door and breathed in the fresh air. They had made a small step toward pushing back the evil at their borders, but as he saw Colten disappear into the forest, he knew the darkness was gathering in Trans-Falls as well.

§

"AND THAT'S WHEN I slapped his hind end with the flat of my blade and ran off. He squealed in pain for a long time after that." Lamora couldn't stop the laughter she tried to hide behind her hand.

Ravillian stomped his hoof, a fierce scowl on his face. "As well he should. He had no right to talk to you or touch you like that."

"I agree. Stephania, did you hear what I said?"

Stephania shook herself back to attention, an unexplainable chill slithering down her spine. She forced her eyes away from the forest to look at Lamora. "I'm sorry." She blushed. "I guess I spaced out."

What might have been hurt flashed through Lamora's eyes, but it quickly vanished as she jumped back into her story.

"I was talking to Arore, and he kept making all kinds of advances on me. I think he's always been infatuated with me since training, but anyways ..."

Lamora's voice faded off again as Stephania's attention wandered back to the forest. She tried so hard to listen, to devote her focus to her friend, but something in the dark shadows drew her in. A *Ñáfagaræy* leapt out of the brush and raced through the leaves, straight for the trail they were on.

Lamora jumped in surprise as the blue rabbit-like creature shot past them and disappeared into the forest again. She and Ravillian quickly resumed their conversation, unmoved by the animal's appearance, but Stephania was enraptured, remembering what Dalton said when they first arrived: "*They're usually nocturnal and actually have four eyes to see better in dim lighting. Obviously, we scared it out of its nest.*" But she didn't sense other Centaurs in the forest besides her and her friends. Something else must have startled the creature.

"Are you okay, Stephania?"

Stephania cursed herself for not paying more attention to her friends. It had been harder to navigate the realm of friendship than she had anticipated, and she felt she was already failing. Not to mention, she didn't want them to worry about her, and now they were. "I'm fine." She tore her eyes from the forest and plastered a thin smile on her face, wishing she could do something more convincing.

They both narrowed their eyes at her, as if they were sizing her up, so she added with a fake yawn, "I'm just tired. Didn't sleep well last night." It wasn't necessarily a lie. She had been haunted by that horrible nightmare again and again, every night since coming here. Sometimes it changed a little, but one thing was always the same: she was the murderer. Nevertheless, her being tired was still a lie and poor excuse—the same one she told everyone when they got too close. *But at least it works.*

Ravillian and Lamora were apparently satisfied with her answer and merely shrugged, talking about how the stars had been in a strange pattern and it seemed no one lately was getting good sleep.

A sigh of relief left Stephania's lips, and she made another effort to listen to what they were saying.

Soon, they reached the grand waterfalls that Trans-Falls had been named after.

"Wow," Stephania whispered at the sight of it. If she had thought the waterfall back in New-Fars was awe inspiring, she had no words or feelings to describe this.

It wasn't necessarily the magnitude of these waterfalls that was impressive, it was how many of them thundered over the cliffs. Nearly ten small torrents poured from the top of the cliff down to a second pool where they then spilled off into three roaring rapids before plummeting to the lake below; all the water then collected into one small river.

"Chief Aeron and Frawnden really outdid themselves with the festival this year." Lamora sighed dreamily and fingered the beaded necklace someone had given her that night.

Ravillian rolled his eyes. "Are you ever going to stop going on about it?"

Lamora slapped his shoulder, and he winced, though it clearly didn't hurt him. "Of course not. If you hadn't had so much wine to drink, I think you would've enjoyed it a lot more."

Ravillain stared at her in disbelief. "You're kidding me, right? You speak as if I didn't have the night of my life with my best friend at one of Trans-Fall's most important and memorable festivals. Besides, you're the one who had seven bottles, not me."

Stephania's eyes widened. "Gods of all, *seven?*"

Lamora blushed and waved her hands in dismissal. "Okay, so I got a little carried away. But that's why I have Ravillian around. To keep me from doing anything too stupid."

Ravillian's eyebrows raised as he coughed to hide his laugh. "Of course. I always keep you from doing stupid things. Like how I let you try to walk on your front legs because I couldn't stop laughing."

Lamora's face turned blood red as Stephania howled with laughter trying to picture how a Centaur would even attempt such a ridiculous thing.

"I am saddened that the festival is all about new birth and the forest awakening from winter but that it doesn't actually wake up anymore." Ravillian's tactful change of the subject spared Lamora any more embarrassment, but from the tone of his voice, Stephania knew he cared more about the topic than just its usefulness as a distraction.

"I thought I might have seen a Faun." Stephania sat up from the rock she had been laying on. "Down in the trees."

Ravillian's eyebrows shot up, and hope lit up his eyes. "Are you serious?"

Stephania nodded, but before she could describe her experience, Lamora laughed. "Yes, but you were also on your third bottle of *uafañoshigo*. There's no telling what you saw."

A hot flush rose to Stephania's face, and Ravillian shrugged.

"Maybe you did, maybe you didn't. I don't see why she couldn't have seen a Faun or forest spirit. The festival is all about the forest coming back to life, maybe this time it worked."

They all knew he was wrong. It hadn't worked, no matter how much the Centaurs wanted the life of the forest to come back, the trees never moved, and the Fauns never appeared to dance and sing.

They spent the rest of their afternoon hiking and swimming around the falls, the cold water offering Stephania an excellent distraction from the unusual darkness of the woods, which only seemed to grow more ominous since their discussion about it earlier. Though she was sure Lamora was right—the wine must have been playing tricks on her—she couldn't shake the feeling that something was watching her from the shadows.

Lamora seemed to feel the same. "Do you ever feel like the forest is watching you?" Lamora shifted her weight, her legs curled underneath her, and plucked a *Leño-zhego* flower, twirling it nervously between her fingers.

Words and images of whispered secrets and moving trees tumbled through Stephania's mind, but it was a long time before she had the courage to break the silence. "It *does* watch you."

Ravillian and Lamora exchanged questioning glances at each other and then to Stephania.

"What do you mean?" Ravillian moved so he could see Stephania better.

Stephania looked down at her lap, forcing herself not to play with the string she had picked loose from the small hole in her pants, almost wishing she had just stayed silent. "I've seen them move—the trees, I mean. They made a path for Uncle Dalton and I when we left New-Fars. They protected us from the Etas. And there was another time when I was given a Lyre." She frowned as if she were saying too much. "Ever since then, I've felt them watching me, and sometimes if I look hard enough, I can *see* them watching me."

"What lyre?"

Stephania was taken back by Lamora's question. "The one I always have with me, wrapped in the blanket on my saddle." She tipped her head in the direction Braken was grazing.

"I've never seen it."

An uneasiness grew in Stephania. "It's the one that glows green and is shaped like an 's'."

Both friends shook their heads at each other.

Frustration grew in Stephania until realization washed over her. *They've never seen it because I've never held it. Not since that day ...* It felt like someone had dumped ice water down her back.

"Can we see it?" Lamora made a move to get up, and something between a strangled cry of "no" and terror leapt from Stephania's throat as she scrambled to her feet, her hand held out in protest.

Her eyes flitted back and forth from Ravillian to Lamora and then to Braken and where the Lyre hung from his saddle as he grazed. Her heart raced in her chest as little beads of sweat clung uncomfortably to her chest. A flash of fear and worry could be seen in their eyes, and she instantly regretted her outburst. How would she talk her way out of this?

Laughter that sounded so fake it hardly sounded like laughter jumped from her throat as she waved her shaking hand. "Oh, I left it at home today. And besides, I want to be able to show you guys it when I can play a few more songs." She silently thanked the gods no one told Lamora and Ravillian she had known how to play many songs since she was just a child.

Neither seemed too convinced as she sat down, but they didn't press further until Ravillian brought up the trees again.

"Why didn't you tell us you can see and hear them?"

Dread mingled with anger flashed through her, but she shoved it down so it wouldn't show and merely shrugged instead. "You never asked, and I didn't want you to think I'm crazy."

A warm smile spread on Ravillain's face. "I don't think you're crazy, Stephania. And I'll make sure to ask more about you instead of telling you so much about Centaurs and Trans-Falls all the time."

Lamora laughed, but Stephania couldn't help but scoff. *If you knew me better, you'd think differently. You wouldn't want to know me. To know all the nightmares, the bullying, the selfishness.* "Thanks, Ravillian."

"Although it does seem a bit far-fetched." Lamora frowned, twining a bit of her mane around her fingers, something Stephania noticed she did when she was pondering. "Even though all our legends say the forest is alive and that all spirits and creatures who once lived inside of it are asleep now, it just seems a little hard to believe. Doesn't it?"

"I believe it," Ravillian defended without hesitation.

Stephania only shrugged. "I don't know. I've never heard your legends. And Uncle Dalton says I should only believe in things I can see and prove."

"But you said you've seen the trees move. Isn't that proof?"

She turned away from Ravillian's intense gaze and shrugged again. "I don't know."

Their conversation lapsed into silence as they lost themselves in the dark shadows of the forest until the suns had set low and Ravillian finally stated they should head back home.

"You're right," Lamora agreed as she stood and yawned.

Stephania couldn't hold back her giggle as she watched her friends stretch.

"What's so funny?" Ravillian's voice was distorted as he extended his back feet and held his arms high above his head.

Stephania shook her head, trying and failing to subdue her laughter. "Nothing, nothing."

She sat for a while longer, feeling as if it were impossible to inspire movement into her heavy limbs. He friends walked for a short distance before they realized she wasn't following. Lamora turned back and called for her, but she shook her head.

"I think I want to stay a bit longer."

"Won't Dalton be worried?"

She slowly shook her head, dragging her eyes away from the forest. "He went to the library again today. Said he would be home late."

"What about Aeron and Frawnden?"

But Ravillian's words floated away as a muffled silence settled over her. Movement in the trees caught her eye. It looked like a dark creature staring at them from behind a tree. Watching. Waiting. She sat completely still, hardly breathing. The *Zelauwgugey* pulled her; the forest pleaded with her. The darkness in the trees grew heavy. Dread settled. Her eyes glossed, staring into nothing; her arms pulled her knees closer to her chest, her hair moved in the gentle breeze. She felt ... everything. And yet her body didn't feel like her own. She felt like she *was* the forest, looking down at herself, calling herself, begging her to—

"Stephania! Are you okay?" Lamora was shaking her shoulders; Ravillian was helping her to her feet.

"It's the power," Stephania stuttered, seeing through them and into the forest.

"What do you mean? What power?" Lamora held out a tankard of water, but Stephania batted it away. Ravillian steadied her as she tried to take a step.

Her heart slammed against her chest as if it were trying to run away. Her body hummed, and her mind crackled with an unwanted power, the kind that sends creatures jumping off a cliff even when they know they'll die. She knew this power. She had felt it before. Images of her killing the humans in New-Fars flashed through her mind along with her dreams of the man who stalked and murdered. It was the power Artigal had said never to speak or think of again. But she couldn't help it. She had promised him, but her promise was long broken. The power surged through her. A memory almost surfaced. She could see a child, a child in her arms, but the child had red hair, like herself. A Centaur stood in front of her—a white Centaur. Voices echoed softly, *"Thanks to the Kijaqumok, I know even more."* Purple eyes were boring into her as his voice rang horribly all around her. "I'm coming for you, Stephania," he hissed. "No matter where you are, I will find you. You are *mine*."

She couldn't stop the scream from rising in her throat, couldn't stop herself from flailing against the arms and hands reaching out, trying to grab her, steal her away, control her, and consume her.

"Stephania! Stephania!"

She screamed against her name, against everything that haunted her.

"Great Emperor, help us!" she heard a man yell.

Then everything was quiet.

She was standing in the tall grass. The waterfalls roared behind her. The suns' light streamed over the trees. Hands held her, softly, gently, not grabbing or demanding.

The arms encircled her, and she cried into her friend's shoulder.

"Shh. It's okay, Stephania," Lamora whispered as she patted her back, and as Ravillian smoothed her hair, placing his head against hers.

They asked her what happened, if she was okay, if she wanted them to take her home, but all she could do was cry and beg to be left alone.

Despite Lamora's soft words and caring touch, Stephania could see in her eyes, sense from her presence, fear.

She fears me because I am a freak. I'm a monster. A murder. And deep down she knows.

"I'm going to send Aeron and Frawnden to you if you refuse to come with us," Ravillian demanded and Lamora agreed.

"No, please don't." Panic rose in her. She didn't want any one of her parents seeing her like this, didn't want to endure their questions and probing. "I'm fine, really. But please, just leave me alone. I need to be alone." She could barely look into their eyes. When she did, she saw the eyes of the dead Centaurs that haunted her dreams, and the eyes of the humans who had stood against her the last time this power had found her.

Finally, after more back and forth arguing, they gave in. As they turned to leave, she heard Lamora whisper, "Do you think she's okay? Shouldn't we stay?"

A long silence issued before Stephania heard Ravillian answer, "No. Obviously, she's not, but sometimes, I think there are places she must go which we can never follow."

Then they were gone, and she was alone. She crumpled to her knees, her face resting in her hands, and the darkness pressing in on her. She knew that at least now, if she couldn't fight this power, they would be safe, no matter how alone she felt.

Finally, she stood, trying to brush the tears from her eyes. The forest closed in around her and Braken, a small sliver of light illuminating the path to him. She walked along it, dreading what she knew she was moving toward, but wondering if she would lose this pain, this weight, this dread, if only she played that Lyre. Her fingers reached out for the instrument, and it hummed, mesmerizing her. Glowing green light filled the clearing as her fingers wrapped around it.

§

TROJAN KNELT TO THE ground, tracing his fingers around the hoofprint in the soft forest floor. The suns were just beginning to set, but everything around him was shadowed in unnatural darkness. He could feel the *Kijaqumok* shifting through Trans-Falls, and the goodness in him revolted against it.

He closed his eyes and let the Synoliki magic flow through him. It took a few minutes of concentration, but slowly, an image formed around him as he peered into the magic realm. It was a hazy image, as if he were looking through painted glass, but it was the best he could do, and it was all he needed.

He could see the three Centaurs as if they were dark silhouettes with shadowy beating hearts inside them and black veins through their flesh. Their figures tramped the prints into the dirt as they headed toward the Trans-Falls. A fleeting image of the falls showed a girl's red, wispy figure standing by her horse, alone, her fingers reaching for the Lyre, which was hidden in the packs on her horse's back. The darkness that moved ahead of the three Centaurs circled around her and crept up her ankles before a bright green light flashed around him, casting him out of the magic realm and back into the physical.

With a cry of rage, he galloped into the forest, his sword appearing in his hand. Of all the times for her to play the *Zelauwgugey* ...

His worst suspicions had been right. The *Kijaqumok* had possessed Colten and his friends, and they were going after Stephania and the *Zelauwgugey*.

§

SHE COULD FEEL the cold darkness swirling around her, but the light of the *Zelauwgugey* encompassed her like a warm blanket, sheltering her from the world around her.

The green glow increased under her fingers as she stroked the smooth black wood, feeling the bumps of the masterfully carved snake scales.

Enraptured and controlled by the calling, all sense of danger left her; she slowly plucked the strings, softly and delicately, as if she were afraid it would break under her touch.

At first, nothing happened, but as she began to play a song, the green light spread through the trees. Coaxing strength from the Lyre and her own magic, she poured the power into the Lyre. But no matter how much she tried, the green glow didn't grow, and the trees didn't move any more than a weak shudder. It seemed she could do no more. Disappointment filled her heart. She wasn't strong enough to break past whatever barrier was holding the forest asleep.

Just when she was about to release the magic and give up, words from a mostly forgotten vision drifted to her on the breeze. *"I will wait no longer. Whether you are ready or not, they will wake. I will make sure of it."* The voice filled her with cold light and strength—the way she thought it might feel if she drank pure star light. Her veins felt as if they were filled with icy fire. Taking a deep breath, she gathered the foreign power to her and released it into the Lyre.

The barrier cracked.

The forest began to move.

The green light rushed through the trees as they bent closer to her and the Lyre; shapes began to form out of the darkness.

Creaking, moaning, and groaning filled the forest as the trees bent, twisting slowly and shifting their arms, stretching in the chilling evening air.

Braken tossed his mane and whinnied, fear widening his eyes.

"Shhh ..." She released a bit of calming magic on him and undid his lead. "Go home," she breathed softly, pushing him home with her mind. With one last nibble to her sleeve, he turned and cantered into the shadows.

She gasped with shock and delight as a deer leapt out of the woods moments later, bounding straight toward her before jumping over roots that had moved up out of the ground and back into the brush.

The sound of tearing dirt, moss, and grass filled the forest as the trees pulled up their roots and sank them back into the ground, pulling themselves toward her until they were standing in a ring around her, their sighs, moans, and creaks filling the air along with the whispers of their leaves and branches, all of it in harmony with the music she was playing.

Suddenly, vines twisted up around her legs and around the Lyre, slowly taking it from her. When they took the Lyre, she only panicked a moment as she waited for the familiar tightness to grip her heart in the Lyre's absence, but when the vines struck up a new song, she felt only peace.

The fresh, powerful notes moved through the air, and something else began to happen—something Stephania had only heard about in legends.

Spirits—with the likeness of gentle young women and men, and a few of them old—began to step *out* of the trees.

Her eyes widened with recognition. *Tree nymphs.*

Spirits by nature, they floated across the ground instead of walking, their bodies constantly moving and waving in the wind as if they were merely shadows or wisps of smoke.

Laughing, they moved among the trees, weaving their way in and out of their physical tree bodies. Dancing, they took each other's hands and sang to the music of the Lyre, their light feet never touching the ground as they spun around Stephania, almost in complete ignorance of her.

Blossoms from the trees and leaves of all kinds twirled to the ground while flowers, moss, and mushrooms sprang up after the nymphs, the glowing green of the *Zelauw-gugey* giving light to everything around them.

Then, another sound filled the air—a bugle horn—a wild sound that caused her heart to race.

Shivers ran up and down her spine. Memories of the night after she got the Lyre flooded her.

Fauns.

Hooves beat against the ground, sounding muffled, as if they were very far away, though she could feel them in her chest as if they were running right beside her.

Faces peered around the trunks of the great trees as the branches bent to give passage. It was hard to make out details, shrouded in shadows as they were, but she could make out what appeared to be horns growing out of the tops of the Fauns' heads and curling around their faces. Drums joined the throbbing music, and a cloud settled over her as if the drug of a dream.

A throat cleared itself behind her, and she whirled around, face to face with none other than the very faun who had given her the *Zelauwgugey* months ago.

His large, sparkling, yellow eyes shone brightly in the mystical green light as he pressed a finger to his lips, quietly hushing her when she opened her mouth.

She could see him more clearly now than on that day, and she was delighted to see that instead of regular ears, his curved out in the shape of a goat's. His face was youthful and clean shaven, save for a long, curly goatee, which grew from the tip of his oddly pointed chin. Hair grew thick on his arms and back, though less so on his chest. From his waist down, he was covered in sleek goat hair, which clothed his strong goat legs and his hooves that danced anxiously against the ground.

Before she could say anything, he took her hand in his surprisingly strong grip and pulled her with him. "Come. Dance with us, Dragon Child."

She could hardly feel the earth beneath her feet as she was thrown into the chaos of the forest's dance.

Every creature had linked hands in three large circles around the *Zelauwgugey*, each bigger than the one inside it. Their feet stomped to the beat of the music, their wild, yelling, howling voices rising high into the dusk sky.

Almost carelessly, they seemed to fling her from one to the other, but despite their wild dances and howls, she never once felt unsafe; she felt only the thrill of the dance, the wild throb of her heart in time with the music and the very life and spirit of the forest as it moved with her.

They stopped twirling her around for a moment long enough to place her between the Faun who had pulled her into the dance and a female Faun. Stephania quickly noticed the males and females looked very similar to each other, except the females sometimes had longer hair with more *Leño-zhego* flowers woven throughout, thinner faces, and mature breasts, which they seemed to neither clothe nor keep covered.

More Fauns and nymphs joined them, some of them yawning and stretching, a few of them stumbling before slumping back to the ground to sleep; the others merely danced around the sleeping ones as if it were all part of the fun.

Then, in one moment, the beauty and glory of their dance was shattered with a piercing scream.

Stephania was violently wrenched away from the golden-haired female whose hand clung to hers. A dark shadow streaked through the circle of trees, and many more screams rent the air. The darkness darted through the female Faun, and she convulsed before dropping to the ground—lifeless.

Stephania screamed and tried to lunge after the Faun but was wrenched the other way. A tree whose spirit had been killed fell right where she had stood only seconds before; its leaves and branches shriveled as a black sickness spread through its trunk.

Blindly, she felt herself being lead through the falling trees and dying Fauns until they reached the center of the clearing again. The vines that had wrapped around the Lyre were being consumed by the dark shadow, the Lyre's magic unable to keep the darkness at bay.

With surprising agility, the Faun who had led her jumped nearly fourteen feet into the air, tore the Lyre from the vines and shoved it into her hands. She couldn't help but remember that day he had done the same, months ago, when life hadn't been so confusing and frightening.

Feeling as if she were either going to faint or throw up, she stumbled backward as the vines instantly died, the light of the Lyre snuffed out, sending the entire forest into dark, murderous chaos.

"Run, Dragon Child! You must protect the *Zelauwgugey*! You must protect the life of the forest! You must not forsake us!" He shoved her away, his glowing yellow eyes the last thing she saw before she fled into the screaming, dying trees.

CHAPTER 8

Mount Drymoore, Far West mountains of old Ravenwood

Present Day

HOW MUCH LONGER DO you think we should stay here looking, Yollen?" A black skinned and bodied Centaur shifted the pack that was digging into his shoulder.

He turned his eyes to the Centaur he was addressing—an older, markedly smaller roan with darkly tanned skin. He was lying on the ground, his legs curled under him, hands held open, face turned to the starry night sky, eyes closed.

"Hmm." The meditating roan barely moved before his emerald green eyes snapped open, the stars shining in his eyes as he searched them for guidance. "Artigal said as long as it takes. So, we shall stay here, Dusan, as long as it takes." As his eyes roved the heavens, his voice grew quiet. "Even if it takes us until the end of the world."

Not another word was said, and Dusan settled down beside his companion, each not moving a single muscle as they stared up at the stars. Sometimes, the stars would write messages across the heavens, but other times, they merely sparkled and stared back, completely silent. This was one of those nights.

"Remember what they taught us? About the stars and the sky realm?"

Dusan laughed then smiled. "Of course. How could I forget? I could hear it a thousand times and never tire of it."

"Me too." Silence stretched until Yollen took a deep breath and recalled their beloved lessons. "Our forefathers came from the stars." He took another deep breath of the sharp, cold night mountain air. "It is said that beautiful, fantastical creatures were made out of the dust of the stars and were created to populate Hanluurasa. Then, when Rasa was created and the foundations settled, some of the creatures were sent to populate the ground, giving their own light to the world. It was here, on the grassy and forest floors, that some of the creatures took the shapes of Fauns, Centaurs, Sphinxes, and other such creatures that displayed a perfect blend of both mankind and the dumb beasts that walked on the land. Others found life in the trees and rivers of the land and melded their spirits with the physical world in that way. They became the water and forest nymphs, and they are our brothers and sisters.

And it was here on the land that the creatures of the forest, the nymphs, and the Centaurs, the Sházuk, spoke to their brothers in the heavens; and the heavens, who could see the fate of all from Hanluurasa, helped the Kin and nymphs to create peace between man and nature. Those fathers blended into the forest, and so the forest is our father, and the suns, and moons, and the stars are all their brothers."

Dusan smiled gently, his eyes tracing the many visible galaxies across the skies, easily picking out constellations as familiar and intimate to him as his own mother.

Yollen continued. "Soon, the Centaurs rose above the other mixed Kinds and were gifted to stand alongside the Dragon Riders, forever in connection to the chosen kind, making us all One under the Great Emperor, and we were given the great task of reading the heavens for the future. We were chosen to be mediators between Rasa and the Stars of Hanluurasa. Then the Fauns were graced with the gifts of the forests and became more one with the land. They were chosen to be mediators between the greater Kinds of the land and the land itself. They, with the land, their brothers, lie in slumber, waiting until the end of the world when they will once more walk freely amongst the other creatures of Rasa."

Yollen sighed heavily, his eyes sparkling with excitement and wonder. "And one day ..." He traced his fingers across the heavens, a wistful longing in his voice, as if he could see Hanluurasa. "The forest will awaken, and I, like many others before me, will go home to the Great Emperor and walk, once again, with my brothers and fathers in the great halls of Hanluurasa."

CHAPTER 9

Eta Stronghold in High Northern Ventronovia

Present Day

P URE AND CORRUPT MAGIC *raged against each other. He could feel their struggle.*

The Corrupt Kijaquomok overpowered the Pure Magic, and he thought he had won. Triumph surged through him, but suddenly, so did something else.

The child in his arms screamed, and a blinding flash of light threw him to the ground. The mark of the Great Lord burned in his mind, burned into his soul, burned everything within him. He screamed, and the child screamed before everything went dark and he was lost in pain and worthlessness.

Like every day before, Thaddeus stirred awake to the wretched soreness in his legs and back from the unrelenting stone throne under him. Only, today seemed especially painful. He had delved into the door between himself and Stephania again last night, just as he had the night before, and the night before that, but all he had to show for it was a few shattered memories of a girl swimming with a young Centaur and practicing archery. He had tried moving closer to the present but had found even less. Usually, more recent memories were easier to recall, but something was wrong about those memories: he hadn't been able to find them. If he didn't know any better, he would've guessed she had been deprived of magic after the age of five. Only non-magical creatures were unable to recall memories.

A string of curses poured from his lips. He had a direct passageway to Stephania, but the Pure Magic spreading its poison through his mind and body kept him just at bay. He could only wade through the dream world and the realm of memories for a brief time before searing pain tore through him and forced him back into his body. Then he faced the issue of her lack of memories past the age of five. No one could take away a Duvarharian's magic unless they bled the Rider out. So either Stephania was dead or Artigal had done something to her, preventing her from accessing her magic; whatever the cause, she had been virtually untraceable the past twelve years.

Anger stirred in him, but he almost couldn't find the strength to nurse it into motivation. Everything he could've wanted was just at the tips of his fingers, but he had no way to break the barrier between it and himself. At least, not without killing either himself or Stephania, which, contrary to what all of Ventronovia thought, he did not want in the slightest.

Finally, he cracked open his eyes. The hall was still dark in the morning light, and he could just barely make out the form of his dragon, not sleeping but not awake either.

With a cry of pain and frustration, he dragged himself from his throne and muttered a small enough healing spell so the aches melted from his joints, but not without painful protest from the Pure Magic raging inside him, tainting his own magic.

Slowly, he dragged himself to the stacks and stacks of books littering the edges of the dark hall, shifting through them until he found what he was looking for.

Feeling all eight hundred years of his age, he sank to the ground and studied the tome's dusty cover. It read: *A Study on the Sleshqumok.*

It was one of his oldest books, having been one he rescued from Duvaharia's antique libraries just before he burned the city to the ground with acid. He had already learned so much from this study's words, it seemed impossible he would learn anything more. Nonetheless he opened it and turned to the chapter titled "Channeling *Sleshqumok.*"

The first half of the chapter droned on about how only certain chosen individuals could channel the Ancient Magic and what the requirements were. He couldn't stomach reading so much about the Duvarharian's Great Lord, so he skimmed most of it, except for the part that mentioned the Great Lord's mark.

He had always been comfortable in the belief that the Great Lord's mark was a brand, one usually found somewhere on their body after birth or a supernatural confrontation with the Great Lord, but one small note caught his eye for the first time. "The Mark has been recently recorded to expand beyond a symbolic tattoo and could possibly manifest as or possess other characteristics not yet known to us," he read aloud with awe.

Stephania's hair is her mark. Kyrell's sleepy voice pierced his thoughts, and he readily agreed. But that would mean it wouldn't be so easy to tell who was marked or not. A strange hope welled up inside him, but he shoved it aside. He had lived much too long on his own determination and ambition to have hope

He flipped a few pages and kept reading. "Those who carry the mark of the Great Lord were initially thought to have been given control over only *Shushequmok,* but it was later found these creatures were simply given the ability to channel all Ancient Magic. It had usually only been their choice to use *Shushequmok.*"

A few more pages later, he read, "... through careful studies, *Kijaqumok* was found to be more physically powerful than *Shushequmok*. Though all properties of *Shushequmok* were unable to be tested, it is our belief that it is the weaker power."

He flipped through another couple of pages and kept reading. "It is believed by some and mentioned in legends that during the end of the world, Ancient Magic will flow once more through the land and not all will have to be chosen to control its power."

He threw the book onto the table and gazed down at his hands. His Shalnoa were glowing very dimly, more dimly than they had for a long time.

Stephania as a child had channeled the *Shushequmok* Artigal had released but had been unable to control. It was the magic she channeled that had caused him to be stranded in this wretched Eta Castle for nearly sixteen years. The lingering effects of the *Kijaqumok* he channeled when killing the Duvarharian rulers had provided enough protection from the *Shushequmok* for him to make a few appearances in the Human Domain. Besides that, the wretched Pure Magic had left him with just enough of itself to render him almost unable to use his any of his own magic—the magic that mattered most to him—but not enough to actually kill him, at least not quickly.

He held out his hand and muttered a string of words in the Ancient Duvarharian language. Even now, he couldn't cast magic without stating his exact intentions.

His hand shook. A bead of blood dripped from his lips. His heart twisted inside him. Sweat beaded on his forehead.

Slowly, as if a small wind had blown through them, the books on the table shook, their pages flipping lazily.

Then white light exploded all around him, burning his mind, his soul, and his body, its fire spreading, raging through his veins.

Screaming, he released the spell and collapsed to the ground, clutching his chest in agony, curses spilling from his frothing, bloody mouth.

Within seconds, he felt the warmth of his dragon's tail as Kyrell comforted him, pressing his enormous head to his rider.

Together, they shared in the pain.

"Curse them all. If only they knew. If only they knew."

Tägäsutyä señekol. It is they who are really destroying the land. Their lawlessness causes their poverty and suffering. If only they would submit. We could build them a new empire with peace and equality where all are able to share in the benefits of magic and bask in the rich wealth of the Duvarharians. Kyrell's thoughts shook with their shared fury.

"But how can I when the *Kijaqumok* has abandoned me along with its Master? I rely on my own magic, my own power, my own sacrifices to renew Ventronovia for all this time, and he does one small thing for me—killing Drox and Andromeda—before leaving me to rot. This is why I curse the gods!" he screamed into the dark halls as if hoping someone would hear, but no one spoke back. "Reliance on deities, ancient powers, gods, and anything not of your own making was exactly what destroyed Duvarharia in the first place. I was a fool to put my trust into the hands of vile scum like Raythuz and his Cursed Magic."

And now it is the only thing that will save you and save the future we have been striving to reach.

Thaddeus's shoulders sagged as he buried his head in his hands. "I know. And that is what I hate most. I need him now. He did a splendid job of making *siv* sure of it."

Kyrell hissed, his huge forked purple tongue slithering in and out of shining white teeth. *Thaddeus ...*

But he wasn't given time to finish before the air tore open around them like fabric and the screaming started.

A dark hole materialized in the center of the throne room and a low roar rumbled through the dark walls.

Thaddeus was already on his feet, his great battle axe in hand, his dragon's acid dripping from its blades. He could feel Kyrell's looming presence behind him, and it offered him some solace. Even without magic, they would be a formidable pair to take down, and gods be cursed if he was going down without a fight.

Loud snorts and the thunder of hooves echoed through the cold air until dark shapes leapt from the demonic portal and filled the room.

A sense of utter awe and terror filled both dragon and rider as they laid eyes on the creatures. They were enormous, some even bigger than draft horses. They had bodies like a horse and heads like a horse, but their faces ended in a horrible beak, their eyes and features almost humanlike. From there, the horse-like characteristics disappeared into a tail like a snake's but with long, matted hair at its end. Their front feet appeared like those of eagles or a dragon's. They seemed to stand mainly on their back legs, which were similar to the legs and paws of a leopard. From just behind their shoulder blades sprouted wings much like a bat's, but with bloody cuts and torn holes.

The stench of death and fear flooded the room and choked anything else out.

Neither Thaddeus nor Kyrell moved. It seemed the creatures chose to ignore them in favor of turning their attention to the portal.

Then, as if the whole room were taking a breath, a swell of air rushed past them before everything went still.

The portal swirled red and black before a long leg shone through, a dark, tall figure following it. The creature's features constantly shifted as it looked back and forth through the room until its gaze landed on Thaddeus.

Its features started to warp and change until it somewhat resembled a man. Standing nearly thirteen feet tall with broad, crushing muscles, it dwarfed Thaddeus, and he couldn't help but suck in a breath of annoyance.

The creature's skin was a pale sea green, which looked rather sickly, and its eyes shone a dark, mustard yellow, though they still managed to glow in the dimly lit hall.

It flexed six long, spindly fingers on each hand, apparently getting used to its new form before its black lips cocked in a smile, revealing more than two rows of razor-sharp teeth.

Mindlessly, a dark green tongue slithered in and out of his mouth.

"May the suns smile upon your presence, Thaddeus." The creature held his hand over his heart and bowed low.

Thaddeus said nothing, only walked through the path the other demons made for him until he and Kyrell were standing in front of the being as the portal closed.

Purple eyes stared into yellow until Kyrell growled low.

"And you as well, Kyrell." The lead demon bowed to the dragon, a certain venom in his tone and eyes. It was obvious he loathed dragons with all his existence.

"What do you want, creature?"

The smile grew on the being's face, but it did nothing to radiate reassurance or trust. "Straight to business. Good. I am here because the End of Rasa draws near and I need a champion."

Thaddeus narrowed his eyes. The last thing he wanted was a deity pulling the strings behind his own reformation of Ventronovia, but the throb of Pure Magic inside him told him he might not have much choice. "Go on."

The being's yellow eyes scanned the room until they landed on the stack of books Thaddeus had just stood by. He nodded with appreciation. "You've done some research. Excellent. So you've discovered you can channel low level *Kijaqumok*."

"Yes, but I have found it to be ... unreliable."

The being's gaze moved back to Thaddeus, lingering on his chest where it seemed he could see past Thaddeus's armor straight to his wound. "Ah, you would, wouldn't you? You know what your problem is, Thaddeus?"

He didn't answer, so the being continued.

"You don't have faith."

Kyrell hissed, and Thaddeus drew his axe in front of him. The demon seemed unfazed.

"It's not just of those who follow the Great Lord or the Great Emperor, you know. Faith goes both ways, just the same as power. It is like a key. A key used to unlock the

EFFIE JOE STOCK

powers beyond your own."

"Get to the point, *ñekol*."

"You are a vessel, and I am stuck being a spirit. I want you to be the catalyst for my reformation of Rasa. You've done a splendid job these last eight hundred years or so, and I want to personally endorse you. You shall have the power you need to do what you will. Nothing shall stand in your way now."

Artigal, Stephania, and the helper promised to Stephania in the prophecy came to his mind. They would all have the ability to channel Pure Magic. Was the *Kijaqumok* really strong enough? Was it really worth it? A sickening dread filled him, but he shoved it aside. He had made sacrifices before, this would be no different. He could take this demon's help, and then when he needed him no longer, he could cast him aside, just as he had with the Eta King Veltrix.

"How do I know if the *Kijaqumok* will be powerful enough to do what I will it?"

The creature raised his hand and twitched a finger, a lazy, almost bored smile on his lips. "It is more than powerful enough."

Instantly, Thaddeus felt the Pure Magic drain out of his body. In a moment, his mind, body, and soul were all healed. He was free from the agony in his mind and body, free from all the barriers between him, the dream world, and his magic.

A cry of elation left his lips as he easily conjured a bow and arrow from his magic, his dragon roaring behind him.

"But as for whether or not it will obey you ..."

In one clean movement, the being stepped forward and clamped his massive, clammy hand around Thaddeus's throat, effortlessly lifting him into the air.

Kyrell threw himself at the man, jaws gaping wide, but chains of black magic encircled him and tightened until his bones cracked.

Darkness swirled through Thaddeus's mind, and the burning pain of Ancient Magic coursing through his blood seared through his body. The most unimaginable pain tore through him until he couldn't hear his own screams, see the room around him, or even feel the demon's taloned hand on his throat.

Then as soon as it began, it ended and he was on the floor, clawing his throat and trying to breath in the air that still smelled like rot and death.

All the humor and nonchalant politeness disappeared from the being without a trace. "It will *never* obey you. It obeys me only. Your end has come, Thaddeus. You did well, but you failed. Stephania, a babe of a rider, laid you low the day she channeled the Pure Magic. Something in you died that day, but I have given you a second chance and a new power to give you life. I've watched you for the last sixteen years and have found your resolve to be compelling. Now I give you your choice. You can either rot in

100

Susahu like you should have years ago, or you can be reborn into my kingdom. What do you choose?"

Tears from stinging eyes streamed down Thaddeus's face as he forced his body to his feet, every muscle, bone, and nerve in his body aching with pain. Kyrell groaned behind him in equal agony.

His fingers traced the hideous scar down his face, the magic he used to cover it now gone, and a memory from the day he obtained that scar rang in his mind. *"I know what you seek, Thaddeus."* Artigal had told him. *"It cannot be found on the path you follow. But there is time to turn back. You must seek out the true Lord of Rasa. It is never too late to turn back. Never."*

The time for turning back was long gone. He could either give up and die, or he could accept this being's request and live out the dream he had started all those years ago. Despite what Artigal had once promised him in the distant past, Thaddeus knew he would find no saving grace from the Pure Magic. Not today. Not for him.

Drawing himself to his full height and shoving this turmoil deep in his mind, he made his decision.

CHAPTER 10

Trans-Falls

Present Day

THE FOREST AIR, RANCID with blood and fear, burned in her lungs. Trails of blood trickled down her face as branches and thorny underbrush grabbed at her while she stumbled through them. No matter how far she ran, she couldn't escape the screaming. It was in front, behind; she was screaming. She couldn't stop as she ran and choked against her tears.

The forest was darker than she had ever seen it. Her thighs burned, her calves cramped, her breath burned through the stich in her lungs, heart throbbing in her ears, but she knew she couldn't stop.

The darkness reached out, dragging her down, herding her through the trees.

Blood splattered up on her legs.

A light shone ahead of her.

She shoved her way out of the forest and into what looked like the light of a fire. The world dimmed around her as she collapsed to the ground.

"*Run, Dragon Child. You must protect the Zelauwgugey. You must protect the life of the forest!*"

"*Run.*"

"*Run!*"

Stephania jerked awake and scrambled to her feet. The Lyre was still clutched in her tight fist. Surely, someone would come to help. Surely, someone had noticed her absence or all the screaming and death.

Mocking laughter rang around her. She tasted bile and couldn't stop herself from vomiting when she fell. Warm blood soaked through her clothes. The *Kijaqumok* had suppressed the magic of the Lyre; the forest, no match for the dark magic, had sunk beneath the Sleeping once again. She could hear the Trans-Falls thundering menacingly as she wiped her face and horror sank deeper in her.

Stumbling, she turned and ran for the trees, reaching out for their protection, but they disappeared, and she was once again running toward the falls. Disoriented, she threw herself back toward the trees only for them to disappear again and again.

She was running in circles.

Panic seized her, and she sank to the ground, sobs racking her body.

"You cannot escape me, Dragon Child." The voice was dead, chilling.

She knew that voice. A flashback from her dreams consumed her. It was the voice, the being, who had possessed the murderer whose memories she relived. The voice was one and the same with the power she had possessed in New-Fars. It was the same as her hate, and the same as her rage, even the same as her fear. They were all one.

"You cannot run from me any longer. I see you. Through the darkness, through the memories you lost, through the traitor you share a connection with, I see you!"

She dragged herself to her knees, lifting her head, searching for the voice, except it was all around her, it was inside her.

Three Centaur silhouettes stepped out of the forest before her, stalking closer. Their glowing, demonic red eyes pierced into hers.

"Look around you, savior of the Dragon Riders. Look at the pain and suffering you have wrought. Your heart, black as night, drew me to them. Look at what you've done!"

Though she willed against all things good and evil to not look, her eyes disobeyed, roving across the clearing. Her heart cried out in horror, knowing the power was taking hold of her again, that it would take control over her again just as it had in New-Fars.

Tears flooded her eyes, a silent scream parting her lips.

The forest had now gone silent; only soft, far away wails could be heard, though she felt they were actually the trees around her crying. Bodies lay strewn around her, woven amongst the fallen trees. Hoofprints dotted the soft forest floor and bent back the thick green grass. Some prints were dry, but others held the blood of those who had danced them into the ground.

Slowly, she dragged herself through the thick, wet grass, smelling the stench of gore and feeling it seep through her clothes, until she was near one of the motionless shapes. The Faun was lying on its side, its back to her.

Her hand shook so hard it was almost impossible to steady it long enough to roll the Faun over onto its back. A sob broke her lips, and she held her hand over her mouth to stop the screams.

It was the female Faun who had clung to her hand while they danced, before her last breath. The one she had watched die.

Her veins were pitch black, streaking across her now grey, clammy skin. Her eyes, still open, stared into the sky, the shimmering green life they had once held now gone.

Dried blood traced a path from the corner of her pale lips to her bare breasts, her hands balled into fists.

"Do not weep for them, Dragon Child. They are naught but wild animals."

Stephania threw herself away from the Faun, scrambling and slipping on the ground, desperate to get away from the Centaurs who had stepped from the forest, and now stood just in front of her.

Fury and hatred raged through her. "They weren't animals. They were beautiful creatures of life and love, and they didn't deserve to die." Just as she surged to her feet, her hand reaching for the knife at her hip, she felt the Corrupt Magic inside her, robbing her of strength, and feeding off her hate and anger.

He mocked her passion with resounding laughter. "Why do you protest this? Why do you deny yourself a power which could be yours? Instead of letting it take only your hate, let it take all of you." One of the Centaurs reached down and grabbed her jaw tightly, forcing her to look up at him. "Let it consume you."

She screamed as darkness swelled around her, piercing pain racing through her mind, throbbing through her blood.

Voices screamed at her, and images mocked her.

"You're just a helpless little demon baby like you've always been!"

"No more shall we be forced to live with the scum of Mordok! This demon will get what she deserves once and for all!"

"Murderer! Murderer!"

She felt the power struggling to control her. She pushed back, but she wasn't strong enough. She had no way to fight against it.

Images of the man and woman being killed on the mountain flashed through her mind again, and blind fury coursed through her, a fury born out of years of hate, though she didn't remember what she had hated. Then Artigal the white Centaur was standing in front of her again. An undefined child in her hands, Stephania was once again in the perspective of the murderer. The hate the man holding the child felt filled her, even if it wasn't her own hate.

"Perhaps you have come to the realization that your Lord is not as powerful as mine ..."

"Bow to Rasa's true Lord! Succumb to his power!"

She screamed against the scorching pain coursing through her body unabated. She could see nothing around her but felt the vise-like grips of the Centaurs as they held her thrashing body, their leader's hand wrapping tighter around her throat.

"Give me the *Zelauwgugey*."

Tears painted down her face and neck. She shook her head slowly, forcing herself to look into his demonic red eyes her, memories and nightmares flashing around her;

the voices overlapped, causing nothing but chaos. She wanted to curl up and die, to be free from this horrible nightmare.

He smirked before releasing his grip on her neck, and letting her gasp for air, the other two Centaurs stepping back as well.

"Fool. I am so much more powerful than you. Your defiance is petty."

Ignoring him, she rubbed her throat, gasping for air. She heaved, but only burned her throat with bile. *I'm going to die, and there's nothing I can do about it. Everyone was right.* She bit her lip against the burning tears. *I'm just a helpless demon baby–a worthless monster–and I always have been.* When Jackson had bullied her, when she had found out she was a Dragon Rider, when she had been ridiculed by the townspeople, when she had tried to take control over her life, she had tried so hard to appear strong, in control, but she never had been. Rage at how worthless and powerless she was and at how life had treated her surged through her, and instead of the darkness taking it away, it empowered her. What if she took hold of this power and used it? She would easily be able to slaughter these Centaurs just like she had the humans. She would be free.

"I'm going to ask you one more time." The lead Centaur bent down, and finally, she could see his face clearly.

All rage and hate fled her in the presence of her fear, leaving her without the dark power and quivering in terror.

His eyes were shining blood red orbs, not a trace of white left. Blood leaked out of his sunken eyes and down his jagged cheek bones. His teeth were jagged and sharp as he grinned, a forked tongue slithering in and out of his mouth; blood trickled from his lips and down his neck. Black veins crept under his skin.

His breath was cold and lifeless on her face, smelling worse than rot and death. "Give ... me ... the ... *Zelauwgugey*."

The Lyre was still in her hand. She could feel the warmth of the weak, green, flickering glow. Slowly, the darkness circled her arm. Searing pain raced through her arm, forcing her to hold the Lyre in front of her, but still she would not let it out of her fist. It wouldn't let her. Magic of its own snaked out of the strings and clutched her arm, bonding her hand to it, refusing to let her drop it. The conflicting magics tore at her, and she felt something pop in her elbow.

She groaned against the pain, her vision blurring around her.

"You leave me no other choice. I will simply have to take your arm with it!"

Her throat burned with bile and her screams as he conjured a massive sword out of the swirling darkness, raising it high above his head.

"For Raythuz!"

The weapon cut through the air above her.

She screamed, thrashing against the inevitable, unable to move with the shadows holding her firmly in place.

Another scream mingled with hers. Her eyes snapped open in confusion as the Centaur convulsed. Blood spattered onto her face, and he roared in pain and fury. Masterfully, he redirected his weapon behind him, and Stephania heard it hiss through the air before thudding into a fallen tree trunk

The magic dropped her mercilessly to the ground, and she scrambled to her feet, the world spinning wildly around her, her legs giving out underneath her.

The clearing was in chaos. The hiss of blades and snapping branches filled the air.

With disembodied awe, she watched as two of the Centaurs' bodies joined the dead Fauns, leaving only their leader standing.

Seeing his comrades dead, the last possessed Centaur quickly abandoned the fight with the new Centaur who had emerged from the trees and galloped back to her. She couldn't force herself to move.

He wrenched her head back, his blood soaked, filthy hand knotted in her hair, and pressed his knife against her throat so hard she was scared to draw breath.

The new Centaur cursed and dragged his hooves into the ground only a few feet in front of her.

Her eyes widened in disbelief. His name escaped her mouth before she could stop it. "Trojan?" Blood trickled down her neck when the knife pressed deeper. She whimpered, all other pleas for help dying on her lips.

Trojan barely let his blue eyes lock with hers before he turned them to the possessed Centaur behind her.

"Let her go, Colten."

Colten roared with unnatural laughter that sounded more akin to a wounded animal. "Colten? Colten is no more. Only the Dark Lord and the *Kijaqumok* are here now. Don't you see? Your Great Emperor is no match for Raythuz. The Dark Lord has more power than any, and he is the one true Lord over Rasa.

Trojan narrowed his eyes, and for a moment, Stephania panicked, thinking he wouldn't do anything to save her.

"I know you can sense the power I possess, Trojan. I know you can sense she has used it too. She reeks of it. Her heart belongs to Raythuz. She is the same as the evil you try so hard to rid the world of. Let me help you in your holy quest. Let me kill her."

Her face burned with shame. He was right. She was no different. She had let the power take over her again, had wanted its power to give her strength so she wouldn't be worthless anymore. She had done more than think about it—she had used it. She had failed herself, Trojan, and the promise she made. Her shoulders sagged, and she found herself unable to meet Trojan's piercing gaze.

"The end has come. It is time to choose a side, Trojan. She has chosen hers, who will you serve?"

For nearly a minute, Trojan stared into his blood eyes and neither moved. Stephania didn't trust herself to speak.

"She has not chosen." Trojan's voice was deathly quiet. "She wasn't given a choice. But if given one, I am positive she will choose the same side I have chosen."

Colten hissed and shook his head. "Such a shame. The Dark Lord would have appreciated a great warrior of your strength on his side. Now, drop your sword, or I will slit her throat and take the Lyre."

The knife traced a red ribbon across her throat; she hissed against the stinging pain, tears sliding down her bloodstained face. *Let me die. It would be better for all of us.* Though she thought it, she didn't believe it. She didn't want to die. Not like this.

His voice rose into a frenzy; his lips frothed with pink foam. "Drop your weapon, *shábda,* or I will kill her and take the *Zelauwgugey!*"

Blood dripped from her throat as pain raced across her skin.

Cursing, Trojan violently threw his sword a few feet away from the traitor.

"Excellent." Colten released Stephania, and she fell to the ground, clutching the stinging cut on her throat and gasping for air. Before she could even think of anything else, chains made from the Cursed Magic twined around Trojan, pinning his arms to his sides and hobbling his legs.

"You are a coward, Colten," Trojan hissed at the laughing Centaur.

"Maybe, but you are a fool." Colten turned to her just as she gained her footing.

Through the painful rasp in her throat, she hissed, "*Shábda.*"

With a deathly cold gaze, he narrowed his eyes at her insult. "Give me the Lyre or your brother dies." He stretched out his hand. His skin was starting to peel off his flesh. Half his face curled away from the muscle, and Stephania dry heaved against the retched sight and smell. His body was failing under the Corrupt Magic's influence, even though it grew stronger with her fear.

The chains tightened around Trojan, and she heard him take in a sharp breath of pain. Their eyes locked, and he shook his head slowly. His face was completely emotionless, lacking fear or even a plea for her to trust him.

"Give me the *Zelauwgugey!*" Colten's magic crushed her, dragging her to him, forcing her to hold out the Lyre.

She tried to open her hand, but the Lyre's magic only gripped her tighter, and she groaned at the pain. She couldn't escape from this.

He conjured another sword from the dark magic again and raised it above his head, a wretched grin on his peeling, bloody face.

A flash of light from where Trojan's sword had once lain on the ground blinded them before blood spattered onto Stephania's face as Colten coughed. Trojan's sword was sticking out of his chest, its glowing blue tip dripping blood.

Stephania gasped as the Centaur's eyes flickered back and forth from red to normal. The magic holding her clenched tighter before slipping away. With a horrid squelch, Trojan wrenched the sword from Colten's twitching body.

The possessed Centaur stood for only a moment longer before he heaved a cough, throwing up a clot of blood, and his eyes rolled into the back of his head. Stephania had to dive out of his way as he dropped to the ground. His legs curled up to his body, his flesh melting off his bones as the Corrupt Magic left him.

If Stephania had anything left in her stomach, she was sure she would've lost it now as her eyes locked on his glassy stare, his blood soaking into her boots.

Before the tears could spill down her cheeks and the screams tear her throat, she felt strong arms wrap around her and place her on a warm, broad back. She clutched his mane in her fingers and tried to pace her breathing to the pounding of his hooves as he took her far, far away from that horror.

"How—" She almost couldn't hear her voice as it rasped, competing with the wind. "How did you do it?"

Trojan slowed to a smooth trot, his shoulders rolling as he took several deep breaths. "The Synoliki magic allows me to teleport my weapon." His answer was rather dry, as if he were teaching a particularly boring class.

"Oh." Her answer was equally dry, but she didn't know what else to say. The blood on her shirt, the guts on her boots, her own screams, and the screams of the dying forest still ringing in her ears began to overwhelm her, try as she did to forget it, and her tears began to fall again.

"Why didn't he just take it from me?" Her fists balled.

"He couldn't. Unless you gave it to him, it wouldn't exist for him. My guess is he wanted to convince you to give in to your hatred and willingly give it over."

"He almost succeeded." She felt vile for admitting it but also as if a weight had been lifted in doing so.

For a long moment, he was silent before he answered, "I know."

She bit her lip, wishing the silence would swallow her whole. *Surely, he hates me now.*

"However, the *Zelauwgugey* has a mind of its own. It won't let you betray it, not unless you truly hate it with all your heart."

"But I do." She didn't mean to let the words out of her mouth, but he said nothing. They knew the truth.

Trojan's shoulder's shuddered, and when he spoke, it sounded as if he were holding back tears. "I'm sorry."

A new ache grew inside her. "For what?"

"For everything."

She didn't want to be this close to him right now, sitting on his back, her fingers entangled in his mane, her face pressed against his shoulders feeling his heart beating through her chest. It took her a long time to push past the emotion to answer. "I'm sorry too."

"I should have been here earlier." Nearly all the muscles in his body tensed, and a darkness entered his voice. "You could've died. I could've lost you. Again."

"What do you mean, *again?*"

He didn't answer, and the coldness of realization poured over her.

He had lost her all those years ago when she had been given to Dalton. She had died to him, left him alone. She hadn't thought of it like that until now. The silence between them stretched until she knew he wouldn't answer, nor would he talk to her again until they arrived home.

§

SHE SAT IN STONY silence, staring down at her hands as Trojan calmly explained what had happened at the Trans-Falls. Her family's worried eyes moved between her and him as they patiently listened.

Gratefully, she realized how little he told them—only that Colten and his friends had been possessed and tried to take the Lyre from her. He made no mention that hundreds of trees and Fauns were dead, not that she had almost given in to the grip of the Cursed Magic, not that she had failed miserably at being Farloon—the protector.

Numbly, she accepted their weeping and comfort, hugs and kisses, and whispers that they were so thankful she was safe.

If you knew the truth, you wouldn't pity me. Perhaps you would even wish I were dead.

Trojan's arm wrapped around her shoulders, guiding her after Frawnden, who mentioned something about a bath and an early night to bed.

"Thank you," she whispered so low he had to lean down to hear her repeat it.

For a long time, he stared into her eyes, looking over her face, searching her for something. Finally, he nodded curtly. "I will inform Artigal of the casualties. He'll take care of it."

She nodded and went to move away, but his arm remained around her, holding her close.

He hesitated only a moment before quickly pressing his lips to her forehead and muttering something in Sházuk.

She watched him go, a strange bit of warmth flickering in her before she let Frawnden pull her to the bath and help her into bed.

The night was cold. The air was stale. The stench of death clung to her, unwilling to let her go. She could still feel the blood on her hands: warm, sticky, thick, wet. When she closed her eyes, she saw red blood swirling in purple eyes. When she opened them, see could see the forest's light wavering through the slaughter in the flickering light of the moon on her walls. And when the darkness consumed her, she became their murderer.

§

HER GLAZED EYES *stared back at him, wild, ferocious, scared, pained. Blood dripped down from her head and bloomed on her fair neck.*

The power surging inside him was both excruciatingly painful and the single most exhilarating thing he had ever experienced. His hands shook, his shoulders twitched, but his mind had never felt more alive and clear.

"Andromeda," he sneered as he intensified her husband's torture curse. He could sense the man's soul pleading for reprieve, but he only pushed it harder. The Duvarharian Lord would die today, and this time he would stay that way.

A dry tongue passed over dry lips. His burning eyes wandered over the woman's body as she struggled to pull herself to her feet. Her body was cut and bruised, her armor dented, some of it having been torn away in the fight. Her flaming auburn hair was ratted, torn, hanging limp in strings around her shoulders. She reeked of death.

Growling with the pain of channeling the power, he grinned wider and raised his palms to the heavens, feeling the darkness consume him.

A dark cloud formed around him and crept toward Andromeda, swirling mockingly around her legs, twining up her body.

She gasped and strained against the power. It filled the air, choking her lungs. It filled her heart, choking the blood. It filled her mind, choking her thoughts. It destroyed her will to live. Slowly, painfully, it drew sustenance from her life, drawing every ounce of strength and soul from her body. Dull green eyes rolled into the back of her head, seeing nothing. Her arms and legs convulsed. Blood trickled out of her mouth.

He threw back his head and took in a deep breath. "Ah, the power. Kijaqumok. The Corrupt Magic." He sneered as he watched her crumble, body, mind, and soul, against the power. "Soon, there will be a day when all will bow before me and this Magic."

Black veins spread under her skin, creeping from her heart to the rest of her body. Her eyes, completely white now, rolled with pain as she curled into the fetal position against the agony.

"Kneel to me, shike. *Kneel before the true Lord of Ventronovia and the true power of Rasa!"*

She screamed loud and long as the magic tore through her body, and she convulsed, the magic forcing her to her hands and knees before him.

Cries of anguish from the husband having to watch his wife's torture drew the killer's attention back to the man.

As his gaze traveled from the dead woman to the dying husband she left behind, his eyes filled with blood, turning them black. No longer did they swirl purple, no longer did only he stand in control of his body and this power. Something else, something greater, had taken his place.

"I am ashamed that this is what you have put against me, Joad!" His voice was not his own as he spoke. "Such weaklings!"

The darkness spread around the wounded Lord and completely engulfed his mind.

"Such a shame. I was looking forward to a good fight after my long imprisonment." He sighed deeply in obvious disappointment. "Still, either way, you and your followers shall fall in the end, and I will have gained back what is rightfully mine, piece by piece, starting with your most devoted."

Effortlessly, the shadowy magic entwined around the Lord's throat and pulled him closer.

He chuckled darkly as the man tried to kick the magic off him and whisper spells against it. His efforts were futile. He meant nothing to Raythuz, the true master of Rasa.

Thaddeus tilted his head from side to side, surveying his victim; he drew a finger down the man's bloody face. "So easily I could kill you. But why deny you the pain of suffering and grief over losing your wife and your dragon?" His shrieking laughter rent the dark air as he threw the man to the ground and spat on him.

Raythuz, the master of the dark magic that possessed Thaddeus, spoke to him. "Find the child and bring her to me."

"Of course, my Lord," Thaddeus answered with a sneer.

Within moments, he was mounted on his triumphant dragon and traveling at an unimaginable speed to where the dark power was leading him.

An image of the man he had tortured flashed before his eyes. The husband was alive, crawling toward his wife.

The voice of Raythuz once again instructed him. "The other dragon scum are on their way. The Lord will live if he is left."

Growling, Thaddeus clenched his fists and laughed when, far away, a knife, made solely out of the Kijaqumok, dug deep into the Lord's side. He wouldn't recover.

"Good. Now, the child."

Loud cracks in the air signaled the arrival of some of the Dragon Riders, but he didn't mind. He had a power none of them could stand against and a being supporting him who surpassed all others. Stephania was his.

CHAPTER 11

The Abandoned Mountain Fortress

Dragon Palace, Duvarharia

Present Day

T HE DARK NOTHINGNESS OF DASEJUBA *abruptly turned into the cool mountain air of the Filate Mountains. The first thing that hit his ears was the screams of dying Centaurs and the unmistakable emptiness that lingered around dead dragons.*

His own dragon dove toward the mountain, and his blood ran cold.

Two mangled masses of flesh lay still on the mountain, swarms of Etas screaming over the bits of flesh that were left. Bile rose in his throat as he recognized them as Aldwyn and Mischievous. His own dragon landed close by.

Seeing the once majestic dragons' bodies being preyed upon by the repulsive shape-shifters, he was unable to contain his rage.

A powerful blast of gold magic exploded around him, disintegrating the remaining Etas on the mountainside.

It only took him a few seconds to jump off his dragon and rush to Drox and Andromeda.

His heart pounded painfully in his chest as if it were driving a knife into itself. His ears rang and his vision blurred as he dropped to the ground and cradled Drox's limp body in his arms.

"Ah, Syrus." Drox coughed and blood spurted onto his chin.

Syrus quickly wiped the blood away, his eyes sweeping to Andromeda. He choked against his own breath. Her once striking green eyes were dull; black veins had spread under her skin; her chest was still. One quick glance told him she was dead. Dead. Andromeda was dead. The only mother he had ever known was dead.

Dead!

Syrus bolted upright, a cry on his lips, his hand groping for his dagger. The sheets were tangled around his legs, his body hot but his skin cold with sweat. Realizing he was in his room and not back at the carnage of the Battle of the Prophecy, he replaced his dagger on his bedside table and clenched his eyes shut but only until he saw her glazed, dead eyes staring back at him, along with Drox's pained, defeated gaze as he too slipped into the darkness.

Digging his nails into his calves, he gritted his teeth against the images and against the burning mark on his back—a mark to the secret he had never been able to share and now never could.

A low groan pulled his attention to the large, dark mass that lay curled, twitching in the corner of his room. All worry for himself vanished as he tore the claustrophobic sheets from his sticky skin and padded across the cold stone.

Galdarian, his Sun-Flash Dragon, turned in his sleep, another groan rumbling from his chest. Syrus knew he was being haunted by the same terrible memory he had woken from.

Taking a deep breath, he opened his mind to Galdarian's, letting the emotions of Drox and Andromeda's death seep back in. He pushed aside the edge of Galdarian's huge golden wing and crawled underneath it, laying close to his warm, soft belly. Taking a deep breath as he placed his hand on golden scales, he let Galdarian's dream pull him in.

The Etas had completely destroyed Aldwyn and Mischievous' bodies. Blood, flesh, and entrails were strewn everywhere. The Etas were ... eating them.

Despite all his experience in war, the sight before him drove him insane.

He screamed to the sky, tore his own chest with his claws, and stumbled around the mangled bodies. His wings dragged the ground. His claws felt too heavy to carry. His snout scrapped the earth beneath him, his senses rank with the stench of death.

He could sense the empty nothingness taking their place, could feel Drox slipping away too. He felt Syrus' grief and the weight of the secret the Dragon Rider was never able to tell his guardians. He could feel the Dark Magic and Thaddeus's joy and triumph.

He could feel ... everything.

Gasping, Syrus wrenched himself away from his dragon's body and quickly severed their connection. He dragged himself to his dragon's head and placed his forehead against Galdarian's massive jaw.

"I'm so sorry, Galdarian. If only I had gotten us there sooner. We could've saved them."

Galdarian growled sadly, now awake. He pressed his head against his rider's chest. *No, Syrus. He would've killed us too.*

He didn't want to admit it, but he knew his dragon was right. They would've been just as powerless as Drox and Andromeda to stop Thaddeus, and if they had died as well, then no one would've been left to lead the Duvarharians, especially since they didn't know what became of Stephania.

They lay in each other's presence, safe from shared past horrors, for a long while, until the earth began to shake under them.

At the first small tremor, they did nothing but ignore it until the second came, and the sound of shattering jars filled the air as one of Syrus' tables toppled over.

Hardly able to stand and using one of his dragon's steady legs to hold him straight, Syrus struggled to his feet, his teeth cracking against each other from the power of the third earthquake.

"What in Susahu ..." Before he could finish, screaming rent the air.

He clamped his hands over his ears and tried to drown it out, but it felt like it was coming from inside him, not just all around him.

"Curse the gods, what is happening?" He couldn't even hear his own voice over the horrific noise.

Together, they stumbled to the patio, the huge glass doors rattling on their magic fashioned, iron hinges. Syrus was grateful they lived in a mountain until rocks from the celling began to shatter and rain down around them.

It was nearly impossible to see even the Dragon Palace as the earth shook and rattled his senses. The screaming was unrelenting and driving him mad, but when the tremors stopped long enough for him to see straight, he couldn't believe his eyes.

The sky was on fire.

Streaks of lightning and flames licked the sky, and stars seemed to shine just inside the mountain ranges as if hovering over the ground instead of in the heavens. Both moons were visible, as were both suns, and yet the sky had never felt more dark.

"Gods of all." He sank to his knees. When he heard the words escape his mouth, he realized the screaming had finally stopped.

Syrus ...

"What—" Syrus turned in the direction his dragon was nudging him, and his words caught in his throat.

A young woman was standing in front of him, asking who he was. She looked terrified. Her neck was bruised, as were her arms, and her whole body was covered with small cuts and scrapes.

"Who are you?" Her voice was drowned out as the wind began to rage around them and the screaming stared again.

He tightened his grip on his dragon, but even Galdarian was having trouble keeping the wind from rising under his wings and tearing him from the mountain.

"Why aren't you talking to me?" Frustration burned in her eyes. "Who are you?"

EFFIE JOE STOCK

He tried to focus on her, on her voice, but it was nearly impossible in the flashing light. She was holding her hand in front of her face as if something were blinding her. Then she started dissolving into the light, fading away from him.

"I am Syrus, rider of Galdarian, of the Dragon Palace!" He yelled it several times, but no matter how loud he screamed, she just kept shaking her head as if she couldn't hear him.

"Are you a dream? Or memory?" Her hair violently whipped, tangling in the wind. His heart lurched when he saw its color.

Blood red.

Stephania.

"Stephania! It's me. It's Syrus and Galdarian!" His heart surged with elation. She was alive! After all these years, somehow she was alive! But then dread replaced it. What if Thaddeus had taken her? What if this was a trick of some sort?

Everything he had learned from being Duvarharia's leader for the last decade screamed for him to alert the Dragon Palace of this possible attack. Every other instinct in his body told him to face it. The possibility that Thaddeus had found and brainwashed Stephania was very real, but if it wasn't, and she needed his help, right here, right now, he could be risking the promise of the Prophecy by not reaching out to her. Without another moment's hesitation, he lunged at her. Instead of touching flesh like had expected, his hands went right through her as if she were only an illusion.

Dread hit his stomach like a spear.

A dark, gaping hole opened beside them, and another form took shape. Her scream was lost in the many others that pierced their ears.

Out of the darkness stepped the last creature on Rasa Syrus ever wanted to see.

A demonic grin was on his cunning, pale face, and elation sparkled in his swirling purple eyes.

Thaddeus.

§

SHE WAS YELLING at the man before her, begging him to tell her who he was. She was sure he was the man from the dreams and visions she used to have frequently back in New-Fars—the man with the dark hair and golden eyes who had always appeared at her piano. His mouth was moving, but she couldn't hear what he was saying.

"Are you a dream?" she screamed into the wind. "Or memory?"

The light swelled around her, blinding her, and she was afraid she would lose this chance to find out who this man was. He lunged at her, but his hands traveled through

118

her. His gaze turned from hopeful, to confused, and then to horror.

Agony seized her.

Images flashed around her—images of dying Centaurs, mangled dragon flesh, trees burning with acid, a girl shooting a flaming target, a young Centaur carrying a girl, a man and woman fighting and dying, two brothers fighting, words of a prophecy, a white Centaur, and then blinding light and excruciating pain.

Everything went dark, save for the flashing, burning lights and fire around her. The pain suddenly left her along with the visions but left her feeling raw and exposed. She couldn't see the room around her. She was standing on nothing, and she could feel nothing. Vaguely, she was aware of the man still in front of her, but her attention was quickly taken by a figure who stepped out of the darkness next to her.

Instantly, she was lost in shining purple eyes, and everything fell silent around her.

A scream left her lips, but she didn't hear it since she was thrown back into a memory.

She was staring up into those purple eyes.

"Everything is going to be okay," he whispered gently. "I'm going to take care of you and raise you'll never have to fear anything ever again. I'll never let anything hurt you."

She felt his warm arms holding her, and she felt herself sinking, sinking, sinking into his magic as she fell into those swirling purple eyes.

"Ah, Stephania," came his smooth voice, clearer than in the memory, and she was violently pulled back into the present, her mind reeling, her stomach roiling.

Voices rang around her, whispering things, some evil, some good, some passive. The golden eyed man from her piano visions was saying something, but his voice was lost in the chaos. The only voice she could hear was *his*.

"You know where you belong, child." He extended his hand out to her, his eyes consuming her, drugging her, seducing her. "Come fulfill your destiny, Stephania. Cast aside the lies you've been fed. This is your *true* destiny, with me."

She couldn't hear herself think, couldn't discern what she was feeling. Rage, horror, distrust, and disgust filled her but then mixed with pity, trust, safety, and a strange understanding, as if this man knew more about herself than she did. Her hand reached out to him, and something stirred in her heart, something small, as if he had left a piece of him in her that fateful day so many years ago.

"No, Stephania."

She could barely hear the golden eyed man beside her; his voice sounded so faint, so distant, as if he wasn't really here with them.

"Please don't do it."

She turned to face him, and his golden eyes met hers.

Something about him was familiar, as if he were more than just a memory, as if he had actually meant something to her at some time. Sad piano music danced around her, haunting her. The voices whispered things she had heard in her dreams, but only the words she could never remember when she awoke.

"Come, Stephania. You've always known they don't truly understand you, don't truly accept you," the man with purple eyes whispered, "But I will, I always have. I have seen you for what you are, and I will not turn from you. Come with me, start over, forget the pain you've caused, and help me bring a new age to Duvarharia."

The wind screamed around them, and the voices rose to a pitch again. The fire was burning hot and then freezing cold. She wanted to claw out her eyes and tear out her heart, wishing she could leave this place, to stop this war raging inside her.

She hated this man before her, with his purple eyes and double headed battle axe, but something inside her answered the call to him; it muted her senses, drugged her, consumed her.

But she also knew the man behind her with his golden eyes and long dark hair. He had known her parents, she was sure. He was the man who haunted the dreams that didn't leave her screaming and wishing she were dead.

They were both yelling at her now, pleading or demanding she join them, but she couldn't choose, couldn't think, couldn't breathe.

Tears burned as they fell down her cheeks, and blood trickled out of her ears and nose. She sank to the ground, pleading with them to stop, pleading the with magic that roiled within her, fighting against itself, to leave.

Then strong arms encircled her and pulled her to her feet. Warmth spread through her, and for just a moment, all the screaming and raging and chaos stopped.

"Stand aside, Artigal," the man with purple eyes hissed, the comfort with which he had spoken to Stephania suddenly nowhere to be found. "This is no longer your fight."

She opened her eyes to see Artigal standing before her, the blond man facing him. Artigal's hands were held out, as if he were shielding her. Golden white magic trailed down his shoulders and mixed into the fire of the darkness around them, creeping up her legs and spreading a warmth and peace with it.

"It will *always* be my fight, Thaddeus, because it is *His* fight."

Thaddeus screamed and lashed at Artigal with his axe. Light formed a shield, and the weapon clashed harmlessly against it, making Thaddeus all the more enraged.

The man from her visions dodged an assault from Thaddeus and ran to her, his arms pulling her out of the way when she was too stunned to move. The axe streaking toward them, just as it had so many times in her nightmares, came within a breath of their skin. *Is this just another nightmare?* If she stood still long enough and tried to breathe, would it all fade away and leave her crumpled on the floor somewhere like it always had? Or was it real? Tears streamed down her face as she struggled back a sob.

"Let me take the girl, Artigal. You can keep the commander; I have no use for him. Level the playing field for once."

Artigal's body was blinding, as if every pore in his body was emitting light. She had to squint to watch. But even among the light, somewhere in the center of his chest a darkness hung, sucking in the light, destroying it, and weakening him.

She lunged forward, but strong arms held her back as Artigal cried out, falling to his knees, his hand clutching his chest.

"The playing field was always level, Thaddeus. You were just never up for the challenge," he barely managed to growl.

Thaddeus screamed, and darkness poured from his body in waves. Each tendril of shadow grappled with the light. His eyes bled as black veins spread under his skin.

"Maybe not, but I am now. I serve the true Lord of Rasa!"

The darkness exploded around them, and Stephania felt it race across her skin, crackling and destroying the white light that had encased her and the man who held her back. Her eyes rolled into the back of her head, her heart pounding against her ribs. Everything in the darkness told her to accept her rage, her pain, her hate and leave the light, to join to darkness where she belonged.

"Fight it, Stephania! You have to fight it!" The man's golden eyes burned into hers. They were the only things she could see through the darkness as it filled her body with cold and horror.

She opened her mouth to cry that she was trying, but nothing came out. She coughed violently, and blood spattered onto the man's face.

"Fight, Stephania! I can't let you go again!"

Then she was looking into Trojan's eyes as he said those words to her.

"I could've lost you. Again."

Her shoulders shook with sobs as she thought of how he had fought against the darkness—had protected her, had said she hadn't made the choice to follow the call of the evil—and how she wanted so badly to now, if only to stop the pain. She was failing him. She was failing everyone.

"Step aside, Artigal," Thaddeus screamed. "The girl is mine. My magic rots in her heart, and she has all but given herself up to the *Kijaqumok*. Let me take her from you; she is nothing but a liability."

Artigal groaned against the strain of the magic. His body had nearly stopped shining with the light as the darkness spread inside of him. "No, I will not. It is you who must step aside. The Great Emperor is preparing his return to claim what is his. You can still come back to the light, Thaddeus. You don't have to stand against victory. You can stand with us."

Stephania watched through her bloody tears as Thaddeus lowered his axe for a moment. A flash of hope sparkled in his eyes before the darkness tightened its hold on him and he sank back into its control. "I don't have a choice."

"Then neither do I."

Stephania cried out in horror as she saw the inevitable: Artigal was fighting against a dark power Thaddeus wielded—one he couldn't win against.

She couldn't let that happen. If Artigal died, so would any chance of her getting her memories back. As much as she hated to admit it, Trans-Falls needed Artigal. *She* needed Artigal. If he was gone, everyone would look to her for guidance, and that was a responsibility she certainly didn't want. And worse, if he had died because she had failed to act, how would she be able face Trojan and tell him she had chosen the Corruption and let Artigal die? Or what about Aeron, Frawnden, Jargon, Dalton, and all Trans-Falls? And what of this man who held her now, pleading with her to fight the darkness? How would she tell him she hadn't been strong enough?

Something like memory or instinct flashed through her mind. She had stood in the path of Thaddeus's magic once and survived; she could do it again.

Raging against the darkness, against the unfairness, against her hate, her pain, and her love, against everything wrong that had ever happened to her, her friends, and her family, she tore away from the man and threw herself in the path of Artigal just as the light and darkness exploded around them.

It filled her, surrounded her, consumed her, and then it came together in one swirling mass of light and darkness.

She took it in her hand and commanded it to obey her, to put an end to this nightmare, to protect those she loved, and then she let it go.

CHAPTER 12

Mount Drymore, Ravenwood

Present Day

USAN'S EYES FLUTTERED OPEN to the starry heavens above him. The stars shone peacefully back at him. Crickets chirped. Frogs croaked. A night bird trilled a few notes, and somewhere in the distance a wolf howled. Everything appeared as it should be.

But something was wrong.

In a moment's breath, Dusan was on his feet, an arrow on his bow string. "What's wrong?"

Yollen's own bow was notched, his steady fingers pulling back ever so slightly on the string. Besides his eyes flickering from side to side, he hardly moved a muscle.

Dusan's gaze followed his as they peered into the darkness, their every sense reaching out to expose what had disturbed this otherwise peaceful night.

Yollen slowly shook his head, his eyes searching the land from his hooves all the way to the tree-dotted horizon and then back to the stars. "I'm not sure, but something stirs in the air. The stars are unusually quiet, as if they don't know what's going to happen or are watching it themselves, and now even the forest has gone silent."

The unnerving stillness in the air spread across the land until it felt almost wrong to breathe.

Then, as if the land were tensing, air rushed past them, ruffling their manes and tails, bending tree branches and swirling the grass.

"Do you hear that?" Yollen's eyes widened, but when his companion listened, he didn't hear anything.

"What is it?"

A strange look overcame the commander's face as he chuckled. "I *hear* the stars. I can actually hear them tonight." A lopsided grin spread across his face. "It's ... beautiful."

Before Dusan could ask what he meant, a roar filled the air, drawing their attention to the north.

Their eyes widened in a mix of fear and awe.

A great band of what appeared to be magic was streaking toward them at an alarming rate. It was over a hundred feet tall, easily towering over most of the trees, and looked very much like lighting inside clouds, only it was black and white.

The forest cried and moaned. The ground shook. Unearthly cries filled the air, and for a moment, it almost appeared as if monstrous creatures made of shining spirits had risen out of the ground and were stumbling across the land in the distance, as if they had just awoken from a long slumber.

Then it was upon them.

They threw up their arms to shield themselves against the sheer force of the magic, bracing their hooves into the rocky soil. Darkness and light engulfed them as the magic swept through them. In only a split second, they felt life in its purest form, and they also felt death the same way.

As soon as it came upon them, it was gone, racing away from them like a giant ripple of water.

"What in the stars was that?" Fear and awe lined Dusan's voice as he watched the forest move, stretching and moaning, coming up from its sleep for just a moment before settling back down. He heard the cries of the legendary creatures, but when he searched for them in the distance, he could no longer see them. With a shock of dread, he realized he hadn't heard his commander since the magic hit them. "*Fom?*" He turned to where his leader was standing, only to find him staring into a doorway made of pure light.

"By the stars."

Yollen held out his hand to the portal, his eyes shining in its light. "My home," he muttered. "The Great Emperor is calling me home. Hanluurasa itself awaits me."

Dusan followed his leader's gaze into the portal, his breath catching in his chest. It was unlike anything he had ever seen. Beyond the doorway, nothing was physical and yet everything seemed so much more real than anything he had ever experienced on Rasa. Everything shone with unearthly light and color, and strange, mystical creatures moved amongst the shining light and swirling darkness.

A wistful longing hung in Yollen's eyes as he turned to face his companion.

"Go, Yollen," he whispered to his commander as he placed a hand on his shoulder. "Go home. I will stay here and complete the mission. It was an honor to serve with you." He yearned to go with his friend and leader, but he knew someone had to stay.

Tears collected in Yollen's suddenly youthful eyes, and he nodded. "It was an honor to serve with you as well. Give Artigal my respects and tell him I will be waiting for him. May the suns smile upon your presence, *fom*."

"As do the stars sing upon yours, *fom*."

They clasped forearms, and their eyes locked for a moment before Yollen turned to give his homeland one last look. "I've always wanted to see the glory of Ravenwood from the stars." A strange smile spread across his face before he stepped through the portal without a second glance back. The doorway closed behind him, dissipating into a small spark of light, which gently floated to the ground.

Dusan bowed his head and placed his fist on his chest. He was just turning away when he saw the last spark of magic plant itself into the ground and slowly begin to grow into a snapping, fiery red plant.

A broad grin spread across his face as he knelt in front of the plant, praising the Great Emperor as four *Negluu* berries formed on the tips of the crackling branches.

CHAPTER 13

Trans-Falls

Present Day

AS IF SOMEONE FLIPPED a switch, all the screaming voices, fire, darkness and light, and the other creatures disappeared. Pain shot through her head, and stars exploded across her vision. She felt something hard under her: a wood floor.

Instantly, shaking hands groped her, pulling her gently but anxiously to her feet.

For a moment, she didn't recognize the voices and started thrashing against them, her screams coming out as dry rasps, until she heard Uncle Dalton's voice.

"Stephania! Stephania, it's okay, child. It's just us. It's your family." His arms pinned hers to her sides until her vision stopped spotting and she was able to hear the other worried voices around her.

"By the gods." Frawnden's teary voice brought some familiarity and comfort, and Stephania sagged against Dalton. "What happened to you?"

As she opened her mouth, though, she wasn't sure what to say; she wasn't even sure what had happened herself. A strange energy surged through her, and she gasped as Artigal's voice rang in her head, saying, *"Come speak with me."*

Frawnden was trying to help her drink a warm, strong liquid, but she sputtered against it, her eyes darting wildly around the room, looking for Artigal, praying she had only mistaken his voice for being inside her head. Instead, she saw Aeron, Frawnden, and was shocked to see even Ravillian and Lamora.

"What—" The world spun around her as she tried to focus on Frawnden's face and Dalton's arms around her. Disbelief shone on her Centaur mother's face, as if she were looking at a ghost.

"Why is everyone here?" Her own voice sounded very far away. "Why am I in the living room?" She tried to still herself but couldn't stop her pounding heart or the tremors that raced through her body. Panic swelled in her as she remembered the darkness swirling around her, gripping her, pulling her, consuming her. She suddenly wrenched herself from Dalton's arms and ran for the door, trying to escape everyone staring at her, trying to escape the feeling that something, *someone*, was chasing her.

Before she could reach the door, reality struck her.

She had met Thaddeus—the traitor of the Dragon Palace, the man whose eyes haunted her nightmares, the man who had killed her parents and their dragons, the murderer of the Duvarharians. It was he whose body she inhabited in the dreams where she slaughtered mercilessly. It was his memory she relived night after night after night. Horror consumed her as she saw the faces of that man and woman who he had killed. That memory ... those people ... those dragons ... they were *her parents*.

Whatever herbs or remedies Frawnden had tried giving her quickly came back up as she retched, her body burning with repulsion.

Every night she suffered, it was her parent's deaths she relived. It was her mother whose life she choked out with the magic, her father's pain that imbued her with power.

She sobbed against the unfairness, the horror of it all, refusing comfort as she collapsed by the coffee table.

"Stephania, talk to me, please. What's wrong? What happened?" Dalton knelt beside her, his warm hand on her back the only thing that felt steady and real.

She shook her head, trying to find the words, trying to push past her tears, runny nose, ringing ears, and the bile rising in her throat. "I saw ..." She hiccuped, her stomach rolling. "I saw *him*, Uncle Dalton." Her fearful eyes pierced his. "I saw him." She tried to close her eyes against the memory but saw his purple eyes when she did.

"Who?"

She tried to say his name, but when she opened her mouth, she only gagged, spitting up acid that burned her throat and tongue.

Frawnden handed Dalton a liquidized herb. "For the vomiting and anxiety."

"Thank you," he whispered before going to feed it to Stephania. When the smell of the bitter herb reached her nose, she thrashed against him, sobbing and crying.

"Stephania, child. Stop. Please. I know you feel horrible. I know you think you're going to throw it up if you drink it, but this will stop the nausea and ease the anxiety. Please trust me. Trust Frawnden."

In a moment of trust and mental clarity, Stephania took the herb. It went down hot, but sat cold in her stomach, and a bit of the nausea went away.

"*Come speak with me.*" Artigal's voice rang in her mind again, but she shook her head violently. She didn't want to see him, not after what happened. That would be admitting it had been real, that it hadn't been just another night terror.

"Can you please try to tell us what happened, Stephania?"

Her eyes met Aeron's, and she slowly shook her head.

"We heard you screaming in your room, so we ran to check on you. Just as soon as we got there, you disappeared into an explosion of what looked like light and dark magic. You were gone for nearly five hours before you appeared here." Aeron's steady voice wavered, and he took a deep breath. "We tried looking for you, we tried to get help, but we couldn't find Artigal either." He crossed his arms across his chest.

A memory of her jumping between Artigal and Thaddeus flashed before her. "Artigal." She tried to push Dalton away and stand. Suddenly, her mind felt a little clearer. "Artigal was with me. He was with me and ... and ..." She could only shake her head.

"What do you mean?" Aeron looked just as confused as she felt.

"Only a few minutes. We were only there for a few minutes." Her lungs struggled to get air as her heart began to pound again.

"Where were you?"

"What do you mean?"

"What happened?"

They were all asking her questions now, but she couldn't hear them. Everything was too loud, too bright. Her head hurt, her body hurt, and she couldn't stop shaking, couldn't stop crying. She had to get away, run away, escape. She staggered to the door.

"Come speak with me!" His voice tore through her mind, and she whimpered against it. She couldn't put it off. She had to speak with him. She needed his help.

Shoving against Dalton and Aeron, she only shook her head at their questions, delirious to anything besides the door in front of her. "I have to get to Artigal. I have to find him. I have to protect him."

"Protect him from what?" One of their questions broke through, and she bit her lip.

"The screaming. The pain. The thunder and fire." For a moment, she saw their confused faces, and anger pulsed through her. "You didn't see it?"

They shook their heads, and she exploded. "How could you not have seen it?" She tried lunging at Aeron, but Dalton held her back, trying to use magic to subdue her. "How did you not hear it? It was everywhere! I couldn't escape it! I couldn't escape it." She suddenly collapsed to the ground, her shoulders shaking, her eyes burning from the tears. *Why am I the only one? Have I gone isane?*

"I'll take her to Artigal." A new voice pierced the air, and she turned her face to him, her eyes meeting Trojan's.

He extended his hand to her, and she was barely able to take it her hands were shaking so much. Quickly, he pulled her to her feet and steadied her in his arms.

Her heart slowed as she stared into his blue eyes. "Tell me you saw it," she whimpered.

Slowly, he nodded, and she sobbed with relief. "Take me to him."

Again, he nodded. His gaze moved to the worried family and friends. "*Zháf wafu zhœk zi mazh,*" he whispered tenderly.

Frawnden smiled sadly. "I know, Trojan."

Effortlessly, he helped Stephania onto his back before he opened the door and stepped into the night.

§

AS HE GALLOPED through the trees, she drifted between wakefulness and restless sleep. Mostly, she kept her face buried in his soft, dark mane, but sometimes she would look up to see where they were.

Brushing tears from her face and wishing she could drink something to wash down the lingering acid in her mouth, she realized the forest around them had changed drastically.

The air now buzzed with a strange, soft energy of which she had never felt before. A gentle, almost warm fog covered the ground, growing thicker and thicker until she couldn't see Trojan's hooves anymore. He slowed to a trot, and she realized she couldn't hear or feel the thunder of his hooves; they must be walking on lush, thick grass or perhaps moss. *So soft. If only I could curl up in it, fall asleep, and never awaken.*

The farther in they traveled, the stranger the forest grew. The fog seemed to fall down from the trees themselves, floating lazily to the ground and swirling in strange shapes as if manipulated by an unfelt wind. Vines dripped down from the branches and glowed soft blue. Whispers from the trees drifted to her on the fog but disappeared before she could hear what they said, and the trees themselves ... she had never seen such ancient trees, towering far above the rest of the trees around Trans-Falls and so unbelievably large.

The forest itself seemed to radiate peace, and she felt her soul still. Her heart stopped racing, her hands stopped shaking, and slowly, the tears dried from her face as her grip on Trojan's mane and sides relaxed.

Pulling her face from his soft mane, she studied his face. His eyes wandered around the forest, reflecting the beauty. His heart didn't pound against her chest like it had, and she wondered if he too felt the peace in this forest.

With a gasp, she caught sight of the markings lining his body. They had begun glowing a fierce blue, practically mirroring the magic around them. Her gaze wandered to her hand, and she was surprised to find her own Shalnoa glowing bright red.

"There he is." Trojan's voice broke her out of her mystified trance, reminding her of the cruel reality she couldn't escape from.

Leaning slightly to the side, she peered down the path. Not too far ahead was a white Centaur down on his knees.

Her heart lurching in her throat, she jumped off Trojan's back.

"Artigal!" She fell to the ground beside him and grasped his slumped shoulders, searching his face.

Bruises, cuts, and dirt decorated his once immaculate hair and skin. The black veins that twined through his body were clearly visible now, reaching as far back as the shoulder blades of his horse body and down his front legs. The inky wound on his chest throbbed, and blood trickled from his skin.

This is my fault. This is all my fault, she moaned to herself, even though she couldn't see how it was. Though she hadn't been able to control what happened, it still felt as if it was her sin to bear.

"The *Negluu* berry." Artigal groaned and lifted his face, dragging his hands away from his head. His eyes were dark, and his eyelids drooped as if they were too heavy to hold up.

"What happened, Artigal?" Though she tried not to, she shook him none too gently, her voice rising. "Who was that man? Was that really Thaddeus? Answer me!"

His head lolled to his chest, and he only murmured again, "The *Negluu* berry."

Before she could stop herself, she struck him across the cheek. "Stop saying—"

He grunted sharply, but the strike seemed to have woken him from his daze.

"Quiet, Stephania." Trojan wrenched her away from Artigal. Though his voice had been harsh, his eyes were wide with disbelief and a flicker of hope as he realized what Artigal was trying to convey. "The *Negluu* berry. They found it. You can get your memories back."

No, this is all too much. I don't want my memories back, not after what I just experienced. I don't want to see what other horrors await me behind the wall in my mind. She violently shook her head. "I don't care about that. I want to know what happened just now. Where were we? Who was that man? Is Thaddeus in Trans-Falls?" She tried to ignore the hurt that flashed over Trojan's face. She couldn't think about that now. She couldn't.

"Thaddeus has been healed from the *Shushequmok*." Artigal tried to meet her gaze. "That's why he was able to use that surge of Ancient Magic to make contact with you."

The ground was softer than she hoped as she dropped from sitting on her heels. "So that's why he never came after me. He was wounded."

Artigal groaned in response, barely able to nod his head. "Yes. Much the same as I am now."

"But you can heal yourself, right? Don't you have *Shushequmok*? Isn't that how you wounded him in the first place? Isn't that how you teleported to ... wherever we were?"

His eyes met hers, and her heart dropped. The look on his face was clear. If he had the magic, he would've healed himself by now. "No, Stephania. *You* wounded him."

"I-I don't understand." Her head was spinning again, and if it weren't for Trojan's hand on her shoulder and his warm body kneeling beside her, she was sure she would've passed out.

"You can channel Ancient Magic. Just like Thaddeus and the ones the rumors speak of—a Wyrider named Doxa and the Empress of Wyerland's daughter."

"Stephania, we need to get Artigal to a healer. You need to stop—" Trojan tried to pull her away, but she pushed against him.

"I have to know." Her swollen eyes were raw with determination. "If Thaddeus can channel the magic to heal himself, why can't you?"

Artigal shook his head and averted his eyes. "Because the Emperor does not will it."

Rage welled up inside her, but before she could lash out against his cursed Emperor, Trojan spoke up. She was surprised he was helping. Maybe he thought if he answered her, she would relent.

"Ancient Magic is divided into two sectors: Pure and Corrupt. The Pure used to be Creative energy, while the Corrupt used to be Destructive, but they existed in harmony as the *Sleshqumok* which used to be ruled by one Master, known as Joad. Long ago, a fallen creature, known to the Duvarharians as Raythuz, took the Destruction, thinking it was more powerful, and corrupted it with hate and malice. The balance was broken then, and the Destruction was no longer useful to the Master, who now only rules over the Pure Magic. One who channels the Magic must chose a Lord—Joad or Raythuz—and they can only channel the magic in accordance with their Lord's will."

"I thought you believed in the Great Emperor, not Joad."

Artigal tried to smile but ended up coughing blood. "To some, they are one and the same."

It was hard to bite back the hateful comment that sprang into her mind. "So are you saying he doesn't want you to live?"

"I cannot say what the Emperor wants, and it is not my place to judge His will. I have lived a long time and—"

"What kind of a wretched god would let that happen?" Tears streamed down her cheeks; her hands balled into fists. She didn't know where the tears came from. She could hardly care less whether or not Artigal died. Perhaps it was more from self-pity at the weight that would fall upon her if Artigal were to die, or perhaps it was from her hidden memories of a time when she had been fond of the old Centaur.

With great effort, he reached out his hand to hers. "He is not a god."

She nearly spat. "Then what is he?"

A sad smile lifted the edges of his bloodstained lips. "He is *kuur.* That's what misled Thaddeus."

"What?" Her tone was sharper than she intended, but she didn't feel like apologizing—not after everything she had just gone through.

Trojan answered her. "Thinking the Great Emperor was nothing more than a pagan god."

"What does that have to do with any of this? Can't you believe in whatever you want?"

Trojan shrugged, clearly frustrated they were still having this discussion instead of getting help for Artigal. "Of course you can, but that doesn't make it true."

She couldn't meet his intense gaze for long as he explained. "Thinking the Emperor is only a god caused Thaddeus to believe that Ancient Magic is the highest power in the world and that *Kijaqumok* is stronger than *Shushequmok.*"

"Is it?"

Artigal's eyes narrowed at her, and she remembered his warning to never think or speak of *Kijaqumok,* but she ignored him. After all, she had already broken that promise too many times to count.

Trojan paused for a long time, searching her face as if he were weighing whether or not it was worth telling her. Finally, he spoke. "In a way, it is. Physically, it is more powerful, but there is more to life than just the physical."

"Why does he want it?"

"To remake the world because he believes it to be impure."

"And he can do that with the Ancient Magic, right?" Fear laced her words, and she felt her face drain of color. Memory of the *Kijaqumok's* power, the way it fed off her hate and anger, the way it drained the light from Artigal, struck terror into her.

"No, because he forgets *Kijaqumok* can only, and will only, destroy, and it only obeys its master, Raythuz. He will destroy the world and will be powerless to make anything rise from the ashes, because he lacks *Shushequmok.* He has chosen the wrong power for what he wants to do."

Realization dawned on her as she turned to Artigal. "So that's why you told him it wasn't too late, that he could still come back to the light."

He nodded his affirmation.

"So if *Kijaqumok* can control the physical nature of things, is that how he was able to bring us all together?"

Artigal shook his head. "No. In fact, Thaddeus was not responsible for bringing us together at all."

She scowled. Why did this all have to be so complicated? "That doesn't make any sense. If he didn't, then who did?"

"The Ancient Magic itself." He coughed violently and groaned.

Her nails dug into his skin as she shook his shoulders. "Curse your riddles. What does that mean?"

"Stephania, be still." Trojan roughly pulled her hands away and scowled. "The great powers of Rasa are waking once more, the *Kijaqumok* and *Shushequmok* are stronger now than they have been for thousands of years. They're extremely volatile. They're trying to reclaim Rasa, and to do that, they need to unite the creatures that can channel their powers. They pulled you and the other creatures together so you could channel their power."

A pit of knots tied in her stomach. "Does that mean it'll happen again?"

Before Trojan could answer, Artigal snarled in pain and slumped over.

"Artigal!" She tried to help him sit up, suddenly guilty for disregarding his condition, but he was too heavy for her. Trojan quickly moved to help. "Oh gods, I'm so sorry. I—"

"Stephania." Trojan squeezed her arm. She hated the tone in his voice.

Artigal coughed, a spurt of blood dripping onto his chin.

"Stephania, the *Kijaqumok* is spreading. At this rate, he'll be dead in an hour."

"Dead?" The word rang in her mind over and over until it began to settle in. If Artigal died, they wouldn't be able to get her memories back. Even if she had been second guessing being able to regain her memories, the idea of truly losing them forever was more than she could bear. "I won't be able to get them back." She turned her terror-stricken face to Trojan and was surprised to find tears streaming down his cheeks.

"I know."

"We have to get him to Frawnden." She could feel the panic settling back in as she clawed at Artigal's unconscious form, desperately trying to drag him with her. He looked so small, lying there in the grass. In fact, he looked so ... normal. He had been intimidating, powerful, and commanded respect and awe, but now he looked so under-average. He really wasn't all that muscular or even very large. His body looked old and worn, and she could even spot wrinkles in his skin. His hands were a little bit crooked, and even his hooves weren't perfect or symmetrical. And his face ... it was so gentle, so tender, it reminded her of the face a father might have—sweet, protective, caring.

Something else caught her attention—a patch of brown on his side. Her eyes widened as she realized it wasn't the only one. Another patch grew on his chest, and spread through his mane. She shook her head in confusion. Was he not naturally white? Her heart beat louder, painfully, fearfully. Whatever was happening, she knew he was dying.

Something woke inside her, and for a moment, she thought she could almost remember a time when she cared about him. Then a horrific realization dawned on her: if he died, she would never know for sure if she had. "We have to save him. We have to save him!" She wrapped her small fingers around his arm and pulled.

"Stephania, no."

She cursed Trojan and pried his hands from her. "He has to live, Trojan. I don't want to lead Trans-Falls! I don't want them to look to me as Farloon. I don't want to lose my memories. If we hurry, we can get him to Frawnden!"

"We can't take him to Frawnden, Stephania. Stop it. Stop it!"

She froze when he yelled and wrenched her away from Artigal. Hot, confused tears poured down her cheeks. "But you just said we could. We have to," she hissed, but he shook his head.

"I know, but we can't." His voice was a harsh growl now. "Frawnden can't do anything for him, and neither can Jargon. The only thing keeping him alive is this forest and the magic it contains."

"So we're just going to let him die? All of Trans-Falls and the Centaurs and the Duvarharians will look to me, and I'm not ready for that. I'm not ready! If he dies, then so does any chance I have of getting my memories back, of actually knowing who I am, or what I'm supposed to do and how!"

He grabbed her shoulders and shook her, his face only inches from hers, the calm composure he had always carried with him shattering. "Don't you think I already know that? Who do you think your memory loss has affected the most? You? Because you're wrong. Look at Mother and Father. They hide everything from you so you don't see the way they cry at night, wondering if they'll ever have you back, if you'll ever call them Mother and Father again, if you'll ever embrace them like family.

"Jargon broke down after he took you to Artigal the other day, nearly crying when he told me you didn't remember him. He put all that pain aside so you wouldn't be uncomfortable. And Artigal practically raised us. He taught us when Aeron wasn't there. He took care of us, protected us, led us, and provided for us. He was everything to you! You looked up to him and admired him and loved him in your own stern way. And now that's all gone."

He shook his head. "And the way you look at me ... All the things I want to tell you, show you, remember with you ..." His voice broke, and he murmured, "Oh,

Stephania."

Abruptly, he threw his arms around her and crushed her against his chest. She clung to him like she would never let go. Their tears mingled in each other's hair and dampened their shoulders, their quiet sobs echoing through the empty, mystical woods.

"I'm so sorry, Steph. I'm just so scared."

She clenched her eyes shut and smoothed his hair under her hand. She had to try nearly three times before she could rasp, "I am too."

A voice drifted to them on the still air.

It was just a quiet whisper, like the ones the forest never stopped murmuring, but this time it was clear.

Do not fear mourning. Comfort will come to those who grieve.

Before they could say anything, magic from the forest began to seep from the vines, the fog, the trees, and even the dirt and sky themselves. Her and Trojan's markings began to glow vibrantly, and as the magic wrapped around her ankles and hands, Stephania felt something move inside her.

"The *Shushequmok*." The tears slowly dried from her eyes as she pulled from Trojan's embrace.

His brow rose questioningly, but she only whispered, "It's here. I can feel it."

She extended her hands. Her markings were no longer red; they were white. With the strange sense that her body was not her own, she crawled over to Artigal's still, crippled, brown form.

Wide-eyed, Trojan stood and stepped back.

Shining light shrouded Stephania and quickly encompassed them, filling their small section of the forest path with bright, warm illuminations. Everything around them hummed with unearthly song.

Taking a deep breath, she placed her hands over Artigal's body, and extended her consciousness to his, searching for the wound. When she found it, she focused on nothing but healing him. White, sparkling magic trailed from her hands and circled itself around Artigal's body. The black veins slowly receded; the cuts, burns, and bruises vanished. The dirt melted away, and the patches of brown hair slowly turned back white. Within a few minutes, his shining, multi-colored eyes snapped open, and he scrambled to his hooves, gasping for air, for life.

The magic abruptly ceased, leaving her reeling as Trojan gently wrapped his arms around her. She could barely keep her eyes open, her whole body feeling as heavy as lead.

For a moment, Artigal stood gasping, staring at seemingly nothing, until his eyes

136

filled with tears, and he held his hand to his chest, his gaze turning to Stephania.

"You channeled *Shushequmok*. You saved me."

She could only shrug as she fought off sudden drowsiness.

"I thought—" Confusion lined his face, and he shook his head. "I was so worried ..." He couldn't seem to finish his sentence, but she guessed maybe she knew what he was trying to say.

"You thought I would choose *Kijaqumok*."

He could only nod, and she shrugged again, not sure how she felt about any of this. She couldn't deny she still felt the Corrupt Magic's pull, and how the distant ache of the magic Thaddeus had left in her and was strengthened, but she didn't want to ruin the moment by mentioning it.

However, a dark mark on his chest caught her attention. "I thought you were healed."

He looked down at his chest, a sad smile lingering on his lips. "I guess it is not in the Emperor's will that I be fully healed."

A scowl marred her face, but she didn't have the strength to argue. "But what if you die? What if I can't channel the magic again to heal you?"

"Then I die."

Trojan's arms tightened around her, and she leaned her head against his chest.

"I don't understand." Tears rose in her eyes, and she wiped them away, cursing their presence, wondering how she even had tears left to shed. If she couldn't control the *Shushequmok*, then why should she trust it?

"I have overstayed my welcome on Rasa. It is only by the Emperor I have lived as long as I have. If it is His will for me to die, then so be it."

She shook her head. "But surely there is something we can do. There *must* be something."

"Stephania ..." Trojan's jaw tightened as if he were struggling with the words.

"The only things capable of staving off this curse are the *Negluu* berries," Artigal interjected. "However, only enough are left to heal your memories."

"That's impossible." She remembered what Trojan had said when they found Artigal. "*The Negluu berry. They found it. You can get your memories back.*" But she wasn't ready for it to be true. "There's only one left."

"Not anymore. The stars informed me that the explosion of magic that encompassed you and I caused just enough for your memories to grow. In just a few days, when I am well enough, you will have your memories back."

She couldn't stop shaking her head. "No. No. It's not fair. I don't understand."

"Stephania, this is what we've all wanted ..." Trojan started, his heart pounding in excitement against her back.

"No," she whispered through her tears. "I don't want them back." The words spilled from her lips, and she hated herself for saying them. Moments before she had been hysterical at the thought of losing them forever, yet now she wasn't sure she wanted them again. She chewed on her lip in frustration. *Maybe I just want to have the choice. Maybe I don't want them to be forcefully given or taken away. Maybe I just want to figure out what I want without the decision being made for me.*

The forest fell silent as a strange horror gripped both Centaurs.

"Why not?" they both asked simultaneously.

She bit her cheek, wishing she had just kept her mouth shut. "Because there are some things I don't want to remember."

Trojan's jaw tightened next to hers, and she wished she knew what he was thinking. *Does he hate me now?* she couldn't help but wonder. *Would I hate myself if I were in his place?* She didn't have an answer.

"I know, Stephania. But your memories are so much more important than me being healed. When you get your memories back, you will have everything you need to face Thaddeus. You won't need me anymore."

She hated hearing him say that. She didn't want to face Thaddeus. Not after what had happened, not after she had wanted to take his hand, to succumb to his power, to leave all she loved for the murderer just because she had been weak. Even now she could feel that seed of magic within her; if she remembered the day he had left it in her, would it grow into something she wouldn't be able to resist? She didn't want to face the demons of her past, the cruel deaths of her mother and father, the carnage of the Dragon Palace. She didn't want to hold this on her shoulders. "But we *do* need you, Artigal," she mumbled, her head hanging against Trojan's arms around her chest as he tightened his embrace.

Slowly, Artigal knelt before her and placed his hand on the side of her face over her Centaur markings. "No, Stephania. We need *you*."

CHAPTER 14

Southern Trans-Falls

A Few Days Later

L AMORA! HOW COULD YOU say such a thing?" Stephania mock gasped at Lamora, who dissolved into a fit of giggles, leaving Ravillian to answer for her.

"Well," he drawled in his deep voice, his light brown eyes sparkling at his childhood friend as she clutched her stomach and stamped her hooves. "Esmeray *is* quite ghastly when you get a close up look at her, seeing as she's got huge scars all over her body and her eyes are milky and creepy. Some say she's actually completely blind and can only read the stars because of dark magic."

"Oh, come on. I'm sure she's not all that bad. You can't fault someone for wanting to be a recluse." How many times had she herself wanted to run away and never see another living soul again? "I mean, isn't Esmeray one of the best star readers in Trans-Falls?"

"Oh, yes, by far," Lamora brushed a tear from her eye and cast a glance at Ravillian. "But she's also really harsh on young children and only comes out of her cave when something really big has been predicted in the stars."

"It *is* pretty strange for a Centaur to live in a cave. We're much more adapted to live in the forest," Ravillian interjected.

"I suppose." Stephania resisted muttering under her breath that caves are actually lovely places to make homes, with strong rock walls and a never-ending supply of darkness, not to mention half of Aeron and Frawnden's home was in the hillside, but she chose to keep her mouth shut.

"I think you're just saying that to seem tougher than us." Lamora crossed her arms and gave Stephania a look that said, 'Prove me wrong.'

For a minute, Stephania could only laugh and shake her head, not sure what to say next. She had never been able to develop witty comebacks, which often made it hard to verbally spar with Lamora, whose mind always seemed to be moving a bit too fast for her own good. It was endearing sometimes, but other times it left Stephania feeling like she had failed some social test she had never been instructed on.

"She *is* tougher than us, Lamora. You forget." Ravillian quickly saved her sensitive emotions, and Stephania shot him a grateful look, which he returned with a wink.

"Oh, how so?"

"Well, for one, she's the only one who can climb the trees to get to the ripe fruit at the top." He shrugged and Lamora frowned.

Stephania quickly caught on. "Yeah, and what about the time you lost your ring in the pond and I swam down to get it for you, and the time—"

Lamora burst out laughing and waved her hands in defeat. "Alright, alright! You win. You're right. You're much tougher than us."

Stephania shifted and nodded, forcing a smile on her face. "Thank you, I am."

As their chuckles fizzled into silence, Stephania shifted in the saddle again, unable to dispel the anxiousness settling within her. It had been hard to keep smiling these past few days. Her appetite was almost non-existent, and sleep hadn't been an option unless Dalton sang her to sleep, but even then, as soon as he left, the nightmares came back, and she never had the heart to ask him to stay with her all night.

Trojan hadn't been avoiding her as much, but he seemed to be in the same quandary as her. They each felt the weight of the *Negluu* berries on their hearts

Hundreds of questions plagued her mind. *Will they work? Will Artigal have the magic necessary to fashion the spell? How much of my memories will I get back? What will I find?* And most pressing, *Who will I become?* It was obvious neither of them could forget that day at the waterfalls, but neither had the bravery to talk to the other, as if something horrible would happen if they did—as if it would happen all over again.

Stephania hadn't been able to tell Ravillian or Lamora about anything that had happened. Every time she thought about trying, she was sure she would throw up or pass out. Artigal had crafted up some half truth to tell the whole of Trans-Falls and, with the help of his elites, had managed to repair the damage done at the falls without word of it spreading. That was the story Ravillian and Lamora had heard, and Stephania wasn't sure she wanted them to know any differently. Even if she *could* tell them about the carnage, the fear of dying, and all the blood and screaming, she would never be able to tell them about the *Kijaqumok* and how she had wanted to follow Thaddeus. *What will people think of me?* The savior of the Dragon Riders wanting to side with the traitor? Thinking of what the consequences of her actions might be if anyone knew the truth caused her blood to run cold and her stomach to start churning again.

Just as her thoughts were spiraling out of control and she felt tears welling up in her eyes, they stopped walking, their focus turned solely to a Centaur standing alone on the road before them.

"Good afternoon, Ravillian." Trojan nodded his head, and Ravillian responded in turn before he turned to Lamora. "And Lamora." She nodded as well. Taking a deep breath, he turned his sharp gaze to Stephania. As soon as their eyes met, she knew exactly why he was here.

"It's time." It was more than he needed to say.

She swallowed and nodded. "I've got to go." She turned to her friends and plastered a grin on her face, willing her body and mind to relax and make this look like no big deal. "I'll stop by later to see you two, okay?" She hoped her anxiety didn't show. As Lamora quickly kissed her cheek and agreed, she knew she had fooled her, but when she looked into Ravillian's eyes as he nodded goodbye, she knew she hadn't fooled him. She tried to give him a reassuring smile, but the worry didn't leave his gaze as he turned away and linked his arm through Lamora's, striking up a lively conversation that sounded about as forced as the ones Stephania crafted daily now.

For a moment, she didn't move, only sat astride Braken as he nervously pawed the ground, her eyes shifting from Trojan's face to the forest.

"Are you ready?"

The words were so simple, spoken so gently, so sweetly, but they instantly called up tears to her eyes, and she bit her lip. *No,* her heart told her. *No,* she wanted to whisper, but she didn't trust she could keep her composure if she opened her mouth to whisper "yes," so instead, she nodded curtly once then twice, as if it made her more sure in her answer.

He seemed to be having the same issue as he opened his mouth and then nodded instead, turning quickly and trotting down the path, indicating she was to follow.

It was too awkward to follow behind him, but she certainty didn't want to ride beside him in case it sparked a conversation she desperately wanted to avoid, so she settled for riding somewhere in between.

She quickly recognized the road they were taking, and a knot formed in her stomach. It would lead straight to the Trans-Falls. Her heart quickened, and she felt her head begin to ring as she remembered the screaming, the blood, the dark magic, the—

"Stephania?" Trojan's voice pulled her from her spiraling thoughts, and she saw him gazing at her with worry from the side of the path. "We're going this way. Through the woods. It's ..." He hesitated as if he wanted to mention something important but wasn't sure if he should. When his eyes met hers, he shook his head and finished, "It's a shortcut." He waited only for her to nod and nudge Braken after him before he pushed through the tall ferns and into the shadowy woods.

She had thought the looming trees, shadows, and grabbing branches would strike fear in her heart, reminding her of the slaughter she had endured less than a week ago, but she found a certain peace had settled over her instead as the wind whispered through the leaves. The trees didn't move; spirits didn't walk out of them. It was just a normal, quiet forest where nothing interesting ever happened. She wished.

A familiarity struck her as white fog swirled across the forest floor, and once more the trees were looming giants with sparkling vines and floating lights. This was the same part of the forest she had healed Artigal in a few days ago.

"It's the *Gauwu Zelauw,*" Trojan whispered as his hand trailed over the bark of one of the gigantic ancient trees, "the Tomb Forest."

The name sent a shiver down her spine and caused more questions to surface, such as the reasoning behind the name "Tomb Forest", but the air was simply too quiet and heavy with sleep that she felt it a sin to ask such a dull, typical question.

"It's only a little farther."

She nodded, though she was too far behind him for him to notice.

It was hard to see in the dark, glimmering fog, and she swore several times she saw something dart through the trees and giant ferns, but neither she nor Trojan mentioned it, though she was sure he had seen it too.

Abruptly, they came to a towering wall of vines, and she dismounted, tying Braken to a nearby tree.

At first glance, she couldn't see anything specifically interesting about the vine wall, but as she looked for longer, she noticed the vines were encompassing something that looked as if it might have been an old structure at one point. It had cylindrical walls and a dome on top and was quite large, though she couldn't see any wood, granite, or other building material under the vines. For all she knew, it was made entirely out of the sparkling plants.

Trojan's hand extended toward the vines but drew short of touching them. For a moment, he stood completely still. She almost spoke up to ask if everything was all right. Finally, he turned to her, a strange glint in his eyes.

"Stephania ..." he started but then trailed off. Slowly, as if he were afraid she would run away, he extended his hand to take hers in his. She let him after a moment's hesitation, a moment of listening to the Corrupt Magic within her hiss lies that he must hate her for not remembering him.

"I just wanted to tell you, before you got your memories back, to tell you as the young woman Dalton raised, I'm sorry for treating you the way I have. I shouldn't have ignored you. I only thought that if I didn't get close to you, it would hurt less for both of us"—he took a deep breath—"but I can see now that I was wrong. I could've at least had you as a friend, but instead, I made you feel as if all this was your fault, as if you are somehow responsible for my emotions and actions. Which, of course, you're not."

He took a shaking breath and looked away for a moment before focusing on her once again. "I understand things will probably never be the same between us like they were, even when you get your memories back. You have new friends now, and I wasn't there for you when you needed someone to be. You've learned to live without me in the way I never was able to live without you. But I'm trying to accept that. I just want you to know that no matter what, I'm here for you. Not just the little dragon I cared for as a sister years ago, but as the young woman you are now, as a friend."

She didn't know what to say. Her heart pounded in her chest, her thoughts running so fast she wasn't sure if they were running at all. His words played over and over in her mind, but she wasn't sure if she understood them fully.

"And I just want you to know that, despite all the pressure everyone is putting on you to get your memories back ..." His jaw tensed, and his hand tightened around hers. He seemed as if he were choosing his words very carefully. His eyes wandered over her head to the forest behind her and then back to her eyes. "They are still your memories. And this is still *your* life. Yes, I think you would do better knowing who you are, where you came from, what you can do, but it may not be the only way. You still have a choice. I don't want you to think you have to get them back because that's what everyone's telling you to do. Even me. I want you to—" He bit his lip and looked away from her as if he were holding back tears. "Stephania"—he squeezed her hand harder as if trying to draw strength from her, even though she knew she had none to give—"I want *you* to want them back."

She didn't notice the tears flowing down her face until she tasted salt on her lips.

"Do you understand?" His eyes sparkled, and it only made her own tears worse.

She nodded. She could choose? Could she? Was she really free to? She thought about all the times she wanted to leave Trans-Falls behind and all the memories with it. She had wanted to run from New-Fars to Duvarharia, wishing she could be someone new, to leave all this behind and start over. If she accepted her memories back, she would never be able to run from them, from who she was, and who others wanted her to be.

"I will stand by you, whatever decision you make. Even if you choose to leave it all behind."

She nodded again, weighing his words in her mind. If he did so and she ran away, he would be forfeiting everything: his rank, his army, his friends and family, his inheritance to Trans-Falls, and his Synoliki position and magic. He would be giving up everything—for her. *But why? Why would he care so much about me?* For the first time since she learned her memories had been taken from her, she wanted to know—to know about her family, her old home, her old life here in Trans-Falls. Mostly, she wanted to know what bond she and Trojan had shared that would motivate him to lay his life down for her.

"I want them back." She was surprised at her own voice ringing through the trees, but it brought a certain peace to her.

"Are you sure?"

She met his gaze and nodded. "I am. I want to know. Everything. I want to remember what I left behind. The nightmares haunt me, even without my full memories. I can't escape them by running. I think it's time to see if there is enough love I've forgotten to outweigh the hate I might find."

A poorly restrained grin spread across his face as he squeezed her hands. "Then let us continue, together."

She took a deep breath and tried to smile back. "Okay."

His hands slid over the vines, his blue markings glowing with a light that traveled from his heart to his hands. The vines absorbed the light and rustled as if breathing before they parted, opening to a tunnel.

Fearlessly, Trojan stepped in, Stephania just to his side, her hand clenched tightly in his.

With one step, she found herself in an entirely different world. The walls of vines and flowers she had spied from the forest looking in were no longer there. Replacing them, thousands of stars and galaxies shone against a black void.

Creatures moved around her, melding into the stars and shaping themselves into images. Images formed in the galaxy, and she saw herself, presumably in the future, astride a black dragon soaring over the Dragon Palace, and then in the present, as if she were looking into a mirror, walking through the tunnel, and then years untold into the past with a young boy who looked strikingly like Thaddeus playing with another boy with black hair and blue eyes; a beaten man and his dragon being bled out as a crowd cheered for death; the waters rising and crashing over an empire of dragons and riders as they fled through a portal, and many more things she couldn't begin to understand. Ten or twenty huge monsters dominated the images around her, and every step the creatures took caused the creation of mountains, forests, plains, deserts, lakes, and rivers; or caused what already existed to morph, break, bend, and change into something else.

Slower and slower she walked, as if the tunnel had stretched to a mile and she was too tired to continue. Her hand reached out to the abyss beside her, and she wondered if she wouldn't see Infinity and be lost in its mysteries forever if only she stepped into it.

Something gripped her other hand tighter and pulled her roughly toward a bright light ahead. Abruptly, the tunnel was gone, and she was standing in a large room.

For a few long minutes, she could do nothing except blink at her surroundings, trying and failing to see what was around her, as if what she was seeing was too bland or common to hold her attention after what she had just witnessed.

Finally, she registered it had been Trojan's hand that pulled her out of the tunnel. She stared at his dark skin and slowly looked up his arm to his face and then lastly to his eyes. She could see the infinity hanging in them as if everything she had seen had been trapped in their sparkling blue.

Quickly, her gaze darted to the other creatures she could make out in the room, but she found nothing unusual. Aeron, Dalton, Jargon, Frawnden—none of them looked any different. But when her eyes found Artigal's, she was finally able to fully gaze into their color changing mystery and realize she had always seen the Infinity in him, she had just never understood it until now.

Confused, she turned back to Trojan, her question obvious in her gaze.

He squeezed her hand reassuringly and leaned down to softly whisper, "Only a few have been shown the Infinity."

Mystified, she turned her attention back to her surroundings, her head clearing enough so she could finally take it all in.

They stood in what appeared to be a great granite chamber covered almost entirely in glowing vines giving just enough light to the room so artificial light wasn't needed.

Small, shimmering white beings floated around the room. They had strangely long legs like hundreds of little ribbons, which flowed behind a circular body, flexing and moving through the air as if they were swimming. The white fog was still present and poured from the vines all around the room, settling on the ground in a thickness that barely allowed her to see her feet. The air was cool and fresh and smelled much like flowers, though none she could place her mind on.

In the middle of the room rested a large solid granite table. It had numerous chips and erosions in it, but it held a sense of power and majesty that made her breath falter. Green markings decorated its surface and glowed much like her Shalnoa, or the Synoliki markings on Trojan. However, the designs themselves were unlike anything Stephania had ever seen before, even in all of Dalton's old manuscripts.

The table had no chairs, but the overall impression Stephania got from the room was that this wasn't a place to sit long and rest.

Besides her family, Jargon, and Artigal, five other strong warriors stood protectively and honorably to the sides of the rooms. They made Stephania tremble with fear. All of them were, head to toe, the darkest black and stood heads and shoulders above even the largest Centaur warriors she had seen. Each of them bore green markings akin to the ones on the table, and all their eyes glowed green. It was instantly clear their sole purpose was to protect this shrine with their lives.

"Shall we begin?" Artigal's voice finally broke the silence, and a low murmur of approval rippled through the room, though Stephania wished she could simply curl up and fall asleep in this wonderous place, waiting for it to divulge its secrets.

Gently, Trojan pulled her to the table. It was bare, save for two items. One was a white handled knife with a shining steel blade. The other was a golden chalice, though the gold hardly looked worth anything compared to all that surrounded it. Inside the chalice was a clear, swirling liquid that seemed to move with its own power. Stephania quickly deduced it was the magic combination that had been formed from the vials and bottles Jargon and Artigal had shown her weeks ago in the small hut.

"Today we gather in a very sacred place, one given to the Centaurs the day the Great Emperor blessed us with the gift of magic. It is only one of five known tombs like it. According to our beliefs, numerous others exist all across Ventronovia but have been hidden from us in this age. They are said to contain the souls of the creatures of Destruction and Creation that once walked Rasa in the dawn of time. It is also said these creatures will walk again at the end of the world."

Stephania's brow furrowed in skepticism. She wasn't sure how much of what he said she believed, but if any place on Rasa existed where a creature like that might lie in a tomb, she was sure this would be it.

A strange tone filled Artigal's voice—one of awe, something she had never heard him express. "Long ago, you could hear the mysteries of the world as they were whispered on the branches of this forest. It hasn't been heard for a long time, but it might be possible again.

"Because this place is so full of the Great Emperor's blessing and the Pure Magic, it is here, in the safety of the *Shushequmok*, we will perform the magic needed to open the barrier around Stephania's memories."

A lasting silence echoed through the room, and none dared even breathe.

A strange surge of magic raced through Stephania. She gasped and blinked a few times, trying to rid her sight of the sparks flitting across her vision. A quick look to Artigal and Trojan told her she was the only one who had felt it. A sense of dread mingled with the peace within her creating an uncomfortable emotion she chose to try to ignore.

Artigal's face broke out into a grin as the vines parted again. "Ah. Dusan has arrived."

The black Centaur wearing the same armor as the Centaurs sent to retrieve the *Negluu* berries stepped into the room. No one else came in behind him, and the vines

146

closed.

Outwardly, the Centaur looked almost exactly the same as he did back in the crude training hut weeks ago, but Stephania instantly noticed a change about him. A calm hung over him instead of the solemnness that had the first time she saw him.

"Trojan," she whispered, trying to get his attention though not sure what to ask. He didn't seem to hear her as his eyes followed Dusan.

The Centaur bowed low in front of Artigal before retrieving a vial from his pouch. "The *Negluu* berries, Igentis."

"He's seen Hanluurasa," Trojan whispered with disbelief.

"What do you mean?"

"Look at him."

She trained her eyes back on the black Centaur as he straightened and turned to face her. For a moment, their eyes met, and she gasped. She could see the galaxies in his eyes.

"Where is Yollen?" Artigal narrowed his eyes at the vines that refused to part for the second Centaur.

As if he couldn't contain his excitement, the messenger abandoned all pretenses and waved his hands excitedly, his eyes shining like a child's. "He was taken home by the Great Emperor into Hanluurasa. I saw it myself. I saw it."

A hush of disbelief hung in the room.

Tears collected in the burly Centaur's eyes. "I got to see it, Igentis. I was able to look into the land of my ancestors. I could feel the stars. I could *hear* them! I wanted to go. Oh, stars, I wanted to go! But I stayed to deliver the berries."

Artigal couldn't mask the joy that shone on his face as he clamped a hand on the Centaur's shoulder. "Thank you, Dusan. You will be rewarded. May the suns smile upon your presence."

Grinning like a fool, his eyes shining with untold joy, Dusan bowed again before turning back to the vines. They parted again, and Stephania just caught the multitude of color in the tunnel. Far more stars shone now than she had seen when she passed through, and somehow, she knew she was looking into *Hanluurasa*. As the vines closed behind Dusan, Stephania got the strange feeling they would never see him again, that he had passed on into the starry realm they called home.

With quick, steady fingers, Jargon took the *Negluu* berries and crushed them before letting their crackling red juice drip into the chalice. Shining white fog with sparks of gold magic flowed over the chalice's rim and down to the ground. Jargon nodded with satisfaction before replacing the chalice on the table and stepping back into the shadows with Frawnden and Aeron.

"Stephania, for this magic to work, you must mix in a drop of your blood." Artigal's eyes locked with hers, and she swallowed dryly before nodding.

Feeling as if she was walking through a dream, she rounded the table and slowly dragged the knife off the surface. Her eyes flickered nervously to Trojan, and he half-smiled before stamping his hoof. She didn't feel much reassured, but she was glad she wasn't the only creature here who was anxious.

Grasping the cool handle of the knife in one hand, she positioned one finger over the chalice. Biting her lip against the pain, she placed the blade against the tip of her finger and jerked it across her skin. The stinging only lasted a second.

A drop of her blood collected at the end of her finger, and she gasped as that same strange surge of electricity rippled through her body. As the drop of blood fell, she saw a shadow following it, and a small flash of recognition sparked in her—*Kijaqumok*. The blood dropped into the swirling liquid magic, and for a moment, the liquid turned red then black, a shadowy fog oozing ominously over the cup's rim before disappearing. She quickly looked around to see if anyone else had noticed. It seemed they hadn't, and she decided against saying anything lest Artigal put an end to it and therefore waste the last *Negluu* berries.

Quickly, so she didn't have time to change her mind, she picked up the chalice to drink from it. But before her lips could even come near the rim, the darkness in it disappeared and the magic began to shift. Strands of the magic shaped themselves into what looked like chains made of blue lightning; they twined out of the cup and wrapped around her arm. With a cry of fear, the chains reminding her too much of the dark chains that had held her and Trojan at the falls, she tried to drop the cup. But she found she couldn't. The magic had taken control of her arm and wouldn't let her.

She couldn't take it back.

The knife slid out of her other hand and clattered onto the table, a horrendous noise in the silence.

The chains wrapped around her neck and torso, cracking and snapping as they quickly covered her body. A strangled cry tore from her throat. *Will it crush me like at the waterfall, dragging me to Susahu?* "Trojan," she whimpered, tears streaming down her cheeks. Her eyes met his, and she tried to reach out to him.

She knew he saw the fear in her eyes when his jaw clenched in anger, and he wrapped his arms around her. His mouth moved, but she couldn't hear what he was saying.

Then the figures around her moved and shaped until she was standing in New-Fars and Nemeth's house. Then it disappeared, and she was standing at a rose bush, cutting roses before Grey beat her. Then it changed again to when she was ten and she was given her mother's ring from Dalton. While the memories flashed around her, trying to drag her into their depths, she kept her eyes locked on Trojan's as if he were her lifeline.

The older the memories, the more pain they brought. She groaned in agony, her mind and soul burning as if on fire. Every day of her life flashed violently before her eyes, stamping themselves into her mind. Her ears rang, her head throbbed, her eyes stung.

She tried to look at Aeron and Frawnden, but for a moment, she couldn't remember who they were. Were they her parents or were they Trans-Falls's leaders? Her sight blurred, and briefly, she could see them all—Aeron, Frawnden, Jargon and Artigal—but they were so much different, so much younger. The old memories melted with the present, and she rolled her head, crying in confusion and pain.

Sweat dripped off her brow, and she swayed, feeling Trojan's hands steadying her.

"Make it stop," she pleaded, her nails digging into his arm. *Can't they see how excruciating this is? Does no one care? Please ... end this ...* She searched for Trojan but could no longer see him. She was alone. Alone in her fear and agony. Her heart beat irregularly, and she couldn't seem to draw enough air. "Make it stop." The images only flashed faster, louder, brighter. The voices mingled into one, and she couldn't tell if it was their noise or her screams ringing in her ears. "Make it stop!"

"It's okay, Stephania." A deep voice broke through the chaos, and she tried to focus on it. She knew that voice. "I'm here. I'm here."

She drew shaking breaths as she concentrated on the voice. The pain subsided as a few memories drew into focus.

Yes, she knew that voice well.

Sleepy. She was sleepy. She was sitting on something. No, she was riding on something ... a Centaur. A young Centaur. He was talking to her, saying something, and she spoke back before he answered, "I'm not sure. But somewhere. Somewhere with the Great Emperor ..." Then the memory faded into another.

She felt disappointment rise in her, but over what? She felt the curve of a bow in her hand and felt the warm sun on her head. The smell of herbs and flowers filled her senses, but she focused only on the voice as it reassured her. "Maybe you just need to practice a bunch more. I *know* you're going to be great at archery."

Again and again she heard that voice, that sweet voice that sounded every bit like what home should sound like.

Then a dark wind blew through the memories, and all the love and joy left them. Fear filled its place. Terror raced through her, and she panicked against her unknown assailant. She felt arms around her and revolted against them but found herself unable to move. They held her tightly, lovingly, protectively. She heard his voice again, but this time, not in joy or love, but in horror and tears. "I love you, Stephania! I will always be waiting here for you! Please don't forget me!" She cried against the unbearable pain she felt radiating from him as the words echoed in her head, "Please don't forget me. Don't forget me. Don't forget me."

She choked against her tears, shaking her head against the pain, against the guilt because she knew she had failed him. She *had* forgotten him ... Trojan ... her brother.

In that moment, she truly remembered everything. It was as if everything that had ever covered who she truly was shattered into a thousand pieces, baring up her soul. She remembered her family, Jargon, all the Centaurs who had loved and cared for her, and her Duvarharian parents, their dragons, and their palace. She remembered the Etas, their blood lust, and all the lives they stole, and then she remembered her hate.

The *Kijaqumok* surged forward, shattering the wall of *Shushequmok* around her mind, brushing it aside as if were chaff in the wind. She felt herself scream but couldn't hear anything over the roaring in her mind as the magics collided and warred, neither wanting balance. The Corrupt Magic fed off the hate pouring from her memories as if it had been hungering for the power for years. The Pure Magic flickered and wavered as the Corrupt consumed her, controlled her, enraging the flames of scorn inside of her, fighting to turn her into the plaything of Raythuz just as Colten had been. Nothing would stand in its way. She was powerless to stop it, and so was everyone around her.

No one could save her.

§

DARKNESS AND SHADOW poured from the vines, mixing with the white fog as each fought for dominance. The air went cold. Wind rushed through the room, howling and screaming. A crow cawed wildly outside.

"Great Emperor help us." Artigal resisted his urge to smash the granite table in his frustration. Hot tears burned his eyes and threatened to ruin his composure. It was going so wrong. Somehow, even in this sacred place, the *Kijaqumok* had found purchase, and he knew it had to have come from Stephania herself. Horror and dread churned his stomach. A searing pain raced through his body from the magic on his chest as he struggled toward Stephania and Trojan, wishing for some way he could protect them.

Black veins spread under her skin as Trojan cried her name, pouring as much of his own magic into her body as he could, but it did nothing against the *Kijaqumok*.

"Great Emperor." Artigal fell to his knees, his hands clutched against his chest. The world fell silent around him. He saw Trojan's mouth moving but heard nothing.

Stephania's back was arched in a scream as her eyes turned white and rolled into the back of her head. However, he couldn't hear her either. He strained to hear the voice of his Emperor as he pleaded. "Just once more. Let me channel it once more." His hands rested on the granite table, and he stilled his soul, reaching out to the creature he believed to lie below. "Rise," he whispered.

An earsplitting crack tore through the room followed by an unearthly roar. The ground shook beneath them, and the roaring grew louder until they couldn't block it out. With the screeching of polished stone on stone, the table split in half.

A shining green creature rose from the gaping tomb.

"The *kazozh kadu*," Artigal whispered and cried with joy.

The creature shook his mane and roared. It looked like a lion but had eight glistening eyes and enormous wings. It slowly turned to Trojan and Stephania.

The terror on Trojan's face quickly turned to confusion, then awe, then reverence.

The being opened its huge jaws, displaying more than one set of teeth, and spoke. Its words sounded like a language but one greater than all others, as if its words held the power of the universe itself.

From out of Stephania's quivering, limp body, the darkness collected into a large dark shadow with red, glistening eyes. It hissed and snarled at the lion, but the creature only spoke again. The creature of *Kijaqumok* yowled in pain, screaming something in reply, before they lunged at each other.

The sound was deafening as their roars and words shook the very foundation of everything around them. The granite shifted and molded like clay, the vines died and then grew again, the air rushed and stilled, the light faded and then shone again. The battle was almost impossible to watch.

An explosion rent the air around them, and all went completely still. Artigal opened his eyes and saw the creature standing before him. It was the same but different. Half of its eyes shone red, and streaks of black melded perfectly in its green figure. It had balanced itself, the Corrupt and Pure, like the Magic had once been at the beginning of time.

Slowly, it bowed its head as its form swelled into a shining orb of both the brightest light and darkest shadow. The orb rested a moment, suspended above the table, then shattered into black and white sparks that floated to the ground and vanished in the white fog.

Blinking against the once blinding light, the Centaurs stepped out from the shadows, shock and confusion on all their faces.

Artigal's eyes widened as they landed on the table. It was completely intact, as if it had never broken open.

Trojan was cradling Stephania's sleeping form, tears slipping from his eyes and down to her face. The black veins were gone from her skin, and her eyes were closed in peace, her chest rising and falling steadily. She was safe, and she was healed. In a few days, she would wake and would remember everything.

At last, Artigal's promise to Stephania was fulfilled.

All was right again.

Frawnden, Aeron, and Dalton rushed over to their children, their words lost in murmurs as they hugged each other and held their daughter. Jargon stood just to the side, a bright grin on his dark face.

Joy turned to sorrow as Artigal turned away. His fists clenched tighter as he remembered the little brown-haired Duvarharian girl. If only he could have given her the same love he had given Stephania. If only he had been able to give her a family who loved and supported her. If only he hadn't destroyed her mind. He bit his lip until blood dripped onto his tan skin.

Tan.

His heart twisted in his chest as he looked down at himself.

"By the stars."

He was no longer white.

His coat was brown, his skin tan and rosy. His hair was brown, and he knew if he could see his eyes, they would be gold.

The air stopped in his lungs. The world spun around him. His hand strayed to his chest. He could no longer feel the *Kijaqumok* or the *Shushequmok* inside him. In fact, he felt ... old.

Tears rushed down his face, and he did nothing to stop them.

His purpose had been fulfilled. After thousands of years, he had finally done what the Great Emperor had blessed him to do.

Before any of the other creatures could notice his transformation, he slipped out of the granite room, trying to ignore the call of the Infinity within the tunnel.

Finally, he was mortal. His days on Rasa were numbered once again. As for death, when it came, he would welcome it with open arms. Maybe, at least in death, he would find forgiveness and peace for all the sin he had dealt to those he loved, and maybe, just maybe, he would be able to see them again.

PART TWO
Thicker than Blood

CHAPTER 15

T ROJAN, LITTLE HOOVES. You need to go take a walk or get some
sleep." Frawnden's gentle voice drifted in from the cracked door. When no
one answered, she called again. "Trojan?"

Kneeling beside Stephania's bed, Trojan startled from his trance, his gaze breaking
away from her sleeping face. "Huh?"

"Did you hear what I said?"

He shook his head and turned back to Stephania, his hand tightening around hers.

"I said you should take a walk or a nap. You've hardly left her side in the last day."

"What if she wakes when I'm gone?"

Silence ached in the room.

Stephania had been in a coma-like state for almost twenty-four hours now since
she regained her memories in the *Gauwu Zelauw*. Thankfully, it had been a restful
sleep, but that hadn't eased the anxiety of her friends and family. Artigal had been
unusually distant since then, and they'd had to do without his help.

"I think you both will be just fine. Please come. You're obsessing."

A scowl drew down his lips, and he muttered something under his breath. Frawnden waited until he stood, his knees popping loudly and a grunt escaping his lips.
He still held on to Stephania's small, pale hand, his gaze focused on her. Finally, he
squeezed before letting go. He cast a glance over his shoulder, just in case her eyes
had fluttered open in the spare moments he had looked away. A grunt of displeasure
rumbled in his chest when he saw she hadn't, and he dragged himself out of the room
behind Frawnden, shutting the door gently behind him.

"What will you do?"

He looked down at Frawnden. Determination shone in her eyes, and he knew she
wouldn't leave him alone until she was certain he would either sleep or get his mind off
Stephania.

"I'll walk, I suppose."

She nodded, seemingly satisfied with his answer. "When you do so, try not to think too much about her, okay, little hooves?"

A smile made its way onto his face at the endearing Centaur nickname. "What else is there to think of?"

Her black hair waved across her shoulders as she shook her head in slight amusement. "I heard Dakar and Lycus are coming home early. They won the battle at the Domain border quicker than expected. I suppose you could think of them."

Dakar and Lycus were his brothers in war. They had all saved each other's lives more times than they could count. They had been with him through training and had served under his command for as long as he could remember. He hadn't seen them for a good six months, but it wasn't until his mother mentioned them that he realized how much he missed them.

"I suppose I shall." He smiled tenderly as he kissed her cheek, and she patted his.

"Good. I'll be making remedial tinctures in the kitchen. I won't be far from her. Neither will Dalton."

He nodded slowly but then added, "I know." He didn't want her thinking he didn't trust her to take care of Stephania. After all, she was her mother and his own too. But after what happened with Colten, the *Zelauwgugey*, Artigal, and then just yesterday with the memories, he knew he could never protect her enough, could never be too careful.

"How is she?" Dalton walked up beside Trojan, his hands cupped around a steaming mug of Muluk. His eyes, bloodshot from sleepless, restless nights, were dark with worry.

Frawnden smiled tenderly. "Just the same. I'm trying to assure Trojan she'll be fine long enough for him to take a break."

Dalton nodded, his usual, easy-going manner absent. "That's right, Trojan." He placed a reassuring hand on Trojan's arm. "I'm going to sit with her awhile. And maybe if she wakes ..." He gestured with the Muluk and Trojan's heart skipped a beat.

Of course he wasn't the only one worried about Stephania, nor was he the only one who wanted to spend time with her. "Thank you. For sitting with her. For ... everything." He found it hard to meet Dalton's empathetic gaze. How could he possibly expect to covet all of Stephania's time when Dalton had raised her?

"No need to thank me. She's always been a daughter to me; I take care of her, and I worry. That's what family does." A genuine smile spread on his face and Trojan couldn't help but return it.

"Good idea about the Muluk, Dalton." Frawnden grinned. "When she wakes, I'm sure that will be the first thing she'll want to drink."

Dalton nodded, his hands tightening around the mug. "That's what I thought too." Opening the door carefully, he took a deep breath in, then out, before quietly slipping inside, pulling the door shut behind him.

Trojan found himself letting out a breath as well as he nervously smiled at his mother.

"Now go. Please take some time to yourself."

Trojan nodded, then, with curt steps, turned and left the hallway. Though Dalton's concern had left him with a certain measure of comfort, it still took every measure of his willpower to walk through their house, out the doors, down the steps, and into the woods. When the branches and leaves finally closed around him, he breathed out a deep sigh of relief. As much as he wanted to spend every second with Stephania, it didn't do him well to leave the forest for too long; his soul was connected to it intimately.

Before he realized how long he had walked, he was standing at the edge of a stream where the water collected into a little pool before continuing.

It took a moment for him to recognize the place.

A warmth of sad nostalgia filled him. This was where he and Stephania had swum the day they went to demonstrate her archery before Artigal. The day she created magic. The day that changed everything.

A whirlwind of emotions stormed within him.

Almost nothing had changed at the pool. A small patch of clover they used to lay in while watching the birds was still flourishing, though a few saplings had taken over the far corners. A large rock jutted out over the deepest end of the pool. He remembered running off it and splashing into the cool water. A rope had once hung from the branch above; Aeron had hung it for Stephania to swing off of. He looked, but couldn't find it. *I guess some things do change over time.*

He closed his eyes, letting the emotions surface: relief that it was almost completely unchanged, nostalgia for all the joy he and Stephania had shared here, disappointment that time would keep changing it little by little until he wouldn't recognize it, anger that it was one of the last things they had done in Trans-Falls before they were forced to take Stephania to New-Fars, and a strange, swirling, anxious joy that Stephania would awaken and she would remember it too.

He clenched his hands, hardly able to quell this strange feeling rising in him. She would wake up. She would have her memories back. He had waited so long for it, now that it was within reach, yet he didn't know how to deal with it.

"I wondered if I would find you here."

Everything in him froze. He tried several times to speak before his voice would let him. "Stephania?" Slowly, he turned around, as if afraid it was all just an illusion.

Her slim frame was silhouetted in the setting suns, the light dancing off leaves and tickling her shining hair as it spilled in curly tangles down her shoulders. Her hands fiddled with a loose string on her shirt—a habit she had picked up living in New-Fars. She wasn't completely changed because of her memories. "Hey, Tro."

His heart lurched at the old nickname she had used for him.

She stepped forward, but he couldn't make himself move toward her.

"I'm sorry I've been such a pain and that I didn't—" Her voice caught, and she shrugged her shoulders as a nervous laugh parted her lips, her eyes darting away. It wasn't something she could apologize for, they both knew. But both held regret as if it was their own fault.

Finally, he regained control over his body and stepped toward her, though his hands shook uncontrollably. "Look at me."

Their eyes met, and he gasped. He couldn't mistake it. Remembrance shone in her shining, red eyes.

A guttural laugh leapt from his lips as he reared in uncontrollable excitement. "You remember. You truly remember."

She nodded through her tears and laughed with him. "Yes."

"By the gods ..." His eyes pierced hers until abruptly he crushed her in his embrace, lifting her in the air and shaking her playfully before setting her down. Every emotion he had bottled up since she had arrived in Trans-Falls suddenly broke open, and before he could stop himself, he was crying into her messy hair.

He quickly pulled away when he felt her sobbing against him. "Steph, Steph. What's wrong?" He quickly dried his eyes and tried to meet her gaze, but she avoided his. "What's wrong?"

"I just—" She rubbed her eyes and sniffed. "I can't believe how I treated you. I ignored you and avoided you, and when I told you I didn't remember you—" She bit her lip against the tears that spilled down her cheeks. When she couldn't say any more, she shook her head.

It wasn't all her fault. His heart ached in his chest. He too had acted irrationally, wanting to heal his wounds alone even if it meant distancing from her and making the wounds bigger. "Oh, Steph." With a heavy sigh, he pressed his forehead to hers. He could never forget how it felt when she had looked up into his eyes with nothing but fear and discomfort and told him he was a stranger. Never.

But he had been just as destructive, pushing her away. He should have been the one showing her around Trans-Falls, teaching her about their culture and the animals and whatever else she wanted to know. He shouldn't have left her alone. "Please don't ever think about that again. It wasn't your fault, and it wasn't fair to you."

She opened her mouth, but he interrupted her with a curt shake of his head. "It doesn't even matter anymore. That's all behind us now. And no matter how you treat me, I will always, always be here for you. Just because we've had a rough few weeks doesn't mean I don't still love you. You're my little sister. I will always, *always* love you." He gave her shoulders a gentle shake. "Do you understand?"

She nodded.

"Good. We don't need to look behind us anymore, Stephania. Only look ahead."

§

THEY SAT NEXT TO EACH OTHER, Stephania's legs dangling from the little outcrop over the water, while his were tucked delicately under himself. Long moments of silence followed, but they never felt the time slip by. The minutes could have been days, and the hours could have been seconds, but neither cared.

Finally, Trojan broke the silence. "I waited so long for you to come see me, after we gave you to Dalton."

She tried to dry her face on her short sleeve, but much of it was already damp. "What do you mean?"

A sad smile spread across his face. "We stayed closed to New-Fars for a few months. Artigal conversed with Dalton every so often to make sure you were adjusting well. Every day, as long as I was able, I went back to the waterfall hoping you would come to see me." Fresh tears brimmed in his eyes, and he struggled against them. "You never came. I nearly went insane from worry and loneliness. Finally, I had to accept that new, horrible reality when Artigal told me you would never come back because he erased your memories." A darkness settled in his eyes. "It ruined me. I was depressed for a long time. I barely trained, hardly spoke to anyone, and refused to eat most of the time. That's when I met my *Fomdaazh*—brothers of war—Dakar and Lycus. They stuck with me when others were too exasperated to care. About a year later, I realized I couldn't undo what had been done, and I decided to apply to become the leader of my own division."

"So young," Stephania breathed in a mix of awe and horror. *What has he endured? How will I ever come close to understanding?* She looked deep into his eyes and found the dark sadness she hadn't noticed before. *He's lost so much but has managed to survive, to rise beyond his suffering. But it will never leave him.*

The edges of his lips curled up momentarily before he looked away. "Dakar and Lycus were put under me along with a few other gifted young Centaurs. They called us Little Hooves."

She laughed at that, and he couldn't help but join her. "We didn't much appre-

161

ciate it at first, but we grew into it." His laughter faded. "This is what I missed," he whispered hoarsely.

"What?"

"Being able to trust someone enough to tell them the things I've suffered. I've always had to be strong for someone: my army, mother and father, Artigal, my people, the humans." His gaze grew distant. "There was one other, someone I trusted my heart to but ..." He shook his head and smiled sadly when she nodded for him to continue. Instead, he passed a hand over the stubble on his face and smiled. "But I missed *you*. You never counted it against me or thought I was weak when I opened my heart to you."

A warmth spread in her as she struggled to remember, to call the memories to her. After a moment, they surfaced. He used to tell her about his yearning to see *Hanluurasa*, or how much he loved the colors of a rising sun on a field of *Leño-zhego* flowers. He liked cardinals best because their red reminded him of her eyes. He always pretended to be annoyed when Frawnden called him "little hooves" but would walk away grinning sheepishly. She remembered the little, strange rocks he used to find and give her. She grinned broadly, tears sparkling in her eyes. "I remember. Tell me what happened to you."

He nodded and took a deep breath. "The Synoliki magic caused me to grow up much faster than normal. By the time I was sixteen, I was in charge of the army itself. I threw myself into battle after battle, hoping I would die." He hung his head, his hands trembling at the memory.

A dark chasm opened in her. *He wanted to die.* She felt as if her heart had broken into a thousand shards. She couldn't fathom her strong, stoic brother wishing for his own death. Even simply trying to understand was more anguish than she wanted to bear. She covered her lips and strangled back a sob.

"Sometimes the thought of seeing you again kept me going, but other times my anger and grief over losing you and failing you drove me to do things I wish I had never done." He paused for a moment, opened his mouth, and then closed it as if not sure he wanted to continue. He took a deep breath and spoke so quietly she almost couldn't hear him. "To love things and people that only hurt me more. Hurt *them* more."

She squeezed his arm, wishing she could do more. Though she knew no words could heal his hurt, she whispered anyway. "I'm sorry, Trojan."

He shrugged and clenched his jaw, his large hand engulfing hers as he held it against his arm. "It's no matter anymore. You're back, and that's enough. The past is behind us."

Something like clarity finally dawned on her, and a peace rested in her soul. "I guess it's better I didn't remember any of this."

He looked down quizzically at her.

"You suffered so much because you knew what you had lost. You remembered everything life took away from you. But I never did. I didn't miss any of this, and I didn't have to suffer what you did because of it."

"Maybe that's one of the reasons why he did it. To protect you from more than just your own magic and Thaddeus."

"Maybe," she drawled, her face contorting in a frown. Two very different emotions and beliefs rose in her. She believed Artigal had done it all for good, for her safety and her happiness; she trusted him completely; she would do anything he asked of her. But she remembered how betrayed she felt when she had been told her memories had been taken away from her, how much she hated Artigal and resented him, how confused she had been because she didn't know who she was.

Quiet curses slipped through her lips as she balled her fists. *So this is how I will suffer getting my memories back.* She would be two people living in one body. Even now, she wouldn't know who she was.

"Stephania?"

She snapped back to reality at Trojan's worried voice.

"Uh, I'm fine. I'm just really tired."

His face suddenly took on a very protective and determined aura as he quickly took to his hooves. "You need to get back home to eat. Come. Let me carry you."

He turned his broad back to her, and she nearly jumped on before something stopped her—a little voice telling her he was a stranger, someone who she avoided and who avoided her. Another voice told her he was her brother and they did this all the time. The voices screamed at each other, pulling her in half until she thought she might cry from the confusion.

When he turned his eyes to hers, one eyebrow raised, she swallowed the chaos, put on a smile, and hopped on his back, trying desperately to ignore the confliction of joy and horror that rose in her, focusing instead on the rhythm of his hooves and the new age that had dawned on them.

Silence reigned during their ride until the cabin loomed through the trees and Trojan broke the silence. "Did you get your cup of Muluk?" The random question caused her to laugh.

"Yes, I did, actually. How did you know?"

She thought she heard a smile in his voice as he answered. "Dalton had just taken it in to you after Mother convinced me to go for a walk." He was quiet for a moment before adding: "He knows you well. He really loves you, really cares about you."

A content smile spread on her face as she laid her face against his back. "Yes. Yes, he does."

Trojan slowed to a stop at the steps and Stephania slid from his back. "I'm glad he was there when you woke up. And glad he was the one who raised you." His hand balled into a fist.

She nodded slowly, finally understanding why he had also been distant to Uncle Dalton as well, and why he no longer would be. "I'm glad he was too. We've shared a lot of memories together, and a lot of laughs and tears. As he always says: that's what family does. And that's what we're going to do, right?" She playfully punched his arm.

He let out a small laugh before grinning. "Yes. Yes, it is."

"Race you inside!"

Before Trojan even knew what had happened, Stephania was already up the stairs and flinging open the doors, their laughter ringing through the house once more.

CHAPTER 16

Odessa, Human Domain

DARKNESS. BLACK. NOTHINGNESS.

Frustration mounted as Thaddeus resisted the urge to shatter something. He had found nothing in Stephania's mind. Nothing but a never ending, impenetrable wall. At least he no longer felt pain as he explored the mind plane. He was just to the point of giving up when he heard something.

It wasn't any more than a whisper, but in the nothingness around him, it was more than he had been able to sense for over a week. Scrambling, he searched for the sound, dragging himself closer to it. A red light grew in the distance. He ran toward it, the sound growing louder and louder until he was standing before a door—the door between him and Stephania's mind.

He dared not hope but reached for the sliver of light shining through. It burned red and hot, thick like blood. His heart raced.

Magic.

For the first time since he had discovered their connection, he could sense her magic.

Carefully, he slipped his fingers through the crack and pushed. On smooth hinges, the door swung open, and standing before him was a very young Duvarharian girl, her red, curly hair cascading down her shoulders. Her ruby red lips parted as she laughed again, the sound crystal clear in his mind.

The wall around her mind was falling.

A sadistic smile spread across his face as he stepped through the door.

His patience had paid off. He would find all he needed here.

Now nothing stood in his way.

CHAPTER 17

Trans-Falls

About A Month Later

A SMALL CREAK STIRRED STEPHANIA from her shallow morning sleep. Dawn rays sneaked through her curtains, and she blinked. Quietly, she waited to hear the sound again. When she didn't, she snuggled back into her pillow.

Her room exploded in chaos.

Someone was yelling, a horn was being blown, and leaves were flying through the air.

Stephania screamed, flailing against the arms reaching for her, her heart leaping into her throat.

Strong hands quickly ceased her thrashing and shook her gently.

"Stephania! Steph, it's just us!" It was Trojan. He laughed and shook her again, dragging her into a warm hug. "By the stars, I didn't think you'd fright so much."

She nearly snapped at him, ready to remind him her flashbacks and night terrors were certainly worth lashing out against, when she heard Frawnden, Aeron, Dalton, and then his own voice singing in Sházuk.

"Kaño daiwzum kiñ zuñi! Daugmoul zuzháf faiwuzh shab da fu zueñi! Yayáfay daiw, blessed birth, little tree! May the suns shine on your leaves forever!"

Tears stung Stephania's eyes as she pulled away from her brother, first gazing into his tender eyes and then to the rest of her family.

"You remembered." She wiped her nose on her sleeve and stifled a chuckle through her tears.

Dalton rolled his eyes before winking. "Well of course, my child. I didn't raise you for thirteen some years just to forget your eighteenth *yayáfay daiw*."

"Wouldn't miss it for the world." Aeron took her hand in his and kissed the top of her head before Frawnden descended and scooped her into a bear hug.

Stephania could hardly believe her eyes as her room turned into the center of celebration. Frawnden quickly piled all sorts of gifts and treats on the bed, and they all gathered around to enjoy.

Every gift she opened was either handmade or purchased with her likes and needs in mind. Never before had she seen so many gifts for her; excitedly, she opened them one after another: hand carved *Yu'jac* playing pieces, a clay mug sculpted with little trees, stars, and Fauns for her morning cup of Muluk, Lyre sheet music for two well-known Centaur folk songs, a colorful new leather grip for her bow, slippers made from *Ñáfagarœy* fur so her feet wouldn't get so cold walking through the cabin's mountain tunnels.

When all the gifts had been opened, her new slippers on her feet and a fresh cup of Muluk in her new mug, she listened with misty eyes as her family read lines of Centaur poetry they had written themselves and combined as one piece—a tradition.

After that, a patch quilt shawl of small animal pelts was draped around her shoulders, and more leaves were thrown over her as Aeron blew a war horn.

"What is it for?" Stephania eyed the different furs used in the shawl, some of which she had never seen before. It wasn't big enough to be of any real practical use, and she decided it must have some deeper meaning.

Dalton adjusted it around her shoulders and clasped the gold chain in front. "It's a Centaur sign of gratitude for the wearer and almost like a promise that those who made it will always take care of you and provide for you."

With a gentle touch, she stroked the furs with new appreciation. "It's beautiful."

Frawnden smiled and brushed her hair from her face, trying and failing to undo a few of the knots she found in the mess. "I stayed awake all last night to finish hand stitching it because someone"—she shot a sideways glance at Trojan—"couldn't pick which furs were the best of what he had."

Stephania laughed and shook her head, trying to catch Trojan's eye, but he had already changed the subject by turning to grab the last unopened packages.

She took it, feeling as if it were a very solemn and serious gift. It was cylindrical and wrapped with a forest green silk ribbon. Careful not to damage the wrapping too much, she slid it off and opened the end of the tube, pulling out a scroll of paper. When she unrolled it, she found herself facing a beautiful artistic rendition of Trans-Falls, every detail hand drawn.

"I drew it myself." Trojan shifted around to her side so he could look at it over her shoulder.

"Tro ..." She could hardly find the right words to express what she was feeling. For him to spend so much time on something like this ...

"I left all the spaces blank. I thought maybe—" He cleared his throat, his eyes darting around the room as if he wished it were just him and her. Frawnden must've picked up the cue because she quickly jumped up and instructed Aeron and Dalton to help her take dishes to the kitchen.

When they were gone, Trojan took the map from Stephania and laid it on the bed, rolling it out to its entirety. "I thought maybe today you would want to go visit all these places." He trailed his fingers over the map, and she followed his lead, her touch tracing all the places she knew and loved so well: Jargon's house, their house, the *Gauyuyáwa*, the falls, and so many other little secret places, some of which only she and Trojan knew from when they had been children. Each place had a small blank spot next to it where a name would be. "And when we get there, we can fill in the names together."

Tears rose in her eyes as she threw her arms around him. "I would love nothing more than that."

"*Yayáfay daiw*, Steph."

"Thank you, Tro." She pulled away and gave his shoulder a light punch. "I'm glad I get to remember spending it with you."

He smiled, though a deeper emotion shone in his eyes. "Me too. Me too."

§

"WOULD YOU LIKE AN UAFAÑOSHIGO?" Stephania held up one of the plump fruits to the trusting bird sitting on her shoulder. She tried her best to hold back laughter as the *Ñáwag-gazu* eyed the fruit suspiciously and squawked.

"Yes, I think I would," the bird chirped in its light, strange voice before opening its beak in expectation.

She quickly popped the tart *uafañoshigo* into its mouth. It swallowed it whole before chortling graciously, "Thank you, beautiful Dragon Child. Thank you!"

"*Talfindo!*" Laughing, Stephania turned to her audience and bowed lavishly to the amazed hoots and praise from her friends. Her eyes roved over the small group of Centaurs standing before her, and a mix between hesitant wariness and tender warmth filled her. She and Trojan had set off almost immediately after they helped sweep the leaves from her room. It was a *yayáfay daiw* tradition to throw leaves onto the celebrated during morning light to signify a new year of bright sun shining on a happy, healthy life.

The suns had traveled their course in the sky, and it had been nearly afternoon when they met up with Ravillian, Lamora, and Trojan's *Fomdaazh*—brothers of war—Lycus and Dakar. Now almost all but a few places on the map were filled in with many

169

new memories made to cherish along with old ones.

"Did you teach him, I mean her, all of that?" Lycus' eyes were wide, and he only dragged them away from the colorful bird for a moment to look at Stephania.

She chuckled and stroked the bird's sleek, colorful neck feathers. "No, actually, I didn't. She just landed on my shoulder when I was out for a ride once and slowly picked up the language. She doesn't always get it right, but she's certainly learned a lot."

"*Kaogouya!*" Hesitantly, he reached his hand to the bird. "Is it—would it be okay if I—"

"Of course." She grinned at the vibrant sparkle in his bright eyes. It was hard to reconcile that he was one of Trans-Falls most skilled and fearsome warriors. "If she'll let you. She's not too partial to new people."

Nodding, Lycus hesitantly reached for the colorful plumage of the bird's chest.

She squawked loudly and pecked his hand, lifting her wings just slightly in protest.

With a muted yelp, Lycus jumped backward, quickly snatching his hand away. "Guess not." He tried to smile but couldn't mask the disappointed shadow in his eyes.

Stephania quickly calmed the bird using the same technique she had been using on Braken for a long time. Within a minute, the bird was once more calm.

"Okay. Try again."

Lycus eyed her skeptically. "Are you sure? I don't want to upset her—"

She smiled reassuringly. "I'm sure. She'll get used to you. It just takes a bit of patience."

Once more, he reached his hand to the bird.

Raising her head in alarm, the wary creature eyed him before slowly letting her head back down and chortling.

Hesitantly, he brushed the blue feathers on her chest while she cautiously watched his every move.

Not wanting to disrupt her or break newfound trust, Lycus accepted the little bit of contact he was gifted and quickly drew away. Once again, his eyes shone with awe and wonder. "You know, I always knew *Ñáwag-gazu* were smart enough to learn language."

"Oh, yeah?" Her fingers mindlessly stroked the bird's head, seducing it to sleep.

"Mm-hm. Before I was sent off to the Warriors, I spent hours studying them. I was never able to get close enough to befriend one, though. They were much too skittish. I wonder what this one saw in you." His eyes caught hers and searched her face, as if looking for an answer.

She quickly looked away and shrugged. "I don't know." Her stomach churned with anxiety. *Different. I'm different. Always different.* The words rang through her mind mockingly. Her thoughts wandered to when she had lived with the Centaurs, how they

170

would bow before her small but commanding presence, then in New-Fars how they had feared her though they didn't know why, how her resentment had given her such courage against the weak-minded humans, about how animals were like playthings in her hands because of something they saw in her, and now how *different* she was. She felt neither confident like her child self nor brave like her young adult self. No matter how her personality, beliefs, looks, or abilities changed, she was always different, always an outcast whether by intention or not.

It seemed to not matter how welcome the Centaurs made her feel, sometimes she couldn't help but either feel they were beneath her—something she thought to be a byproduct of her superiority complex from youth—or wait for them to make fun of her and bully her like the New-Fars humans.

"It's probably just her charming personality and obvious good looks." Lamora quickly wedged herself between Stephania and Lycus, her arms crossed over her chest in her usual attitude. Her eyes burned warningly into Lycus'.

His eyebrows raised and then furrowed before he nodded and laughed with a nervous shrug. "I mean, of course."

"Well, I guess you proved me wrong, then, Lycus." Dakar slapped Lycus' shoulder, and Lycus punched him back.

It was one of the few times Stephania had heard Dakar talk, and she couldn't help but stare in wonder at how such a smooth, caramel voice could come out of such an imposing body. It was intimidating but also caused her to realize why the other Centaur woman would often fawn over him.

"Oh, yeah?" Lycus raised an eyebrow. "How so?"

Dakar winked one of his dark eyes at Stephania. "There *are* pretty girls in the *Ñáwag-gazu* business."

A furious blush raged across Lycus' face. "I'm not interested in the *Ñáwag-gazu* because of girls."

Dakar smirked. "Maybe not, but you do think Stephania is pretty."

Lycus' jaw dropped as he tripped over his words. "I do not!" His eyes met Stephania's, and she raised her eyebrows. "Oh, *zuru*, I don't mean it like that, you're very pretty, beautiful even, maybe one of the most beautiful girls I've ever seen ..."

Dakar roared with laughter and began rattling off something mocking in Sházuk.

Stephania didn't think Lycus's face could get any more red, but it did as he realized everything he had just said. *"Zuru fuñofufe,* Dakar!" He lunged on an unassuming Dakar, instantly instigating a brawl.

Her own cheeks hot with Lycus' embarrassment, Stephania covered her mouth, hiding her awkward laugh, the bird on her shoulder squawking in protest and quickly taking to the trees.

Trojan quickly jumped beside Stephania and drew his shining blue sword. "Must I slaughter yet another one of your relentless and unamusing suitors, Stephania? Perhaps we need to lock you away in a castle and let the men kill themselves trying to win your hand." His face was stone serious, but his eyes sparkled deviously.

Her eyes widened, her mind drawing a blank at what to say. *I should say something witty or do some dramatic scene like Lamora would.* But two competing ideas fought in her mind instead: be seductive and take the compliment or stoically turn her head up and demand they treat her less familiarly and with more respect. Awkward laughter left her lips instead as her stomach did a summersault.

"Oh, no." Lamora shook her head fiercely. "If there are any unwanted suitors, they'll have to go through me first, Trojan."

He pretended to look hurt, but she waved him aside with a smirk. "Sorry, but that's just how it works since she's my best friend."

Ravillian gasped. "Lamora!" His eyes were wide with horror. "I thought *I* was your best friend."

Though she was almost sure he was joking, Stephania was so convinced by his wounded expression, she couldn't stop herself from desperately assuring him she wouldn't get in the way of his and Lamora's lifelong friendship. Lamora suddenly cupped Ravillian's face in her hands and quickly kissed his nose.

"You still are, *koyuwuk*. But she's my sis. Not sure you want to give up your special place for that, right, *gumewa?*"

Ravillian's eyes lightened with joy as he stared triumphantly down into her face. "No, you're right. I'm just fine where I am, *fazub.*" He gently tucked a lock of hair behind her ear.

"Kiss her! Kiss her!" Dakar's deep, silky voice rang through the clearing, causing Ravillian and Lamora to jump at least five feet away from each other, hardly able to look anywhere in the remote vicinity of the other, their faces suddenly bloodred.

"Oh *uyuy*, Dakar." Lycus was sitting on Dakar as well as a Centaur could, having clearly won their scuffle.

As Dakar continued to chant, "Kiss her!", Lycus punched him, shouting at him to shut up.

A huge grin spread across Stephania's face as she tried and failed to suppress the girlish giggles that rose to her lips. It had been obvious to her, perhaps more so than it was to Ravillian and Lamora, that they were deeply in love with the other. She wished they would be mated. Faintly, she heard a voice whispering in the back of her mind, *Do I have a right to have fun? To laugh like this? To enjoy myself? To be among friends like this?*

What if they end up making fun of me? I should be with the adults, with Artigal, planning our next move against Thaddeus and the Etas, moving on to lead my people in Duvarharia.

She did her best to ignore it. Today, she wouldn't worry about being something other than a regular eighteen-year-old girl. Today, she wasn't the savior, Dragon Child, or Farloon, and she wasn't some god-like child to be worshiped by the Centaurs or some misshapen human whom the others feared and hated. Today, she was just Stephania ... a sister and a friend.

"You really have no shame, do you?" Lycus shook his head at Dakar, who only smirked.

"No, not really. Look, *fom.*" He tried to adjust himself to a more comfortable position, but with his legs stuck under him as Lycus pinned him to the ground, and his torso at an odd angle, he could only grunt uncomfortably. "You may be able to best me in a fight, but I have always bested you at females. I know an opportunity when I see one, and even you can't deny they are perfect for each other."

Lycus quickly glanced over to Ravillian and Lamora, who were doing their best—and failing miserably—to ignore what was going on around them. Trojan tried to stare Lycus and Dakar down but only accomplished in looking like a mildly amused father of two naughty children.

Lycus lowered his voice to a hiss Stephania could barely hear. "I mean, you're right of course, but do you have to yell it? And so ... shamelessly?"

Dakar winked through one of the black dreadlocks that fell into his eyes as his gaze met Stephania's. "Nah. I just wanted to." He grinned wickedly and dodged a playful punch before shoving his friend off him and brushing himself off, smoothing the thick locks out of his dark face. "You couldn't ever beat me in a fair fight anyways. You either cheat, or I let you win."

"You keep spreading wretched lies like that, and I'll take that hideous face of yours right off."

Dakar groaned. "How dare you. My face is beautiful, like a god's. It's the most *zuru* beautiful thing ever to grace this planet."

"Oh, stop it, you two." Lamora rolled her eyes before adding under her breath with a sideways glance to Stephania, "Males."

Stephania nodded in agreement, though she wasn't entirely sure she knew what Lamora meant. She cocked her head as Dakar and Lycus brushed the dirt and leaves off their coats and made their way back to the rest of the group, their eyes constantly darting to the other as if expecting an attack.

"Are they always like that?" She glanced toward Trojan, doing her best not to burst into laughter and therefore encourage the ridiculous friends. She was surprised at this teasing, cocky side of Dakar. She never would've guessed such a brooding, stern Centaur would find it in his heart to be so amusing.

Trojan shrugged, a smile tugging the corners of his lips. "Yeah, they are."

"*Medozud*, don't think your precious big brother isn't the same. He may act tough and brooding all the time, but you give him enough time and take him away from his bloody wars long enough, and he's the worst of us." Dakar pointed an accusing finger at Trojan and sneered. "He just doesn't want to show his true colors around his baby sis, lest you think less highly of him. You should've seen him with his girl—" Before he could finish, Trojan shot him a look that chilled even Stephania to the core. He shook his head slowly, and Dakar looked away, bowing his head.

The clearing had gone cold and quiet.

Stephania awkwardly shifted her stance and elbowed Trojan, desperately trying to save the mood. "Oh, is that true?"

He ran a hand through his hair, a scowl on his face as he muttered something under his breath.

She frowned at his dark mood, suddenly feeling more than a little uncomfortable, before he gave her a smile that was hardly reassuring.

"I don't believe you," Lamora laughed at Trojan's muffled answer and winked at Stephania. "I have to agree with Dakar on this one."

Trojan was spared any further jabs when Lycus tactfully challenged Ravillian to a brawl.

Stephania heard Ravillian protest he wasn't sure he could win before Lycus teasingly responded by saying he'd go easy on him to make him look good in front of his girl. A blush raged on the younger Centaur's face, but he agreed to the challenge, and in moments, they were circling each other, their sleek bodies glistening in the bright sunlight.

Lamora's face flushed with pride as she watched her friend warm up to the fight.

After bowing respectfully, the competing Centaurs drew their daggers and lunged at each other.

It was almost impossible to tell who was who as they fought each other with matched speed and skill.

Stephania couldn't ignore the eagerness with which Lamora watched the fight, and she knew if given the chance, Lamora would be fighting side by side with Ravillian.

Dakar's jaw fell slack as he beheld the incredible fight. He scowled, and Stephania was just barely able to catch him mutter something about being born too scrawny and good looking before he grinned and shook his head, engaging Trojan in a hushed discussion in Sházuk.

Stephania didn't mean to eavesdrop, but she was sure she caught the tail end of a heartfelt apology before they clasped arms and hugged. Trojan's demeanor lightened a bit afterwards, but she saw a familiar darkness in his eyes and knew he was thinking of something long ago.

Not wanting to bother him and unsure if she should ask if he was all right, she turned her attention back to the fight.

Ravillian and Lycus ducked and weaved their way around each other, somehow barely managing to escape the careful attacks of the other. Each had maybe one or two hits on them at most. Dirt flew around them as their tails snapped in the wind, their muscles straining and rippling as their hooves dug into the ground.

Trojan whispered to Stephania that he had bet against Lycus; he was sure Ravillian could beat him in a fight. It was becoming quickly apparent Trojan had bet well.

With one final, masterful movement, Ravillian knocked both blades out of Lycus' hands, his own dagger under his opponent's neck in seconds.

The fire died out of their eyes as they began to laugh and shake hands.

The friends congratulated each other, teasing each other while Stephania stood to the side, her hands clasped in front of her. Sometimes, in moments like these, she wasn't sure what to do or say, so she contented herself to watch. To enjoy their friendship from a position where she didn't have to overthink her actions, battle between the competing personalities inside her, or worry if she missed a joke or was smiling enough.

Ravillian suggested they walk into Trans-Falls and get dinner. Dakar and Lycus challenged each other to a race into Trans-Falls; it didn't seem like their competitive nature ever ended, though Stephania was sure that drive was what kept them alive in war. They challenged Trojan to come with them, but he had caught Stephania hanging back from the group, and she knew he declined their invitation to be with her. A stab of guilt shot through her, but as he smiled with his shining blue eyes and motioned for her to climb astride his back, she shoved it down with all the other conflicting emotions she wanted to keep locked away.

Trojan started out down the path, slow enough so the dust from Dakar and Lycus' hasty departure had time to settle, and Stephania looked back to see Ravillian and Lamora standing close to each other, their hands entwined and their foreheads almost touching, their mouths moving in quiet whispers.

Stephania couldn't help but think if she only focused hard enough, she could hear what they were saying ... *No*, she chided herself. *This is not New-Fars where I can do whatever I want. I have to be respectful and give creatures their privacy.* She wondered if having friends would ever become easier or if it would always be a struggle between her social awkwardness, fear, and trying too hard to do the right thing.

Soon, hoofbeats grew louder behind them until Ravillian and Lamora caught up, a new twinkle in their eyes.

"Have you enjoyed the day, Stephania?" Trojan's voice rumbled in his chest, and she felt it through her hands as she braided little strands of his mane.

"Yes." She smiled. "I couldn't ask for a better *yayáfay daiw* celebration."

Trojan nodded solemnly. "Good."

A moment of silence stretched between them, but she got the feeling he was wrestling whether or not to tell her something, so she let the silence grow.

Finally, he cleared his throat. "Stephania, about what Dakar said, about the girl—"

She shook her head and gave him a quick hug. "It's okay. You don't have to tell me about it if you don't want to, or aren't ready."

A heavy sigh left his lips. "Thank you."

She nodded and rested her cheek against his back.

The suns' light was warm on her face, and she was beginning to feel the wear of sparring, hiking, and adventuring. Her eyes drooped low though she blinked furiously to keep them open. Trojan's voice repeated itself in her mind. *Good.* She thought of her friends, Ravillian and Lamora, and now Dakar and Lycus; of her family, Trojan and the precious moments she spent walking and training with him or gazing at the stars; of Frawnden and Aeron waiting to hear about her day and give her advice on friendships; of Dalton and the new books and tomes he would have brought back to the cabin as treasures to share with her, and when he would come in to check on her if he thought she was having a night terror.

She couldn't help but think it *was* good. Unexpected tears filled her eyes. *Is this what it's like to be happy? To be loved? To have a home and people I love to go home to?* If it was, then she never wanted to forget this, never wanted to lose it.

"I sure love you guys." She was almost shocked at her own voice, but she couldn't deny the peace that settled in her from saying it.

Lamora smiled, her eyes trailing from Ravillian to Stephania. "Love you too, Stephania."

A lump rose in Stephania's throat, but she pushed past it. A sudden overwhelming urge to speak her feelings overcame her. "I'm not sure what I would do without you."

Ravillian laughed, and for a moment she thought he was making fun of her, but then she saw the pleasure in his eyes. "Oh, you would be just fine. You're stronger than you think, you know. Although one thing's for sure."

She raised her eyebrow.

"You wouldn't get so many free rides."

Trojan roared with laughter, and Stephania shook her head, brushing the tears from her eyes as she chuckled. "See, I do need you guys."

"You sure do." Lamora winked.

Their laughter faded into the soft spring air, and Stephania rested her head on Trojan's shoulder as Lamora and Ravillian spoke in soft tones to each other.

The air was warm, though the breeze was refreshing. The sunlight was hitting the trees just right, and it looked like the suns had come down and kissed the land. Everything was peaceful and calm. Everything was perfect, and for just a moment, for just one day, she forgot about the nights she woke up drenched in sweat and screaming at terrors only she could see.

"Thank you for staying with me, Trojan."

He smiled and pressed his cheek to hers. "Of course, Stephania. That's what a big brother does. I'll always be here for you. Always."

§

"**DID YOU HAVE A GOOD DAY TODAY?**" Dalton picked up a few leaves from her bed, placing them on the nightstand.

"I really did." She pulled back the furs and sheets before sliding under them. "It was absolutely *kaogouya*: the celebration here with the family, the gifts, traveling around with Trojan, messing around with our friends ... it felt almost ..." her nose wrinkled as she struggled to think of the right word.

Dalton sat on the bed next to her, brushing a lock of her hair from her face. "Normal?"

She nodded. "Yes. Normal."

He smiled down at her. "Good. I'm very happy to hear it." His eyes searched hers for a long moment before his voice dropped to a whisper. "Do you want me to stay with you again tonight? In case the nightmares come back?"

A breath hitched in her throat. She hadn't thought about the nightmares all day. As foolish as she knew it was, she had secretly hoped the nightmares would simply go away if she forgot about them. *But maybe ... maybe after today they won't come. Maybe I can start to move on from them now. Afterall, I'm eighteen now. I can't always rely on Uncle Dalton to spend the night protecting me from night terrors and purple shards.*

Quickly, she shook her head. "No, I'll be fine."

"Are you sure?" His eyes narrowed.

She wasn't sure, but she put a smile on her face. "I'm sure."

Though he didn't seem convinced, he nodded. "Alright. But if you need me, I'm—"

"Just down the hall. I know."

A small grin graced his lips as he planted a quick kiss to her forehead. "Alright. Sleep well, my child."

"I will," she promised.

But after the door was shut, minutes turned to an hour, and the moonlight faded behind trees and clouds, she realized how wrong she had been.

The night terrors returned and in response to her screams and crying, so did Dalton.

CHAPTER 18

Trans-Falls

BRAKEN'S HOOVES DRAGGED through the dirt, his head swinging low.

Stephania sighed and let the stallion stall to a stop and nibble on a roadside fern. She had been putting this day off for over a week now, trying to bask in only the good memories she had obtained, but the night terrors had gotten worse—more vivid, more frequent, more horrifying. She was seeing things she didn't understand. As much as she had tried to avoid it, it was time to face the memories she dreaded.

"Come on, boy. Just a bit further." She gently nudged his side with her heel, and he snorted, quickly picking up the pace to a slow trot. A flower dropped from his lips and floated gently to the ground.

The return of her memories had brought the joy of feeling truly whole and understanding who she was, where she came from, and the people she had loved. But with them came not only complicated personalities that were hard to reconcile with each other, but also answers to some of her darkest questions—questions she had secretly wanted to remain unanswered.

After last night, when she had been completely inconsolable and Dalton had held her as she screamed, frothed at the mouth, and even pulled her dagger, he insisted she go see Artigal. No one had heard from the Igentis since she regained her memories, and the last thing she wanted to do was seek him out, but Dalton had been right; she needed to put an end to this, if it was even possible.

She lifted her eyes from the saddle horn to the path ahead of her. Over and over, she had the same nightmare she had always experienced: dragons, Centaurs, and black mutated animals. She knew what it was now. It wasn't just the product of Dalton's many stories or the intense fear she had of creatures she wasn't sure existed; it was the past. It was *her* past. Those dragons and Centaurs weren't just figments of her imagination; they had been real creatures who had died ... to protect her.

Her grip on the reins tightened as she bit back the torrent of emotions flooding her. "Curse the gods."

It wasn't just her past, though. Tears collected in her eyes as she remembered the night terrors, and for once she let them fall. After all, no one was around to see her suffer, no one for her to pretend to be strong for.

"Kill her!"

The chilling voice from the visions haunted her even now. It wasn't just anyone speaking. It had been *her* speaking, even though she was sure it had been Thaddeus's voice. But then why was it from his eyes that she watched him kill the man and woman?

She choked. It wasn't just any man and woman. They were her parents. She sniffed and wiped her nose on her sleeve.

She remembered them now ... her parents. They were beautiful memories, so full of love, so gentle and peaceful. She could remember their voices, the way they and their home smelled, their faces, and the way they laughed. But the memories were tainted with their death—a death she remembered from the murderer himself.

"How?" she snarled as if someone would answer, but no one did. She clenched her jaw, fury rising in her. She hated them: Thaddeus and Kyrell. Her stomach churned when she thought back to the Ancient Magic anomaly that had dragged her, the mysterious man on the mountain patio, Thaddeus, and Artigal all together. She had been so easily swayed by Thaddeus's words, had so desperately wanted to give in to whatever he asked of her. Her heart pounded in her chest. All she could think of was how much she wanted to wrap her hands around Thaddeus's throat and slowly squeeze the life from him, just as he had to her mother.

Nausea welled up, and she had to take deep breaths to keep from throwing up as she remembered the vision of when Thaddeus killed her mother and how she knew what that moment felt like to him. She had seen from Thaddeus's own eyes, and felt with his own hands, as he had crushed the life from Andromeda, how her pulse had gone weak and her muscles spasmed, how her eyes had rolled and then dimmed before stilling and glazing over, how her breath had risen one ... last ... time.

"Why?" she whimpered, biting her lip to distract her from her runny nose and teary eyes. She forced her mind away from the memory but couldn't stop as another took its place—the mystery man on the patio.

She thought she might know who he was: Duvarharia's military commander, Syrus. He was the man who had first taught her about Etas, saying they could kill all the Etas together. He had been the one to play little sword fights with her, and he watched her more than once. She remembered his face well from when she had been young, but he was so much different now. The way she had seen him on the patio caused something in her to twist uncomfortably.

He was much older now and much unhappier and desolate. Why? Was it her parents' deaths? The weight of the Dragon Palace resting on his shoulders as military commander? What had he gone through to look so dead inside? Perhaps it was a bit of everything. Her heart ached for him. She understood so little about this world, about the Dragon Riders—her people. Perhaps she hadn't been the only one to suffer in this hell of reality.

Now all the worries that used to plague her, like whether or not the villagers in New-Fars would like her, if she could beat Jackson in a fight, or if she could control Gray seemed like such childish, petty problems.

Perhaps I have been too selfish.

Her thoughts wandered back to Thaddeus, and she had to struggle to push back her hate. One memory of him stuck in her mind more than she wished it did. She had tried many times to forget it again, but had found the efforts futile. Now she let it come forward. No one could see her shame over it now, not here in the darkness of the forest.

She closed her eyes, drawing upon her magic, willing it to show clearly what had once been hidden from her.

The slaughter of the Centaurs stretched out before her again. She felt their blood on her, smelled the carnage of their bodies, and heard their dying screams. She remembered being picked up, not harshly, but gently, lovingly even. Those purple eyes stared down into hers, and even now she clearly felt the way she had felt when she first gazed into them: safe.

"Do not worry, sweet child. I will not harm you. No, I will never harm you." He brushed red hair from her face, his magic sweeping away the blood from her small body. *"You are beautiful, little child. And so intelligent. You are powerful and important. You know this?"* He gently rocked her, humming something under his breath. *"Yes, there now. There now. Do you see? You need not fear. You have nothing to fear. I will take care of you."*

She shivered at the memory, though the late spring air was warm. *All those years ago I had stared into the face of that murderer, the blood of my parents fresh on his hands, and I had felt safe. Safer in his arms than I had ever felt in Artigal's after he saved me.*

"Gods of all, what is wrong with me?" She tried to replace this sickening guilt with hate, but only succeeded in feeling pity.

She had experienced the exact same memory in her dreams, but instead of looking up into his purple eyes, she had stared down into her own red eyes. She had felt what he had, and it hadn't been hate or anger. All the rage he had possessed when killing her parents had vanished when he held her, and had been replaced with sorrow—such a soul-destroying grief.

And she pitied him for it.

She shoved aside her emotions. She had no room for pity or mercy or hate. He may have felt the pain she felt now, but he had also been the cause of her agony and she couldn't forgive him for it. *Somehow, I have his memories. That is the only explanation. And yet ...* She drew a shaky breath. *And yet it is not the explanation I wanted. I have begged for answers since the day Dalton told me I was a Dragon Rider, but now I am not so sure I want the truth.*

Braken snorted and pawed the ground, suddenly coming to a stop.

She shook herself into the present. The *Gauyuyáwa* loomed in front of her. No one had gone in or out of it since her memories had been returned. The emptiness made the hollow tree seem almost unbearably foreboding.

Straightening her posture and gritting her teeth, she brushed the tears from her eyes, dismounted, and knocked as loudly and confidently as she could on the towering door.

Whether she wanted them or not, she was here for answers.

§

"THADDEUS'S MEMORIES." Artigal frowned and crossed his arms.

If he hadn't been a Centaur and wasn't standing, Stephania was sure he would have sunk deeper into his chair. Instead, he only shook his head and muttered something under his breath. His eyes snapped to hers, and she quickly looked away, knowing it was obvious she was staring. How could she not? He wasn't white.

It had been so shocking to walk in and see him a very average tan with age touching his features, she hadn't recognized him and actually asked him if she could speak with the Igentis. It hadn't been until he stared at her sadly with his golden eyes that she had *seen* him. It had taken everything she was to not gape in horror or disbelief. She had resolved to keep her mouth shut and eyes glued to the floor. He hadn't mentioned his coloration, and neither would she. Now she understood why no one had seen him since she got her memories back.

After her initial uncomfortable shock had subsided, she told him everything about her nightmares and flashbacks, what Jargon had told her the day they discussed the *Negluu* berries, and anything else she could think of that related to those things, including her assumption that, somehow, she had been left with Thaddeus's memories. She tried not to leave too much out, but most of Thaddeus's deeper emotions she had felt were too heavy or complicated for her to explain, so she left them unsaid.

After a long moment's silence, he sighed and shrugged, his hand passing over his wrinkled chin and scraggly beard. "I think you are right."

"Oh." Though Artigal couldn't, she *did* sink deeper into her chair, a darkness settling inside her. "Why?"

His tail swished nervously, and she wondered if this was the first time she had ever seen him nervous. "I think, if you remember correctly as I do, an explosion of magic freed you from Thaddeus at the Battle of the Prophecy."

She only nodded. She hadn't told him how she had felt in that particular memory nor how she knew Thaddeus had felt. It felt evil, knowing that even if she hated it, she did pity the murderer of her parents and the whole of Duvarharia. It was something she desperately wanted to keep to herself.

"You know now it was Ancient Magic that caused the explosion."

Again, she nodded, too numb to do much more.

"Ancient Magic has power over everything spiritual and physical. Anything you can imagine, it can accomplish, even transferring memories."

"But why me? Why not you? You're the one who released the Pure Magic. Why don't you have the memories?"

His face darkened. "Do you remember me telling you someone has to have a key of sorts to access Ancient Magic whether it be a deity like Raythuz, Joad, or something else?"

She frowned, trying to remember, then nodded anyway.

"It is possible to be born as the doorway itself."

Her mind fell blank. *Gods, I've had enough with riddles.* She crossed her arms. "What is that supposed to mean?"

"Stephania, has there ever been a time you experienced a power that was not your own? One that was, perhaps, driven by hate or anger?" He stepped closer to her, his eyes dark, his voice low, his presence almost menacing.

Her heart raced. The faces of the villagers of New-Fars flashed before her. Their blind, dead eyes stared back at her through her memories. A sweat broke across her brow as she played with the hem of her shirt. "Yes," she whispered so quietly she could hardly hear herself.

"A power that possessed you? Controlled you? Consumed you?"

"Yes," she snapped, her voice catching on the lump in her throat.

He stepped back. "Yes, I figured you had." A sadness hung in his eyes as his shoulders slumped. "Ever since you arrived in Trans-Falls, I could feel the darkness surrounding your being. I could feel the trace the Corrupt Magic had left on you. I assume that is why you are able to recall your memories much better than I expected. The *Kijaqumok* within you must've risen to destroy the "invading" *Negluu* berry magic.

In doing so, it fed off your emotions toward your memories and then attacked the Pure Magic used to make the wall I made. With the wall gone, the magic from the *Negluu* berries was able to build an even stronger bridge to your memories."

She chewed the inside of her lip, her arms tight across her chest. *He had known all along and said nothing, did nothing to save me from the Kijaqumok. How could he betray me like that?* She expected him to lash out, curse her, or punish her for her evil, but he did nothing.

Her eyes met his, and she found nothing but sorrow and compassion in them. She quickly looked away.

"However, Stephania, you are a gateway. Your path with this power is not determined. You can open and shut this door on anyone and anything you desire. If you want to be led by *Kijaqumok*"—he sighed heavily, shaking his head—"then nothing will stop you. Not even I. However, you have a choice. You can channel Pure Magic too, just like you did when you healed me."

She couldn't help but wonder if she had truly healed him when she had never seen him look so weak, old, and mortal. It wasn't just the whiteness that had been stripped from him. Something else was missing. Something that had made Artigal ... Artigal. At least, the Artigal she had always known. She wiped the unwelcome tears from her eyes. "I thought I was given the power that day."

He grunted. "No. You took control of the magic yourself, and let it and its will flow through you. It is not the first time you have done this."

"What's that supposed to mean?"

"You channeled it first the day your parents died in the Battle of the Prophecy."

"When?"

"When Thaddeus captured you from my soldiers."

The memory of the butchered Centaurs flashed before her again, and she thought she was going to be sick. She could still hear the moaning and screaming of the dying and the horrible squelch of footsteps in blood. *How many of those Centaurs had Artigal trained? How many of them had he known personally?* She found her answer in the anguish in his eyes. *All of them.*

He paced back and forth, a slight limp in his step, before studying a map on the wall opposite her. "That explosion of magic, the one that allowed me to take you to safety, was not of my doing. My magic had been swallowed by Thaddeus. Something else had come between he and I." Artigal turned back to her, his eyes piercing into hers. "You."

"Me?" She sounded less skeptical than she felt.

"Yes. Even as a child, you recognized the evil Thaddeus released and fought it back with goodness. That burst of *Shushequmok* came from *you*, Stephania. It wasn't I who wounded Thaddeus enough to send him back to his castle to brood for all the years you were in New-Fars. It was you."

Her face paled. "So then, that means—" She was unsure if she wanted to acknowledge what she now knew to be true.

"*You* took Thaddeus's memories and in turn may have given him yours."

§

THAT NIGHT, STEPHANIA tossed and turned against the raging memories and the overwhelming sense of fear and abandonment, of resentment, of forgetting. She tried to wake, but sleep dragged her deeper into the dark things she now remembered. The pull of a familiar dark magic grew stronger, forcefully dragging the memories from her mind.

Sounds faded. Everything dimmed. All familiarity washed away, and nothing but strangers were left. Darkness consumed ...

CHAPTER 19

Odessa, Human Domain

Because, Artigal decided *it would best if you didn't remember any of it.*"

"*What? What do you mean?*"

"*He took them away, Stephania. Your memories ... It was the only way ... He promised to give them back to you ... you'll get them back. I promise ...*"

Thaddeus opened his eyes, unable to stop the smirk that spread across his face.

Kyrell's voice rang through his mind. *So that is how she was kept hidden from us.*

Thaddeus threw back his head and laughed before jumping from his throne. "That *guxo ñekol.* I didn't think he had the guts, but I underestimated him. Our searching has paid off. I didn't expect the passage between her and I to be so difficult to navigate, but I couldn't be more pleased with the results."

If we are able to see so clearly into her past ...

"Then the walls around her memories have been torn down, and a new, much more powerful bridge has been built to them."

Only Artigal could have done that.

Thaddeus rubbed his hands together. "Indeed." A spark of magic trailed up to his face, erasing any remnants of facial hair and covering the scar that ran through his eye. With the wave of his hand, his clothing morphed into armor. Kyrell slid out from the shadows and followed as Thaddeus blasted the enormous hall doors open, sending the Eta guards on the other side scattering for cover.

He lunged for one of the slower Etas who had disgusting crab claws for arms and a beak that seemed too large for his spindly body. The Eta screamed as Thaddeus's acid seeped into his already rotten skin, its red eyes wide, his full attention on the Dragon Rider.

"Find your worthless King and bring him to me. Tell the commanders I want my army assembled in the courtyard, fully armed by midnight."

Unceremoniously, he threw the Eta to the ground and watched as its body dissolved into snapping red sparks. It changed its form into something between a bat and panther before racing down the halls to fulfill the orders.

"Now for the finishing touch."

Something personal we can use against her.

"Something that will drive her insane."

He closed his eyes and delved into the places of Stephania's mind she kept hidden, even from herself.

A horrible laugh bubbled up from his throat. *This place is riddled with Corrupt Magic. Someone's been a bad little dragon.*

He followed the corruption as it led him to the heart of New-Fars, to one fateful day when the Magic had taken over her, spilled out from her, and turned her into a murderer.

Though Stephania had left New-Fars, she had left a piece of herself there—a form of the Corrupt Magic. It was just enough to prepare an attack so horrible and twisted, it would haunt her for the rest of her life.

Thaddeus drew a hand down one of the spines that grew from Kyrell's tail as it curled around him. "Tomorrow, they march for Trans-Falls while I pay New-Fars a special visit for a bit of unfinished business. Then our little game will finally begin."

CHAPTER 20

Trans-Falls

Two Months Later

THE MORNING WAS CRISP and bright—the kind that was wonderful at first but soon turned into a blazing summer day where the suns beat heartlessly down on anyone not lucky enough to find reprieve.

Stephania rested her head against Trojan's shoulder, her eyes falling shut as they trod silently down through the misty grass.

Neither spoke a word. They didn't have to.

For once, it was just like it had been nearly fifteen years ago. For once, she didn't feel the war between the different people inside her. Right now, she was simply Trojan's sister, and that was enough.

She wrapped her fingers in his silky black mane and took a deep breath.

The air was soft. The suns sparkled through the trees and scattered through the thick green foliage. Everything seemed so perfect, as if it were nothing but a dream.

That's how the last few months had felt—as if she were living someone else's life. It was too good to be her own.

She didn't train often unless Dalton was trying to teach her new Duvarharian magic from the old tomes he brought home from the library, or she was sparring with her friends. He still comforted her when she woke up screaming, but she had found a study on magic that allowed her to seal her voice for the night so she wouldn't wake him. She couldn't do anything to mask her red, tear-stained eyes in the morning and the worried glances he shot her way because of them, but she was searching for a tome on that too.

She hadn't seen Artigal since their disturbing discovery about her shared memories with Thaddeus. In fact, few had. It seemed he spent most of his time in the Tomb Forest, and the one time he had stood before the city, she had been mildly surprised to see he had somehow rid his body of coloration, most likely with Jargon's help and some magic. The façade hadn't fooled her, though, and she could still see the age pulling at his body and the way, if the light hit him just right, the brown was almost visible. Without his solemn presence, the threat of her destiny, the Ancient Magic, and everything else that had previously plagued her hadn't seemed as great a deal.

Trojan had voiced concerns about increasing Eta attacks on Trans-Falls's borders and mentioned several times that he needed to re-assemble his forces to run drills up north, but he too seemed to be caught up in the lazy summer months and hadn't done more than talk about it.

Time itself seemed to be suspended and with it the wills of all those in Trans-Falls. Plans for traveling or going off to war were quietly put off one day to the next. Stephania hadn't even talked to Dalton about continuing on to the Dragon Palace for nearly a month. She had brought it up several times, but he had responded with such anxiety, she eventually let it drop.

She knew she wasn't the only one grateful for the distractions Trans-Falls had to offer—more old documents needed copying and restoring at the library, they needed new maps for the journey, Stephania needed the Duvarharian tomes to hone her magic, she had friends, she wanted to spend time with her family, she was happy for once—all excuses to keep putting off their journey.

"Do you ever feel like you're just walking through a dream? As if nothing is actually real, that time doesn't really exist, and neither does anything else you can't see?" She felt like she was rambling but kept trying to explain anyway, as if it would do something to wash away the rapidly growing unease in her. "Or that maybe even what you are seeing isn't real? As if you're living someone's life, not your own?"

Trojan didn't respond for so long, she wondered if he would. Finally, he spoke. "Yes, many times in my life." He let out a heavy sigh. "But," he drawled, "I've felt that a lot recently. It's the same feeling many get before they go into battle. Everything seems especially quiet and still, as if the world is taking a breath before its breast is rent open by violence."

A sullen silence hung in the air, and she adjusted her weight uncomfortably. *Rent open by violence.* It wasn't exactly the answer she had wanted. "You don't think—" She shook her head, wishing she hadn't started that thought.

"What?"

Her brows furrowed. "I just ... I mean ... you don't think that all of this"—she gestured nervously around her—"is going to be rent open by violence, do you?"

The silence only dragged, and she hated how long he hesitated.

"I don't know, Stephania," he whispered very quietly. "Maybe."

Frustration rose in her, though she wasn't sure at what. Perhaps it was just the dread that comes when everything is going too well. Perhaps it was just both of them overthinking the precious time they had been given, sure it would end in heartbreak like it had before. Or, perhaps it was something more.

Their walk had suddenly changed from relaxing to very strained, and where the morning air had once felt peaceful, it now felt heavy and unexpectedly quiet.

"Tro?"

"Hm?"

"What are you going to do when Uncle Dalton and I leave?"

"Oh." An emotion she couldn't place hung in his voice. "I guess I'll go with you." He shrugged his shoulders uncomfortably. "My place is beside you, wherever you go."

A frown pulled down her lips. "No," she whispered, shocked at her own answer.

"What?"

She winced at his sharp tone. *Gods, why did I say that?* But she didn't want to take it back. As much as she didn't know why she had said it and wished she hadn't, she knew deep down she was right. Now she owed him an explanation. She bit her lip, trying to think of one. "I don't think your place is to follow. I mean, your tribe needs you and—"

"You don't want me to come with you." He stopped walking and turned his head slightly. She was glad she didn't have to face him directly, but she also suddenly didn't feel comfortable sitting on him.

"No, that's not what I'm saying." She shook her head, tears blinding her eyes and emotion making it hard to find words. *Then what do I mean?* Her hands balled into fists. "I want you to come with us, more than anything. I just don't feel like you're supposed to. Or that it's a good idea for you to."

He didn't respond, and her stomach rolled as a wave of uncomfortable heat crashed over her.

"I just don't think Duvarharia is where you're needed most—"

"You don't need me?" His voice was quiet. Too quiet. His face was a mask she couldn't read.

Take it back. Take it back. Take it back, she screamed to herself, but the words that left her mouth were far from an apology. "No, Trojan. I *do* need you. I need you more than Uncle Dalton, or Mother and Father, or anyone else. But I—I think your tribe needs you more."

"Are they more important than my sister? Do you really think I'm going to let you travel across half of Ventronovia and fight Thaddeus alone?"

"I don't know. I think you might have to let me. I mean—" She fiddled with her cloak and licked the tears off her lips. *What do I mean? Why don't I want him to come with me? Why do I feel like I have to do this by myself? Who am I trying to prove myself to? Am I scared Trojan will get hurt? Or perhaps ... perhaps I'm still wishing for a new life, a completely new start, with nothing tying me to an old version of me.* She hated the icy cold horror sinking into her stomach, telling her she was right to want a new start. She couldn't tell him that. No, she couldn't tell anyone that. So, instead, she only said, "Maybe this is something I just need to do on my own."

"Oh. I see." His tone told her he *didn't* see, not at all, but neither of them pressed it.

Her shoulders dropped with her tears, instant regret filling her. How could she be so selfish to want to run away? When things had gone wrong in New-Fars, she had considered running away, leaving Dalton behind. Now she wanted to leave him, Trojan, and everyone else behind; if she could just start over, then she could do it all right. *Do what right? Could I ever run from any of this?* She didn't want to answer that. "Tro, I'm sorry, I just—"

"No. It's fine. I understand." His words were curt, emotionless. "I just need some time to ... think about it. That's all." A small smile spread unreassuringly across his face, and he turned back to the road, his hooves echoing through the darkening forest.

"I'm sorry," she whispered again through her tears, but he didn't respond.

Her blood ran cold as the scream of a Centaur violently rent the air, then was abruptly cut off.

"Trojan—"

"I know. I heard it." He stopped walking.

They held their breath.

The forest stood still.

The air was stale and cold.

Stephania gasped as she felt something hit her head. "Ow." She rubbed the back of her head and looked around for the object, but she saw nothing. The pain steadily grew worse. "Trojan." She shook his shoulders.

Instantly, he was on the alert. "What? What is it?"

She tried to tell him, to describe what she was feeling, but only a strangled croak came out. Tears poured down her face as darkness swirled around her. She felt her breakfast rising into her throat. Pain exploded through her mind, and she blacked out.

Shapes moved past her vision. Red sparks blinded her. Screaming rang in her ears. Death's stench and icy hand reached for her.

Her eyes flung open. She was sucking in air, but her lungs burned as if she hadn't breathed for a long time. Trojan was holding her in his arms, resting her gently on the forest floor. His eyes were wide with worry and terror.

"What's going on? What's wrong?"

A chill crept through her body as a presence stirred in her mind. *Gods, no. No. No. No.* Pushing him away, she scrambled to her feet, her head reeling with dizziness, her eyes wild with fear.

More screams rent the distant air.

"This can't be happening. Not again." She staggered in the direction of the screams, feeling the blood rush from her face, tears burning her eyes. "*Kijaqumok,*" she whimpered before covering her ears against the screams.

Trojan's pleading voice faded into silence as a new pain racked her body. She tried to remember her training, everything she had read from the tomes Dalton brought home and all the exercises he had drilled her in, but she only drew a blank. She searched for the Pure Magic deep inside her, pleading with it to protect her, but only found hollow emptiness instead.

"Stephania, what in Susahu is going on?" Finally, his voice found its way to her.

She clasped her hands over her ears, trying to block him out. *Be quiet. Please just be quiet!*

He pulled her to her feet, shaking her shoulders, trying to snap her out of her trance. "Say something, Stephania!"

Groaning against the ringing in her ears, she pushed against him. "They found me. They found me," she slurred, her head lolling to the side. She tried to focus on his face but saw only his blurry outline. Nausea rose in her throat, and the bitterness of bile followed.

"Who?" His voice was deep, quiet. He stopped shaking her. "Who found you?"

She shook her head against the tears. It took her a few tries to make the words come out of her mouth. "The Etas. The Etas are here."

CHAPTER 21

A BLOODCURDLING SCREAM RENT the air just to the right of them.

In a split second, Trojan dropped her, drew his bow, and nocked an arrow to the string.

In a moment of clarity, or perhaps habit from when she was a child, Stephania drew her sword and held it in front of her, but her hands were shaking so uncontrollably, she was barely able to keep hold of it. She remembered when she had fearlessly fought off Etas as a very, very young girl. *Where is that fearlessness when I have need of it?* But those memories were like watching someone else. Sometimes they felt like her, but mostly, she hadn't been able to become both the little Dragon Child who fought side by side with Centaurs, like a true warrior; and the frightened, bullied young woman who never did more than best her abuser in a single, non-deadly swordfight.

The thundering of hooves and feet tore through the forest in front of them. Another scream pierced the air before a Centaur leapt from the brush, black blood covering her body.

"Synoliki, they've infiltrated the northeastern side of Trans-Falls."

Every muscle in his body tensed. "How many of them?"

She galloped within a few feet of him, bowing slightly. "Over two thousand at the least. Artigal said we have reason to suspect Thaddeus has discovered Stephania's location and they are now tracking her by—" Her body convulsed as if struck from behind. A gurgled cry left her lips before she collapsed to the ground, two long black arrows protruding from her back. Her legs kicked as her eyes glossed over, staring blankly at the forest canopy.

Without hesitation, Trojan fired three quick arrows into the forest in the direction of the arrows and was rewarded with two screams.

Every muscle in Stephania's body refused to move, her eyes fixed on the twitching body of the young Centaur woman at her feet, the warrior's red blood mixing with the black that still trickled from her hair.

"Stephania. Come. We have to get you home to Dalton." When he didn't hear her answer, he turned, his eyes flashing. "Stephania, come *now*. If we wait any longer, we won't be able to make it home, and I won't know how to find Dalton. He's the only one here who can cover your trace—Stephania, what is wrong with you?"

Tears poured down her face, and she could only shake her head, her sword falling limp to her side. He was pulling her, trying to get her to either run alongside him or jump onto his back, but she found she wasn't able to move. "It's my fault." Her eyes never left the dead Centaur's. "They followed me here. I did this." She remembered Artigal saying she may have given Thaddeus her memories. If that were true, he would know all he needed to successfully infiltrate and annihilate Trans-Falls. He would know their commanders, their numbers, their strong-holds, where her home was. They were probably already there, and Dalton was most likely already ... dead.

"Stephania!" A stinging slap rocked her back. For a moment, she could only blink her eyes and rub her throbbing cheek before her eyes widened in horror and she realized Trojan had slapped her. A fleeting glimpse of sympathy flashed through his eyes before it was taken over with determination. "This is not your fault, do you under-stand?"

She nodded, wishing he wasn't speaking so loudly.

"Gods." He roughly shoved her behind him, an arrow whizzing through the air where her head had been. Within seconds, he had fired two shots, dropping the hid-den Eta, and dragged her onto his back. She barely had time to grasp hold of his mane before they were galloping through the forest.

Some near miss encounters slowed their pace, but after a few minutes, they were far enough away to pause. As he let her down off his back, he grabbed his second quiv-er.

"Stephania."

Her eyes were focused on the forest, waiting anxiously for another Eta to launch itself from the brush or an arrow to cut the air and split her skull.

"Stephania, look at me." His hand pulled her face up, and she lost herself in his strong, blue eyes. "This is not your fault." Deft hands tightened the straps of the small patches of armor he was wearing. "We have to get you out of here. Out of Trans-Falls. Okay? But to do that, I need you to look back and find that little girl who charged into battle with me once. Can you do that?"

"I don't know that girl."

Pain flashed through his eyes before they flickered and focused past her.

Again, she was shoved out of the way. A chain with a small spike ball at the end whistled between her and Trojan before slamming into the road in a cloud of dust.

Trojan's bow was in his hands, and two more arrows fired. Animalistic screams rent the air along with the unmistakable crackle of an Eta changing form.

Cursing, Trojan dragged Stephania back onto his back before galloping down the road, the Eta's screams fading into the distance.

A small group of Centaurs broke out of the trees onto the road, instantly snapping to attention.

"Where do you need us, Synoliki?"

Trojan didn't miss a hoofbeat as he yelled at them over his shoulder. "Cover our tracks. I can't have any Etas following us. I'm getting Stephania out of Trans-Falls."

The Warriors obeyed without question and thundered down the road, some flanking Trojan and Stephania at a distance, and others rising to meet the pursing Etas. The siblings would be safe for a little while, as long as the rest of the Eta army didn't catch wind of her magic trace.

Once it seemed they were far enough away from the initial breech and the fighting, he slowed his pace. "See? This is why I have to come with you to Duvarharia," he growled low. "You can hardly defend yourself. Stars and galaxies," he cursed, running his hand through his hair and readjusting the belt of his sword. "And you think you don't need me."

Her cheeks burned with shame, and she pressed her mouth shut. He was right, but his words still stung.

A heavy sigh sagged his shoulders. "I'm sorry, Steph. It's not your fault. I just ... I don't want to lose you." His voice suddenly caught on tears, and he tried wiping them away. "I can't lose you. Not again."

She nodded against his shoulder, not trusting her own voice, her arms wrapped around him as tight as she could.

"I will find Dalton for you." His back was tense, his voice harsh again with determination and decision. "You will grab your things from your room, and you and he will take the western road into the mountains and out of Trans-Falls. You will not come back, not for anything, do you understand? They won't follow you if Dalton can manage to cover your magic trace."

She couldn't leave him here. And what about Lamora and Ravillian? Jargon? Artigal? Mother and Father? She couldn't just leave them. What if she never saw them again? What if they died and she couldn't even say goodbye?

"I can't. I—"

They ground to a halt, and she felt the ground smash into her as she was thrown from his back. Panic seized hold of her. Were they under attack again? But through the dizziness, she saw only him standing over her.

197

"No. It's too dangerous for you here. You can't stay here any longer. You must go to Duvarharia."

She struggled to her feet, wincing at the new pain in her side. "Too dangerous? What about all the training Dalton gave me in New-Fars? And even what Artigal and you taught me years ago? Isn't this what all that was for? To fight the Etas? Isn't that why I got my memories back? So I'd remember everything I was taught?" She staggered on her feet, the world spinning around her. The metallic taste of blood hung in her mouth, and she knew her lip was bleeding. Anxiously, her hands brushed the dirt and grass from her clothes. "I know I froze earlier, but I was taken by surprise. If I could just have a chance—"

"No." He shook his head slowly. "It's too dangerous. You're not ready."

"Please. I have to—"

"No, *zuru fuñofufe*!" He stamped his hoof, his eyes flashing violently.

She flinched and took a step back.

"Battle is all about being taken by surprise. There are no second chances, there are no re-dos, or breaks. There is only death until there is no more life. If you were ready, you would've killed that Eta before I even had the chance to. I know you can't use your memories. I've talked to Dalton about how you struggle with combining your old self with the girl who grew up in New-Fars. Everyone was a fool to expect if of you so quickly." He stepped toward her, and she stumbled back, shaking her head.

"Stop," she whispered, but he ignored her.

"You changed, Stephania. That is fact. You may be able to gain information from your memories, but you cannot *be her.* It's not fair to you or anyone else to expect that from you. If you could, it would've happened already. The girl you are, the one from New-Fars, blanches at the sight of dead friends. She can hardly hold her sword when faced with real death. The only fighting she has done has either been in hunting or in a non-life-threatening situation. She cannot kill, not in battle. You want another chance? The enemy does not give any chances. They do not wait until you are ready. When you hack down one, there will be another, and another, until they are all dead or you are. It doesn't matter if you're wounded, if you're tired, or thirsty, or want to throw up and scream. The battle goes on, and you either survive or the land drinks your blood."

She felt the rough bark of a tree dig into her, and she could back up no further. A pit opened inside her. She wanted to scream, to throw herself at him to prove he was wrong, to prove she wasn't a failure. "Don't say that." She knew she was weak. She always had. She may have her memories back, but she had lost so much more than them all those years ago. He was right; she *had* changed. She was a fool to think not, but when would she become strong enough to fight for herself so others didn't have to?

198

She should have left for Duvarharia weeks ago. None of this would've happened if she had.

The screams of Etas and Centaurs grew louder in the distance and mingled with the clash of metal on metal and the wretched sound of death. Their guard wouldn't be able to hold off the Etas for much longer. In a few minutes, they would have to press on.

This was all her fault.

It had always been her fault. She had to take responsibility for it. If not now, then when?

"I have to fight." She forced her eyes to meet his. "I caused this, don't you understand? I'm the reason why they're here. I have to fix this. I have to. I can't run away. Not again." Pressing her hands against her sides, she tried to hide their tremble.

His countenance softened as he cupped her face in his hands, forcing her eyes to stay fixed on his. "No, Stephania. This isn't your fault. You can't think that. None of this was ever your fault. You didn't call the Etas to you or ask that they hunt you. It wasn't your fault you stayed here either. You can't put that upon yourself. Understand?"

She nodded through her tears. She understood; she just didn't believe it. "I can't let them die for me."

He opened his mouth then closed it before taking a shaking breath. "You don't have to worry about that, Stephania. Everyone in Trans-Falls is willing to fight and die for you. They—"

"I *know*, Trojan." Sobs racked her body as her voice rose to a fervent pitch. "And I can't stand it!" She furiously tried to wipe away her tears, but it did nothing to help. Nausea churned her stomach. Her head throbbed with her heartbeat; her ears rang. *Why can't anyone understand?* "I don't *want* people to die for me. Ever."

Trojan pulled her into his embrace as tears began to trickle down his own cheeks and into her soft hair.

"What if *you* die? Or Artigal? Or Mother and Father? Or anyone? It would all be my fault. Your blood would be on *my* hands. And then I'd have to live without you."

She felt his heart hammering his chest, felt his tears on her head, and she knew he too had the same fear.

"Stephania," he stroked her hair before taking a deep breath. "Once, a long time ago, I saved you from a Susahu Viper. I made a promise to myself that I would never cease protecting you, no matter what the cost would be. I'm not the only one who has done so, Steph. I know I'm not. I know you don't want everyone to be entitled to protect you, maybe even die for you, but you must understand this is bigger than us, and each warrior gives what they want freely. *You* are bigger than this. Today, here, this isn't your fight. And Stephania?" He gently pulled her away so he could look down into her face. His gaze searched her face before he looked away, his hair rustling in the light breeze that pushed past them.

A dull ache settled in her as he took a deep breath.

"You have to let me die for you, Stephania, if it should come to that."

She started shaking her head, trying to say something, but he shushed her.

"No, no, listen. I know how hard it would be for you to live without me and with the false guilt that I had died because of you but—" He cut himself off, shaking his head, his arms tightening around her. "Please, Stephania. I can't live without you. Not again. I did once, after Dalton took you to New-Fars, and I died that day and every day after. I can't do it again, especially if I knew I could have saved you. Especially if I chose my life over yours."

She could barely hear his voice over the ringing in her ears and the way her head spun.

"I'm just—" He gritted his teeth. "I'm just not strong enough."

"Tro ..." She couldn't push past the illness churning in her. "How can I—" She bit her lip, trying to find the words. "I can't be stronger than you." Her eyes searched his face in exasperation. "You're, you're—" Tears cut her off.

"I am weak, Stephania. I am. I can't bear to lose you, so if it comes to it, you will have to do it for me. You will have be stronger to live without me."

Unable to find words and tired of trying, she threw her arms around his neck and squeezed, her tears mingling with his, her heart racing.

The distant clash of fighting grew louder.

After only a few seconds, Trojan took a deep breath and pulled away from her. His face was suddenly hard and emotionless, his voice commanding.

"But that's not even going to happen. You should be much more worried about Ravillian and Lamora. This is their first battle, and they don't have even an eighth of the training I do. Two thousand Etas is nothing compared to what I'm used to, and Trans-Falls is heavily fortified. Now, I'm going to take you back to the house. You are going to pack your things, and Dalton will take you to Duvarharia. You must move on. It is time. The Emperor wills it."

Her mind went blank as his words recalled those Artigal spoke to her so long ago. *"No, child. You cannot stay. This is not your life anymore. This is not your home anymore. You must continue to push on. You must put all of this behind you and become what you were meant to be."* She bit her lip, bile rising in her throat. A feeling surfaced in her, one she thought she had put behind her long ago. *Will I never be home? Will I ever get to stay with the people*

I love in a place I love? What is home?

"Promise me, Stephania, that you will not fight in this battle and will not turn back to Trans-Falls for any reason. Even if it is burning to the ground, or we win, or even, Stephania, if I die. Promise me."

Her eyes widened, and she pushed away from him. "I refuse to promise that! I can't run while everyone I've known and loved is being slaughtered. What kind of a coward does that?

He recoiled, repulsion painted on his face. "Coward? Are you serious? You are living to fight another day. And by the stars, Stephania! You've only just begun to tap into your potential! You have no idea what you're capable of, and you'll never have the chance to know if you die today. This isn't your fight today, no matter how much it seems like it is. What else can I do to make you see?"

A long, ringing bugle blared in the distance, and several more followed. Trojan's face hardened.

One of their Centaur guards broke out of the trees, black blood smeared on her face. "They're coming, Synoliki. They're heading north."

Trojan nodded curtly, and she disappeared back into the brush.

"The Etas are heading for our house." He shook Stephania's shoulders none too gently. "Come on. We don't have much more time. Please, Stephania. Promise me."

Her heart lurched in her chest. She felt his iron grip on her hand, felt as his eyes pleaded with her. It was so hard to think. She just wanted to lie down and sleep, for everything to slow down, and for time to reverse itself so she could try again. But it wouldn't, and every moment she spent waiting, more Centaurs were dying because of her.

"I—I—" She sucked in a deep breath. "I'll try."

The corners of his mouth tugged down with disappointment, but he hadn't the time to press for a better promise.

Within seconds, she was upon his back again, and they were galloping through the trees.

He reached back to her, something clamped tight in his closed fist.

"Take this, Stephania. And if I don't make it, then you must look for a Centaur named Roan who claims to be the first son of Frawnden and Aeron. Give it to him."

Her jaw dropped. "Gods of all ... *what?*"

He ducked under a branch, and part of it scratched her cheek. "I'm not the first-born. Roan was, but he was sent off to war as soon as he turned of age. His battalion marched to the remote lands of Wyerland. It was strongly believed at the time that the Wyriders were sending Thaddeus supplies, so they went as an investigative team. They never came back. A phoenix returned to tell us that he watched their progress, but as soon as they had crossed the Wyerland border, they'd simply vanished. They were marked as missing in action and then later accepted as dead. And I've always thought ..." His eyes grew distant.

"What?"

He shook his head. "I've always thought if he was still alive, if anyone had a chance of finding him, of saving him ... it'd be you."

Feeling disembodied, she took the ring from his hand and turned it over. *Why hadn't I been told of this earlier? Am I not part of the family? I have another brother, and no one cared enough to mention it.*

"I don't mean to throw this on you,"—he grunted as he leapt over a log—"but I want to make sure the ring is safe in case—"

"In case you die." Her voice was bitter.

"But I won't. And I think you deserve to know, since you are leaving for Duvarharia, and because you are an heir to this ring and Trans-Falls. You can remember us by it. Someday, when everything settles down, I'll tell you all about him, the girl Dakar mentioned, and anything else you want to know."

Before she could answer, another bugle rent the air, this time much closer, but it was abruptly replaced with a scream and then silence.

"Oh, gods." Trojan quickly wrenched to the side, nearly throwing her, before releasing an arrow into the brush. A small explosion of brown magic knocked the arrow aside.

"Uncle Dalton!" Stephania slid off Trojan's back and dove into the brush just as Dalton staggered out, black blood splattered all over his chest. She stopped shy of embracing him and instead recoiled.

"Child, it seems they've already made it to Frawnden and Aeron's home. It's not safe there anymore." He yanked on something he had a loose hand on, and Austin shied forward, his eyes rolling from side to side in fear, Braken was tied to his saddle and following in tow. Besides a small limp, Dalton didn't seem to be injured, but the darkness that had settled in his eyes told her enough.

A string of curses left Trojan's lips. "You must leave by the western road into the mountains and on to Duvarharia. After the fight is over here, I will make sure to send an escort, but your main priority is to get as far away from here as you can and hide your trace."

Dalton nodded solemnly and grabbed Stephania's arm, pulling her to her horse.

"Wait!" She broke free. "Trojan—" She flung her arms around him, her heart slamming in her chest. She was leaving, truly leaving. It could be the last time she ever saw him. Even if she couldn't say goodbye to anyone else, she wouldn't walk away without at least telling Trojan. In the distance, she could hear the clash of steel and the unmistakable, agonizing screams. She swallowed hard, resisting the urge to gag. She was repulsed by this day, by the Etas, by her whole life, by herself.

"I'm sorry," he whispered. "I shouldn't have been so harsh to you. I was too hasty in my words. Forgive me."

"Of course I forgive you. I—"

He cut her off with his rambling, half of it in Centaur and half in the common tongue. "I will survive. I'll find Ravillian and Lamora and protect them. I'll watch over Mother. Trust me, Stephania. I will find you when this is over. You must stay alive. You must be strong. Do not be afraid. The Emperor goes with you. You must trust Him. He will keep you safe. I will see you again. I love you, Stephania. *Me yuwuk fu muyaa fáfád.* You are everything to me."

She tried to speak, to say something, anything. Words failed her, and she only groaned through her tears and held him tighter. These seconds were falling through her fingers like sand. Everything was going by too fast, but she could do nothing to slow it down. She could do nothing to say everything she wanted to, *needed* to.

He pulled away, staring deep into her eyes one last time before nodding and cantering off into the woods.

"Don't leave me." Her plea remained unheard as it trailed after him. She stared longingly at the trees that he disappeared into, her heart thundering numbly in her chest, her eyes stinging with tears.

In a blur, Dalton helped her onto her horse, untied the reins from Austin's saddle, stuffed them in her hands, and in seconds they were galloping through the forest. She was glad Braken knew to follow Austin because she was blinded by tears. She thought of all the things she was leaving behind, even the little things she wouldn't be able to collect from her home: a small carving of a sleeping dragon Ravillian had made her, a bracelet made of rare stones Lamora had labored over though she wasn't a crafter at heart—both *yayáfay daiw* presents—the first sword Aeron had made for her, along with the first bow Frawnden had made for her. Would the Etas leave their home alone if no one was there? Or would they tear it apart and burn it to ashes like her and Dalton's home had been in Trans-Falls?

"Oh, gods."

She looked up at Dalton's whisper.

They were atop the first ridge, looking out over the valley of Trans-Falls.

All she could see before her was ruin. She cried, feeling as if her soul had been crushed, wishing she could wipe the image from her memory, wishing it was just another dream she could wake up from.

Huge plumes of black smoke rose high into the sky. The flashing, raging red-orange fire snapped and lashed out from the trees. A dark shadow hung low in the trees, seeping into every corner of the once peaceful, gentle forest. The *Gauwu Zelauw's* shining blue magic looked horribly dim; its borders were encroached upon by the darkness. The air reeked of *Kijaqumok* and Eta stench.

This can't be happening. This isn't happening.

Hadn't she only been walking with Trojan just this morning? It had been so peaceful. Had that been just a dream? Maybe it had been, and this hell she was in had been reality all along.

The fire consuming Trans-Falls burned in her mind, and suddenly she saw their old home in New-Fars. Her home ... on fire. She had walked away when it burned, when she had lost everything. She had run away. And she was running again while her other homeland, the second of the only two lives she had ever known, burned as well.

Her fists tightened. The tears stopped, and something changed inside her.

She had to make a stand. This was her life, no one else's. She had to be better than this.

She was going back.

CHAPTER 22

BRAKEN'S HOOVES TORE UP the earth as she spurred him on, both with magic and her heels. She could hear Dalton yelling at her, and Austin's hooves as they raced after her. She knew they wouldn't be able to catch up. Austin had never been a match for Braken, and she knew these woods far better than Dalton.

The seconds felt like minutes as the wind stung her face, the trees a blur around them. She could barely keep control of Braken as his nostrils flared with the rancid smell of Etas and death, filling him with terror.

Screaming, he suddenly dug his hooves into the ground and reared. Her neck burned from the whiplash. As soon as his hooves hit the ground, he bucked to the side. She felt the sting of an arrow as it caught the back of her shirt, another arrow skimming Braken's flank.

Before she could think, her sight clouded with a strange red haze. She felt oddly disembodied from herself, as if something else had taken control of her ... like it had that one day in New-Fars.

In a heart's beat, her bow was drawn and an arrow pulled back to her check. She aimed instinctively for where the assailant's arrows had flown from and released.

A scream rent the air, but before she spurred Braken on, she paused. For a moment, she didn't know what she waited for, until she saw the red sparks in the brush. Her memories hadn't failed her; she had remembered to wait and see if the Eta was truly dead. With no time to ponder it, she quickly pulled out another arrow and loosed it on the Eta. This time, she didn't see the sparks.

Then she realized she didn't know where she was, let alone where Trojan might be. Braken had charged off the path and into some part of the forest she couldn't place right now. A pang of fear shot through her, but she shoved it down. She had made her choice; she couldn't turn back now.

The sound of Centaurs calling for reinforcements by horn caught her attention, and she urged Braken in its direction.

The smell of burning flesh met her nose, and she resisted the urge to gag. As she weaved Braken around small fires eating through the forest, her senses tuned in to anything that might be a threat. A darkness had settled in the forest.

She swallowed uncomfortably. It was the same darkness that had seeped through the woods before she had played the Lyre, the same darkness that had overcome everything when the forest had been slaughtered, the same that had driven Colten to try to steal the Lyre, and the same that possessed her to kill the New-Fars humans. Subconsciously, her hand strayed to her back; she had made a sort of backpack for the Lyre. After that day, she hadn't been able to be away from it, even for a few seconds. The few times she had left it behind, she had dissolved into such uncontrollable panic attacks, she vowed to never let it out of her sight again. Even now, she hated that she had it, wishing she could cast it away into one of the fires burning around her, but she couldn't. No matter how hard she tried to get rid of it, she failed. She owned it, and it possessed her.

Instinct took over, and she ducked, an arrow whizzing over her head. From nearby, she heard a Centaur roar in effort. An Eta screamed before the thudding of a weapon on flesh silenced it.

She broke into a clearing. Five Centaurs stood in front of her, battling nearly twelve Etas, though more seeped in from the forest and even more lay dead on the ground. Two of the Centaurs were wounded, and one seemed too old to be in combat. The other two were completely overwhelmed. A cabin and its garden burned behind them, and she faintly thought that maybe it was the old Centaur's home.

As she rode Braken into the clearing, all eyes turned to her, Centaur and Eta alike. For a moment, only silence could be heard in the small clearing. Then the old Centaur whispered, "Farloon."

All the Etas screamed, lunging for her.

Braken whinnied and bucked, his hoof connecting with one of the dog-like Eta heads, sending the creature flying into a tree like a rag doll. Her sword caught the neck of another one of the canine Etas; black blood splattered on her leg as the Eta stumbled backward, its face engulfed in red sparks. One of the Centaurs whistled, and Braken charged through the Etas toward them, grinding to a stop at the old Centaur.

Stephania quickly dismounted, and the old Centaur smiled at her. Gratitude and hope shone brightly in his eyes, and a strength flowed through Stephania. Her memories were helping her. She wasn't helpless anymore.

Taking her quiver from the saddle, she made sure she didn't need anything else before she slapped Braken's flank. He whinnied before charging into the forest. She prayed he would find safety.

Now she turned her attention to the battle.

She sent an arrow between the eyes of an Eta that looked uncannily like a horse but with crab legs and a beak, watching it stumble to the ground and trip another Eta behind it. She remembered faintly Artigal telling her and Trojan long ago that most average Etas could only shapeshift into creatures they had seen or encountered. That made most of them just mutated combinations of animals she was used to hunting and didn't have an issue killing: deer, canines, rats, eagles, *Zelauw-fafu,* wolves, *Raffudafaf.*

Giving over to instincts, she stopped thinking about what she was doing. Trojan was wrong. She *could* do this. The training was in her memories. All she had do to was trust it. Deeper, darker instincts churned within her, clawing to the surface, but she ignored them; she only had to push them down long enough to win this battle, to prove she wasn't a burden.

Dodging a swipe from a bear-like Eta's claw, she rolled under its follow-up attack before driving her knife between its ribs and deep into its heart. Stinking, rotting flesh pinned her to the ground as it collapsed on her. One of the Centaurs quickly lifted the Eta off her and dragged her to her feet before she was once again thrown back into the fray.

A leopard lost its head to her sword; its dying swipe clipped the skin of her shins. She gritted her teeth against the pain but was relieved when she didn't feel the telltale burning of Eta poison. *Apparently, not all Etas have the poison.* She distantly remembered the poison consuming her once on their journey to New-Fars and how it had taken Artigal, Frawnden, and Jargon to heal her. She tried not to think of what would happen if she were poisoned here, so far away from anyone who could help her.

A groan of pain dragged her attention away from the fighting for a moment. *I can heal them.* She weighed the risk of healing. If she was successful, then she might be able to move through the ranks of the Centaurs and heal them. She would be an asset, not a liability. She made her decision.

"Cover for me!" Her sword missed a mangled Eta's head, severing its arm off instead. Within seconds, an Elcore stood before her. She cursed under her breath, but the axe of her fellow fighters took down one, his eyes meeting hers enough for her to know he would protect her.

She quickly ducked in between the Centaurs as they were pushed back to the charred garden fence. She explained to the two wounded Centaurs what she was going to do, and their eyes shone in awe and gratitude. Their neediness and admiration for her was empowering, almost addicting, and she felt a surge of pride flood her. *Yes, I will heal them. We will fight and we will win. I will keep fighting until every Eta in Trans-Falls is dead. I am Farloon, after all. It's time I start acting like it.*

It took her several tries to get the concentration she needed, and she ended up having to whisper her intent in the few Ancient words she knew, but slowly, the wound on one of the Centaur's legs began to stitch itself back together. The warrior cried out in joy, her voice rising high with praise.

It was a miracle, but something was wrong.

Stephania gritted her teeth as she forced her magic out, sweat beading on her forehead. She shouldn't be struggling this hard. Dalton had been training her in healing, and she had healed worse with much more ease before. Panic began to grip her. Her red magic, which had so confidently sprung from her hands and over the Centaur's wound, began to flicker, some of it turning black. She was sliding back into the mindset of thinking magic wasn't real, that it was only miracles or myth. The personality of fear and doubt, once so familiar in New-Fars, was clawing its way back into her mind and suffocating her magic. Even now she couldn't escape being the little demon child of New-Fars.

Oh, gods. She choked against the wave of emotion crashing over her. The flashing red magic and the darkness swirling around her feet overwhelmed her. It was too much like those days at the Trans-Falls and in New-Fars. Flashes of the possessed Centaurs raced through her mind, and she stopped her magic. Horror, hate, and pain bubbled up inside her. She could feel the dark magic. It was all around her. It was in the trees, in the Etas, in the air. It was moving, feeding off the fear of the fighting Centaurs, and off her. It was *in* her. Even after getting her memories back, after knowing how much she abhorred the Etas and the dark magic that drove them, she wasn't strong enough to push it aside, to move past the horrors it brought up in her.

Faintly, she heard the Centaur she had been healing ask her if she was okay and why her leg wasn't fully healed. Stephania stared down at her hands, unable to answer. Her Shalnoa glowed red, but streaks of black wormed their way through the designs. *No. No. No. I can't channel it. Not here. Not now.* She thought of how the men in New-Fars had fallen like wheat before her. She couldn't control who it killed. Yes, it would kill the Etas, but she couldn't stop it from killing the Centaurs too.

"Why didn't you finish?"

Stephania shook her head, stumbling to her feet. The other Centaurs were yelling too, asking what she was doing. One cried out in pain as he took an arrow to his side.

"I can't," she whispered softly as she realized something terrible. Trojan was right. She didn't know her on potential. She was dangerous—dangerous to Trans-Falls, to the Centaurs she was trying to help, and to herself. It wasn't just the Etas Trojan had been trying to protect Trans-Falls from ... it had been from her too.

Tears streaked down her face. She tried to run, but the Etas were pressing in on them. One of the Centaurs threw her from the inside of their circle, saying if she wouldn't heal, then she had to fight. He was right. She had to do *something*, even if she was worthless.

She barely had time to raise up her hand in defense as an Eta, blood dripping from its circular mouth, lunged for her. She realized her mistake too late.

Magic raced from her hands to protect her. The Eta lit aflame, stumbling, screaming, into other Etas, catching them on fire as well.

But the magic didn't stop.

It poured from her with abandon, streaking through all the Etas in the clearing. It tore their bodies apart in a violent, bloody mess until she couldn't control it any longer.

It exploded through her, tearing through every seam of her mind and every weak sense of control she thought she had over it. Ancient Magic, both Pure and Corrupt, surged forward, flooding through her, casting her own magic and mind aside.

Screaming, she arched against the torment. Fire burned in her eyes from the magic; her hands came back red with hot blood when she tried to cover them against the pain.

The magic rushed from every pore on her body, sending a wave of energy in a huge ring from her, tearing through the forest. White magic swirled and tore against the black magic, fighting it, becoming it, balancing it, and then succumbing to it before fighting again. The sound was like a thousand galloping horses and screaming eagles rushing into battle.

She collapsed to her hands and knees, blood dripping down her face from her eyes and trickling out of her mouth, ears, and nose.

Everything was black.

Everything hurt.

She turned her head to the side, blinking back the blood, her rasping breath slow in her chest. The face of the old Centaur stared up lifeless, magic having torn through his body. His veins were both white and black, his face frozen in horror and fear. She tried to look around her. All the Etas were dead. One Centaur was healed and another staggered in shock. The others were dead.

Tears mingled with the blood.

"Oh, Trojan," she sobbed, droops of bloody tears decorating the grass. "What have I done?"

§

FRUSTRATED SNARLS AND THE hissing of blades, arrows, and ripping flesh filled the forest. Sometimes a scream, Eta or Centaur, would break the monotony, but it was ignored.

Trojan's sword moved so fast, its shining glow left a streak of blue hanging in the air with a fine mist of black blood trailing it. A red haze had settled over his gaze, his nostrils flared, his muscles burning with exertion and adrenaline. Though every movement of his body was calm and graceful, a fire in him raged with the exuberance of a berserker. Nothing stood long in front of him before being reduced to a mass of blood, flesh, and shattered bone.

Faintly, he felt Dakar and Lycus just behind him and to his right, and Ravillian and Lamora to his left. He had done what he had promised Stephania and found them, bringing them into his circle of elite warriors. They weren't good enough to keep up, but at least they were safe.

His battalion pressed on under his leadership, easily cleaning their section of the forest of Etas.

Images of Stephania flashed before him; the thought of her being killed if he were to fail protecting Trans-Falls haunted him, driving him on, urging him to fight harder than he had ever before. He had something to fight for again.

In his hands, his sword turned to an axe, and he threw it twenty paces into the Elcore of an Eta with the body of man and the head of a bird. His jaw worked against itself as he replayed his and Stephania's last conversation over in his mind. He wanted to take so much of it back. He had been too harsh to her, too distrusting. Using his magic, he teleported his weapon back to him and in seconds molded it into three small knives, sending them through the hearts of nearly ten Etas before him. With every Eta dead, they moved deeper into the forest; their line of defense was nearly impenetrable as Centaurs stretched in a line from his left and right.

The bugle horn of a Centaur blew in three short bursts before them, and his line came to a halt. They had met up with the other defensive line. This section of the forest was clear. A cheer of victory rippled through the ranks, but he did not join them.

They had to keep moving, to keep fighting until all the Etas were eradicated.

His eyes met Dakar and Lycus'. They nodded, assuring him they were well and ready for the next command.

Taking a deep breath, he closed his eyes and let the Synoliki magic flow through him. He could feel the heat of the fires consuming so much of Trans-Falls, and he saw not only the bodies of the living all around him but also the bodies of those who had passed on, the magic and life slowly receding out of their charred, bleeding corpses.

Forcing his horror at the destruction of his home from his mind, he focused on the living, on those ranks and battalions still standing strong. The majority of both the Eta and Centaur army was headed toward the *Gauyuyáwa*. From what he could tell, that was where Artigal was rallied at. Trojan knew if the *Gauyuyáwa* was destroyed, not only would the very heart of Trans-Falls be stabbed, but it would also lead to the destruction of the *Gauwu Zelauw*, Trans-Falls's last place of defense against dark creatures.

His eyes snapped open, and he instantly shouted out his orders.

"Fifth division under Lycus, take to the north and circle around toward the *Gauyuyáwa*."

Lycus nodded curtly before he gathered his troops. In a whirl of hooves and wild yelling, what was left of the fifth division galloped into the forest, Lycus at their lead.

Trojan turned to Ravillian and Lamora. "You'll come with me. Stay close." They nodded without questioning, their weapons tight in their hands. Blood decorated their armor and faces, but they were unharmed. He was determined to keep them that way.

"Eighth division, follow me!" He and Dakar had just started to gather ranks again when Trojan felt a wave of electricity surge through him. His eyes snapped to the forest and caught sight of something racing, roaring, and surging through the forest toward them.

He didn't have time to warn anyone or to put up any sort of defense.

With the force of a raging bull, the wave of magic struck him, slamming him to the hard ground.

For an instant, he felt the magic pass through him; the Corrupt Magic battled against the Pure Magic until he felt the Pure Magic win. The magic quickly passed them, leaving him empowered.

Lunging to his feet, he chanted in Sházuk, shouting for his warriors to join him. Only a few responded.

The bit of courage and strength the Pure Magic had left him with dimmed as his gaze washed over the forest.

Not many others had been fortunate enough to have walked away unscathed.

Nearly twenty good, strong warriors lay strewn across the ground, black and white veins spreading under their skin, their eyes open wide and staring blindly into the forest.

The Centaurs who were left staggered to their feet, stumbling around incoherently. Many of them sank back to the forest floor, too dazed to move. A few lunged to their feet, much like he had, the Pure Magic racing through their veins, giving them strength and hope.

"Lamora and Ravillian." His heart slammed in his chest as he whirled around, searching for Stephania's friends. He spotted Ravillian first, but his hope was damped when he realized Ravillian was kneeling beside a still form on the ground. "Emperor. Please ... no."

Trojan raced over to him, skidding to a stop just beside her.

Lamora was stretched out across the ground. Black and white veins trailed under her skin.

"Ravillian ..."

"She's alive," he whimpered pathetically, his hand desperately clutching one of hers. Tears sparkled in his eyes. "She's alive."

Trojan's shoulders sagged. He had failed. Again. He went to place his hand on Ravillian's shoulder, to drag him away, saying what no one wanted to hear—someone they loved was dead—but they had to grieve later or else they too would be dead. They had to keeping moving.

His eye caught something.

Lamora's chest twitched in breath.

Ravillian howled and clutched her hand to his chest. "Help her, Trojan. Please. You have to help her." His eyes begged, shining with pain—a pain Trojan knew too well.

"I don't know if I can ..." Trojan knelt beside her and took her other hand in his. He could faintly feel her pulse. It would take the Pure Magic to heal her. His Synoliki magic might be able to heal her, but he wasn't sure if he could channel enough of it.

"Please, Trojan."

Their eyes met, and Trojan's heart lurched.

"Please. I never told her—" He shook his head, his knuckles turning white as he clung to her hand, to hope. "That I—that I love her." He broke out in sobs, his shoulders shaking as his tears fell down onto her.

Without another second of hesitation, Trojan closed his eyes and pushed forward with all the Synoliki magic he had and all his faith in the Great Emperor. *You have to heal her, Emperor. Please. Please heal her. Please don't let this love die.*

For seconds that felt like hours, nothing happened. Then she coughed up blood, her eyes blinking against the light. "Ravillian ..." Her hand moved from his, to his face.

Ravillian laughed through his tears and quickly helped her to her feet. He crushed her to him, and she melted in his arms, their tears mingling as the black and white magic faded from her skin.

"I love you, Lamora. I love you so much. I never want to leave you. I love you," he muttered into her hair, and she responded by pressing her lips against his.

Trojan smiled but staggered as he felt the weight of the magic he used crushing his body and soul. His hands shook, and he could hardly draw his weapon. He wanted to stay and celebrate with Lamora and Ravillian, but the battle wasn't over. They had to stay focused, had to keep moving.

For a moment, through the fog clinging to his mind, he couldn't remember what had happened. He thought back from the black and white veins fading from Lamora's skin, and then his eyes traveled to the dead and disjointed Centaurs around him.

The Pure and Corrupt Magic ... it had exploded around them ... traveled through Trans-Falls ... from the north.

Etas in the distance screamed in unison; the sound reminded him of hound dogs when they caught on to the scent of their prey.

Rushing feet thundered behind him, and he drew his bow, aiming it for the trees, positioning himself between the oncoming Etas and Ravillian and Lamora. The Etas poured through the forest, screaming and shape-shifting as they ran. His bow took down nearly five before he realized they weren't attacking any of the Centaurs. It was as if he and his Warriors were invisible. They were running toward where the magic had exploded from.

His mind began to clear, and horror sank into him as he realized the truth. Only Stephania could've channeled both Corrupt and Pure Magic, and she would only have cause to do so if she were in danger.

"Oh, gods, no."

CHAPTER 23

GET UP. MOVE. The world spun around her. Her head rang. She tried to wipe the blood from her face but only smeared it. *Get up!* she mentally screamed, trying to pull herself to her feet. She swayed, swallowing the burning bile in her throat.

She staggered a few feet before falling to her knees, unable to stop the world from spinning around her. She heard the last two Centaurs shouting at her to get up, that the Etas were coming, but everything hurt. She couldn't move her arms, her legs, her eyes. She could barely draw a breath without coughing up blood.

She had to get up. She had to keep fighting, had to move. They were coming for her. She could hear them screaming like bloodhounds, coming for her, coming for her blood.

Again, she tried to push herself to her feet, forcing her attention on a tree in front of her, forcing herself to focus. After a second, she was able to see clearly. Her eyes had stopped bleeding, but her ears hadn't, and neither had her nose.

One of the Centaurs who was left took the bloody, cracked bugle from a dead ally and blew one long, loud note. Stephania wondered if anyone would actually be able to come. No one knew where she was. Would anyone come? Was anyone left alive at all?

Her hand tightened around her sword, which she was surprised to see she was still holding. Her bow was a few feet away. She faintly heard the Centaurs telling her to collect her arrows and prepare to make a stand. They were being surrounded. They couldn't run. They could only hope someone, anyone, would come.

"Stand firm, Farloon," one of the Centaurs whispered, and she nodded, an arrow nocked to her string. She was surprised they hadn't turned on her. *Perhaps they don't realize the magic came from me. That I killed their comrades.*

Thundering feet in the forest grew louder and louder until the darkness in the trees was a mass of moving bodies instead of shadows. Stephania's breath caught in her throat as the first few broke out into the clearing.

They were humanoid in form and brought weapons with them, most of which were large, crude metal workings that looked to be made for a slow, painful death. A new putrid smell carried in on a stiff breeze assured her these Etas were dripping in poison.

In a breath, they collided.

A sword streaked for Stephania's neck, and she ducked just in time, only to see a spiked ball on a chain come whirling toward her feet. She lunged forward with her sword, her blade piercing through the rat-headed, man-bodied Eta. Jumping over the ball and chain, she watched as it whirled under her and smashed into another Eta's knees with a meaty smack.

She called upon the reserves of her strength and threw herself back into the battle. Every so often, she blocked an attack and saved one of her fellow warriors, and every so often they did the same for her. But no matter how many they killed, more and more came.

At last, the fighting slowed and then stopped. No more Etas remained alive. However, something told her the battle was far from over.

Ten Centaurs galloped toward them, quickly setting up ranks around her and the remaining two Centaurs.

"Reinforcements are coming, but we were only just able to break through the Etas." Their leader nocked an arrow to her bow, her eyes dark. "It'll be a miracle if anyone else can."

Dread filled the air and their hearts.

A still, uncomfortable silence settled over the clearing until laughter broke through it, sending a chill down Stephania's spine.

Etas gently moved out of the forest and into the carnage of the small clearing. Her instincts and training told her they were much stronger Etas than the ones she had just fought, but they were nothing like she had expected. These resembled ... humans.

One was a girl of about ten years old. She had soft brown hair and pure golden skin that would've been Stephania's envy. She wore a pretty little pink and white flowered dress and fairly skipped through the plants and trees with a delicious, trilling laugh, a basket of flowers in her left hand, and a ribbon in her right.

Another was a handsome young man with a loose brown shirt, dirty jeans, and a woven straw hat on his fair head. His eyes sparkled happily as his arms swung freely at his sides.

Every type of person she could imagine walked out of the woods: old to young, male to female, blond haired to black haired, dark skin to fair skin, even wealthy to poor. It was as if a whole city had come to greet them.

Like New-Fars. As soon as she thought that, her eyes caught the little girl's, and her heart stopped. *Diana?* It couldn't be. *Oh, gods, no.*

Stephania began to back up, her bow falling lifeless by her side. "No, no, no."

"Ready!" The lead Centaur held up his hand as the others pulled back their bows.

"Oh, gods, no." Her eyes followed the arrows to their targets. She recognized more and more faces. *Lacey, William, even Gray. It isn't them,* she tried to tell herself. *It isn't really them ... right?* But when she looked into their eyes, they weren't red like the Etas. It was her past come to haunt her again.

Only this time, it wasn't a nightmare.

"Fire!"

A wave of arrows soared through the air.

Everything seemed to slow down.

The first ten creatures whipped back as the arrows struck them. She couldn't mistake the color of their blood as it spurted from their soft skin.

Red.

It was them. Stephania retched as spots covered her vision and she dropped to her knees. It was everyone from New-Fars.

"Some are Corrupt Humans!" the leader shouted to the rest as they fired their second wave of arrows and knocked another ten of the creatures to the ground. Some were black blooded Etas that only looked like humans, but a shocking majority were not.

"Oh, gods."

The humans who hadn't died from the first round of arrows were dragging themselves to their feet, pulling the arrow shafts from their bodies, and brushing themselves off. She could see no pain, or horror, or fear in their eyes as they marched onward.

"Aim for the hearts or head. They feel no pain and will not stop until they are dead! Fire!"

The next wave of arrows hit the humans, and she watched, too numb to raise her own weapon as the little girl, Diana, took an arrow to her neck. She sputtered, her eyes wide, before she grinned, snapped the shaft, and twirled her ribbon, her eyes locking on Stephania's. Blood splashed up onto the hem of her flower dress, but she didn't seem to notice.

Suddenly, the little girl threw her ribbon at the Centaur next to Stephania. Stephania saw metal flash at the end of the ribbon and realized it was a knife. She tried to open her mouth to warn the warrior but couldn't find her voice. The Centaur saw it in time, stepped to the side, and then in one quick, merciless stroke, decapitated the girl with his sword.

Stephania screamed as she watched Diana's severed head roll across the ground to her feet, the girl's eyes wide and dim, her mouth dripping blood.

She backed up, shaking her head as she wiped bile from her lips and tried to spit the wretched taste out of her mouth before she retched again. She couldn't fight them. These were the villagers of New-Fars. Corrupt or not, she grew up around them. Even if they had hated her, she knew them all by name, knew their professions, where they lived, what they wanted to do with their lives, knew who they were going home to, and in whose arms they felt safe. She came to fight Etas, not them. *This is one of my nightmares.* She was sure. *I'll wake up from it soon. This can't be real. I just want it to end. I just want all of New-Fars to be over, done, behind me.* A sob escaped her lips. *Why can't I escape from it? Why is it still haunting me?*

"Little girl, would you help me find my doggie?"

Screaming as a bony hand touched her shoulder, Stephania whirled around, coming face to face with a kind old lady with a dainty dress and apron on. "Mable?" she whispered. The old woman was the baker's wife, whose discarded scones Stephania would try to sneak away and eat.

"Did you like my scones, Stephania?" Mable grinned demonically before lunging at Stephania, knife in hand.

Before the blade found its mark, Mable's back arched, the tip of a sword barely showing out of her chest, patterning blood on her apron, before she felt to the ground.

Stephania dry heaved and sank to her knees, her head swimming, her ears ringing with the sound of battle, her stomach churning at the gore, her lungs burning for air.

As she looked up, a young woman about her age took an arrow to her side. She was sobbing, clutching a young boy, pleading to be spared. *Jessica,* Stephania thought numbly. *And her little son, Harmon.*

Jessica bawled for mercy as one of the Centaur's axes streaked toward her.

Stephania couldn't stay to watch. Before she knew what she was doing, she was up on her feet and running into the woods, past humans who reached out to her, moaning her name, slicing at her with kitchen knives, swords, and shovels, everything she had nightmares about them killing her with.

"Stephania!" Someone was screaming her name. She ignored it, staying focused only on running, on trying to flee from this horror she could never escape from.

Her flight created confusion for the Etas. Tracing her magic had led them to the clearing where she no longer was. Confusion and chaos rippled through their ranks, and they hardly noticed her as she rushed by them.

"Stephania!" The voice was louder, and she screamed against it, crying out as she tripped over a log and fell face first into a pool of what most likely was blood. Sliding on the slick grass, she struggled to her feet when a hand clamped on her arm, jerking her upright.

She lashed out, screaming, clawing, and kicking against her assailant. She couldn't see or make sense of anything. *I just want to be far away from here. I just want to undo all of this. I want to change; I want everything to be different. I want a new start. I don't want to die. Not here. Not like them, covered in red and black blood. Please spare me. Please!*

"Stephania, my child! It's me!" His voice caused her to pause long enough to see his face.

"Uncle Dalton?" She knew he must be like the others—dead to reason, to thought, to feeling, and to pain, only wanting her dead.

She broke from his grasp, but he was back on her in a second, his warm brown magic twining around her. "I'm not one of them. I'm not one of them!" He kept shouting to her until she stilled.

Finally, she felt clarity overcome the panic and threw herself upon him, sobbing into his shoulder, pleading with him to make it all stop, to protect her, to save her. Instead, he tore her off him, took her by the hand with a vise-like grip, and started dragging her through the forest. "Don't grieve now. You can't stop now. We have to keep going. We have to keep fighting."

His sword cut through the Etas that came too close.

He was right. She couldn't stop now. But she couldn't bring herself to raise her sword against the Etas lest they end up being human.

Together, they stumbled through the forest, half running, half tripping and limping. Finally, the Etas around them stopped looking like humans and appeared more like animals again. She took down a few with her sword, feeling her courage returning to her.

"We're almost there. Almost there."

She wasn't sure where he was taking her or what he meant, but she thought she might've caught Artigal's name in his mumblings.

They were running out of time. The Etas were learning their quarry had fled, and they were back on the hunt. More and more came after them.

"Gods of all," Dalton cursed and jolted. An unmistakable grunt of pain escaped his lips.

"What—" Her eyes widened in horror as she caught sight of a long shaft sticking out of his leg. "No—"

Wrenching her bow and arrows from her back, Dalton shot the Eta that had wounded him and thrust the weapon back at Stephania. He took a shaking step, but his leg collapsed under him. His face paled as his eyes met hers.

"Stephania, listen to me—"

"No!" She knew what he was going to say. "No, I can't—"

"Quiet, child! I'll drag you down. Artigal is waiting for you at Jargon's house. The whole army is waiting. You have to get to them. It's not much farther. I'll hold them off for as long as I can, but it's you they want. You have to go."

"No." Tears sprang into her eyes as she threw her arms around his neck. "I don't want you to die for me," she sobbed and crushed him to her.

"It's okay, Stephania. Ever since the day your parents chose me to be the one to raise you, I have dedicated my life to you. That's what an uncle does."

She shook her head, but he only hugged her tighter.

"I won't die. I promise. I'll stay alive. But you have to promise me you'll stay alive too. That you'll go *now*. You must chase your destiny." He held her at arm's length, searching her face. "I love you, Stephania. My child. You know that?"

She nodded. "I love you too, Uncle Dalton."

"Promise me."

But he didn't see what she did.

"No!"

She threw herself behind him, forcing him to the ground. Her hands flew up to protect herself, expecting the arrow to pierce her flesh deep into her heart.

It never did.

The crackling of a fire caused her to open her eyes. The Eta that had loosed the arrow was twitching on the forest floor, consumed by a raging inferno. The arrow was in ashes at her feet.

"Gods of all," Dalton whispered in horror as the forest went silent.

Tears raced down Stephania's face as she looked down at the magic swirling around her hands—a clear beacon to every Eta in Trans-Falls.

The screaming started again.

"Run, Stephania." He staggered to his feet, groaning when the arrow in his leg dragged him down.

The screams grew louder.

"Run." His eyes pleaded with hers as he tried shoving her away.

The thunder of feet crashed through the forest.

"Please."

They were coming for her.

"Stephania ..."

It was already too late.

Centaurs rushed past her as the Etas poured from the forest. Black and red blood flew through the air. Screams mingled with metal.

She grabbed Dalton and dragged him behind her, running straight into the wave of Centaurs rushing into battle. Tears blinded her vision. She heard Dalton yelling at her to leave him. His cries of agony wrenched her heart when she fell and it strained his leg, but she couldn't leave him. She stumbled to her feet, trying to help him up.

"Come on, Uncle Dalton. Stand up. Please. You have to. We have to keep moving."

He couldn't.

The Centaurs were pushing back the Etas, creating a barrier between Stephania and the Etas, but more of the shape-shifters were racing through the woods from the rest of Trans-Falls. Though the fighting was dying into the distance, and a strange peace had settled around them, Stephania knew they wouldn't be safe here for long. If the Centaur's front broke, they would be at the mercy of the entire Eta army. Time was running out, always, always running out.

"Uncle Dalton, please! We have to keep moving. They can't hold the Etas for long. We have to go *now*!"

She tried to ignore how pale his face was, how shallow his breath was, how much agony shone in his eyes as he struggled once more to stand and then crumpled under his own weight.

"No." She cupped his face with shaking hands, unable to accept the inevitable.

"Stephania—"

But before Dalton could speak, another voice shattered the strange calm around them.

"Stephania, thank the Emperor!"

Trojan was galloping toward her, and before she knew it, she was in his arms, crushed in his embrace. Hysterically, she sobbed and dug her fingers into his back, sagging into his arms.

"You have to take him, Trojan. He can't walk, and the Centaurs—" She couldn't finish past her sobs.

"No, Stephania." Trojan smoothed her hair and kissed the top of her head before turning to Dalton. They shared an intense look before Dalton nodded.

"What are you—" Stephania started screaming as Trojan dragged her away from Dalton. His arms were unmoving, his grip hard as iron on her small frame. All her thrashing and screaming did nothing against him.

"Let me go! I can't leave him!"

"We have to keep moving, Stephania. Jargon and Frawnden are coming to the front lines. They can save him. But we have to leave. Now." Trojan's face was stony cold; he didn't look back once as he dragged her with him.

"He's going to die, Trojan! You're leaving him here to die, do you understand?" She beat her fists against his chest. "Do you understand? Look at me, Trojan!"

But his eyes wouldn't meet hers as a single tear slipped down his cheek. "I know. I know." His voice was a deathly quiet whisper. "But you have to embrace your destiny, Stephania. I'm going to save you. You're going to survive. No matter what."

Time slowed.

In one horrible movement, he shoved her to the side, shielding her body with his.

She saw it all too late: sinister red eyes shining from under a dark cloak, a long beak curving out in front of them, an evil hiss of triumph, an arrow streaking through the air.

In a breath-taking moment, his sword turned into a bow in his hands and his own arrow passed the Eta's as it streaked toward them. The blue arrow struck the assassin Eta in the head, tearing a mass of dark flesh and blood with it just as the black knotted arrow sunk deep into Trojan's chest.

A scream tore from her throat as his body jolted from the shock and he staggered. *No.*

Trojan growled against the pain as his hand cupped around the arrow's shaft. The arrow protruded from his back; red blood shone stark against the black, triangular arrowhead.

With deft hands and a great roar of pain, he snapped the shaft off at his chest, then reached around and snapped it off at his back.

Stephania didn't realize she was screaming until his hand covered her mouth and he shook his head. His eyes burned with determination and pain.

"Don't cry. Don't scream. And don't you dare try to heal me. The Etas will sense your magic, and we'll never make it out of here, do you understand?"

Sobbing against his hand, she nodded. Try as she might, she couldn't tear her eyes away from the dark wound, directly where her head came up to his chest—his heart.

With a shaking hand, he grasped her arm and tried to pull her onto his back. An animalistic cry of pain tore his lips and he lost grip; she was barely able to catch herself before she tumbled to the ground. Blood pumped from his wound, splattering on her face.

"Trojan, you can't carry me. You're losing too much blood. You'll kill yourself." Tears raced down her cheeks.

"It doesn't matter," he growled and grasped her arm again, steeling himself against the pain.

The fighting grew louder. The Centaur frontline was being pushed back.

"Trojan, you can't do this—"

"Stephania, for once, please be quiet. I have two hearts. One is enough to get you to safety, but I don't have much time left. Get on my back, *now*."

She clamped her mouth against her screams of protest and mounted his back, resisting her heart, mind, and soul telling her to run back to Dalton, to use her magic, to save both of them, even if it killed her. He took two then three shaky steps before forcing himself into a staggering trot. With every hoof fall, new blood seeped from the wounds.

"Dalton—" She strove to see her guardian one last time, but already she was too far away. She tried pressing her hand to Trojan's back, struggling in vain to stop the blood. It only seeped through her fingers and dribbled down her arm, saturating her clothes. The sticky warmth and the reality that her weight was too much for him to carry made her lightheaded.

Centaur bugles ran out behind them, and the cries of "fall back!" and "regroup!" as the Centaur front broke rang through the air.

She couldn't stop herself as she screamed for Uncle Dalton, knowing he would be caught in the fighting.

Trojan's hoof dragged against a rock, and he staggered. Another step, and then his leg froze. He fell to his knees.

"Trojan—"

He was trying to stand again. He managed to balance himself, sweat pouring down his face and back, and take a few more steps before his legs gave out.

"Trojan, stop." She slipped off his back.

"No. I have to make sure you're safe."

She shook his shoulders, pleading with him to stop as he tried to stand again.

And again.

And again.

"Stop it!"

Panting, he fell to his knees, his head hanging low.

"I can't carry you any farther. You must run. Jargon and Frawnden will find you."

"No." She threw her arms around his neck. "I won't leave you alone. Don't make me go."

"You have to. It's over for me, but for you—"

Hands grasped her, and she screamed, thrashing against them.

"Stephania! Calm down!" Jargon's familiar voice reached her ears, and she stilled only for a moment before begging him to save Trojan, to save Dalton, to save all the Centaurs she had left behind.

No one listened to her.

"Dalton is only a short way behind us. He took an arrow to his thigh. I don't think the Etas have reached him yet. You have to take her. You have to make sure she's safe." Trojan's voice was surprisingly steady, though unnaturally quiet.

"I will find him. Frawnden will take Stephania."

Trojan's eyes closed with relief as he took in a shallow breath. "Good. Thank you, Jargon. Thank you. Thank you."

Jargon placed a hand on Trojan's shoulder, tears glistening in his eyes. "May the suns smile upon your presence, *fom*. Rest well." He took to the forest in the direction of the fighting.

"Take her, Mother ... make sure she's safe ..." Trojan coughed, wincing against the pain.

Frawnden nodded before quickly grasping Stephania, pulling her away. "Stephania, let's go. Artigal is waiting for us."

"You're not going to save him." Horror filled Stephania as she gazed up into Frawnden's emotionless face. "You're going to leave him, your own son, to die. You monster! You can save him! You have to save him!"

Tears broke through Frawnden's stony mask as her eyes fell on her son. "There's no time. He can't be healed."

Stephania beat against Frawnden and tore herself from her mother's grasp, rushing back to her brother.

"Stephania—" he started, but she cut him off.

"You should have let me die!" she screamed, shaking his heavy shoulders. "You should have let me! It should have been me!" Her hands slid across the horrific amount of blood on his back. "Gods, I want it to be me!"

He was barely able to bring his shaking hands to her face, barely able to open his eyes to meet hers. A soft smile lifted his lips. His shallow, chill breath smelled like blood. He sagged into her touch. "My little sister ... you must ... fulfill your destiny ..." His eyes moved past her to Frawnden, pleading with his mother. "Please, take her away. Make sure ... she's safe."

"No!" she yelled in protest, as Frawnden pulled at her, pleading with her to go to safety. But the mother's efforts were half-hearted. Stephania wasn't the only one who didn't want to leave Trojan.

Jargon galloped back to them; Dalton was astride his back, alive but barely conscious. "They're coming. The Centaur front has fallen. They're regrouping at the ridge. We need to move. I'll get Stephania." He transferred Dalton to Frawnden. "Go, Frawnden. He cannot be saved. Let him go to the Emperor in peace."

Frawnden took one last look at her son. Her mouth parted with silent tears. Finally, she held her right fist to her heart in salute and galloped into the woods.

"I'm glad I got here ... in time." Trojan's words were barely audible. "I couldn't lose you ... not again."

"Stephania—" Jargon wrapped his arms around her waist. She twisted and punched his nose as hard as she could, causing him to reel back, cursing and clutching his face.

"Go with them. Be strong ..." Trojan whispered with a small smile, his eyes sliding out of focus, "... for me."

She bit her lip, hardly able to force the words out. "I don't know if I can."

It seemed he hadn't heard her.

"Remember that time ... with the Susahu Viper ..." A strange, almost silly smile had spread on his face as his eyes glazed.

"Yes, yes?"

"I think ..." His gaze softened as if he were seeing it play out in front of him.

Jargon wrapped his strong arms around her once more and with a final tug, wrenched her from Trojan and threw her over his shoulder.

"No!" she cried. "I have to hear what he's saying! Let me go! He's trying to say something to me!"

The scream of Etas filled the air as they rushed through the trees. Stephania could see their bloodthirsty eyes shining through the darkness, hunting her. They would tear Trojan to pieces.

She beat her fists against Jargon's back and kicked. "No! They'll kill him! Let me go! Let me go!"

Tears spilled down Trojan's face as his glossy gaze met hers. "No matter what," he whispered before he lifted his head to the trees above and gathered all that was left of his magic into his hands.

"Trojan, no!" But she was powerless to stop him.

Blue fire leapt from his body and raced across the ground, creating a boundary that would protect them even as it drained the rest of his life.

They couldn't go back. All hope of saving him was gone. It was over. The seconds had run out.

Lifting her head, she screamed into the forest.

Centaurs rushed past them into the battle as Jargon climbed the ridge to safety. A Warrior was assigned to restrain her lest she run back into the fighting, back to where she saw the last of the blue fire die out, signaling the death of the one creature she had loved more than anyone. Her lips moved silently, saying all the things she had wanted to tell him, wishing he could hear.

As the battle faded, her cries mingled with a hundred others as those left behind mourned the sacrifices given in the cruel name of love.

PART THREE
Seeds of Vengeance

CHAPTER 24

SOFT HOOFBEATS VENTURED out then, bounded away. A gentle breeze blew, dark with lingering smoke. Birds piped quietly as if too tired to sing. Low voices whispered last goodbyes and "I love you." Silence suffocated it all. Not pure, golden silence, but mournful, aching silence—the silence heard in the depths of hearts that have only an echo of the loved ones they lost.

Stephania turned her face to the darkening sky over the Trans-Falls forest that stretched out from Frawnden and Aeron's house. No tears ran down her face, but in their place, a hollow pain shone from her dark eyes.

Spots of burnt grass and foliage dotted the landscape. Though a few embers had singed the cabin, it luckily hadn't caught fire. But Stephania found it hard to be grateful the fire spared the home when the attack had claimed something much more irreplaceable.

Vaguely, she remembered them tearing her away from Trojan's still body, saying the forest wasn't safe, that they would come back for him. Vaguely, she remembered them later lifting him onto a ceremonious carriage then taking him to the Forest of Tombs, the *Gauwu Zelaw*. She remembered Frawnden's wailing and mourning, and Aeron's ashen-white face of disbelief and horror. She remembered Frawnden holding her while she had stood frozen and numb, having cried all her tears, but she didn't remember feeling the warmth of her mother's embrace piercing the dark pit inside her.

"Stephania, little dragon, you didn't kill him. It wasn't your fault," the mother had whispered, consoled, sobbed, over and over and over again.

Yes. Stephania's hands trembled, and her stomach turned. She ground her teeth, fighting the tears that chose to stay rotting inside her. *Yes, I did kill him. Of course it was my fault. All of it. Can't they see that?*

No one blamed her. They never once spoke ill of her.

She wanted them to—to scream at her, hit her, curse her, banish her, hate her. How could anyone love or forgive someone like her? As much as she wanted them to, she was terrified of what would happen if they did throw her away. She would be so alone. So, so alone.

She had learned why it was called the Forest of Tombs. After Artigal and Aeron dug a perfect grave with magic and had laid her brother's body to rest, the Centaurs had joined in a song of such despair, she felt as if her own soul had cried the words. The forest turned the song to magic, and the magic mingled with the forest, wrapping around Trojan's body, covering him in vines, which twisted and turned until a tree of despairing beauty stood before them. It was younger than the other trees in the forest and possessed a different soul, but it was then she realized all the other trees must be tombs as well.

It isn't good enough for him. The significance of his burial in such a revered place was lost on her. *He deserves so much more.* A lump rose in her throat, anger burning in her chest. *He deserves ...* Her heart lurched inside her. *He deserves to live.*

She buried her face against her knees, drawing her legs closer to her. She sobbed on air; no more tears would fall from her eyes. She was glad she could no longer cry. Her eyes felt heavy, and they burned; her nose was raw and stuffy; her lips were swollen; her lungs ached for breath. But now it all stayed inside her, rotting, festering, growing.

The cabin door opened behind her. She didn't look up.

"Stephania?" Frawnden's voice, raw from her own tears, floated gently toward her daughter. The mother's voice, usually so comforting and safe, now felt and sounded like screeching metal.

She didn't answer.

"Stephania—" Frawnden's words caught as she struggled back her tears. "You need to sleep. It's too late to stay out here."

I don't care.

Her second answer of silence hung uncomfortably in the air.

After a few long moments as Frawnden nervously pawed the deck, she turned back inside, shutting the door gently behind herself.

A new wave of loneliness washed over Stephania. *Why won't they come sit with me? Where's Father, Dalton, Ravillian, Lamora? Why did Mother have to leave? Why won't anyone just give me a hug?*

Sleep, sleep, sleep, her body and mind pleaded with her. *All I want to do is sleep. At least in the darkness, I cannot know pain.*

Yet sleeping would bring tomorrow—a tomorrow without Trojan—a tomorrow that didn't seem worth living.

Gods of all, I dread it. I don't want tomorrow to come. I don't think I can do it.

A cry welled up inside her. She wanted to scream, to tear something apart, but instead, the sound stopped in her throat, choking her, and her body only sank deeper under an unexplained weight. Every moment she sat on the steps made it harder to find anything in her that wanted to continue on.

A deer slowly walked out of the forest not far from her, its head raised, ears perked, wondering if Stephania was a threat.

She hardly looked up; she barely even moved with breath. She sensed the presence of the deer with her mind but ignored it, wishing it would go away. Even the gentle company of the wild animal felt like a violation.

The deer snorted before turning back into the woods.

The air blew cold. She shivered, wondering if her heart had stopped beating and would become cold like the earth at night, wondering if it would ever wake back up and want to love again.

The door behind her opened again.

"Stephania."

It was Aeron. His quiet, low voice was steady, unmoving, unchanged by emotion.

She felt herself wanting to turn to him, to rush into his warm, loving embrace, but everything in her refused. She continued in her stony silence.

Everything felt wrong: breathing, talking, crying, eating, sleeping, caring, loving. Anything but sitting and doing nothing, even thinking, felt so wrong now.

"Stephania, come inside. It is too late for you to sit out here. Come in with me."

She gave him the same answer she gave Frawnden: silence.

Why don't you just come sit with me? she pleaded in silence. *Why must I move from this horror I am in?*

The wind blew gently. A cricket chirped but then fell silent. Still, he did not leave.

His hooves clopped hollowly on the deck, pausing at the top of the large stairs before slowly stepping down them.

She ignored him until he was standing beside her.

"Stephania?"

She looked up into his face.

His eyes were red and swollen, and dark circles colored his lower lids. A black silence hung in his eyes.

"Oh, Stephania." He held his hand out to her.

She sniffed, feeling as if her heart were breaking all over again. "Father." She clung to his legs, burying her face into the soft fur of his horse chest, feeling his long mane falling onto her face.

Why can't I cry? A lump rose in her throat. She wanted to scream and cry, but nothing came out. *Why do I feel as if I am the one who died?*

His hand gently stroked her head, traced the curve of her ear, holding her close to him.

She listened to his strong heartbeat. For a moment, just a moment, she could almost imagine it was Trojan, that they were lying beneath the stars, her head rested on his chest, his black mane blowing into her face ... but never again. Never again would she feel his soft mane on her skin, hear his warm voice whisper the secrets of the forest to her, watch his blue eyes light up as he taught her something new.

Finally, tears stung her eyes. Her nose was clogged; she sucked in a breath through her mouth and bit her lip. A strangled croak left her lips as she wrestled past her emotions, struggling to suppress them and the ugliness of her grief.

"Stephania, little dragon, fate has been so unkind to you." His voice was so quiet, she wondered if it would be taken away on the night breeze. "Do not stop your tears, do not lessen the pain, do not let it be buried inside of you. If the night must last for a hundred years, then let it. Better to sleep in the night than to burn in the day."

She frowned, confused. She didn't respond. *What do I say to that? Do I even understand it?* She sniffed again, wiping her nose on her wrist, pulling away one of his long hairs that had caught between her lips. *Nothing. Just say nothing. Nothing matters anyway. Is time even moving?*

Their silence together carried into the night. Seconds moved on past them, waiting on no one. A single tear ran down her check; the rest had abandoned her again, leaving her feeling crushed under the wight of her turmoil.

His fingers stroked around her pointed ear, gently massaging her stiff neck, running through her curly, tangled hair.

"Come with me, Stephania."

She shook her head.

"It's time to go to bed."

"No." She barely heard her own voice, muffled as it was by her stuffy nose and watery mouth. She hardly cared enough to swallow. "I don't want tomorrow to come."

He shook his head, wiping a tear from the corner of her eye, smoothing her hair from behind her ear. "Neither do I." His jaw tightened, but he never broke their locked gaze. "But it will come, whether you or I want it to or not. It will shine its face upon us again and again. Your grief is not big enough to stop the world, just as your love for Trojan wasn't big enough to stop death. That is the cruelness of life. It neither waits on, nor answers to anyone."

Her chest ached. Nausea rose in her throat.

"And yet"—He shook his head and chuckled sourly—"how beautiful it is, to not have to hold such a weight on your shoulders as making the suns rise again. What a relief, to know that no matter how low you sink, the suns will rise on you again."

She sniffed again and tried to wipe her nose. "I don't ... I don't understand."

He smiled sadly down upon her. "I know. But one day you will wake from this nightmare, and you will understand." He held out his hand to her. "Come. Let's go to bed. You need to sleep."

Yes, sleep. I want to embrace the darkness. Let it come. She took his hand, letting him pull her to her feet.

"Let me carry you, daughter."

She climbed onto his back. She hadn't ridden with him since she had been just a child. It was comforting, and she felt as if she were very young again, without a care in the world—without the confusion of three parents, the death of her brother and the discovery of a second, Artigal's sudden change, her connection with Thaddeus, and the uncertainty of her life ahead—without the weight of destiny crushing her.

She closed her eyes, letting her fingers entwine in his mane, feeling him carefully step up onto the patio and into the house.

Low voices and the soft glow of lantern light caused her to blink and gaze around the room.

Dalton was speaking quietly to her very tearful mother.

She barely caught her name in their words that trailed off into silence. It was obvious they were wondering how best to help her deal with her loss.

I wish I knew. I wish I knew how you could help me. Please help me. She couldn't form the words to ask them.

She caught Dalton's worried, pained gaze, and her heart ached. She wanted to rush into his arms and let him rock her to sleep like he had done for so many years. She wanted him to tell her it was all going to be okay, that everything would just be okay. But she couldn't move. Nothing in her would move. She could only look into his eyes, her gaze lifeless and dead, and watch the pain grow in his heart, a mirror to her own soul. A pang of guilt shot through her. Should she be with Aeron when Dalton so wanted to comfort her? Was that fair? Why did she even have to worry about that in a time like this? *Gods of all, this hurts too much.*

Aeron quickly passed through the stony silent living room and into the dark hallway.

Oblivious to everything except the death inside her, Stephania felt him slowly lower her from his back to her bed and tenderly cover her with the fur blankets. He muttered Centaur endearments before exiting the room, the door shutting hollowly behind him.

Her heart thumped in her chest. The room was unnaturally silent, unnaturally dark. She felt it all around her, all inside her. Time moved past like a breeze; she could feel it pass but could do nothing except lie still. Sleep did not come, but neither did she feel like she was awake. There was simply ... nothing.

No. Not nothing. Fear and emptiness still consumed her heart and soul.

She shivered though the blankets were warm. A lump rose in her throat, and then the tears came again, spilling silently down her face, dampening her pillow. She clutched the covers to her chest, but it did nothing to shut out the cold seeping from her soul, nor did it diminish the feeling of being so exposed. She felt as if she had been torn wide open before all of Rasa, as if judgement had come upon her.

"I guess I'll go with you. My place is beside you, wherever you go."

Her teeth dug into her lip, trying to fight back the memories. She could still hear him so clearly—his sadness, his despair.

"You don't need me?"

She couldn't stop the cry from parting her lips. *I need you, Trojan! Gods of all, I need you so much.* She shook her head, sobbing. "I'm so sorry. I'm so sorry." She stared up at the dark ceiling, her chest aching as if she had been thrown off a cliff. *This is all my fault. I should've left. I should've promised you. And I never told you—*She felt as if her heart were going to stop. She wanted it to. She couldn't face this reality—this living, waking nightmare. *I never told you I'm sorry. Not really. Not like I should have. Not like I meant to.*

You never got to tell me about our brother. About the girl I think you loved. I spent so much time telling you about what I had gone through, I didn't get to hear about you, about your life, your stories.

She wailed, unable to contain the sheer, gut-wrenching pain inside her. *And–and I never will. I will never again speak to you, or hear your voice, or see your face, or touch you again. Never again. Never again. Gone. Gone forever!*

She screamed into her pillow, her eyes burning with tears.

"Why?" she moaned. "Why? Why?" She thrashed against the furs, wanting to tear something apart, wanting to tear herself apart. Nothing made sense anymore. Everything was pointless. Nothing mattered.

Gone. Forever.

"Why?" she yelled, sitting up, not caring who heard the turmoil of her soul. She wanted them to hear, to come to her, to stop ignoring her. "Why!" She tightened the blankets around her, clutching them to her chest, wishing they would swallow her whole. "Why?" she whispered once more, so quiet she could hardly hear herself.

Uneven, heavy footsteps rushed down the hall. Her door flew open then shut again.

For a moment, just a moment, she wished it were Trojan.

She squeezed her eyes shut, wishing the tears would stop, but they didn't. She drew her knees closer to her chest, her sobs the only sound filling the room.

Soon, warm arms wrapped around her, pulling her close.

"Uncle Dalton," she rasped.

He nodded against her head before shifting his weight, grunting painfully from his wounded leg.

"I am alone. I am so alone," she moaned as she gripped his shirt, pressing her head against his chest.

His fingers brushed through her hair.

"No, Stephania. You are not alone. I am always here for you. Always."

She continued to cry until the tears stopped again. Her head ached, her stomach churned violently, her chest felt constricted in an iron vise, her tongue was dry with thirst. She wanted to scream, throw up, thrash, to die, but she only sat still, as if already dead.

She focused on his arms around her and tried to remember what it was like to feel young, small again. If only life wasn't so cruel. If only she were back in New-Fars when she had been younger, when things had been so much simpler, when she had loved a little less.

She felt something warm and wet on her face. A flashback reminded her of the blood in the battle—dripping, dripping, warm, and wet—and her heart began to race, but Dalton's chest rose against her as he sniffed and shuddered, and she remembered she was in her room, not fighting for her life. It wasn't blood, it was tears. He was crying with her.

A raging in her relaxed in peace. Something about the tears of someone else mourning with her, for her, beside her, calmed her pain and stilled her anger and fear.

Here, in his arms, she felt comfort; she felt at home; she felt safe. She was sorry they hadn't seen as much of each other the last few months, having been so wrapped up in other friends and activities. She hadn't realized how much she needed him. A new grief welled up in her, but she pushed it back. She could only take so much pain right now. At least he was here right now. That's all that mattered.

He stirred, and she felt him take a deep breath. His quiet voice shook, full of tears. Though he sang, he could hardly hit the notes. "Sleep my child, just close your eyes—" He paused as if the words had stuck in his throat. He shook his head, unable to continue.

She struggled to breathe then forced the words out of her mouth, ugly as they sounded through her tears and stuffy nose. "And wait for the morning of suns' rise. A light will come and ... and ..." She bit her lip. She couldn't continue either. Would the light really come? It didn't feel like it. It felt like there was only darkness—an eternal, painful darkness.

She remembered when he sang this song to her when she would have nightmares. He remembered those nights too. How could he not? He had sung her to sleep, wishing her fears away, many, many nights. It had always brought the sweetest visions to her—a man and woman holding their young daughter, singing to her. She knew now they were her parents.

His arms tightened around her, seeming to draw courage. She focused on his embrace, on his voice, forcing everything else—the pain, loneliness, anger, fear—out of her mind.

"A light will come and lead your life," he continued, "and wash you from your strife. Always now in dark and fear, we will know that He is near."

If she thought hard enough, she could see that man and woman again, and she could see their faces as they sang that song to their daughter—her—and she drew strength from that.

"So sleep, my child, just close your eyes, and wait for that morning of suns' rise." His last words rang in the air, his voice now stronger and clearer than it had been when he'd started.

Silence stilled the air until Stephania broke it, her voice muffled in his shirt. "Thank you."

He sighed and nodded.

She could never understand the peace that came with that song. Somehow, she felt warmer, a little less sad, a little less alone. She thought of the lyrics *"Always now in dark and fear, we will know that He is near."* She frowned. *Perhaps, just maybe, this darkness isn't so dark and unending after all.*

They sat still, their arms around each other for a few minutes more, before Dalton shifted away.

"No," she whispered roughly. "Please. Don't leave me." Fresh tears brimmed in her eyes. She knew the night terrors would come for her tonight. She knew she would see the face of the corrupted New-Fars villagers as they fought for her blood. "I don't want to be alone."

He nodded. "Okay. I will stay. I will always stay for you, my child."

He pushed himself up onto her bed, gingerly moving his leg, before pulling her back to him. She nodded against his chest and sighed.

"Is your leg okay?"

He nodded again. "Jargon did a good job. I shouldn't even have a limp in a month."

"That's good."

"Yes, it is." She could almost hear the smile in his voice. "Now, go to sleep."

She closed her eyes, feeling exhaustion drag her down. *Yes, I will sleep*, she thought as the darkness closed around her. *At least, for now, I am not alone.*

§

THE SOUND OF LAUGHTER, once so joyful and pleasing, grated across the air, sounding like the hissing of a snake or the screeching of metal.

Stephania drew her arms around her body. *I feel like I'm going to throw up.* She gritted her teeth and closed her eyes. *Why am I even here? I should be home, crying, screaming, throwing up, tearing something apart. Not ... not this.*

She looked around her.

A large gathering of young Centaurs was laughing, joking, eating food, and playing games. They were celebrating Trans-Falls's victory. For many, it was their first time in battle; they were celebrating that as well. Stephania knew many of them hadn't seen the full extent of the battle. They had been strategically placed in low danger situations because of their lack of experience. Most of them hadn't seen the carnage and horrors Thaddeus had sent for Stephania.

Ravillian and Lamora stood close to one another, engaged with other friends, their joyful voices rising above the trees. Stephania caught glimpses of their conversation. They were relaying how Lamora had nearly died from the Ancient Magic and how Trojan had saved her. They didn't mention that the Ancient Magic had come from Stephania, though perhaps they simply didn't know. It seemed no one did.

Stephania didn't understand how they could speak of Trojan's last acts with such irreverence, as if he hadn't died only minutes later, but she supposed if one stared death in the face, another meeting it didn't seem as significant.

She blanched and turned her face away.

"*Go with them, Stephania,*" Dalton had told her. "*It'll be good to keep your mind off everything that has happened.*"

Better to keep occupied than obsess over the pain and anguish is what he had meant. Maybe he was right. Maybe she just needed to get away from it all and forget about it.

She had seen Aeron's disapproving gaze when she had readied herself this morning to meet with her friends, and his words from the night before echoed hauntingly. "*Do not stop your tears. Do not lessen the pain. Do not let it be buried inside of you. If the night must last for a hundred years, then let it. Better to sleep in the night than burn in the day.*"

She knew he had seen how sick she was mentally, emotionally, and physically. She had thought she was going to retch in front of everyone or pass out, but she had forced it down, covered it up.

After all, how did she know who was right? What should she choose? She had agreed with Dalton, trusted him, knowing he understood her better than anyone, except for Trojan of course. But as she had left the house, she instantly knew she had made the wrong decision and should have listened to Aeron.

These Centaurs ... She looked around her. They had no idea. Some of them had fought, had seen the carnage, but only a small number of them had lost a friend or family member. She could easily tell them apart from the others. They weren't laughing and joking. They looked the mirror of how she felt.

Why are we here, then? What good is this laughter when so many have died? What are we trying to prove? Are we trying to grasp on to something normal, even though our lives have been ripped apart? Fresh tears stung her eyes. *I want to go home. I want to sleep. I don't want to do this. I don't want to do today.*

"Stephania! Come here! Ravillian thinks he can beat you at *Yu'jac*."

Stephania stapled a grin on her face and pushed herself off the tree. "Oh, does he now? That's a pretty tall claim." She winked at Lamora who giggled. Lamora knew Stephania was an unbeaten champion. Ravillian, however, did not.

Any other day, Stephania would've given anything to beat Ravillian at her favorite strategy game, but today ... today it felt so wrong.

As they chose their dice and spread out the impossibly large game board, she started to get nauseous again. Her eyes roamed over the small Centaur and mythical creature pieces. Trojan had loved this game. He had taught it to her long, long ago, and they had spent hours playing it, him beating her time and time again, though she had never minded. She loved playing against her cunning brother and learning what he had to teach. She wondered if the person she became in New-Fars would've felt threatened by his superiority.

She clenched her fist tightly over the dice, relishing in the way their sharp, metal edges cut into her skin. Her eyes burned, but she forced the tears away. She would not cry here in front of all these Centaurs. She was Farloon; she had to be strong. Her weakness was what killed Trojan in the first place.

When her eyes met Ravillian's, they flashed with hot fire, angry determination masking the desolation.

"Ravillian challenges me to *Yu'jac*. Will anyone join this challenge?" She raised her fist over her head, gaining the attention of the majority of the Centaurs. *Yu'jac*, though initiated with one creature challenging another, could evolve into a multiplayer game like a mock war. However, the first two challengers were the main competitors, leaving the other players to take the roles of allies, neutrals, or third parties.

"I!" A dark grey female pushed through the crowd. She had scars along her body and a stony face. A darkness past her years hung in her eyes along with the lust for battle. Stephania instantly knew this warrior played *Yu'jac* to sate a bloodlust. She would be a formidable opponent; it would be a strenuous game—something Stephania needed to drown her emotions in.

She crouched over the fabric, scrutinizing every detail as the playing pieces were arranged by the other Centaurs.

Ravillian had challenged her, which put her on the defense and him on offense. *Good. This was how Trojan trained me.* Surveying her troops, territory, and resources, she felt confident she would win. Trojan had taught her well.

Two more shouts indicated another two players. They would complicate her strategy, but she was sure she could make allies or crush them.

As soon as the game was declared in progress, she started shouting out her decisions and movements, rolling her dice to determine the outcome. She never once looked up from the board, forcing herself to concentrate and push aside the bloody images fighting for her attention when she thought too long about sending troops to their death. She played more aggressively than usual, and she quickly felt the difference. A hate burned in her and moved through her decisions. She showed no mercy, and when she annihilated a fraction of Ravillian's advancing army, she took no prisoners.

An opening came up to make an ally with the player to her left. She had carefully forced his troops into a position where he could either align with her or be destroyed by Ravillian. A smile curved her lips, and she stood, ready to announce her terms of alliance to the player.

"I, Stephania, defender of the highlands, request a meeting with the leader of this army. Will he comply?"

He responded with a short, gruff answer. He clearly didn't like being beaten. "Aye. I comply."

"I beseech you to align yourself under my command and push back Ravillian's army. Do you agree—" She paused when she realized she didn't know his name. When she looked up from the board, planning to ask for his name, her mind screamed to a halt.

Rich, golden brown hair, black mane, black tail ... a buckskin.

Gods of all. She swallowed painfully, her heart pounding a million miles per second, a strange joy racing through her veins. "Trojan?" she whispered quietly, doubtfully, hopefully. *He is* ... She looked up into the Centaur's face.

A strange cry left her lips as she felt as if someone had run a sword through her.

The confused Centaur was frowning. "Jacobi. My name is Jacobi."

A vehement laugh sprang from her lips. "Yes, of course." She bit her lip until she tasted blood. *Of course. I'm a fool.* The tears rushed back along with the nausea. *I think I'm going to be sick.*

"Excuse me." She spun on her heel and shoved her way past the spectating Centaurs. *Fool! You will never see him again! Never! You watched him be buried, watched his body turn into a tree. He is* dead.

Blindly, she ran into Lamora who had chased after her. "Stephania, what's wrong?" Her eyes were filled with worry, her hands gentle as she gripped Stephania's shoulders.

What's wrong? She choked back her sinister laugh, resisting the urge to scream what she was thinking. *He's dead, Lamora! He's gone. Forever. And it's my fault.* She balled her fists, forcing air into her lungs. The world spun around. She was sinking, sinking, sinking.

"Oh, nothing. I'm fine." She sniffed, feeling as if she were cutting the smile onto her face with a knife. "I just, uh ... I just needed to gather my thoughts before thinking of the alliance terms," she lied easily. "I was just getting a little claustrophobic, I think."

"Are you sure?" Lamora's eyes pierced hers.

She looked away, hissing the words as if they were poison. "Yes. I said I'm fine. Thank you."

Lamora frowned, her mouth opening then closing. Stephania could feel her eyes on her, but she continued to look away. She knew if she looked into her friend's eyes, she would lose it. She could feel the eyes of all the other Centaurs on her. They were waiting for her. Ravillian, Jacobi, everyone who had fought in the battle a few days ago, they were all expecting her to pull herself together, to be fine. If the Farloon couldn't, then who could?

But I'm not fine. Gods, I'm furthest from fine. Take me away from this nightmare. Hug me. Cry with me. Please, Lamora. Please just ask me one more time. Please ask me if I'm okay, and maybe the gods will give me the courage to say no.

Lamora pulled her hands away and bit her lip. She shook her head before whispering, "Okay, Stephania. Do you want to keep playing or do something else?"

Stephania's shoulders sagged, and she shook her head. "I'll play."

Dead. Dead. Dead. The word repeated over and over in her mind, driving her mad. She rolled the dice again and again, and the game went on. She was winning, and then she had won. Though instead, she felt like the world's biggest loser.

The Centaurs' cheers and praise rang through the forest, but to her, they only sounded like the screams of the dying warriors, echoing endlessly in her mind and heart.

She smiled, laughed, joked with them, put on a mask and danced to their carefree joy, but instead of it lifting her spirits, it only crushed her, pushing her deeper and deeper into herself until she felt like the person they saw wasn't even her anymore. *It's as if they are so far away and the light from their laughter that once inspired me to be a better person is only drowning me. I am alone in this pit, alone with my grief, belonging nowhere with no one.*

Now she was walking home, waving a cheery goodbye to Ravillian and Lamora, promising to see them soon. The instant their backs were turned, she deflated. She felt nothing now. No sickness lay inside her, and the tears had left her. Her anger from earlier had left her weak and tired.

Tired. So tired. I want to go home. I just want to sleep.

She looked down at her hands, hands she felt were stained with Trojan's blood. "Home." She tripped over a rock, struggling to catch her fall. She dragged her feet, one after the other, tripping again and again.

The laughter of the Centaurs behind her had faded. The trees, dark and tall, loomed over her, sheltering her. She wanted to go back, join their laughter, feel their joy, but she knew she didn't belong. She wanted them to be happy. She could still see Ravillian and Lamora's smiling faces. They had lived through a miracle. She didn't want to spoil that with this darkness she carried. She didn't want them to have to feel the way she did. It was better this way—to be alone. It was better than dragging someone else into this nightmare.

She tripped again, but this time she let herself fall. Sharp rocks dug into her legs and hands, drawing blood, but she didn't move away. The pain in her body helped dull the agony in her mind.

I can't go home because my home is dead. A cry rose in her throat, but her lips stayed silent. She planted her palms on the road and let her head hang between her shoulders. *He won't be waiting for me. He won't be there when I go home. I won't see him again.* The same wretched reality kept crashing down on her, but it never really became her reality. Instead of accepting it, she could only feel as it hacked and slashed at her, leaving her more raw, more anguished, with every blow.

Hooves crunched the road's rocks. She didn't move.

The two Centaurs stopped in front of her.

She expected them to rush to help her, to ask if she was okay. Any Centaur of Trans-Falls wouldn't have hesitated. Unless ... unless they knew her.

Slowly, she lifted her eyes. She easily recognized those dark brown and golden hooves.

"Dakar. Lycus." Her voice was unnaturally cold and foreboding.

"Stephania." Only Lycus spoke.

An uneasy apprehension hung in the air.

As if her body were full of lead, she dragged herself to her feet. Her eyes met Dakar's first, and her blood ran cold.

He growled, taking a step toward her, a horrid snarl twisting his face.

"I—"

"Shut up, *wozauñouk!*"

A loud smack rang through the air as Stephania felt the palm of his hand collide with her jaw. Pain exploded through her face and down her neck. The gravel once more dug into her knees as she hit the ground. She could taste the blood in her mouth. Tears collected in her eyes.

"Dakar, please. Don't do this." Lycus' voice was quiet and uncertain. She could hear the anguish in his voice and instantly recognized the unease.

She heard Dakar wrestle himself from Lycus' restraint.

"Don't do what, Lycus? Hit her? Yell at her? Hate her?" He spat on the ground near her. "She knows what she did. This pain she feels now is nothing. She knows she deserves to rot in Susahu."

"I don't think—" Lycus' voice caught. "I don't think this is right." His pleas were barely audible and extremely fruitless.

Stephania watched her tears fall from her face and darken the gravel. *Dakar is right. I deserve Susahu.*

"Everyone thinks you're some kind of great hero, that you're their savoir. They bow before you, bend over for your every need, kiss the cursed ground you walk on." Dakar stepped in front of her, his hooves anxiously pawing the gravel.

She stared at his hooves but didn't lift her face any farther. The words stung. But he was right.

"You think you're some kind of chief's daughter? Or goddess? Huh? Someone who deserves everything served to you on a silver plate, right?"

"Dakar." Lycus tried to pull him away, but the black Centaur violently shoved him.

"Shut up, Lycus! Just *shut up!*"

Lycus backed away slowly, muttering something under his breath.

"Is that what you think?" Dakar kicked rocks at her, and she flinched.

No. I never wanted this.

"That everything should just be given to you without thought or consequence?" His breath was hot on her neck as he bent down, roaring in her ear. She recoiled but did nothing to move or push him away. "Even their very lives? Even Trojan's?"

She sobbed, clutching herself in her own cold embrace. "No."

"Shut up!" Dakar dug his fingers into her shoulders and wrenched her small body to her feet. She was slack in his hold but weightless to his strength. "You have no right to those tears. Whatever did you do to earn them? Who fought by Trojan's side in countless battles? Who endured the whip of the commander in training by his side? Who saved his life time after time after time? Huh? Who helped him up when he was at his lowest?"

She shook her head, her eyes blinded with tears. *I know. It was never me. I never deserved his love. I was nothing. Nothing.*

"Look at me, *wozauñouk*," he hissed vehemently. "Look at me!"

She forced her eyes to meet his violent gaze. Her heart raced with fear.

"I did, Stephania." Her name sounded like death on his tongue. "And what did you ever do?" His face was inches from hers, his voice unnervingly quiet.

She wanted to look away, to hide, to cower, but she forced herself to stare back, to feel every bit of this pain. *I deserve this,* she whispered to herself. *This is my punishment.*

"You went and got him killed. *Killed*, Stephania." He spat on her face. "Do you even understand that? Trans-Falls's next leader, a Synoliki warrior, the military's commander, *Fomdaazh* is dead!" His nails dug into her flesh, but she resisted the urge to cry out.

"I know." She could barely hear her own voice through her tears. "I'm sorry."

Dakar roared in anger and threw her to the ground.

Her head struck a rock, and her vision blackened. Something collided with her stomach, and a memory of lying in a road as Jackson stood over her degrading her and beating her flashed through her mind. It was happening again.

She groaned, tucking her legs to her chest, pain shooting through her body, throbbing in her mind. She felt Dakar standing over her, though for a moment, she couldn't tell if it was really him or the memory of Jackson that held her mind. He lifted his leg to kick her again. She could've moved, could've fought back, but she didn't. His strong hoof collided with her leg. She held back her cry and instead bit her lip, blood trickling down her chin. She couldn't feel her leg now, but she really wished she couldn't feel her soul.

Faintly, she sensed Lycus standing a few feet away. She perceived his confusion and horror, but she felt something else as well—something that prevented him from stopping his friend.

"You called yourself his sister, his family." Tears swirled with the anger in Dakar's burning eyes. "You know nothing of love, or of his sacrifice. *Nothing.* You are not fit to call him a brother. You are not worthy to call yourself one of his family. You are *nothing!*"

"I know," she whispered again. "I know. I can't live with his sacrifice. I can't live with this guilt."

"Then don't." In one fluid movement, he drew his sword and plunged it toward her.

She held her breath, waiting for the cold steel to blessedly end her suffering.

Instead, the clash of metal on metal rang through the woods.

"Dakar, stop this. This is wrong. Trojan wouldn't have wanted this. *You* don't want this."

She opened her eyes.

Lycus' sword was under Dakar's, blocking the would-be-fatal strike.

Dakar's ragged, uneven breath was obnoxiously loud in the aching silence as his eyes burned into Lycus'. For a moment, everything stood still.

Dakar looked down at Stephania.

She turned her face to his and waited.

Slowly, the fire died out of his eyes. He looked down at his sword, and his hands started shaking. With a cry of horror, he threw his weapon away and collapsed to his knees. His hands lay open in front of him. Tears spilled down his cheeks. "Stars, what have I done?" He covered his face and wept.

Stephania swallowed hard, hugging herself. She wasn't dead. She hated herself for it, but she was glad—glad she wasn't dead, glad she wasn't bleeding out slowly on the ground, glad the last thing she would see on Rasa wouldn't be Dakar's pain and fury.

"Stephania," he groaned. "How can you forgive me? I'm so sorry. I'm so sorry."

She felt her heart break again, and she wondered if it would ever stop breaking.

Hesitantly, she dragged herself over to the broken Centaur. Every bone and muscle in her body screamed in protest, but she forced herself forward. Cautiously, afraid his sudden humility was a trick, she wrapped her arms around him.

He stiffened under her arms, and she almost pulled away, but a strange cry parted his lips, and he sagged into her embrace.

"I'm sorry," she whispered again and again, knowing that even if she said it a hundred times, it could never be enough. She had stolen something precious from Dakar, and she knew she could never pay it back.

She glanced over to Lycus. His eyes were dark and dull. He stood turned away from them, his head hanging low. A quiet rage burned inside him. She knew he was bottling up his anger, trying to do the right thing, but it was rotting inside him. Her chest ached. She wanted to hug him too and tell him she was sorry, that it was going to be okay, but she knew the latter was a lie and he wouldn't accept the former.

Silently, she gave up on comforting and reconciling with Lycus, knowing she could do nothing to help him. How could she? She couldn't even help herself.

Finally, he walked away into the forest and left them.

"I'm sorry, Stephania." Dakar pulled away, his head still hung in shame. "I really wanted to kill you, to hurt you somehow the same way you hurt me."

At least he admits I killed Trojan. At least someone does.

"I thought—" He looked up but then quickly turned away. "I thought your death could atone for what you did, but ..." He shook his head. "It could never bring him back. And of course that's not what he would have wanted. I don't know why he loved you so much, Stephania. I really don't. You're childish, selfish, weak, impulsive, and stubborn. But he did. I have to accept that. He thought your life was worth his. I have to believe that it was."

She could only nod. Her whole body throbbed with dizzying pain. She could feel the bruising and swelling on her leg and stomach and could still taste the blood in her mouth, but none of it compared to how she felt inside.

"I—" She swallowed, trying to find the words. "I wanted you to. To kill me." Her voice shook, but she forced herself to continue. "I wanted to die. I still do. I don't know how I can live with his blood on my hands." She looked at her pale palms, but all she saw was red. "I don't know how I will continue without him. I just wanted this pain to end."

He cursed under his breath, wiping away his tears, struggling to regain his usual composure. He looked her in the eyes, searching her face. "I'm sorry, Stephania. For everything. I'm sorry."

She looked away, unable to bear seeing the peace and compassion in his eyes. "I am too, Dakar. I am too."

CHAPTER 25

STEPHANIA DRAGGED HER FEET across the gravelly road, aiming a kick at a rock. She watched the pebble tumble and turn as it flew through the air ahead of her before bouncing on the ground and coming to a rest. Her hands in the pockets of her black traveler's cloak, she shuffled up to the rock and kicked it again.

Stephania's foot stubbed against something misshapen. She looked down. The tip of her boot rested on what was left of the hilt from an intricately carved wooden sword—a child's toy. The rest, from the tip of the blade to the hilt, was nothing more than a thin rail of burnt wood. Slowly, cautiously, she bent down, her fingers hesitating just over the hilt of the sword. It was nearly three weeks since the attack, but the Centaurs had yet to fully piece back what was left of their homes and lives. A toy, burnt on the ground, was just another piece of that past life, left to be kicked, trodden upon, forgotten.

A lump rose in her throat as she gingerly picked up the hilt, but no tears gathered in her eyes. The blade broke away and shattered against the rocky road. With a heavy heart, she studied the hilt and the masterful designs of the carvings upon it. Not many children were able to have such a splendid training weapon. Perhaps it had been the child of a carver who had been given this small blade. Perhaps it had been a gift from a loving parent to an adored child.

It had been carved like the trunk of a tree. The roots knotted together at the base of the hilt and twirled around a very detailed carving of a stone moon. The trunk of the tree extended from there, the twists and turns offering a surprisingly comfortable grip, before turning into two mighty branches at the hilt. The rest of the little branches had been fashioned to look as if they were climbing up the makeshift blade, hugging it, holding it to the hilt. But there it ended, broken off where the fire had eaten its fill. Just at the base of the hideous demarcation was a stain. She peered closer.

With a startled gasp, she flung the toy from herself, her heart racing, her ears ringing.

Blood.

She felt a presence behind her before hearing hooves snap a twig and crush the leaves.

She didn't need to turn around to know it was Artigal. She could've been angry with his appearance. He hadn't said a word to her since Trojan's funeral, and she knew it was awkward for both of them to be together since she seemed to be the only creature besides Jargon, and possibly Aeron, who knew of his drastic change. But in this moment, when the air was too quiet and the grief too heavy, she could find no other emotions than those of darkness and despair.

"Stephania?"

She didn't answer. *Silence.* It had become her friend, her constant companion since Trojan's death. Usually, if she was just silent, the tears didn't come, the pain remained locked away, her soul could rest in numbness, and people would just give up and stop pestering her.

"May I walk with you." It was more demand than question.

She muttered something vile under her breath. He ignored it.

"You have something you want to ask me about."

She almost stopped walking. *Do I? How would he know?* She tried to remember.

The wind blew again.

Crunch. Crunch. She liked the sound of the dead leaves. Something about seeing them fall to the ground and lie waiting to be trampled underfoot reminded her so much of herself.

What had she wanted to ask him? She looked up at the trees, squinting against the beams of sunlight. *Oh.* She frowned. Now she remembered. *I wanted to ask him: why did all of this have to happen? Why did I have to leave for New-Fars in the first place? Why did my parents have to die? Why did the Centaurs have to adopt me? Why did my memories have to be taken away? Why did the people of New-Fars have to hate me? Why did we have to leave for the Dragon Palace? Why did I have to get my memories back? Why have we all had to suffer this pain? Why must I follow this destiny?* She clenched her fists. *Yes. I wanted to ask him,* "Why?"

But now ... Her hands relaxed at her sides again. Did it really matter? Why did she have to continue on this path? What was the point? It was supposed to save Ventronovia from suffering, and yet so much suffering had already been endured because of it. *What does it even matter if Thaddeus takes over Ventronovia? What does it even matter if the Duvarharians are all wiped out? We aren't living anyway. Not really.*

She didn't realize how long she had been quiet until she saw how far they had traveled down the road. She stopped walking.

He stopped by her side. She glanced at him.

The white magic around his body wavered, faltered once, then fell away, revealing the oddly average brown Centaur underneath. An unnerved shiver ran down her spine.

He narrowed his eyes as if expecting her to comment on his appearance. When she didn't, he relented. "Did you forget your questions? Or have you remembered?"

"Both and neither." She turned her attention back to the road.

"Ask me."

She shook her head but asked anyway. "Why did you give me a family if you knew I would never be able to stay with them? That death would take them from me?"

It was a long time before he answered. "We cannot experience a love and joy deeper than family. I wanted you to understand that."

She clenched her fists. "And yet it brought only sorrow."

"Love often does."

The wind blew, and she shivered. "Why?" she whispered and then added, "Why did any of this ever have to happen?"

He looked to the leaves above them. A bloodred leaf landed on his face and trailed off. She thought it looked uncannily like he was bleeding. She wondered how much protection the magic that had made him white had given him and how vulnerable he was now that it was gone. She watched the leaf fall to the ground, lost in the sea of color.

"Because of the prophecy." He paused. "The Dragon Prophecy."

A sour taste filled her mouth. *Yes, of course. The Prophecy.* She sneered. "This Dragon Prophecy. My whole life has been dictated by it, ruined by it, and I still do not know its words." She did nothing to hide the bitter contempt in her voice.

With a moment's hesitation, Artigal took a deep breath, then spoke the words she had waited so long to hear.

"Dragon folk now heed the call, from the wars of man's great fall.
In your days of sloth and peace, the hands of death shall find release.
But up from you, there shall rise, a keeper from this fear and demise.
Features pale with dark blood hair, eyes of red beyond compare.
Guide this girl, whether to or fro, she must come to the Stone Plateau.
Raise her up, to love not hate, never straying from her fate.
And to this girl, marked with my hand, a helper too, both fierce and grand.
Beware her helper, though young and wise, will need be steered from lust of prize.
Soon hard years, from death you cannot run, for a traitor from your ranks will come.
A young boy, Quinlan's own dear son, will bend to evil and then be won.

Listen, riders, that all may know, all this could be avoided so.

Turn back, my children, back to me. I'll set you from the Dark Lord free.

But if my voice, you do not heed, my urgent warning, I now plead.

Then know that I will then set forth, destruction, terrible, from the North.

And if you turn away from me, know this quite for certainty: no rider will retell your lives, no help for you shall then arise.

So, Quinlan, stand, the Stone Plateau, for in five years the moon will throw, the fate for all, written in stone, knowledge to learn and skills to hone. Follow its riddles, follow to know, what the future then may show.

Go to your leaders, speak of this hope, to fight the evil and to cope.

Remind the people to seek me out, with a whisper or a shout.

For I, your Lord, am never far, and know each one for who they are."

She listened to his voice and the words he spoke. She felt the weight of the message settle on her shoulders. She tried to shrug it off, but the words haunted her.

"That is the prophecy given to Quinlan nearly nine hundred years ago by the Great Lord of Duvarharia Himself."

She spoke before she thought. "Dalton said he doesn't believe in the Great Lord. He said He isn't real."

Artigal stomped his hoof and even without the imposing aura the Pure Magic had always given him, his rage still sparked a flare of respect and fear in her.

"Then he is a fool."

Silence reigned for a few minutes as they continued to walk. She watched in mild fascination as Artigal muttered a few Centaur words under his breath and the faux white magic covered his body, making his skin and hair look almost as snow white as they used to. Not long after, they passed two female Centaurs who bowed reverently as their Igentis and Farloon passed.

Stephania wanted to run at them, screaming, raging, and demanding they stop bowing to her, but instead, she remained silent and ignored them, burying those raw emotions deep within her. Dakar's words about how everyone worshiped the ground she walked on echoed in her mind. He was right, and she was sick of it. She was no different than them, no more special or worthy. She didn't want any of this. She wanted a world where she could walk among people, not above them or in the shadows. She wanted to throw this stupid prophecy away and determine her own fate—a fate where people didn't have to die for her to take on the safety of the world.

As soon as the two Centaurs were out of sight, the magic around Artigal disappeared, and once more he became almost unrecognizable.

"Child, I know these last few weeks have been hard on you, but you must continue—"

She couldn't stop the mocking laughter that bubbled up in her. "Hard on me?" she seethed. "You have no idea what I've gone through, Artigal. Don't pretend like you care."

She could hear his teeth grinding against each other as he stopped walking. His voice was quiet with anger and hurt and sent shivers down her spine. "Do not speak of things you do not understand, Stephania. I have loved and hurt more than you will ever know. If anyone knows what you are going through, it would be me." His head hung low, and she could feel his anger and agony seething from him. She had never felt such strong emotions from him before, and she took a step back. "Do not ever let me hear you speak of what you think I don't understand. And don't ever assume you know me. You know *nothing* about me, Stephania. No one does, and no one will." His golden eyes bored into hers.

She winced at his words and felt heat rushing into her face. She instantly regretted saying it. He was right. As she thought about this Centaur standing before her, once imbued with a magic powerful enough to keep him pure white and young for thousands of years, now an old, wrinkled brown Centaur with greying hairs and a limp, she realized she knew nothing about how he had come about that magic in the first place or who he had been before it.

She thought she was looking at Igentis Artigal, but when she looked into his eyes, she wondered if this was a different Centaur, someone he had been before the Pure Magic. How many lives had he lived? How many loved ones had he watched die through the centuries? Had he ever been mated, had children? Had there been a time when he was ... normal? When he hadn't the weight of all the Centaurs on his shoulders? Had he laughed then? Or danced or sang?

No, she didn't know anything about him. Shame filled her. Again, she had been too selfish, too self-absorbed, to think about anyone else. She didn't apologize for her words, though. Instead, she stopped walking and turned to face him, pulling herself back together and banishing the guilt behind her mask of icy indifference.

"What must I continue, then, Artigal? This destiny that was thrust upon me?" She stepped toward him, and he glowered down at her with near disdain. "This life which I didn't chose but have been forced to live anyway? Should I continue this pain? This suffering?" Her stomach churned with emotion. Her throat constricted, and she could feel the tears collecting in her eyes. *No, do not be weak!* she screamed to herself, but her thoughts couldn't stop the tears from gathering. "Should I continue on this path that has only brought pain and death? What good will it do?"

His eye twitched, and his mouth contorted in a mix of emotion. "Because you have to defeat Thaddeus, Kyrell, and Veltrix. If you don't, think of the hundreds upon thousands of lives that would be lost. He has already wiped the creatures of Chioni off the face of Rasa. Do you want the same to happen to the Duvarharians? And then to us? Do you not care for this world and its inhabitants enough to make the sacrifices necessary to save the rest?" His eyes glared menacingly into hers, and she couldn't help but look away.

"What does it matter, though? Too many people have already died for it to be worth it. Too many people I *love* have already died."

"Think of all the families like your own that would be killed. Would you wish the suffering you have endured on someone else?"

She bit her lip and balled her fists before whispering almost inaudibly, "Yes."

His eyes narrowed. "What?"

"Yes!" She met his hardened gaze, her own eyes blazing. "Why should I care if they suffer? Life is hard. Life is ruthless. We are all dealt something in life. Mine has been nothing but pain. Why shouldn't someone else's be as well?" The tears spilled quickly and silently down her cheeks.

"And you would not save them when they could be saved?"

"No! Let someone else be their savior!" She gestured wildly. "Why me? Why is it always me, me, me? Why in Susahu do I have to do this? What makes me so special? Why is it my family, the people I love, the ones who have to suffer so much? Why don't the Duvarharians save themselves? What have they been doing these past hundred years? Sitting around drinking *muluk* and *uafañoshigo,* waiting on me to do their dirty work of salvation? Better yet, if you're so keen on Thaddeus's destruction, why don't you kill him yourself?"

"Enough!" Artigal's voice shook with more than rage as his eyes shockingly brimmed with tears. "Do you think I have spent my whole life fiddling my thumbs and standing back to watch people die? Do you think that just because I am thousands of years old that I no longer feel? Do you have any idea what it's like to live on after everyone you know and love is dead, just because your destined purpose has not been fulfilled yet? Do you think I haven't done everything in my power to kill that traitor and wipe his memory from Rasa? Why do you think I look like this?" He gestured to his dark wound and lack of magic; she blanched.

"For nearly sixteen years this wound of *Kijaqumok* has fought against the *Shushequmok* inside me. It constantly drains my energy and magic, spreads when I have even the slightest of negative thoughts, and feeds off the things I fear. I have suffered to use the Pure Magic to protect my people, to protect you. And Thaddeus is the only one responsible." The tears rolled down his face.

Her vision blurred, and she realized she was crying too. She had never seen him come so undone before. It unnerved her, rocked her very core. Now she knew why he couldn't let anyone see he had lost his power. Everyone had placed all their confidence in him, and now he couldn't protect them.

"This is not my age, Stephania. It is not my fight. I destroyed the evil I was presented with thousands of years ago. You want others to feel your pain, Stephania? You want others to share in your suffering? They *have*. I sacrificed everything I loved when I had to fight to save my people. I gave up *everything*. My home, my family, my mate, my own adopted child. But I had to because I was chosen. I was the only one who could do what needed to be done."

She shook her head. She didn't want to hear about him. She didn't want to know others had suffered like her. She didn't want to know what he had gone through. She didn't want him to feel the same grief and despair she felt. She didn't want to be just one more hurting person in a sea of pain. She didn't want him to understand her, because then she would be the selfish child she knew she was and hated to be. Most of all, she didn't want to think the pain of losing everything she loved would extend for thousands of years, never growing less.

"I can't defeat Thaddeus. Only you can because you have been chosen. No one else is able to no matter how hard they try or what they sacrifice. You are the key, and Thaddeus is the lock. Everything that has happened in your life, all your love and loss, experiences or lack thereof, has prepared, sculpted, *created* you to be the only one. It doesn't matter how many people lay down their lives, only you can stop this!"

She sobbed through her tears. "I was chosen by who? Some Lord or god who has done nothing but curse my existence. I don't even know who he is! Why should I trust him? Why should I follow whatever destiny He has chosen for me?"

"Because He is *kuur*!"

"I don't even know what the *yeazh* that means!"

Disgust at her use of the extremely vulgar Centaur word crossed his face, but she ignored it.

I don't care about anything anymore. But deep down she knew that was wrong. In truth, she cared far too much.

He breathed deeply, the air hissing through his lips. "Thaddeus, Kyrell, and Veltrix killed your parents, Stephania." His voice was low and shaky. "They forced you from your first home. They forced you from your second. Then they forced you from your third. Would you let them get away with the destruction of your life? They took everything from you. Everything. You would really let them walk away when of all those in Ventronovia, you alone have the power to stop them? To set things right?"

Her hands balled into fists. A spark of rage took flame inside her, but she tried to put it out. Hadn't it been better when she had not felt at all? But he was right. She clenched her jaw. *The Etas, Thaddeus, the Corrupt Magic, they've taken everything from me. It doesn't matter why, whether I am Duvarharian, daughter of a lord and lady, savior of the prophecy or not, they had no right to take what was mine. They had no right to destroy my parents or Trojan.*

"They ransacked your life, took it from you, stole it from you. *They* killed Trojan, not you."

Her heart pounded in her chest. Her ears rang. She bit her lip. The world went quiet around her.

Her mind was finally clear. Why had she not seen it before? If the Etas had never attacked Trans-Falls, Trojan would be alive. If it weren't for Thaddeus, she would be living in Duvarharia with her family without a care in the world. If it weren't for all of them, she would be safe and happy. Even if Thaddeus had used her memories against her, even if he would continue to do so, Artigal was right. If the prophecy was correct, then she had been given the power to stop him. She could stop the nightmares, stop the memories they shared, stop the death, and avenge those who had died. A coldness swept away the indifference within her and fueled the flame.

Even if all of Ventronovia should fall and burn, those she loved would be avenged— she would have her revenge. She met his gaze, a new fire burning in her eyes.

Artigal clenched his jaw. "Do you not want to at least take back what is rightfully yours? Don't you want to finish this fight?"

A bright flame danced across her palm. *Yes.* She had made up her mind. She closed her fist, and the fire disappeared from her hand. Scorn radiated off her. What had once been depression and despair now molded into determination in the flames of hate.

"Yes. I will exact my revenge. Thaddeus and his followers will burn in Susahu. I know what I must do now. I do not do this for you, for Ventronovia, the Prophecy, or for the Great Lord. I do this for myself, my parents, and above all, for Trojan. I will see their efforts rewarded, their sacrifices acknowledged, and their deaths avenged." Without a second glance back to Artigal, she spun on her heels and stalked away.

§

THE AIR FELT DARKER in the forest, and a feeling of discomfort passed through Artigal. When Stephania had disappeared down the road, he shivered, though not from the autumn breeze. A sense of defeat exasperated the discomfort. He had come to convince her to follow her fate, hoping to inspire her. But what had he done? He'd dug up his past, and vented his own anger and pain. It had been so easy to ignore his emotions and memories when the Pure Magic had protected him, but with it gone, he had become raw and undone. It was harder and harder to leave his past behind him along with all the regret and pain he had tried to hide with it. And he had dumped it all on her. To what end? He had only fueled her hate, not inspired her to do good. He had only further opened the gateway of evil within her.

He bowed his head and held his arms around himself, trying to ignore the ugly brown his hair now was, a color that brought back the memories and pain. Would nothing he do ever be blessed? Would everything he attempted for good always bring about a greater evil?

The words of the prophecy loudly repeated themselves in his mind. Dread gripped him in its icy claw.

"Raise her up to love, not hate, never straying from her fate." More unwelcome tears brimmed in his eyes. He tried not to think of the last time he had been so weak to sorrow. This was all wrong, so wrong. This wasn't how it was supposed to happen. He had only made it all worse. In forcing her destiny upon her, he had cursed her fate. Bile rose in his throat, and his head spun.

What have I done, Emperor? He turned his face to the skies, holding back his cries of desperation as he asked the same question Stephania had asked him.

"Why?"

Why? Why do you leave me on this planet? What good am I for? You have stripped me of my magic, my power, my control. I have fulfilled my purpose, and yet you leave me to linger on this dying world, only to create more pain. Please take me home, please, please, please let me finally die and let there finally be an end to all the suffering I have caused.

The wind blew, and the leaves fell around him.

He received no answer.

§

THRUST, PARRY, SPIN, BLOCK. Again and again and again.

The forest swallowed the dull sounds of metal against straw and fabric. Sweat poured down Stephania's face, and she grunted with exertion. Her arms burned. Her legs throbbed. The dark blue of her shirt was black with sweat.

"Stephania?"

At first the whisper was too quiet to pay any attention to. The forest had called her

255

many times, and she had ignored it. Why answer now? She cut the dummy with her blade again and again, not bothering to turn around.

"Stephania?" The voice was closer now and too loud to ignore.

Her shoulders sagged as she recognized it. *Lamora.*

The tip of her sword dragged through the soft forest floor as she turned around. Her eyes remained glued to the composting leaves under her feet. Two hooves danced nervously back and forth in front of her.

"Stephania, please stop this."

Her teeth ground against themselves, and her eyes darkened. "Stop what?" Her gaze rose to meet her friend's.

Lamora's usually bright eyes were sparkling with tears and clouded with worry and gloom. Her mouth was turned down at the corners, and her hands were clasped firmly in front of her until they pushed her long hair behind her pointed ears. "All of ... this." She gestured lamely around them, and Stephania's gaze darted to the forest.

Everywhere, makeshift targets hung from the trees, some littered with arrows, others chopped to pieces. An extra dummy lay strung out across the ground, its stuffing of straw and leaves scattered about itself. Stephania had made and ruined them all. It had been too hard to train under the peering eyes of the Centaurs, and she had needed somewhere she felt safe to train. It was always better on her own.

Annoyance wormed into her heart. "No." She turned her attention back to Lamora, her voice stale.

Lamora crossed her arms. "This is all you do anymore. It's not healthy, Stephania. Dalton says you only talk to him if you want to know more about Duvarharia, or the Etas, or something of the sorts. Your parents say you barely talk at dinner, and you've hardly spent any time with Ravillian and I."

Silence hung in the air. Stephania couldn't bear to look into her friend's eyes.

"We miss you. We all do."

Tears stung the back of her throat. She missed them too. Gods of all, she missed them. But mostly, she missed the way it had been just before ... just before ... she clenched her fist. Those days were gone now. She could never get them back. Time had slipped through her hands, and she couldn't scoop it back up.

"I'm sorry, Lamora. I really am. But I can't stop this. Can't you see? This is all I have left. I have to do this." She waved about herself, forcing herself to look anywhere but at her friend.

"That's just the thing, Stephania. This *isn't* all you have left! You have me, and Ravillian, and Dalton, and your parents, and Jargon, and even Artigal. You have Trans-Falls, and soon you will have Duvarharia. You may have lost so much, but you still have the world in your hands."

Stephania couldn't stop the tears that spilled down her cheeks. She scrubbed them away, cursing their existence. "I know," she said but then again even softer, "I know. But it was too much, Lamora. It was still too much for anyone to have to lose."

Lamora stepped closer, hesitant, waiting for Stephania to push her away, but she stood still. Slowly, gently, Lamora's arms snaked around Stephania and pulled her close.

She could smell the faint musk of horse mingled with cinnamon and rose, the familiar scent of her friend, and she closed her eyes, letting herself feel the warmth from the embrace. If only they could stay like this forever. If only time wouldn't move.

"You know what your problem is?" Lamora's voice was quiet, as if she were afraid it would scare Stephania away.

She shook her head when it became obvious Lamora wouldn't continue until she answered.

"You have a heart bigger than Rasa itself. You care more about others than anyone I know, more than I think you even know. That's all."

Stephania laughed, just once, before it turned into a strangled sob. Perhaps Lamora was trying to cheer her by assuring her she was still good, that her heart was still wholesome and pure, that she wasn't selfish. But she could feel the love her heart held, and it was rotting inside her. It wasn't a blessing, it wasn't a virtue, it was a curse. She loved too much, and everything she loved died. "I know. I know. I just—I can't—" She choked on her words, pausing for a moment. Lamora waited quietly.

She took a deep breath. "I can't bear to see people anymore, Lamora." The tears flowed fast and silent. "Every time I see them smile, or talk, or look into their eyes, I see those hideous *things* coming at me; only they weren't things. They were the people of New-Fars, corrupted with magic, people I knew and grew up with. When I close my eyes, they're there, marching toward me, looking so innocent but with blood between their lips. I—it's so awful." She sobbed, throwing her arms around her friend.

"I'm sorry. I'm sorry. I'm sorry," Lamora whispered. But as much as she knew Lamora meant those words, it would never be enough to heal the damage she was left with.

"I can't bear it. I can't. I can't bear to see everyone start to move on when I feel like I'm falling backward. All I can think of is Trojan's still, glazed eyes staring up at me. And the *weight*. Gods of all, the *weight*, Lamora. He was so heavy when he leaned onto me, when he could hardly hold himself up any longer. So, *so* heavy."

She tried to push the memory from her mind, but she couldn't. She could feel his weight in her arms, she could feel it now. It was crushing her, destroying her, pushing her deeper and deeper into the eternal darkness. And her last words, the last words she had said to him: *"I don't know if I can."* She wanted to take them back. She wished she had said: *"I promise I will be. I promise I can be strong enough."* She wished she could've meant it. Most of all, she wished she could've heard what he had wanted to say.

She felt Lamora's tears on her neck, and it brought her back to reality. "Don't you see?" Stephania pulled away, turning her tearstained face up to her friend. She saw something like the beginning of understanding in Lamora's eyes. "I can't let them get away with this. They've crushed everything, taken everything away, and I want to take it back." Abruptly, she shoved Lamora away and turned, her own arms encircling herself. Once more, she avoided her friend's gaze, and the locks around her heart clicked shut.

"That's why I can't stop this. This is my life now. Nothing else matters."

"Nothing?"

Stephania's heart lurched at the desolate tone in her friend's voice. It stabbed like a cold knife. *Was she really a friend? What did it mean to be a friend? Wouldn't friends understand me better? Wouldn't she see what I'm going through and understand what I must do?* She swallowed her emotions. She had to be strong to do what needed to be done. "Nothing."

A strange sob echoed from Lamora's lips, but Stephania forced herself to not look up. She knew if she did, she would be lost. *Or, perhaps, I am lost now. I don't know anymore. I don't want to know. It's better living in the dark.*

Soft hoofbeats on the leaves started, then stopped.

"Stephania." Lamora waited for answer. She sighed when she received none. "Revenge is not worth it. I know it seems like the only way out, but it's not. There are so many people who love you, who need you, Stephania. One day, you will sate your lust for blood, and you will realize that was not what you thirsted after. Remember that."

Without another word, or even a pause for answer, Lamora disappeared down the shrouded path. When the last of her hoofbeats could no longer be heard, Stephania collapsed to her knees and screamed into the wind, crying until the birds had all flown away and her eyes felt like sandpaper.

Maybe Lamora is right, and I am wrong. But now I have gone too far. Too far. And I cannot turn back.

The last rays of the suns were just disappearing behind the tops of the trees. Dark shadows lay cast all around her, and she tried not to let them remind her of the Corrupt Magic. She clenched her fist in front of her and closed her eyes. *I did the right thing. Didn't I?* Somewhere in her heart, in the emptiness that suddenly arose, she disagreed.

Dragging herself to her feet, she shouldered her bow and quiver, sliding her sword into its tattered sheath. The sword was nearly as worn as its scabbard, and she knew she would need a new one soon. It was the fourth sword she had destroyed in just two weeks. No sword could withstand the strength of a Duvarharian, she knew, and though she should have been proud of her own strength, she was only bitter—bitter of another reminder she didn't belong here.

Artigal's voice echoed mockingly again, as it did more often than she wished. *"This isn't your home anymore."* Blood trickled down her lip as she bit it. *If this isn't my home and neither was New-Fars, and Duvarharia has been taken away from me, then where do I belong? Where can I go home?*

After walking blindly down the darkening path, she found herself standing in front of the peaceful cabin she had once called home. Apprehension filled her as she stared up the steps. Inside, her family would be waiting. They would want to know how her day went, where she had been, how she was feeling. They would try to cheer her up. Frawnden would have made one of her favorite foods, and Aeron, though he wasn't good at humor, would have thought up another horrible joke. Dalton would be waiting to share his progress with re-recording the old legends he had lost when his house had burned, or something else he had brought back from Trans-Falls's library. They would all want her to smile, to talk, to laugh, to forget, to move on. As she always did, she would only disappoint them, and she hated that.

Maybe she could just quickly slip into the night and sleep under the stars. A brisk autumn breeze rustled her hair, and she shivered, goose bumps rising on her bare arms. The promise of a roaring fire and thick fur blankets instead of cold, wet leaves and the possibility of the frost kept her feet rooted to the bottom of the stairs, along with the inevitable looming darkness of nightfall. She could never tell anymore whether the darkness was just a shadow cast by the moons or if it was the Corrupt Magic trying to steal her from herself.

To stay or to go? *Why is every little decision so hard to make anymore? When did I lose my confidence?* A lump rose in her throat.

Voices rose inside the house from a cracked open window. Without realizing it, she crept closer, stepping up the stairs just enough to hear well and peer inside, but not enough to be seen.

Dalton, Aeron, and Frawnden were all in the living room. Sure enough, a fire had been built in the stove and was crackling happily, oblivious to the dismal air in the room.

"I just don't know what to do." Dalton's breath shuddered though his voice remained steady.

Stephania stood on her toes to see in better. Dalton was holding his head in his hands. Frawnden was standing next to him, her hand on his shoulder, tears sparkling in her eyes. Aeron stood in front of the fire, staring blankly into the flames, his tail swishing back and forth.

"Why don't you just talk to her?" Frawnden's voice cracked.

Dalton scoffed and hissed under his breath. "Why don't you?"

She frowned but didn't answer.

He sighed. "I don't know how. A few years ago, she started building these barriers against me. She stopped confiding in me and began smiling a lot more. It was clearly forced. I knew she believed if she hid her feelings from me, she wouldn't be a burden, but no matter how much I tried to convey the exact opposite to her, she only hid it more."

A sharp breath stung Stephania's lungs. *So he really had noticed from the very start.* Her stomach rolled. She had never truly fooled him with her charades as she had thought. A flush of embarrassment decorated her cheeks.

"I don't want to overstep her boundaries. I don't want to make her uncomfortable, or cause her to feel like she's forced to talk to me. The last thing I want is for her to hold something else against me."

"Oh, I don't think she holds anything against you, Dalton. I think you're being too hard on yourself." Frawnden sounded so sure, so confident, but Dalton only laughed bitterly.

"I'm afraid you don't know her like I do, then. I have been at the center of all her pains, whether they were my own doing or not. I am there like the track of an animal, or clouds before a storm."

The silence grew uncomfortable.

I don't hold anything against him ... or do I? Stephania pulled on the edges of her cloak, her teeth grinding against each other. The little lies that built her childhood, the fire consuming their home, how long it had taken him to reach her when she ran back to Trans-Falls—perhaps she held more against him than she knew. Petty, childish things they were, but they poisoned her heart nonetheless.

"She needs time to heal." Aeron's deep voice broke the painful silence. He turned away from the fire, his arms crossed on his bare chest. "She hasn't had a moment to grieve since Trojan's death. She had just gotten him back before the Emperor took him away. She hasn't had time to process that."

A scowl crossed Dalton's face. "No, she's had plenty of time to grieve. It's been almost three weeks. She spends all her time alone. Ravillian and Lamora come, asking for her, and she slips out the mountain tunnels to avoid them. I'm her guardian, and I barely see her more than just at dinner time. You're her legal parents, and she hardly talks to you. Don't you think it's time for her to come back?"

She stifled the cry that rose to her lips. Though the anger was plain in Dalton's voice, Stephania could sense the overwhelming hurt radiating from him. They had missed her more than she knew. Perhaps, she had thought with Trojan gone, they wouldn't miss her if she simply left as well.

Aeron's tail swished sharply. "No, that is not grieving. That is burying her hurt in search of the fleeting comfort gained in physical pleasures."

"I hardly consider continuous training pleasure."

Aeron shrugged. "Each finds pleasure in different things. Some find it in love from others, some find it in hate. And sometimes, it's difficult to tell the difference." He turned to the window, his piercing gaze stabbing out into the dark.

Stephania covered her mouth and ducked under the windowsill, her heart pounding in her chest. *Did he see me? Does he know I'm listening?* Her hand pressed against her chest, willing her racing heart to stand still. Tears stung the back of her throat, but she shoved them down, only breathing a sigh of relief when Aeron didn't come outside.

What is truth? Dalton was right, but so was Aeron, and even so was Frawnden. She wanted Dalton to talk to her, but she also wanted space. She didn't feel like she had fully grieved, but she didn't know what grief looked like; she didn't know if she wanted to find out.

On her tiptoes again, she peered back into the home.

"You pushed her too soon to heal after the funeral. She should have stayed with her grief instead of forcing herself into the brightness." Though Aeron's voice was low and steady, Stephania could easily hear the undertone of resentment.

"Oh, so I should have let her sit at home, alone, wallowing in depression, lying to her everything's going to be okay? She needed to be with her friends, her family—the people who love her. What she *didn't* need was to think or feel like she was alone."

"Dalton, Aeron, please let's not argue." Frawnden had stood up between then.

Aeron shook his head, his hands balled into fists. "There is a time for joy, and there is a time for sorrow. Stephania was not alone. She has the Great Emperor."

Dalton barked a mocking laugh. "The Great Emperor! As if there is such a thing. How could she be comforted by a legend, by some distant god? She doesn't need some remote deity, she needs what she can see and touch."

"She could see and touch Him if you would let her open her eyes and extend her hands." Aeron's voice was cold. Stephania shivered. She had never heard him so upset. She wanted to tell Dalton to let it go, but she wasn't inside. She was out here, removed, like she always was. The tears stinging her throat welled up in her eyes. Again, she was intruding upon something in which she didn't belong. Again, she was only causing more pain.

EFFIE JOE STOCK

"Let her open her eyes? Do you accuse me of deceiving her? I have taught her nothing but truth."

"Perhaps it is not the right truth."

"Stop this! Your bickering does nothing for Stephania, and it will continue to do nothing." Frawnden was pushing against her mate, but he wouldn't move.

Stephania bit her lip and let herself slide down the splintered wall. The sharp edge of the steps dug into her thigh, but she didn't move. A cry of horror caught in her throat. *Why are they arguing? Why must they do this?* Her fists were clenched tight as she hugged her knees to her chest. *Please stop. Please stop.*

"Our differences have done nothing to help her either. I can't imagine how confusing it must be to have three parents."

"Confusing indeed. And more confusing as to whether or not to trust fact or myth!"

Stephania clapped her hands over her ears, but she couldn't drown out the yelling. It pounded against her as if driving a stake deeper and deeper into her heart. She could hear Frawnden weeping as she pleaded quietly with the males to stop.

"The Emperor is not myth." Aeron's voice was seething. "Just because your sorrow and anger at Andromeda's choices and faith fueled your hate against the Emperor, doesn't make our beliefs any less true."

Frawnden gasped at her mate's accusation. "Aeron, that's enough—"

"How dare you bring Andromeda into this." Dalton's voice, which had earlier risen loud in anger, dropped to a low, dangerous whisper. Stephania's blood ran cold. What did her mother have to do with this?

"But it's true, is it not? Your unforgivable actions against the Dragon Palace were because of Andromeda, even though they were crimes against even her."

Dalton laughed chillingly. "Perhaps. Looking back, perhaps they were. And yet, even after all that, she was bringing her daughter to me. Not to the Centaurs, but to *me*. I am Stephania's rightful guardian, not you."

No. No. No. This is all wrong. Horrible, aching dread settled into Stephania. They were fighting because of her. If it weren't for her, they wouldn't have a reason to argue. She created distention in everyone she met, in everyone who loved her.

"You know what your problem is?" Lamora's voice from only hours earlier rang through her mind again. *"You have a heart bigger than Rasa itself. You care more about others than anyone I know, more than I think you even know. That's all."* Lamora was right. Even despite her selfishness, she cared far too much about others, far more than she had any right to. Even now, because she loved Trojan too much, her parents were quarrelling, unable to mend the problem of her grief and over-caring heart. She had to make them stop arguing, but she knew the only way to do that would be to break them

262

apart.

Their relationships had been complicated since she and Dalton had arrived in Trans-Falls, and though they had formed close friendships in an effort to create a family atmosphere, it was now painfully clear they couldn't all be together anymore. Her inconsolable grief was driving them apart. A cry, muffled behind her hand, left her lips when she realized what she had to do.

If only she could find the courage.

Her hands found the ledge of the next step above, and she pushed up onto it, her body feeling like lead. *Just one step at a time,* she miserably told herself as she climbed up the steps. *Just one.* She was level with the windows now, but she hardly had the energy to worry about being seen.

"You may be her rightful guardian, but we are her legal parents. She is our daughter, not yours."

"Aeron, Dalton, by the Great Emperor, stop this!" Frawnden's voice had reached a frenzied pitch, but her plea was lost.

"By theft!" Dalton smashed his fist against the tabletop. "You stole the right of parenthood from me. I was, by Duvarharian rights, her legal guardian, her father in the case of her parents' death, but you and your precious Igentis stole that right from me. It was never yours to take, but take it you did. And for what worth? She was always destined to leave you anyway. It was only ever doomed to end in heartbreak, so why? Why did the oh so mighty Artigal think it best to resign a child to a false family, only to tear her away from it along with her memories? Do you call that love?"

Frawnden had no answer. She only sagged against the couch, her face buried in her hands, her sobs echoing in the room.

Aeron stepped closer to Dalton, their faces only a foot apart. "Yes. I do. Artigal understood she needed to learn love, to learn what it was like to have a family. He knew, because of her destiny, she would live a life of burdens and heartache. He knew she would lack joy and compassion, that she could never be comforted for she would be the comforter. It was mercy, what he did. He provided her a glimpse of what happiness could look like. He did what he saw best."

Just one more step. Stephania pulled herself up, tears streaming down her face. Their words pierced her like daggers. She didn't know who or what to believe anymore.

"Oh *suluj* her destiny and *suluj* Artigal. On what authority did you decide I would not be a good enough father or family for her; that I would not teach her love? What about her choice? Should she not be given an option of what her life will look like?"

Aeron scoffed. "On the authority of Duvarharia, the same authority that had you banished, and gave her this destiny. Your record would have been enough to take away your rights to Stephania's upbringing, despite Drox and Andromeda's wishes. You should be thankful we even gave her over to you in the end."

Banished. All energy drained from Stephania's limbs. *Banished.* The word repeated like the sound of an execution gong. *Dalton was banished from Duvarharia.* A wave of emotion she couldn't explain washed over her. *Why? Why? Why?*

"It's been nearly a hundred years since then. Do you think I haven't changed? Why else would they have been bringing their daughter to me?"

"I couldn't guess, Dalton," Aeron hissed quietly. "Perhaps it was because Andromeda hadn't let you go after all."

"How dare you defile her memory!"

"And how dare you disprove my rightful claim as Stephania's father! She is Centaur, blood or not, she is one of us. You cannot change that."

"But she is Duvarharian by blood and by soul, and *you* cannot change *that*. I spent more years raising her, caring for her, loving her, than you. I cried, and bled, and almost died for her. I gave *everything* for her. You were barely even present for the few years she was with your family. You were lost in the woods, if I recall. What claim do you have, then?"

The door flew open and smashed into the wall with a resounding crash.

Everyone froze. The room fell deathly silent.

"Enough!" Stephania stood in the doorway, tears streaked down her face, her eyes swollen and red, her nose running, her fists clenched tight.

Aeron and Dalton's faces went ashen. Frawnden looked up from her hands and muttered, "Great Emperor help us."

"Stephania—" Aeron started, but Dalton interrupted.

"I don't know how much you heard, but—"

"I heard enough." Her voice quavered; her hands shook at her side. She was angry, scared, horrified, desolate.

"Stephania, I'm sorry—" Dalton started.

She held up her hand. "Don't. We're leaving."

"What?" Frawnden's face drained of color as she stood on shaking legs.

Stephania had to take several deep breaths before she was able to push back the tears and speak. "Dalton and I are leaving for the Dragon Palace. Day after tomorrow."

"No." Frawnden covered her mouth, her eyes wide with horror.

Aeron's head and shoulders dropped with regret.

She could see how her words cut them, tore them apart, made them hurt and ache, but she pushed aside her pity. She was suffering too; she couldn't take on everyone else's pain. This was the right thing to do. She had to leave. Only then would those she love begin to live in peace again. It would be easier for them if she was gone—she and Dalton both.

"Stephania, wait. Please don't be rash. Perhaps there is something we could work out," Dalton pleaded.

"No," she whispered through her tears. Red curls fell into her face as she shook her head, but she didn't push them away. "No. There isn't another way. We have waited and lingered long enough. We must continue on. *I* must continue on."

Tearing her eyes from the stricken faces of her devastated family, she forced her gaze to the floor and dragged her feet across the living room and to the hall. Before she ducked into the long, dark walkway, she muttered once more under her breath, "Day after tomorrow."

She wasn't surprised when none of them followed her or called after her. She closed her bedroom door softly behind her and collapsed to her knees, letting her forehead drop to the floor.

It would be better after she left. She could have a new beginning. She would leave behind all she loved and with it her heart, if she could. With nothing to lose maybe she would be strong enough to stand before Thaddeus and do what she must.

A psychotic laugh bubbled up through her tears. *Oh, how ironic! To leave behind what you love just to fight for it back! Lamora may be right, and I may have the world in my hands, but even so, I have still lost too much, and now I have lost my family as well.*

She drew herself straight, her hands clutching her cloak tightly. Hot tears burning like fire streamed down her face. *I will not rest until I have bought it all back, bit by bit, by blood and tears, body and soul. On this I swear.*

CHAPTER 26

Unfinished Castle, East of the Cavos Desert

Present Day

HATE. THADDEUS SUCKED in a deep breath and smiled. How familiar Stephania's hate felt. It was like home. He opened his eyes and drew himself from his throne. His purple eyes blinked slowly at the groveling forms before him—two Duvarharians and an Eta King.

"I have filled her with hate. It burns brightly in her, brighter than her overwhelming love. She hates everything about me, everything I stand for, everything I have done. Our recent attack on Trans-Falls was a success."

Without trying, he could feel confusion radiating from the forms in front of him, and he laughed as Kyrell grumbled, *They are so stupid.*

Indeed. He took a few steps down the dais, his eyes piercing down on their bowed heads. "Ask your question, fools."

The Duvarharians muttered something, but it was the Eta King, Veltrix, who stood and asked what they were wondering. His voice shook, but he maintained some of his former glory as he tried to stare back at Thaddeus with his eight sparkling red eyes. "I thought we wanted her to convert to our side. Wouldn't her hating you be the opposite of that, *Mraha*? I don't think it was wise to corrupt the New-Fars village just to break her. I think it was foolish and only ruined what we have been trying so hard to achieve. Isn't this a step backwards?"

Thaddeus smirked, and Kyrell grumbled from somewhere in the dark, expansive hall. "So it would seem, which is exactly why it is so wonderfully perfect for what we want." He descended the platform and walked slowly around the quivering figures.

Wretches. They know nothing of this world, of the mind, or of magic. They are children. I loathe dealing with them.

It is necessary.

I suppose.

"You see, each of you want something. Veltrix, you want the Duvarharian's blood to feed your people. And you—" He turned to the Dragon Riders, bringing his face close between the two of them. They wouldn't look up. "Want power, revenge, or perhaps you're just tired of fighting, of losing, or merely surviving, and you are ready to live." His eyes burned into them as they quivered with fear. He stood, glaring down at them and began to pace again, his boots clicking on the polished black granite.

"But the one thing you all have in common is the simple-minded belief that there is good and evil in this world. That you are either all good or all evil, that someone is the good guy and someone is the villain. You have all been tricked into thinking you are villains because of your betrayal, but if you had lived as long as I have, you would understand a grain of sand is all that lies between being the hero or being the villain. You may think 'good' always wins, but that is because only victors write the stories."

Sparks encompassed Veltrix's body as he morphed into a humanoid creature with a long, reptilian tail and bat wings—something he did when he was thinking. The Duvarharians shifted their weight uncomfortably, but none dared interrupt.

"Stephania's hate for me will drive her over that line, and before she realizes it, she will have become the very thing I am. She wants something, just as we all do, and, eventually, just like you, she will stop letting the world tell her she can't have it. When that happens, she will see the monster she has become, and she will realize that I am the only creature who understands her, who accepts her, and supports her. And that my arms are the only ones that will hold her."

CHAPTER 27

Trans-Falls

Present Day

A BREEZE SHUDDERED THROUGH the trees, and a swirl of color drifted around her, landing softly on the ground and crunching beneath her feet. The beauty, usually drunk in with fervor, was lost on her, though she wasn't the only one.

Once the celebrations of their victory had died out, the reality of the death and loss had taken their toll. The once excited, bustling of the tribe had fallen into a slow groan, as if even the land itself was sighing with regret and sorrow. She had never heard Trans-Falls so silent and still. Even the young Centaurs who had once laughed, drank, and played games in their exhilaration hung their heads low. It seemed, with the short passing of time, they had all settled into the melancholy hum of grief, letting it fill the hole within them—a chasm the joy of victory had left when it departed.

"Stephania?"

She jumped as a hand touched her shoulder. Flashes of humans who felt no pain and yearned for blood consumed her until she recognized the voice. "Ravillian."

"Are you well?"

She quickly stood from her crouch and turned, meeting his dark, worried gaze. *No*, was what she wanted to say, but instead, she smiled. "Yes. I'm fine. I was just startled. That's all. You're much quieter than one would expect."

"Oh?" He chuckled, but the worry never left his eyes. "And why is that?"

"For starters, you're so ... um—" She stared up into his eyes, and he roared with laughter.

"Are you size shaming me, Stephania?" He tried to pout, but it was difficult to take seriously when he was still such a towering wall of muscled horse and man.

"Oh, no, no. But when my head just barely clears your abs, I find it surprising you can do any amount of sneaking."

He grunted and puffed his chest out in mock pride. "Well, I guess I'm just that talented." He winked, and she rolled her eyes.

"Oh, I doubt that," she muttered with amusement under her breath.

"I'll pretend I didn't hear that."

She smirked. "As if I was trying to hide it." Yipping, she dodged his lighthearted swipe, and they roared with laughter. For a second, she thought of how proud Lamora would be at her easy banter, but she wasn't here.

Unnaturally, the joyous sound turned rank, and they fell into silence.

Lamora would have something to say, something to make us laugh again and lighten the mood. She always does. But Stephania had already said goodbye to her, just as she had already done with Ravillian. So why was he here?

"Stephania." He reached out to her, and she flinched away. She instantly regretted her reaction when she spotted the hurt and confusion on his face. "Are you well? Truthfully?"

Barriers and alarms muddled her mind. If she told him how she felt, how she really felt, she would collapse right then and there. She couldn't allow that; she had to continue. Her eyes turned cold, and she looked up at him, trying desperately to murder the old, happy, teasing, awkward Stephania—the Stephania who felt too much. "As I said, I'm fine."

He bristled in defense and took a step back. "I don't think you are."

"Well, I don't think that's up to you to decide!" She clenched her fist, wishing she hadn't yelled. When she met his gaze, her heart lurched. A look hung in his eyes—the look of unfamiliarity, and she knew he didn't believe he was looking at his friend.

"Ravillian, please. Just let me go." Her teeth dug trenches into her lips. "The Stephania you knew died."

"I can see that."

Her eyes snapped up in disbelief. His gaze was almost as cold as hers except sorrow hung beneath his. "But that doesn't make me care for you any less. No matter how many times you die, I will always be your friend. And Lamora will too."

Tears blurred her vision. Trojan had said something like that before she got her memories back. She remembered what Lamora had said: *"You may have lost so much, but you still have the world in your hands."* And for the first time since hearing it, she thought maybe she could believe it.

"Thank you," she muttered awkwardly, her fingers playing with the hem of her shirt.

"Stephania!" Dalton's voice rang out through the forest, and she flinched.

"Coming!" Shuffling her feet, she turned, facing down the road to where Dalton and her family waited. "Goodbye, Ravillian."

"Wait," He placed his hand on her shoulder. "At least let me and Lamora come with you, just to the Cavos desert. Please. Let us at least have that."

She shook her head. "No."

"Please—"

"No!" She shoved his hand off her.

"Why?" His voice cracked with emotion, and she felt her barriers weaken.

"Because," she chuckled sourly. "I wouldn't be able to let you go if you came." Before he could answer, she ran, letting her pounding feet, and the stinging air beat away the tears.

Some part of her wished she would hear him behind her, unwilling to let her go so easily, but another, horrible, part wished she had never met him or Lamora in the first place, if only it would have prevented this ache in her chest at leaving them.

She stopped a few feet away from the back of the *Gauyuyáwa* where Dalton, Aeron, and Frawnden stood, while Jargon and Artigal waited in the tree. They were gathered not to say goodbyes, but because she herself had called them all together.

Though she tried to ignore it, she couldn't help but notice the awkward tension between the three parents. They hadn't spoken much since their big argument, and while Stephania was glad they weren't still upset at each other, she wished they were back to being a big happy family, like how they had been before the *Luyuk-daiw*. But that was exactly why she and Dalton were leaving. Nothing could go back to the way it had been.

"I'm ready, Uncle Dalton." She drew close to him, her eyes studying the ground.

He slipped his arm around her, and she laid her head on his chest, drawing in the strength of being a child in her parent's arms. After she entered the *Gauyuyáwa*, she wouldn't be able to rely on Dalton or anyone else; she had to act like the leader she was seen to be; she had to grow up. But until then, just for a moment, she could forget it as his arms gave her a reassuring squeeze.

"So are we, my child." Dalton nodded, struggling a smile, before motioning Frawnden and Aeron to lead.

With hesitant glances at their daughter, they turned and strode up the steps to the platform around the *Gauyuyáwa* tree, arms linked together, their heads held high and proud.

Though Stephania had insisted on her departure to be private, it seemed word had gotten out and traveled faster than Eta poison. Most of the tribe was standing before the *Gauyuyáwa*, waiting for her or one of their leaders to say something, anything. But the words Stephania had to say were not for them. At least, not yet.

Taking in a deep breath, Stephania turned from the expectant faces and followed her parents into the tree. The somehow familiar and foreign interior of the structure mixed together a sense of awe, fear, anxiety, and comfort in her. Shaking her head, she pushed aside the confusing emotions and focused on what she had called everyone here for.

Once the door closed behind her, Dalton, and her parents, the room fell silent. She could see Artigal and Jargon in the middle of the room, but also distinctly felt the two other presences lurking quietly under the stairs. She nodded in their direction.

"Please join us." She beckoned to them, and Dakar and Lycus stepped forward. As soon as her eyes met theirs, she felt her heart break all over again and tasted bile as her stomach churned. She had to think of them as just Warriors, not Trojan's brothers of war; if she could just push aside her emotions for only a few more minutes, then she could truly move on and put all this behind her, knowing she did what she was required to do.

They all gathered into a circle, gazing expectantly to her. Their eyes bore holes in her skin, bones, and soul. *Waiting. Waiting. Waiting.* Her heart raced. Her blood went hot then cold. Her breath caught in her chest.

Put it behind you. Set it right, and then leave it behind. She took one deep, long breath, and closed her eyes. Her old memories surfaced: the ones from when she had been the impossibly stoic and intelligent Dragon Child who walked by Artigal's side with pride and power. Remembering the little girl who bowed to no leader but herself, who commanded Centaur warriors to carry her or teach her what she wanted in the days before New-Fars had weakened her soul, she let the memories take control. Right now, she could use her memories and split personality to her advantage; she could be strong enough to lead. She opened her eyes feeling entirely the little Dragon Child who had known her place in the world and had confidence in her own strength and position. "I called you all here because I have come to realize something since Trojan's death."

At the mention of Trojan, the air went cold. A hundred different thoughts and emotions raged against each other as the Centaurs shifted uncomfortably from hoof to hoof, avoiding meeting each other's and her gazes. It was only going to get more uncomfortable, so she didn't wait for the turmoil to calm. "I am heir to Trans-Falls."

A solemn huff resonated around the room as the truth settled in. She knew they had all thought of this many times since Trojan had died, but she knew, like herself, it had been a hard potion to swallow. She, a Duvarharian, heir to the Duvarharian throne, and the Farloon, was direct heir to the Chiefdom of Trans-Falls. It was almost too much power for one creature to have. It was certainly more power and responsibility than Stephania cared to have, but also more than she cared to let go of.

The simple yet harsh truth had brought up a whirlwind of questions that demanded answers, but before anyone could voice their thoughts or opinions, she wanted to make sure they knew she was serious about claiming her rights and executing them properly.

"As Aeron and Frawnden's legally adopted child, I claim my right to the Chiefdom of Trans-Falls and all acting duties as such."

Though it didn't seem possible, the air grew quieter and colder.

"I understand I am also heir to Duvarharia, but I have no desire to give up that claim either. I know this puts us all into an awkward situation since I will be leaving for Duvarharia with Dalton today, but I have put great thought into how I will resolve this. Dakar and Lycus, please step forward."

The two Centaurs moved from being outside the circle to the center of the room, facing Stephania.

"Dakar"—she nodded to him and then to Lycus—"and Lycus, if you are willing to share the burden with each other and bear it for Trans-Falls, I will name you acting heirs of Trans-Falls while I am away. You will fill my role in ceremonies, leading battles, and will cast votes for me should there be matters to vote on with the council of advisors. When I am present in Trans-Falls, I will resume all such responsibilities and any other time I am able to. You will not inherit Chiefdom if Aeron is to die, but you will hold the title until I can return and properly name a Chief should I decide not to be it myself.

You are both Trojan's brothers of war. You were closest to him in all his hardships and struggles, in his victories and joys. You knew him better than anyone, knew his heart and desires for this Tribe better than anyone. It is you two alone who I entrust this to. Will you accept?"

All eyes were upon the two Centaurs. They looked at each other, then to Stephania, and then to the ground. Whatever contempt Lycus held for Stephania was hidden well under his gaze, and though her reasoning for naming him as part acting heir was not to mend relations with him, she hoped it would be a natural side effect. Dakar looked as if he were holding back tears, but it could've been a trick of the light as well.

They stepped forward slowly before kneeling in front of Stephania.

"We accept," they said in unison before standing.

Stephania searched the faces of the other leaders around her. "Does anyone object?"

Silence.

Though the atmosphere was solemn, she easily sensed pride from her parents and Dalton. Artigal was stony faced and hard to read, and she sensed skepticism from Jargon but did her best to ignore it. She didn't want to overthink their reactions and let it eat at the insecurities already knotting her stomach. She didn't have time to think any more about whether this was the right thing to do or not. If she left Trans-Falls and didn't name an acting heir, chaos would tear the Tribe apart as they fought champion to champion for a new leader, and if that got out of hand, it wouldn't stop at heir; soon Aeron and even Artigal's place as Igentis would be challenged. It was unthinkable, and Lycus and Dakar were her best shot at prevention.

"Good. Their duties start immediately." Her voice sounded more confident than she felt as her stoic persona wavered under the old habits of insecurity, but she continued. "I also understand I am the Farloon." She pulled the pendant out from under her shirt and let it rest against her chest where the light played tricks with its red jewel. "But I also understand I never fully accepted the title." Her eyes locked with Artigal's. "I accept it now. I, Stephania, heir of Trans-Falls and Duvarharia, am the Farloon and will adhere to the duties of protection and diplomacy assigned to the creature under that title."

For a moment, no one moved. First, Lycus and Dakar bowed low, then Jargon, Dalton, and her parents. Artigal neither bowed nor broke eye contact with her, and neither did she.

"And finally"—she clenched her first, diverting her eyes anywhere but the other creatures—"I vow I will return to Trans-Falls. I will go on to Duvarharia alone, save for Dalton, take on the title and duties as Lady of the Dragon Palace, and rebuild the armies and power of the Dragon Riders. Once that is done, I will return here, to fully claim my right as heir to this Tribe. I will master the power of the Lyre, awaken the forest, and I will lead the Centaurs and Dragon Riders against Thaddeus, combining our powers to rid the land of his, Kyrell's, and the Etas' blight once and for all. On all the gods and stars, I swear this."

Her Shalnoa and Centaur markings were burning bright red with her raging emotions. Hot tears rose in her eyes but didn't trail down her cheeks. Hate at Thaddeus, Kyrell, and the Etas poured off her in overwhelming waves. The confidence her old persona provided her also came with the unavoidable burning hate for her enemies. She was almost frightened the Corrupt Magic would feed off it and take over her mind again, but for once, the Ancient Magic left her in peace.

"Let it be so." Aeron nodded before placing his fist over his heart.

"Let it be so." Frawnden echoed and did the same. Soon each of the creatures in the room had mirrored the Chief.

"Let it be so," Stephania mumbled before returning the salute.

She sensed a certain unsettling aura from Artigal, but when she met his eyes, she saw something in their depths she knew to be confidence and pride.

"That is all I have to say. Thank you for gathering."

One by one, the creatures trickled out of the tree, but as Jargon passed her, he paused.

"Stephania." He hesitated, his hand reaching out to hers. She made no move to close the gap. His skin came mere centimeters from hers, but he drew away. His searching gaze met hers, and once again she was under the impression she should both hide everything from him and expose everything to him. "Do you know what you're doing?"

The simple question hit like a cold knife to the heart, bringing all her insecurities and worries rushing back, banishing the little Dragon Child she remembered being. Her blood ran cold. *Do I?* She hadn't consulted anyone before making these claims, decisions, or promises. She had made them on her own free will. She had wanted so long for control, but now that she had it, it was much more unsure than she had thought. For her to be able to move on to Duvarharia, she had to make sure things were set into motion here that would last until she needed the Centaurs in the battle against Thaddeus, but was she really doing the right thing? Were Dakar and Lycus really the best choices? Was she thinking with the Tribe's best interests in mind or only her own?

"Stephania?" Jargon touched her shoulder, and she snapped back into the present.

"Um, yeah. I think so."

He narrowed his eyes at her, searching her face for something she was sure he wouldn't find. Eventually, she was forced to look away. His soft, worried gaze brought unhappy, discontent tears to her eyes, dragging her back from being a strong leader to a soft child again.

"Emperor be with you, Stephania, and may the suns smile upon your presence."

She bit her lip. "As do the stars sing upon yours, Jargon."

Then without another word he left, leaving her with Artigal.

The silence between them stretched for a few seconds, though it seemed like an eternity. He said not a word about the decisions she made or what Jargon had said, only gestured to the door. "Come, Farloon. Your people await you."

Her stomach dropped as she stepped outside and met the faces of the hundreds of expectant Centaurs before her.

It was one thing to make lavish claims about being able to lead entire peoples and tribes, but it was another to stand before them and make the same claims. Bile rose in her throat.

At the sight of Stephania and Artigal next to Aeron, Frawnden, Jargon, and Dalton, the crowd roared with excitement.

Revulsion slammed into Stephania as she stumbled forward. Jargon's words had shattered something inside her and the confidence she had felt only moments before, dissolved into an anxious pit in her stomach. It was almost as if they had shattered some reality she had created—one where she had truly moved on from her past and grief, had become someone new and different. It was as if they had instead revealed the harsh reality that she was still the same Stephania who had lived in New-Fars, lost her memories then found them, and made the foolish decision of staying in Trans-Falls when she should've moved on to Duvarharia.

These creatures thought she was some sort of hero since she had stayed to help fight when she could have fled. They knew of Trojan's sacrifice for her, but somehow, instead of hating her for it, they rejoiced, as if they too believed she was worth the sacrifice.

She hid her face, biting back her screams of protest.

A cheer rose up, and she blanched as the jumbled yelling united into one voice: "Stephania, Farloon, Dragon Child!"

But it wasn't their praise she heard, it was the screams of dying Centaurs and Etas, rushing toward her, killing each other, protesting the horrific act of war as they partook in it. The chaos was around her again, taunting her, mocking her, driving her mad. "No, no, no." She violently shook her head and stepped back. She wanted to run, to go anywhere but here.

"Stephania, they're calling for you, child." Dalton reached for her, but she revolted from his touch.

Aeron and Frawnden stepped aside, baring her to the world. She cowered further. "No. Please. Make them stop."

"Stephania." Her eyes snapped up to meet Artigal's flashing eyes. "Stephania," he repeated, his voice hard. "You must step up. Right now, you are their hero, their Farloon and protector, their hope. Right now you have to live the words you just spoke to us in the *Gauyuyáwa*. The time for waiting and being a child is over. You must be the leader they see you as. Remember, with Trojan gone, you are heir to this tribe, to this kingdom. These are the people you want to lead to war. You must face them. This is the responsibility you are bound to live with and to respect. Remember your destiny. Remember who and what I raised you to be."

His eyes were filled with double meaning, and for a moment, a connection formed between them, and she felt his innermost thoughts. He was asking her to do what he had been forced to do thousands of years ago, to give up all she loved, even the pain and sorrow she clung to so desperately, to be something more, to be who they needed her to be, to do what needed to be done. She knew what he was trying to tell her: if he had been able to do it all those years ago, then she could do it now.

For a moment, a hush fell over the tribe.

Stephania's heart slammed in her chest. From where she had hidden behind Dalton and Jargon, she could see the rows upon rows of Centaurs standing before her, waiting for her. They were relying on her. They expected her to be some mighty warrior or hero. They expected her to take up the mantle her Duvarharian parents had left for her, that Trojan had left for her.

"Heir of this kingdom," she repeated in a hushed whisper, her fists tightening. "And of Duvarharia." She thought of Drox and Andromeda, who died protecting her to ensure she would follow her destiny. She thought of Aeron and Frawnden, who had taken her in, loved her, nurtured her, and never given up on her. She thought of Dalton, who had raised her, loved her more than anything and left everything behind for her. She thought of Trojan, who had given her more than any other, who had loved her truer than any could, and who had given his life so she could carry on everything he believed in. Every single one of them had lost something, having given it to her so she could destroy Thaddeus.

Hot tears ran down her cheeks, but she no longer felt sad. Whatever Lamora had said about revenge ... she had been wrong. This *was* the only way. She had been given the world in her hands to take back all she had lost, and by all the gods that existed, she was going to take it back.

Artigal met her eyes and nodded when he saw the resolution in her eyes. Without hesitation, he stepped forward and presented her to the crowd. "Trans-Falls, your Farloon and your heir!"

Again, the tribe exploded into joyous noise.

Pulling herself straight, she gritted her teeth and pushed past Dalton. She spared not a look to her parents or Jargon, focusing only on the people, *her* people, and her mission.

The tips of her boots came just inches shy of the edge of the platform. She felt as if she were standing at the edge of the world. As thousands of eyes stared up to her, expecting her to be something, and someone, she wasn't sure she could properly be, she balked only a moment.

Focusing her gaze just over the tops of their heads, she dismissed the doubts from her mind. Right here, right now, it wasn't about her, or even them. It was about Thaddeus and the filthy Etas. It was about everything that cursed traitor had taken from her.

"Centaurs of Trans-Falls ..." She hesitated for a moment, playing with Trojan's ring around her finger next to her mother's ring. "My people, I stand before you, not as the young girl I was when I first came to you, but as your leader, your protector, and your savior. When I was hunted down by demons, and orphaned because of scum; you took me into your arms and nourished me, sparking a flame of hope. You took that hope and made it yours and all of Ventronovia's.

When you could no longer shield me from the demons and scum, you sent me with the burdens of your hearts to the village of New-Fars. It was there, through the darkness of mankind's heart, I was tried and punished, but I persevered. Despite the humans' weakness, the hope you gave me and the strength of the Dragon Riders brought me back to you. Though I must leave you for Duvarharia, I do not leave you helpless. Already, I have made plans to care for your leadership and best interests. I will return to lead you one day, and until then I will be watching and protecting you from afar.

As I continue on to my destiny, I go before you reformed, a weapon in your right hand, a shield in your left. But most of all, I go before you as your beacon, your shining light, your redeemer. I go on to fight for Synoliki Trojan, son of Aeron and Frawnden, and I go on to fight for Lord Drox and Lady Andromeda, and for all those who have fought and died alongside you."

The Centaurs roared, calling out the names of those they had lost.

Tears flowed freely down her face as she listened to their sorrow and rage, so full of passion and power. They were hers in that moment, of that she was sure, and if she spoke to them with confidence, they would be hers forever, even until after the day she bought back all that had been taken from her with their blood.

Slipping the Farloon necklace over her head, she clutched it in her left hand, the cold metal digging into her palm and grinding against the metals of her two rings. Her Shalnoa burned and glowed, lighting up along with the markings on her neck—the raging of magic mixed with a promise. The confidence and conviction she had felt back in the *Gauyuyáwa* once more coursed through her veins. She proudly held her fist high above her head so all could see.

"I hold in my hand the greatest symbols of our people. The ring of Chiefs and of Trans-Falls, given to me by Trojan, given to him by his father, and back until the day Trans-Falls fought for the right to be their own tribe. Aeron and Frawnden are my parents, and their kingdom is mine."

The crowd shouted wildly, but she only spoke louder until they hushed. "I hold the ring of my mother—a cherished memento to her reign and the reign of my father, and to Duvarharia, the place of my birth. Lord Drox and Lady Andromeda are my parents, and their kingdom is mine.

"And finally, I hold the Farloon pendant, a token to the bond shared between our two Kinds—a promise to uphold each other's laws and beliefs, to protect each other, and stand by each other even in death. Its power and its duty are mine.

"Upon these things and all they stand for, I swear, I will spill the blood our broken hearts cry out for, and slay those who dared stand against us. Upon these things and all they stand for, I swear, I will bring an end to the tyranny of Thaddeus, Kyrell, Veltrix, and all those who follow them. None will be left to speak of their deeds, just as they planned to leave none to speak of ours!"

The tribe roared, stamping their hooves, shouting battle cries, and adding their own promises to hers.

They were hers—she held them in the palm of her hand, just as she did the world. It was all hers, but as she turned away and pushed past her family, she couldn't help but feel how empty it was.

Empty it may be for now, but I will fill it with the blood of those traitors over and over until the void is no longer there or until none of us are left.

"Stephania, wait!" Dalton cried after her, but she marched on, her blind tears of determination and anger clouding her path. Vaguely, she took Braken's reins from a Centaur who had been waiting patiently with Dalton's horse as well.

Subconsciously, she stroked the stallion's muzzle while listening to the cheers and exultation of the tribe. Through blurred eyes, she watched as Aeron and Frawnden trotted down the platform stairs, Jargon and Artigal close in tow, Dalton at their lead.

They drew near, but no one said a word.

How strange it was to be both their leader and their little girl.

She focused on the tips of her boots as she dragged a design in the dirt with her heel. The time had come for goodbyes, but the air was simply too sour for sweet endings one might dream up to say.

Finally, Artigal broke the silence. "They are yours, Stephania. They will follow you to the ends of Rasa if you ask it of them."

She met his gaze but only for a moment.

"Even so, take warning that you do not sacrifice them as petty pawns. Even just one of their lives is worth far more than any simple lust of your heart."

Her jaw tightened, and her stomach flopped. She wanted to snap back at him, but instead she nodded. "I understand."

He moved closer to her, his body language suddenly very different. For a moment, she remembered what she had thought when he had nearly died a few months ago. *He looks like a father.*

"As you know, my condition is in the hands of the Great Emperor. If he takes me before I see you again, I pass my blessing to you." He placed a gentle hand on her shoulder, and she felt a warmth spread through her. She could see the wave of white magic falter, and caught a final glimpse of the brown underneath. The realization that this might be the last time she saw him sickened her.

"May you find and keep His ways, and be filled with His goodness and peace."

A kind of comfort she hadn't felt for a very long time settled over her, and she sighed. "Thank you, Artigal. May the suns smile upon your presence."

He allowed her a sweet, fatherly smile, a sadness lingering in his eyes. "As do the stars sing upon yours."

As he turned to leave, she wondered: if in a different world where destiny hadn't pressed so harshly on either of them, if he would've been the one to adopt her and if they would've been a happy family together. But the thought, the wish, was fleeting—they didn't live in a world like that. She and Artigal were too much the same. Too much was expected of them, and they had too many shadows they wanted to keep hidden. With a heavy sigh, she realized she would never truly know him, not like she wanted to, and she regretted that more than she cared to admit.

Then, without a second look behind him, he disappeared into the forest.

Jargon wrapped her in a bear hug, nearly squeezing the breath from her lungs. "*Fuyushu*, little dragon. You must tell me about the birds in Duvarharia when you get there."

She nodded, biting back her tears.

"Don't forget me again, alright?"

She laughed through her tears and shook her head. "I won't."

"Good." He nodded, winked, and then followed after Artigal into the forest.

Her eyes lingered on the branches they had vanished behind before Frawnden stepped in front of her, soiling the strange feeling of time being suspended.

"Goodbye, Stephania. My little dragon. I pray you find happiness."

Her heart lurched in her throat as she wrapped her arms around Frawnden—the only mother she had ever really known.

Saying goodbye to her parents was harder than she had anticipated. She found her stoic, grim exterior crumbling at the sight of Frawnden's tears and the sorrow in Aeron's deep voice. She found herself wishing to let them come with her and Dalton to the desert, but she knew she would never be able to say goodbye if she didn't do it now.

She pried herself from Frawnden's last embrace and quickly mounted Braken. Aeron squeezed her hand, looking her deep in the eyes, and tried to smile. "I'm so proud of you, my daughter."

She had to hold the saddle horn to keep from throwing herself onto him and never letting go.

Dalton embraced Frawnden, then Aeron, thanking them for everything they had done for him and Stephania, promising them he would continue to take care of Stephania, and whispering his goodbyes. Finally, he mounted his horse.

"Come on, my child. It's time we leave." He placed a hand on Stephania's shoulder and smiled sadly before urging Austin down the northern road.

"Fuyushu," she whispered softly one last time, more to Trojan than anyone else, before urging Braken after Dalton.

Slowly, the cheers of the crowd faded behind her. An ache filled her, and her chest became heavy, her stomach churning with revulsion. With every step her horse took, she wrestled with the urge to yank his reins and gallop back to her family, back to her home. But she had done that once before, and she now knew the cost of such selfish actions.

Her shoulders slumped; her head hung low. Braken sensed her regret, and his hooves dragged the ground. A few times, Dalton had to grasp the stallion's reins and tug him along; Stephania let him, her soul too dark to do more than just sit in numbed disbelief.

This wasn't how she had pictured leaving Trans-Falls. She had thought it would be exciting, like it had been sometimes after leaving New-Fars. She thought Trojan would be with her, or her friends would come along; she thought it would feel like a wonderful adventure or a dream come true. She hadn't known how much it would hurt to leave a place that truly felt like home.

Resentment grew in her. What had happened to the joy she felt about going to Duvarharia? What had happened to the sense of wonder the thought of magic, Etas, and dragons had once brought her? Had that delight and happiness only been an illusion like so much of her life? Perhaps that had all been a dream and she was waking back up. Or perhaps something was wrong with her now and she could no longer feel joy.

"When we get to the main north road past the first mountain line, we'll meet up with the warriors Artigal assigned to our protection."

She could feel his eyes searching her for an answer, but she denied him.

"They will follow us only until the desert. Then we're on our own. Aeron said another tribe lives just on the outskirts of the northern desert plains. We can stop there to restock our supplies and rest. They'll accept us because you are Farloon."

She muttered something under her breath and gripped tighter the reins laced around her fingers.

Dalton continued, obviously uncomfortable with the dark silence. "I don't remember the name of their tribe, but I did mark the location of it on the map. It's by another waterfall. It seems Centaurs like waterfalls, wouldn't you agree?"

Again, she refused to answer.

"From there, it's only a few weeks journey to the border of Duvarharia and then, from there, a week's ride to the palace. We'll be there before the end of the year."

She lifted her head, and her eyes met his. It took a surprising amount of effort to nod, but somehow she managed, and he seemed satisfied with her answer.

Before the end of the year. It didn't seem real, but then again, nothing in her life did anymore.

"Stephania! Wait! Please!"

The voice jerked Stephania alert, her eyes widening. "Lamora?" Her head snapped around.

The pounding hooves came to a halt, and Stephania found herself facing her two best friends.

"Ravillian. Lamora. What are you doing here?" A tremor of fear crept into her voice. She had told them to stay. *Gods of all, why didn't they stay?* She had already said her goodbyes. She didn't want to say them again.

Lamora bent, taking in deep breaths, winded from the hard ride. Ravillian too was panting and struggling to find words.

Stephania exchanged a glance with Dalton. He didn't seem as shocked as she felt.

Ravillian caught his breath first. "Please. We have to come with you. At least to the desert. They're letting a band of Warriors ride with you, so why can't we? We can camp with them and even take turns with the guard, but just let us see you off. Officially."

Stephania slowly shook her head, her mouth hanging open.

"Come to your senses, Stephania. We're friends. That's what we do. It doesn't matter where you go, we will follow you." Lamora laid her hand on Stephania's leg, but she could only stare in disbelief, rooted to the spot.

"Say something, Steph." Ravillian ran a hand through his mussed, dark spotted mane as Stephania finally found her voice.

"Leave."

"What?"

Shock turned to anger. "I want you to leave. Now. I can't have you come with me. I don't want you to come with me."

Lamora stumbled back, tears filling her eyes. "I don't understand. Do you not love us anymore? Did all that time spent together in Trans-Falls mean nothing? Were we only for your short-term enjoyment until you tired of us?"

Stephania stuttered on her words. *No, no, no. That's not it! Why do my words have to hurt everyone so much? Why can't I just be left alone?*

"Lamora, that's not what I mean. I mean, I *want* you to come with me, but if you do, I won't be able to say goodbye again. I won't be able to let you go."

"Then don't!" Ravillian stepped forward, his eyes flashing, Lamora's hand gripped comfortingly in his own. "Let us go with you to the Dragon Palace. You will need good friends to help you through the stress and hardships. We can learn with you and help you grow. We'll go as ambassadors for Trans-Falls and all the Centaurs."

Lamora nodded. "But most of all, we'll go as your friends. We could—"

"No, no, no!" Stephania suddenly yelled, her eyes flashing wildly. "I have to do this on my own. I can't have you two with me. You'll only end up getting hurt. This is somewhere you *can't* follow me."

Tears flowed freely down Lamora's face, but her eyes burned fiercely. "We have already been hurt, Stephania. Love transcends all. There is no place it cannot go."

"No," Stephania's rage turned icy cold. "There is one, and that is death."

Realization dawned on Ravillian's face, and he wrapped his arm around Lamora. "You just don't want to see us die."

Stephania nodded slowly. *Finally. He understands me.* "No. I don't. I guess I'm just too selfish, but even if you die here, at least I won't have to watch it happen like I had to with Trojan. And at least you won't be dying for me."

Lamora bit her lip, straightened herself, and dried her eyes, matching Stephania's gaze. "I understand. I will stay. But know this. If you should ever need aid, I will not hesitate to come, and I will not hesitate to die. That is what friends do whether they are the Farloon, or Prophesied protector, or not. That is love. And love *does* transcend all, even death. In that I believe." She placed her right fist over her heart and waited until Stephania did the same.

New tears poured down Stephania's face as she held her hand to her heart. Never before had the salute felt so much like a promise.

"And I as well." Ravillian agreed and saluted.

"We love you, Stephania. Even when you don't want us to, we will keep loving you." Lamora laced her arm through Ravillian's, and he nodded in agreement.

Stephania choked back her tears. "I love you too. I'll miss you and think of you often."

"And we, you."

She turned Braken, locking eyes with Dalton. He smiled sadly, a tenderness hidden in his eyes before he spurred Austin. The gelding and stallion moved forward together, trudging down the path.

"Oh, Stephania?" Ravillian's voice pulled her back.

She turned her head.

Lamora was gazing lovingly up at Ravillian, a blush on her cheeks.

"We're to be mated, Lamora and I. Only a few weeks from now. We thought we could tell you and celebrate if we went to the desert, but now, it seems, is our last chance."

Stephania felt as if someone had shoved a frozen iron rod through her heart. Her two friends were to be mated, and she wouldn't even be here for it. She wouldn't get to watch them take their vows or fight the ceremonial duel; she wouldn't get to see them as a couple. She would miss all of it.

A stinging lump rose in her throat, and she had to blink to see them through the watery haze in her eyes.

"That's ... wonderful. I'm so happy for you two. I wish you happiness."

"Thank you, Stephania," Ravillian answered before she turned back around.

Braken walked on, moving farther and farther away. She didn't look back. She waited for what she hoped would be their voices, detaining her forever in the place she loved, but she heard nothing.

She clenched her fist, shoving down the cries that rose in her throat. *Oh, why didn't I say something more? Why didn't I rush back to congratulate them? I should have hugged them, wished them well, and blessed them in their language. Gods of all.* But she had only said the barest required—something a stranger would say—and that was all. Everything she had done to lock her heart away was finally working, but instead of rejoicing, she only felt horror and fear, as if she had stepped past a point of no return.

Finally, she could bear it no longer. "Ravillian! Lamora!" She yanked back on the reins, turning Braken around.

Only an empty path through the trees stared back at her.

They were gone

She had waited too long.

"Oh, gods," she sobbed, covering her face in her hands.

She felt Dalton take Braken's reins as she cried, felt as the stallion lurched forward underneath her as he was led down the road.

She had finally gotten what she wanted, what the mask on her emotions had been crafted for—a world where no one she cared about could be hurt by her love, including herself. She had never imagined how lonely and full of regret it had started to become.

CHAPTER 28

THANK YOU ... YES, I UNDERSTAND. Sure ..." Dalton nodded as he spoke in low tones to the lead warrior. Stephania barely caught the leader's familiar eyes before she glanced away, unable to meet his dark, piercing gaze. "Absolutely. I'll make sure of it ... thank you."

She crossed her arms and sucked in a deep breath as Dalton urged Austin over to her.

"They are going to travel with us through the rest of the Filate Mountains, through the plains, and all the way to the edge of the desert. They will help supply our journey across the Cavos, and send word ahead to the Sankyz Centaur Tribe. They ask that we don't wander off or cause any disruptions that might attract rouges from Thaddeus's army. We can practice magic, however, as long as we are quiet and careful about it."

Stephania nodded as he spoke, showing she understood. For a moment, they sat still, him looking intently at her, and her ignoring his gaze.

"It bothers you to have them with us—Trojan's battalion." A sad sigh parted his lips.

Sharply, she bobbed her head, resisting the sting of tears rising in her throat.

"They wanted to continue the protection Trojan gave for you. They don't mean it as a continuation of your pain."

Her eyes lifted and caught the gaze of the leader's again, just behind Dalton. *Dakar.*

His dark eyes narrowed before he dipped his chin and held his fist to his heart.

She hadn't expected to see him past assigning him and Lycus as temporary heirs, and this was so much worse than just making a decision quickly and not having to address them personally; now she'd be forced to spend time with him. And seeing Trojan's battalion led by someone else only made his absence so much more real. She bit her lip and forced herself to focus on Dalton. "I know. But it hurts nonetheless."

A small smile lifted his lips, and he placed his hand on hers. "Let them serve you. I think it eases their pain as well."

"I don't want to talk to them," she whispered before she could stop herself.

Dalton didn't seem worried or offended by her plea, though. "You won't have to. Dakar promised us we would be in relative seclusion except for routine check-ins. He also promised you wouldn't be bothered by any of the Warriors."

"Okay."

"Now come, my child. They have pitched us a camp for the night. We'll rest now and then ride on tomorrow."

Numbly, she let him lead Braken to the tents and fires the Warriors had made. True to Dakar's word, the Centaurs paid little attention to her, and if she caught any of them looking at her, they quickly busied themselves elsewhere. She barely remembered untacking Braken and sipping a few bites of soup.

"What's on your mind?"

"Huh?" She looked away from the mountain peaks looming over treetops.

"What do you keep looking at?" Dalton put down his bowl of soup. "You seem like you're looking for something."

Am I? Am I looking for something I've lost? This was the first night in months she wouldn't spend with those she loved in Trans-Falls. The weight of loneliness started settling on her, but she tried to remind herself she had Dalton and that, before Trans-Falls, he had been all she had known and loved. He had been enough. She wanted it to be that way again. Maybe that's what she was looking for—a time that had passed and would never be again. She frowned. *No. There must be something else.*

"I recognize these mountains."

She could feel his frown as she gazed back to the Filate ranges.

"What do you mean?"

She shivered against the cold air, and he quickly sacrificed his cloak to wrap around her shoulders, his arm encircling her protectively.

"I'm not sure. But I've seen them before. Like in a dream."

"Was it a dream or a memory?"

She couldn't answer and instead shrugged. "I don't know. I guess it could be either."

Silence stretched between them, and she rested her head on his shoulder. He was warm, warmer than she was, and she started to feel sleep drag down her eyes. It had been a long ride from Trans-Falls to meet up with the Warriors. Of course, she had ridden far longer distances when they had left New-Fars, but it had never felt so exhausting, and she hadn't been able to tell if it was all the emotions and regret or if it was the mountain terrain. *Maybe it was both.*

"You know, your parents might have passed over these very mountains years ago when they were bringing you to me."

She shifted to look up into his face. He looked down at her for a moment and then drew his attention back to the darkening sky where a few stars started to sparkle.

"I never thought about that."

"Mm-hm. It wasn't very far from Trans-Falls that the Battle of the Prophecy was fought."

"Why didn't anyone take me there?"

"Do you really want to see it? The place where your parents were brutally slaughtered along with hundreds of Centaurs?"

Unease settled in her as she thought of the memory she shared with Thaddeus: of the dead and dying Centaurs, of his purple eyes looking down into hers, and of the memory she had from him killing her parents. She really didn't want to see that. It was enough that she had recollection of it, enough that she had been there in dreams. If she saw it in real life, it would make it all seem that much more ... real. She wasn't sure she wanted it to be real.

"No. I guess not."

He nodded. "Maybe someday you will be ready to see it."

"What do you think happened that day?"

Instantly, he tensed, and she wished she hadn't asked him. Often times, she forgot he had been close friends with her parents, had known them better than she would ever, and that their deaths affected him more than her.

"I don't know." A catch formed in his voice as it dropped to a whisper. "But it must have been horrible."

"Will I ever know? Will I ever understand?"

"Why do you want to know?" He pulled away from her, and she shrugged.

Trojan's face just before he died flashed before her, and she shook her head. *I want to understand how you could love someone so much you would die so willingly for them. That's what I want to understand.* She didn't tell him that. Instead, she only said, "I don't know."

"Well ..." he drawled and shifted his weight. "I read in a scroll back in Trans-Falls that sometimes memories from Duvarharians are gifted to others they are emotionally close to, most often to family members, like parents to children. Maybe they gave you those memories and others from your childhood. Maybe someday you will be able to see them."

"Really?"

He stood abruptly, a strange look on his half-lit face. "Maybe. But it's very unlikely. It hasn't been done for a long, long time, and I'm not sure why parents would gift their child with the memories surrounding their deaths."

Her heart fell, but she only nodded. "You're right."

For a long moment, silence stood between them until he extended his hand to her. "Come, child. It's time to sleep. We have another long day of traveling ahead of us tomorrow."

She took his hand and let him pull her to her feet. He made no move to take his cloak back, so she slid it off her shoulders and whispered, "Thank you."

He took it with a nod and gently pulled her into his tight embrace. She felt his arms around her, breathed the smell of autumn on his clothes, and closed her eyes before hugging him back.

"Please, try not to dwell on it too much. I know it's hard with Trojan's death and traveling across the same land your parents crossed before their deaths, but it won't help to think on it all the time. Tomorrow we'll practice some new magic, maybe spar a little like we used to, and move forward. No more looking back, okay?"

"Okay," she whispered, but as he squeezed her one last time and then turned away to his tent, she knew she could never move forward, not when the past hunted her so relentlessly.

Though sleep hadn't been far from her only minutes before, all it took was Dalton telling her to not dwell on death for her to dwell on it and chase sleep far, far away. When her eyes finally did close and she tried to clear her mind from blood, screaming, battles, and sacrifice, she was haunted by the cries of a young girl.

"Mama! Mama!"

She groaned, tossing and turning under the furs, which only filled her with claustrophobia.

"Mama! I don' wanna go that way!"

She bit her lip against her own cries. The voice suffocated her when she closed her eyes, it echoed ominously when she opened them. She couldn't escape it if she sang to herself or if she tried yelling her own thoughts as loud as she could. The Filate mountain ranges loomed over her, swallowing her whole as she heard the girl scream, and scream, and scream.

§

Filate Mountain Range
Night of the Battle of the Prophecy
Nearly 17 Years Ago

"MAMA!" STEPHANIA TENSED, *her little chest rising and falling at a furious pace.*

"What is it, sweetheart?" *Andromeda's eyes were wide with panic and concern.*

Stephania quickly turned around on the dragon and clung to her mother, burying her small face in the protective folds of Andromeda's thick, warm cloak.

"I don' wanna go that way!" *Stephania screeched even louder this time, tears now streaming down her face.*

What's wrong? *Drox's heart slammed in his chest as an unknown dread filled him.* Something is happening. Something is wrong.

I don't know. I can't see anything that might be frightening to her. She's never feared heights before. *Andromeda took a moment to calm herself before carefully questioning her daughter.* "What way, Stephania?"

Her child frowned in terror and frustration and pointed to the valley directly ahead of them before she once more hid her face. "That dragon too scary!"

Andromeda gasped and shivered violently. She blinked a couple of times as she tried to shake off the sensation.

Drox shuddered with unease. He too had felt something. He strained to see what Stephania was seeing, but whatever it was, it had not made itself visible to him. What was that? Andromeda? Did you feel that? *Drox demanded answers from his wife, but she had thrown up barriers to keep him out of her mind. Fear rose in the man. Andromeda never shut him out.*

"But, honey, there isn't any dragon there, just the trees!" *A sickeningly sweet smile spread across Andromeda's face. Sweat beaded on her forehead, her nostrils flaring, her breath coming in quick gasps.*

"Yes, there is," *Stephania argued.* "I wanna go a different way."

Andromeda snarled and dug her nails into her daughter's arms, her eyes glinting strangely in the light. "Now, honey, what other way would we go?"

Drox instantly noticed the change in his wife. Dragons and Lords. Mischievous, what is wrong with her? *Both Drox and Aldwyn's minds melded together as one mind in their worry while they questioned Andromeda's Poison Dragon.*

Mischievous groaned and shuddered; the only words passing through her mind were strained and painful. She's possessed!

Stephania didn't seem to notice the change in her mother, and her chubby face wrinkled into a pout, her bottom lip jutting out as she turned slowly to look at the mountains. Suddenly, her face broke out into a smile.

"That way." *She pointed toward a valley much farther away and very much off the course of their original path.* "That a bery beautiful dragon. Bery shiny."

Andromeda turned her face away from the valley, growling unnaturally. "No. No. No. We can't go that way. It takes us too much off our course." *Something in her voice made it obvious more than just direction and planning were keeping Andromeda, or whatever was possessing her, from going that way.*

Possessed? By who? How? *His mind rang with the voice of his dragon as Aldwyn yelled at Andromeda, trying to reach her.* Aldwyn, we have to do something.

But what? *Adlwyn's thoughts snapped out angrily, but Drox could sense the worry and helplessness underneath.* It's been so long since we've had to fight back mentally. I don't even know where to begin.

Mischievous' flight faltered, and she let out a plea for help. It was clear her rider's pain weighed heavily on her as they struggled against whatever was controlling the woman.

The air grew dark around them. The crisp mountain air was now warm and heavy, constricting.

Stephania shivered in fear. Tears shone in her eyes as she gazed in the direction she had said the beautiful dragon was. "Bu—"

"No!" *Andromeda screamed. Her eyes flashed a bright red, and her face distorted, as if superimposed with the face of a demon.* "We want to get you to safety as quick as we can, do we not?"

Stephania looked up at the monster gripping her and started screaming.

Drox drew his sword and readied his magic. He licked his lips, his ears ringing. If whatever was controlling Andromeda tried to hurt Stephania, he would have no choice. He would have to kill his wife to protect his daughter.

He felt the magic prickling his finger, tasted the bile in his throat. The words to the spell jumped at the tip of his tongue as he watched his wife raise her hand to strike their daughter. A sharp pain tore through his mind. He screamed, clutching his head as an intruder attempted to enter his thoughts. The pain was almost unbearable. Aldwyn was right; It had been a long time since they had been attacked mentally, and he wasn't ready for it. Memories flashed through his mind as the demon tried to find something to grab onto—some sort of weakness. Drox felt himself being dragged under. He felt himself slipping into the darkness—felt as he was being pushed from his mind and body.

A dragon roared.

Stephania screamed.

"Joad, help us!"

All at once, he could see everything.

Ahead of them in the mountains were the two dragons Stephania had seen. The white, shining dragon now grappled with the rotting, black dragon, their riders engaged in deadly combat.

Drox felt the evil inside Andromeda as she tried to fight it with her own light. He cried out, feeling wretchedly helpless.

The white rider cut into the evil rider, and the dark dragon and rider spiraled through the air, shattering into a dark shadow against the ground. However, an evil presence still lingered. Andromeda still thrashed with the demon.

Stretching his hands to his side, the white rider locked eyes with Drox and nodded slowly. Blinding white light gathered at his fingertips as he brought them together. Pulling his right hand to his cheek and extending his left in front of him, a bow and arrow appeared, made of the light. He aimed for Andromeda.

Drox started yelling for the man to stop, but it was too late.

The arrow from the white rider's bow cut through the air.

Time seemed to slow.

Drox felt like he was going to throw up. He cried out, reaching out to his wife and child, but he could do nothing to protect them.

When the arrow reached the Duvarharians, it hit Stephania first. The light passed harmlessly through Stephania and Andromeda, but tore a dark shape from Andromeda's body, effortlessly shattering the evil that had possessed her.

Drox opened his eyes, for he had never really opened them in the physical world, only in the magical and spiritual one.

Stephania was hugging her mother, who was clutching at her daughter, tears pouring down her face, her body shaking with fear. She kept kissing her daughter's head, whispering how sorry she was, tears pouring down her face while Stephania pleaded to go home.

Drox's heart ached. His wife was spent and scared. Nearly all her energy had been drained fighting the demon. Even the extra energy in the Vuldaheshab she carried flickered weakly.

His daughter was terrified and hysterical.

He wanted to land and regroup. His mind reeled. He hurt, not only in his mind, but in his body as well. He ached all over like he had been beaten, though not a single physical blemish was on his body. He wanted to console his family, to tell them everything was over and they were going to be fine. But they had to keep going. Time was slipping through their fingers, and their Wings back at the Dragon Palace needed them.

Something on the horizon caught his eye.

A huge black cloud was rising over the mountains at an alarming rate. The very moon and stars seemed to darken. Unnatural screams filled the air.

A pit of horror opened in Drox's stomach. "Joad save us."

§

Filate Mountain Range

STEPHANIA SAT UP, HEAVING FOR AIR.

"Are you okay?"

It took her a moment of reeling before she could focus her eyes on Dalton kneeling beside her. She wasn't sure how to answer as she tried to rid her mind of the fear coursing through her veins. *It was just a nightmare. Just a nightmare,* she tried to tell herself, but she knew better. She knew those mountain caps, she knew those Duvarharians and their daughter. It was her parents, it was her, and it was memory.

"I saw—" She bit her lip and shook her head before trying again. "I saw ..." She couldn't seem to form the words. She remembered what Dalton had said about her not being a burden, but old habits died hard, and she didn't want to bring him worry that the very land they were walking on was triggering nightmares of her parents. "I don't know," she finally whispered.

"Just another bad nightmare, then?"

She nodded.

"From the battle back at Trans-Falls?"

She lied with another nod. She could feel the helplessness radiating off him, much like her father's own helplessness so many years before. It was obvious he wanted to help her but didn't know how. She wished she could tell him, help him heal her, but even she didn't know how.

"When you're ready, the Warriors made us breakfast. It's still fairly early, so I was thinking we could spar a bit before leaving."

"Okay." She lay back down, turning her back to him.

"Unless you want to practice magic? I was able to bring a few smaller tomes on covering magic traces along if you wanted to study them. You might be at that level now."

The thought of reaching into her magic again, of opening those channels linking her to the Ancient Magic, sickened her. *What if I lose control again? What if the Ancient Magic pushes aside my own magic and kills my friends again?* But she was Duvarharian, and Dalton had taught her magic was life itself for the Duvarharians and everything they did was an extended use of magic, even breathing or eating. It all went hand in hand. Just as eating and breathing were necessary for life, so was magic.

But she hadn't wielded magic stronger than a calming, or warming spell since Trojan died. Even now, she could feel the toll it was taking on her. It was harder to focus, harder to quench the anxious knot balling inside her. She couldn't hide from it forever; especially if she would need it to fight Thaddeus. The thought of her resolve to defeat the traitor struck a flame within her, and she found herself casting aside the furs and following Dalton out of the tent.

The morning chaos of a Centaur camp assaulted her. Centaurs were stretching and rolling up furs and tent canvases. Fires burned and food cooked over them. A fresh deer hung from a tree nearby as two Centaurs quickly stripped it of its hide and preserved its meat for the trip ahead. The clash of weapons on shields rang loudly with grunts of exertion.

"I thought you said we wouldn't be bothered."

Dalton laughed and shook his head. "Either this will be the only time, since we stole a corner of their camp last night, or they don't understand privacy as Duvarharians do."

Stephania couldn't help but smile. "What are the Duvarharians like?"

A strange look crossed Dalton's face, and she thought for a moment he wouldn't answer, but he hummed softly to himself and stared off into the distance, his hand rested thoughtfully on his chin. "They're very loud," he chuckled. "Very prideful and headstrong, much like yourself."

A blushed raged on her cheeks.

"But they aren't as close as the Centaurs. They like their space, their privacy, their solitude. Most likely because they have to deal with being bonded to a dragon all the time. You're never really alone."

"What's it like?" She took a bowl of the leftover soup from Dalton and settled down to eat.

"Hm?"

She had to swallow before answering. "Being bonded to a dragon. What's it like?"

Dalton opened his mouth to speak but then closed it slowly. His eyes grew distant as his hand lowered the spoon back into his own bowl. For a few long minutes, he didn't speak and didn't look anywhere but the trees around them. She didn't dare disturb him. Months ago, she might have; she might have pressed him for an answer or demanded it, asking what was wrong with him, but now she knew the lull of silence and how hard to was to drag yourself back from the deep places of the mind.

"It's ..." He shook his head as if he couldn't quite find the right words. "It's wonderful. You feel alive, whole, complete. You never understand how alone you are until you bond with your dragon, and then you wonder how you could ever bear to be without them again." A mist rose in his eyes, but he smiled tenderly at her before taking a bite of his soup.

"Can you bond with another dragon?" She lost interest in the food, her attention focused solely on him. These were questions that had sat inside her for a long time, questions she had truly wanted answers to but had never felt worthy enough to ask.

"Not really." His jaw tightened, and he stared down into his food. "You can, but it's never really the same."

She nodded and gazed at her shoes. They were splattered with red clay, and for a moment, she thought it was blood. A chill ran down her spine, and she had to force herself to look into the fire, concentrating on the present.

"Will I bond with a dragon?"

Their eyes met, and for a moment, she remembered asking him a similar question many, many years ago when she had sat on his lap in his study in New-Fars. *Will I have friends?* Though it was clear now he had lied to her, she now knew he had only meant eventually. Would his answer to this question be similar?

His eyes narrowed as they searched her face. "I don't know."

"Why not?"

"You know why, Stephania." He downed the last of his soup and took the small wooden bowl to the Centaur who was gathering eating utensils.

The answer left her empty. He spoke truth. Of course he couldn't know. After all, weren't the Duvarharians nearly extinct? Obviously, that meant the dragons were too. The harsh reality left her empty and unsatisfied. She wished he had at least answered with: "Maybe someday," or anything else more hopeful.

Tears stung her eyes, but she forced them back as she tried to focus on her food. She sat still, staring at the soup, willing herself to eat it for longer than she would have liked. If even eating was so hard, how was she going to defeat Thaddeus? And Kyrell? *And* Veltrix? For the first time since she claimed her heritage rights in Trans-Falls and made her promises to the Tribe, she was starting to feel the crushing weight of her words and vows, which quickly became strong doubts that she wouldn't be able to do what she was bent on accomplishing.

Abruptly, she stood, took her bowl in shaking hands, and forced herself to take bite after bite until no food was left. Her stomach rolled and protested, but she determinately shoved the empty bowl toward the Centaur who was cleaning, and willed herself not to throw up.

She may not be able to love herself after all the mistakes she had made, but she would take care of herself, if only so she would be strong enough to take her revenge.

Dalton was standing beside his own tent, tome in hand, quiet words pouring from his mouth when she stepped up to him, a coal-like fire burning somewhere inside her. When he looked up, mild shock crossed his features.

"I want to try to master covering my magic trace before we reach the desert." She tried to force confidence into her voice, the confidence she used to have when demanding he teach her.

Something between confusion and pride flashed across his face before he shut his tome with a loud smack and nodded. "So be it."

§

BY THE TIME THEY arrived in the small camp the Warriors had pitched for them that night, Stephania was barely able to dismount, untack Braken, and sink herself to the hard ground beside the fire.

She had easily bested Dalton multiple times when sparring, but training in magic had been much more taxing than she could have predicted. It seemed all the progress she and Dalton had made on their trip between New-Fars and Trans-Falls had been lost. It didn't help that the spells for covering magic traces took an extraordinary amount of energy and concentration, and she had found it almost impossible to focus on anything other than her regret over not learning the spells sooner or being able to stop the Ancient Magic.

"How are you feeling?" Dalton carefully lowered himself beside her with a grunt and sore shrug of his shoulders. He'd taken one or more heavy hits from her, and though she felt a little guilty for causing him pain, she couldn't stop the twinge of victory that surged through her.

"Tired. And a little sick." A small smile lifted her lips. For once, she really *was* tired and not just saying it to get people to stop talking to her.

"That's to be expected. The magic we've been practicing takes an unusual amount of energy. When you get to the Dragon Palace, they should have gems and crystals called *Vuldahesh,* or *Vuldaheshab* if there's a collection of them, that store energy so you can call upon it at any time."

"I know."

He raised a brow at her. "How do you know?"

A chill ran down her spine. She tried to remember a time when he or someone in Trans-Falls had told her, but she drew a blank until a flash of memory echoed in her mind. *Vuldahesh.* Her brows furrowed. Her father had mentioned the energy-storing crystals in her dream last night. "I read it in one of your tomes back in Trans-Falls." The lie jumped easily from her tongue.

He frowned, obviously not convinced, and she was forced to look away from his gaze. She knew she should just tell him about the memories. *But why is it so hard to? Why is it always so hard to open up to anyone?*

Dalton hummed and shrugged. "Well, I guess—"

"Actually ..." Her heart slammed against her ribs as she interrupted. "I didn't read it in your books."

He shifted his weight to face her, but she refused to look into his gaze. She was thankful the Centaur warriors weren't here to intrude. In fact, it was almost as if they were traveling alone, it was so quiet—more quiet than she had experienced for a long time.

"I didn't think so."

She felt her face burn.

"How do you know, then?"

Taking a deep breath and shoving aside her fear and distrust, she told him about how she recognized the mountain peaks and the memory she had from her parents. She didn't know how much to tell him about Andromeda supposedly being possessed or how she as a child sensed the ambush and almost prevented it, but whether she wanted to divulge details or not, she found herself telling him everything, down to the very scratches on Mischievous' neck and the way the clouds had played with the moonlight. The memory played out before her, almost as clearly as it had last night, and she felt as if she were reliving it all again, just the same way she always felt when Dalton had told stories to the children in New-Fars.

By the time she finished, his face was pale and his eyes wide. His elbows were propped up on his knees as he stared blankly into the fire. Something like tears glistened in his eyes, but she sensed his shock and pain went deeper than tears could heal.

She didn't know what to say, didn't know whether to hug him or simply leave him alone. Her own heart ached, but she knew it was nothing compared to what he was feeling.

"You have to tell me if it happens again." His voice was hoarse as he looked at her, a slight craze in his eyes. "You have to tell me."

She played with her thumbs for a moment before nodding. "Okay. I will."

He sighed and ran his hand through his hair. "If you can't stop the memories, it might be best if you embrace them."

Shock covered her face. "What?"

He met her gaze, his hands finding hers and squeezing them harshly. "You cannot run from the past, Stephania. You understand that." It was more statement than question, but she nodded. "Then you have to embrace it. Thaddeus can access your memories, and you can access the memories of your parents. That is how things are. Pathways between you, and other creatures, exist; you cannot close them, or hope they simply go away."

She couldn't still the rapid breathing or beating of her heart. She hadn't seen him this intense for a long time, and it scared her. Everything he was saying was true, she knew that, but it was hard to grasp, hard to truly understand what he meant. "What do you mean?"

He scooted close to her and tucked a lock of hair behind her ear. Once again, his eyes misted, but a small smile spread across his lips.

"I have spent years protecting you, Stephania, from everything I could—villagers, wild animals, fear, uncertainty, self-doubt, Etas, Thaddeus—and there is nothing more in this world I want than to see you, my child, safe and happy. You know that, right?"

She nodded, her own tears rising to her eyes.

"But I can't protect you anymore." His voice was raw with emotion as he bit his lip, hanging his head. "Everything in the last few weeks, even months, in Trans-Falls taught me that. You're basically an adult now. I can't protect you or shield you from everything anymore. I knew I would have to let you go someday, I knew that, but every parent fears their child growing up, fears what the world may do to them."

"Uncle Dalton ..." She swallowed past the lump in her throat as he placed his forehead on hers.

"I am weak, Stephania. I can barely protect you with my sword, let alone my magic. I could do nothing for you in Trans-Falls, and your enemies are the greatest in the land. I can't do much more to help you. I cannot follow you where you need to go. But I can help you face these demons. I can help you face the past so you can move forward into the future."

He drew away from her, searching her face. She held his hands tighter in hers as something between relief and dread settled in her.

"You must harness power over these memories. Thaddeus can use them against you; I am confident that is how he found New-Fars and corrupted the villagers. You must find a way into his memories and use them against him, do you understand?"

Fear rolled over her like ice. *Use Thaddeus's memories against him? Crawl into the mind of the most murderous traitor Ventronovia has seen in thousands of years? Live through the suffering he has wrought in this world? See destruction through his eyes like I see the death of my parents?*

Bile rose in her throat at the thought, and she started shaking her head. "I can't. I—"

"No. No, don't say that, Stephania." His voice was harsh as he gently shook her shoulder and brushed away the tears trickling down her cheeks. "You *can* do it. I know you can. You are strong. You're stubborn, hardheaded, even a little selfish, just like your father."

Her eyes widened at the mention of her father.

"And your father was the strongest man I knew. He never backed down from a challenge. He never gave up. Ever." Tears collected in his eyes, but he only gritted his teeth. "And your mother was just the same. You are so like them, Stephania." Tenderly, he pushed another lock of her slightly tangled hair behind her ear. "I see them so much in you. I see their determination, their power, and their strength ... If you put your mind to it, there is nothing in this world you cannot do. Do you understand?"

She nodded and wiped her nose on the edge of her cloak.

"You can do this. I'll train you as best I can, and you will learn how to control these paths between you and them. You will conquer this, and you will prevail. You will make these demons your friend, and you will never look back. Right?"

Sniffing, she nodded, trying to absorb his confidence and strength. "Right."

He pulled away and straightened his shoulders. A light filled his eyes, and she recognized it as the determination he had when translating old documents, or instructing her on a new sword fighting technique, or even the same determination he had when fighting her stubbornness.

"We're traveling across almost the exact same land your parents did. It triggers the memories, correct?"

"Correct." She banished the last tears from her eyes and met his gaze, pushing her fear aside, focusing only on what he was saying.

"Good. Now, the dream you had last night, you were in it as a child, right?"

"Yes."

"So you should have your own memories of the event."

Realization dawned on her. *Of course.* She *should* have her own memories of it. She nodded her head quickly, a strange flutter of excitement building inside her.

"Then you should be able to use what you know about the dream and the land around you to trigger the memory, but this time, you must try to see it from your own perspective. You need to focus on what you might have seen as a child, such as the marks on Mischievous' neck."

"Then I will see the dragons," she whispered quietly as her eyes strayed to the mountain peaks. She would be able to see from her own eyes what had frightened her so much as a child—what would have been a warning to her parents had they believed her.

"Exactly. Can you do that?"

"I think so." She dragged her eyes back down to his and couldn't help but smile. Finally, she had a goal, something to reach toward, the first footstep in her long plan to avenge those she loved. She was still terrified of where that road led—into Thaddeus's mind—but she didn't have to think so far ahead, not yet anyway. "Thank you, Uncle

Dalton."

He smiled back and pulled her into his embrace. "Of course, child. I would do anything for you."

"I know." She nestled her head against his chest and closed her eyes.

"You are incredible, Stephania. You are precious, and beautiful, and kind, and determined, and stubborn, and you are perfect the way you are. Don't let anyone tell you that you are anything less, especially yourself."

She smiled and huffed. "I'll try not to."

"And you know I would love you even if you weren't that amazing?" He ruffled her hair, and she pulled away, rolling her eyes with a laugh.

"Yes, you've said."

"Good." He winked before turning away. "Sleep well, my child. I hope you find what you're looking for in your dreams."

"I hope I do too," she whispered before she ducked into her tent.

After peeling off her grimy top layer of clothes, she drew the furs over her, shivering in the cold autumn night.

She tossed and turned for a while, trying to focus on the mountain peaks she could barely see through the flap of her tent, and the marks she remembered seeing on Mischievous' neck. Nothing happened. Finally, too tired from the day's earlier lessons, she stopped trying and let her mind wander to the stars.

She could see a few shining above the mountains, and she quickly recalled the constellation as the Leaping Faun—one of the first constellations Trojan had taught her. Suddenly feeling ill, she rolled onto her side and clenched her fists. Would everything be tainted with his memory?

The last time she had read the stars was the night before she lost her memories. With the return of those memories, she still remembered how, but now the act seemed so foreign instead of natural. She knew she should practice more, but the few times she *had* read the stars as a child, their messages had seemed so trivial or confusing; she didn't want to deal with more frustrating riddles at the moment. Even so, she wondered if they would ever speak about what her future would be. Would she defeat Thaddeus, or would his reign of terror never end? Would she meet the prophesized helper? Who was it? Did the stars ever speak of such things?

The thoughts only made her feel more exhausted, and finally, her eyelids dropped low. Somewhere outside, a dragon roared—or perhaps it was just the wind in the trees. Before she could wonder any longer, she was astride a green dragon, her small chubby legs bouncing happily as she traced her baby fingers across five long red marks.

FOR MOST OF THE NEXT DAY, Stephania rode in silence, tears choking her vision and throat each time she thought about what she had seen the night before. From her own child eyes, she had seen the shining, white and gold dragon and the black, wretched creature they had been flying toward. She remembered screaming at her parents to go a different way, begging them to, knowing danger had been ahead. She remembered staring up into the possessed eyes of her mother and remembered how they hadn't changed course from the one that led them to their deaths.

Murderer. The word echoed over and over in her mind. She couldn't banish the guilt from herself. If only she had been more adamant, if only her parents had listened to her and believed her, if only her father had seen it before it was too late, they would be alive right now. It would be them she was going home to in Duvarharia, instead of strangers.

She had told Dalton as she promised, and he seemed to be just as disturbed as her. Was he angry at Drox and Andromeda for not heeding their daughter's warning? She knew she was.

Neither could stay sullen for long. The mountains grew taller around them and then stretched out into valleys they could see through for miles. Birds sang, and the wind blew, and colorful leaves fluttered to the ground like feathers. It was quiet, it was peaceful, and neither ever wanted to leave. Even the horses needed constant urging so they wouldn't slow to a walk and wander off the path.

"I wasn't your fault." His eyes met hers for a moment, and she nodded.

She had lost count how many times he had told her that, but she needed to hear it each and every time. *It wasn't my fault. It was Thaddeus's. It wasn't my fault. It was Thaddeus's.*

By the time the suns sank low over the mountain tops and they had come into the already made camp, her hate and anger toward Thaddeus fueled her determination, and she finally felt like training again.

They trained in both magic and swords until they couldn't see any longer, and then Dalton had her practice her knowledge in Duvarharian culture and ancient language.

It became easier to recall her memories after Dalton gave her exercises to recall events from a week ago, six months, a year, and then older and older. Eventually, she was able to stand at the edge of a cliff near their camp, look out over the moonlit plains that stretched until the Cavos Desert, and listen to the wind as it whispered words from a memory trying to surface.

"Mama. Watch. Watch. Mama."

Stephania sank to the cold rocks beneath her and closed her eyes. Her chest rose and fell as she forced herself to take long, deep breaths and clear from her mind anything but that sweet, young voice.

A smile spread across her face as she felt the earth fade from under her, and the sounds of the night quieted. Then, softly, she felt the wind rise around her, tugging at straight auburn hair that spilled down her shoulders and felt the warmth of a child in her arms, a green dragon beneath her ...

§

Filate Mountain Range
Day of the Battle of the Prophecy
Nearly 17 Years Ago

ANDROMEDA SOON TIRED *of watching the moonlit forest rush beneath her and turned her head to the horizon where the mountains loomed ever closer. She abruptly heard Stephania giggle happily, and the proud mother smiled, looking down at her daughter who had apparently finished her nap. She squirmed a bit before complaining about the straps on her legs.*

After gently instructing Stephania that the straps had been quite necessary, Andromeda stared, amused, into her daughter's solemn eyes.

"I flown witout dem before." Stephania crossed her chubby little arms and pouted, her head tilted back so she could see her mother.

Trying not to laugh at how diplomatic and stubborn her young daughter was, Andromeda shook her head.

"Oh, let her go, Andromeda! She's perfectly right, you know."

Andromeda rolled her eyes at her exuberant husband before turning her attention back to her daughter. "And what if you fall? Then what?"

Stephania shrugged. "You'll 'atch me."

Drox roared with laughter, and Andromeda was suddenly bombarded with Mischievous and Aldwyn saying she should let Stephania be the Dragon Rider she was meant to be, and that they shouldn't be afraid of her falling, seeing as she was such a good rider.

Unable to stay so serious, Andromeda finally gave in. Within only a few seconds of being untied, Stephania scooted up a few feet on Mischievous' slick green neck and was clutching two large protruding scales.

She will be a wonderful rider. *Mischievous spoke gently to her soul mate.*

Indeed, she will. *The woman smiled with pride as she watched her little girl.*

"Mama," Stephania suddenly pouted, again crossing her arms.

"Yes, my flame?"

"Mi'tibus has a red mark on her neck." Stephania ran her soft fingers over a gash on Mischievous' scales as she frowned, drawling out her words in premature speech. *"Dos stupid Etas! Dey should all be killed! All of dem!"*

For a second, Andromeda was shocked speechless at her daughter. Stephania knew the Etas were a threat to the Duvarharians and were the cause of all the constant fighting at the Dragon Palace, but she was stunned to hear Stephania expressing that she wanted them all exterminated. It was the first time Andromeda had ever heard her daughter be so impassioned about something, and so violent.

"Stephania, what makes you think they should all die?" Andromeda cautiously questioned.

The girl shrugged her shoulders and fidgeted with her leggings, suddenly timid.

"I just talked wit my fwiend. He said we should kill dem all. T'addus too" Stephania tilted her head back and looked at her mom. Her chubby, soft face broke out into a little grin. *"He said we could do it togetter! He said it our dest'ny!"*

"Oh?" Andromeda crooned, dread settling in her stomach. *"Who is that?"* While she and her husband had taught Stephania about the Etas, they hadn't mentioned Thaddeus much around the young girl, preferring she not be raised to understand such evil so young. A tense knot tied itself inside Andromeda.

"Just him." Stephania quickly looked away, a small blush on her little cheeks.

Through her mental connection with her daughter, Andromeda caught a brief picture of a younger dragon man. It was the new Susokxoch–Syrus Vespucci.

§

Filate Mountain Range
Present Day

STEPHANIA OPENED HER eyes to the moons and brushed the fresh tears from her eyes.

She called me little flame. Her little flame. She laughed and smiled through her tears as she pulled her knees to her chest. With a flush of appreciation, she realized a fur had been wrapped around her shoulders. *Thank you, Uncle Dalton.* Syrus had known her and her family well. He was waiting at the Dragon Palace. Something between joy and dread filled her. Would he recognize her? Would he care for her as he once did? Or would it all be different now that she had grown up? Too many years had gone by for her to consider him more than a family friend, let alone someone like an older brother.

Would she be able to look to him for help and company, or would he be a stranger?

The stars demanded her attention, and as she focused on them and opened her heart to them, she could hear the stories they told about her parents' last flight across Ventronovia. A sweet bitterness hung in her heart as she listened to them sing, only able to understand a few words from their celestial song. They had loved her parents, the stars had. They had seen their deaths, and they had mourned even before the tragedy.

They had been beautiful people, loved people, cherished by many, even by the stars. Her eyes opened as she shook her head, placing her chin on her knees. *And I shall never know them. Never.*

She cried until the moons were small and high overhead.

Not never. A strange peace settled over her. *I can know them through these memories. I can cherish what little bit I have from them in the small way I can. I will remember the good, remember how beautiful they were, and I shall look past their end and the ugly way death painted them.*

PART FOUR
Shadows of Light

CHAPTER 29

I T WAS AN HONOR TO TRAVEL alongside you and offer my protection." Dakar placed his fist over his heart and bowed low.

Stephania raised her head and placed her own fist over her heart. "It was an honor to be protected by such Warriors as you and your battalion. Trojan would be proud of your service and expertise. He left his army in the best hands. As is Trans-Falls now." Her voice cracked, but she still sounded more confident than she felt.

Dakar straightened his shoulders and nodded. A mist covered his eyes as he stepped forward and abruptly embraced Stephania.

She was too shocked to react, but as he whispered in her ear, she put her arms around him and squeezed hard.

"Thank you, Stephania. For everything. I will bear the title of heir with pride and honor. Lycus and I will lead our people with pride and strength; we will make you proud."

She nodded against him, biting back tears

"Now, you must carry the mantle Trojan left you with pride and resolve. I believe his sacrifice was worth it now. You must too." He pulled away, his eyes searching hers.

She swallowed past the lump in her throat and nodded. "I will. I will make it worth it. I promise."

"Thank you. May the suns smile upon your presence."

She bowed her head. "As do the stars sing upon yours."

He trotted back to the forest line where his army stepped out into the plains, their fists over their hearts.

She saluted them back, her heart swelling with purpose and sadness as their chant rose into the air.

"*Shafalœ ray zi zoud, Farloon, lear, ray zi rok, Farloon.* Emperor be with you, Farloon, and be with us, Farloon."

Stephania nodded before she turned and mounted Braken, holding her hand high in the air in farewell as the Centaurs turned and galloped into the woods, their thundering hooves fading into the distance.

Dalton was saying something about the supplies the warriors had gathered and left for them and then something about rationing water, and then about plans if they got separated, but she found it hard to concentrate on what he was saying as the grass turned to sand and the horses' hoofbeats were lost.

This was it. She was really moving forward.

Something about this desert felt like the end of everything behind her and the start of everything before her.

"Stephania, did you hear me?"

"Huh?" She tried to recall what he had said but drew a blank. "I'm sorry, I spaced out."

He didn't seem to be too annoyed, though, and simply repeated what he said. "I don't plan on passing through the old Cavos Hatching Grounds because it would be an extra day's trip, but if we get separated on the way, I want that to be our meeting place. It's possible an oasis may be at the center of the grounds, and it would be better than wandering around the desert looking for each other. If we travel north of it and then get separated, we'll meet up in Sankyz. Is that alright?"

"Yes, I understand."

"Good. As you know, we're going to be traveling in the late night and early mornings. It'll take roughly five to seven days to cross, but I'm hoping we make it in five. I was thinking ..."

Stephania spaced out again, his ramblings fading into the darkening night.

Taking a deep breath, she searched inside herself for the now familiar sense of magic and tapped into it, coaxing it forward. Focusing more on the thoughts needed to cover her trace rather than create a complex spell, she released the magic, and the sand lifted around her. Beads of sweat that had nothing to do with the lingering heat of the desert spotted her forehead. She held the spell for a minute and then two. Dalton never turned around. With a gasp of relief, she released the magic, and the sand dropped around her. A smirk of pride crept onto her lips.

Dalton had promised her he would tell her if he could sense her magic while she was practicing the covering spell. This was her first successful attempt.

She practiced a few more times before rejoicing to Dalton and showing him her newfound skill, one she had vowed she would learn before she came to the desert. When she tired of that, she fell to imagining shapes in the sand. It wasn't hard; a sort of hypnotic air hung around them, lulling her into a sleeping wakefulness in which her imagination ran wild.

Time didn't seem to apply to the desert. She could see the rise and fall of the dunes ahead of her, to the side of her, and then after a while, behind her. It was the same expanse over and over. They were only a few hours in, and already she could easily see how it could drive someone mad.

Without any distractions, she found it easy to call up memories, and before she knew it, a memory from her parents' dragons effortlessly surfaced.

§

Cavos Desert

Night of the Battle of the Prophecy

Nearly 17 Years Ago

ALWYN, DID YOU SEE THAT? *Mischievous angled her head to better see the land beneath her.*

No. What is it? *Briefly, he let his mind join with his mate's, and he saw through her eyes.* There. Just below us.

He snapped back into his body, his mind going blank. Is that—

I don't know. *Mischievous' throat rumbled nervously, her eyes fixed on the shape below them. It looked like another dragon, but it appeared to be only a shadow.*

I think it is one of our own shadows, dear. *He sounded slightly amused, but she didn't return the humor.*

Dread crept into the crevices of Mischievous' mind. But it's not. Look. There's one, two shadows from us, and then there's that.

The shape continued to glide close to the desert sands, its form indistinct. Sure enough, two more shadows slid across the desert sands, one on its right, and another on its left.

It is still a shadow, though. See how its shape moves with the dunes. Perhaps it is from a dragon above us. *Though he tried, Aldwyn could not mask the unease in his own voice. Another dragon could bring a whirlwind of problems, especially if it was wild.*

They checked the skies above them. Nothing. When they turned their attention back to the sands, the shape was gone. No trace of the shadow was left.

A chill traversed between their minds. Nothing could explain what they had seen.

Let's not tell Andromeda and Drox. They needn't more to worry about than they already have.

Mischievous grunted in agreement.

§

309

Cavos Desert

Present Day

STEPHANIA GROGGILY PULLED herself from the memory. It had been harder to hold on to their voices because they were thoughts rather than words spoken by a mouth. Her shoulders sagged with a sudden exhaustion, but even so, her heart pounded with excitement.

What had they seen? Could it really have been a dragon? Her eyes darted across the vast expanse of sand, but she saw nothing more than the dunes, a cloudy night sky, and the moons. Disappointment wormed its way into her, but she didn't let it dispel the hope within her. Perhaps wild dragons weren't as extinct as everyone had been led to believe. Perhaps dragons still inhabited this desert, and perhaps, just perhaps, she would be able to bond with one.

She continued to search the horizon for even a glimpse of the shadowy figure her parents' dragons had seen, but nothing moved. Eventually, she gave up and sank back into the strange waking dreams the desert seemed to induce.

After what seemed like only a few minutes and an eternity, the suns began to shine over the golden sands and it soon became blindingly bright. Dalton quickly taught her a light dimming spell to shield her eyes from the light, but she was so tired, she wasn't able to maintain the spell well enough make a difference.

Finally, he declared it high noon. She nearly fell off Braken, barely able to take a drink from their flasks and offer some to her stallion before she flopped down on the sand under the small tent Dalton had pitched. Her exhaustion overtook her, but it was miserable trying to sleep on burning sand under glaring suns, even with a tent overhead.

When Dalton woke her up after the suns had just begun to set, she felt no more refreshed than before she had gone to sleep. As they mounted and slowly started back into the darkening plane, she vowed she wouldn't let the memories overcome her again; she feared her exhaustion would affect her ability to sustain magic. If she lost control of her magic, the memories could take all her energy and she could end up killing herself.

Even so, it was almost more work to push the memories back than it was to embrace them. Finally, she had to keep awake by making conversation.

"I had another memory vision last night."

"Oh?" He sounded just as tired and through with the desert as she did.

"It was a memory from Mischievous this time."

"Oh. What was that like?" He turned in his saddle, his curiosity piqued and his

310

eyes regaining a bit of their usual sparkle.

"Difficult. Sometimes it almost felt like they weren't speaking the common tongue. It was more like I was feeling what they were saying." She paused. "Kind of like listening to the stars."

With a grunt of humor, he turned back forward and nodded. "That's about what it's like to be bonded with a dragon. You have to learn to not only hear each other and understand, but to *feel* and *be* each other."

"It sounds so strange."

"It is, until you're bonded, and then it feels like the most natural thing you've ever done. But what was the memory of?"

Her brows furrowed as she shifted in the saddle. "I'm not completely sure, but Mischievous and Aldwyn thought they saw another dragon."

Dalton pulled against Austin's reins until the horse slowed enough for him to be walking side by side Braken. "A dragon? Here? In the Cavos?"

She nodded quickly. "But it wasn't really a dragon. It was more of a shadow. It moved against the dunes like a shadow anyway, and they couldn't see any other dragon around that would've cast it."

A clear laugh rang from Dalton's lips as he shook his head. "Incredible. Absolutely incredible. I can't believe they didn't realize what they were seeing. I guess it makes sense, though. No one's seen one for thousands of years."

"What?"

A boyish grin spread across his face. "A Shadow Dragon. They have the ability to shift their form into a shadow, nothing more than a wisp of pure darkness. They can pass through physical objects and melt into the night. The only way to kill them in that form is by a direct wound to the heart, but even that is nearly impossible."

Her heart thundered in her chest. *A Shadow Dragon.* Could such a legendary creature really exist? Had that really been what her parents' dragons had seen all those years ago? And, if so, was the dragon still here?

"Do you think it's still here?"

Their eyes met, and she knew he was thinking the same thing she was: could she bond with it?

"I don't see why not." His hands fiddled with the reins in his excitement, but he suddenly shook his head. "But I don't know if you could bond with it. The dragon would have to be at least fifteen years old and more wild than the ocean. I'm not sure we could even get close to it. Not to mention, I haven't seen many documented records of Duvarharians bonding with them. They seem almost impossible to bond with."

Her heart sank, but once again, the spark of hope in her would not be dispelled.

A thirst waved over her. She wanted a dragon. She wanted a Shadow Dragon.

Thoughts of what it would be like to ride high above the land, possibly even above the clouds, to be able to go where she wanted, anytime she wanted, to see the world below her so small and insignificant, soon turned into daydreams that matched with the rhythm of the horse beneath her. Shapes and shadows on the sand jumped and wavered into dragons that swooped and flew just above the ground. Remembering how Dalton used to be able to tell stories that listeners could almost see playing out in front of them, and realizing he must have used some sort of magic illusion to do so, she tapped into the magic in her mind and let the shapes and shadows lift from the sands and soar in the clouds. As long as she didn't focus too much on the details, she could almost believe the dragons were alive around her.

Slowly, as her magic let go of reality around her, the vivid daydream faded into the darkness. But despite the lack of the daydream, she couldn't shake the feeling that she hadn't fully awoken.

"Uncle Dalton?" Her voice sounded muffled. It was most likely a trick on the sandy wind, though. However, he didn't acknowledge her. "Uncle Dalton?" She raised her voice to be heard but couldn't seem to shout any louder. Subtle panic rose in her, but she perceived nothing to worry about. Something seemed to be wrong, but she couldn't find what.

"Stephania ..." Dalton whispered, sounding eerily close as if he were only a few feet to her side and not in front of her, facing the opposite direction. "Stephania, don't draw too much attention to it, but a creature is following us on the right."

She turned to look, but he snapped at her. "By the gods, I said don't draw attention to it! We don't want to instigate it."

The reins cut into her hands as she gripped them tightly. By slightly turning her head, she could just make out the shape of a dark creature about one hundred feet to their right. It looked similar to an Eta on a horse, but both the horse's eyes and what she could only assume to be the Eta's eyes glowed a sickening yellow.

The creature turned to look at her.

With a sharp breath, she snapped her eyes back to between Braken's ears. Oddly, he didn't seem frightened, and neither did Austin. Usually, the horses were reliable with sensing danger. Either this creature wasn't an Eta, or something was wrong with their horses. She hoped it was the former.

"What is it?" Her voice, which had seemed muffled earlier, now sounded too loud. The creature started closing the distance between them. It was only eighty feet away.

She didn't like how Dalton wasn't answering her. "Is it an Eta?"

Finally, he shook his head, and Austin slowed his pace. "Get close to me, Stephania."

She urged Braken forward until she was beside him. She tried to look at his face, but he wouldn't look up. Perhaps he was avoiding the gaze of the creature like she had, but something told her he would've at least looked at her.

"It's something much worse."

Her blood ran like ice in her veins.

It was only sixty feet away now.

"What is it?" She couldn't stop her voice from trembling.

"It's a *Zeufax*. A demon of Susahu, and warrior of Raythuz."

Horror froze her limbs. Raythuz, the fallen warrior, the master of the Corrupt Magic—one of his followers was here. She didn't have to think long to realize why.

"It wants the Lyre," she whispered just as Dalton did the same.

He nodded slowly. "We may stand a chance if we can make it to the Hatching Grounds."

Dread dropped in her stomach. "But it's so far away."

He nodded slowly. "I know. But it's our only chance for protection."

"Right, okay." Stephania could feel the weight of the Lyre pressing on her mind, and the more she thought about it, the more the overwhelming urge to take it out grew on her.

"It's going to go after you; it knows you have the Lyre. Give me the Lyre; we have to protect it. I'll take it to the Hatching Grounds. You distract the creature, and I'll come back for you when the Lyre is safe. The most important thing is to protect the Lyre." He held his hand out to her, but still he refused look at her.

Her heart thundered wildly. Something was horribly wrong. Dalton would never value the Lyre over her life. "What? You want me to give it to you?"

The creature was less than fifty feet away now.

"Yes, Stephania, give me the Lyre. It's the only way. Do it now!" His voice has risen to a horrible pitch she had never heard him use before.

Franticly, she looked around, trying to find her Uncle Dalton, not whatever cursed form of him this was. She screamed for him, but her words were muffled in her ears.

The creature was almost to them.

Dalton was grabbing at her saddle. "Stephania, please! It will hurt you if it finds the Lyre with you!"

For a moment his voice sounded almost human. "Uncle Dalton?" *What if he's possessed?* In the second she hesitated, the creature slammed its dark mount into Austin, but instead of it pushing Dalton and the horse aside, it simply melded all together until the creature, lunging, clawing, snapping, and screaming her name, was not Dalton at all.

Stephania firmly grasped the Lyre and violently pulled on Braken's reigns in an attempt to escape, but the horse couldn't move fast enough on the sand, and he fell, screaming, on top of Stephania, pinning her to the ground. The cloth around on the Lyre disintegrated as the darkness of the *Źeufax* wrapped around it and her, pressing the air from her lungs and Braken's.

"Give me the Lyre, you wench." Two sets of flaming yellow eyes bore holes into her as the rancid darkness pressed in around them. It slithered up her arms and chest, around her neck, and slowly, painfully, into her ears, nose, mouth.

She tried to scream, tried to breath, but as the darkness filled her body, she found she could do no more than cry and desperately hold on to the Lyre that wouldn't allow her to let it go.

The darkness was in her mind, working its way into her muscles. It was physical, but it was magical, and she was powerless to fight it. Its control took over her arm. She tried to resist it, but when she felt the bones in her fingers begin to weaken, she let it take over. One by one, her fingers loosened and let go.

Her last two fingers clutched furiously to the Lyre. Stars spotted across her vision as the lack of oxygen and pain forced her to the brink of unconsciousness.

Whatever gods protect this Lyre, she pleaded, *let them now protect me too.*

Her last finger began to peel away from the Lyre, and the green glow started fading to black. As her eyes fluttered close, she heard a horrible snarl from just behind her.

A flash of brilliant blue arched over her as a massive form collided into the darkness, knocking it off her and Braken.

The two creatures tumbled in the sand before viciously tearing into each other, their grunts and cries filling the once calm night air.

She took only a moment to force air into her lungs without choking on it before she began shoving against Braken, yelling, pleading with him to stand.

Blood foamed at the horse's mouth as he tried to breathe. Black seeped through his veins under his skin, reminiscent of Artigal's wound. Tears filled her eyes as she frantically called her horse's name, willing him to stand. He didn't have much more time, but she needed him to at least move off her pinned leg, if nothing else.

After a few struggled attempts, the horse miraculously leapt to his feet, the burning fear in his eyes. She barely had time to remount him before he bolted.

Against the biting wind and sand, she kept taking as steady of breaths as she could manage, both to calm herself and to resupply oxygen to her muddled brain. When she looked back to the creatures, she thought she saw something like a giant wolf fighting what she could only describe as a spawn of Susahu.

Confused, she forced herself to focus only on the empty terrain in front of her. It was too dark to see anything more than what the bit of moonlight shone on, but she was too panicked to create magical light to see by. Dalton was nowhere in sight.

An ear-splitting howl drew her attention back to the fight far behind her. The shining blue creature was racing after the demon as it chased her down.

"Braken ..." She fumbled with the magic at her hands, trying desperately to urge the horse on faster, but his wounds were catching up to him, and he was already galloping as fast as he could across the loose sand.

It would only be a matter of seconds before the demon was upon them. Its hungry yellow eyes burned into hers.

The wolf leapt onto the back of the demonic atrocity and bit down on its neck. The demon screamed with rage.

Claws sprouted from its back as it tried to tear the wolf from itself. Blood speckled the sand, but the wolf's hold on its neck didn't loosen. With a final, blood curdling crunch, the wolf sunk its teeth into the creature's spine before ripping it out. A piece of dark flesh and bone fell from its jaws as the wolf tumbled to the ground.

With frantic thrashes, the creature screamed, struggling to its feet, still desperate to close the space between it and the Lyre.

A cold voice rang through Stephania's mind as her eyes met the creature's, her neck aching from looking back so long. *The Zelauwgugey will be mine. In the void where magic doesn't reach, where your calls to the Shushequmok won't be heard, I will be waiting for you. I will be waiting for the Zelauwgugey. You cannot be safe forever.*

The voice faded, leaving terror vibrating in her veins and memories of the Corrupt Magic pressing to the surface.

The burning light from the creature's eyes consumed the rest of its body before pouring into the sand beneath it. A loud rumble split the air, and the ground shook under her. Braken fell to his knees, and she tumbled off him. "No, no, no." As soon as she could find footing on the shaking sands, she quickly stood again, furiously trying to pull Braken to his feet. He was barely able to stand, but as soon as he was upright, she mounted him again, fearful to touch the sand lest the creature was in it under her.

For a moment, everything was still and silent.

Then the earth fell out from under her.

Her scream was cut short as sand filled her mouth. She felt Braken's body slam on top of her, shoving her deeper into the sand, the horse's blood-chilling screams piercing the air.

She heard the angry howl of the wolf and something that sounded like someone calling her name, but she couldn't cry out as sand burned her throat and swallowed her body in a gritty hug. Braken rolled off her just as something under her crashed into her body and threw her out of the sand, leaving her tumbling and sliding down an impossibly steep slope.

Before she could even attempt to pull herself to her feet, she heard the most wretched, high-pitch scream rend the air from the center of a black crater that opened in front of her. In the flickering moonlight from behind clouds, she spotted rows and rows of something sharp lining the crater. Her blood ran cold as she realized what she was looking at: a gigantic mouth.

Sand scratched her throat as she screamed in horror, flailing to find some sort of traction in it. She pulled out her sword and stabbed it into the ground ahead of her, but it was as if the ground were liquid, pouring down all around her, sweeping her toward the gaping, hungry mouth.

Adrenaline dumped into her veins, and she had to bite back the bile rising from her nauseous stomach. Tears streamed down her face as she screamed for Dalton, but she heard no response.

A thick limb, similar to what had thrown her out of the sand, slapped the sand beneath her, wiping it out from under her. Whatever traction she had gained was lost as she slid hopelessly toward the dark pit. Before she reached the gaping mouth though, a dark shape reached out and wrapped itself around her in a constricting grasp.

Without thinking, she began wildly stabbing and cutting at the arm. With another ear-piercing screech, the creature let go of her, but before she could even stand, another large tentacle wrapped around her, this time pinning both arms to her sides.

A smaller tentacle reached out toward her, something like a mouth opening and closing at the end of it.

"Gods of all," she whimpered before the barbed tongue lashed out and pierced her leg. She felt no pain. In fact, she didn't feel anything at all. Her whole leg was numb. She screamed for Dalton, for the Trans-Falls warriors, for Trojan, for her parents, for any god who might be listening, but no one came. Another tentacle stabbed her other leg, her thrashing completely useless, and she knew it was only a matter of time before one lashed at her head and she was dead.

Another howl tore through the air.

Instantly, the paralyzing tentacles retracted from her, and the arm wrapped tight around her loosened ever so slightly.

Before she could search for the wolf or even comprehend why the sand creature was losing interest in her, she heard a voice calling out to her.

"Stephania! You must relax! You must go completely limp!" The voice sounded strange, as if it were one she had heard before, but she didn't have time to think why.

"Are you insane?" She continued to thrash against the arm, and what little slack it had given her disappeared as it squeezed harder. She felt her back pop, and she had to gasp for air.

"Act dead! It won't be able to sense you if you don't move! It's not hunting right now. It's only been awoken because of the *Żeufax*, and it will let you go if you just relax!"

She tried desperately but only succeeded in panicking more, tensing her body. The creature sensed her movement, and the barbs snaked their way back toward her.

Another howl rang out across the desert just above her, drawing her eyes skyward. She could barely see through the sand and tears in her eyes but was able to make out a dark wolf shape standing on the edge of the great chasm she and the creature were in. The glowing blue markings on the wolf wove together and grew until they formed a wolfish figure of absolute magic that hovered around the wolf, taking the creature's attention.

Just then, the clouds rolled back from the moon, bathing the creature holding her in pale light.

Her blood ran cold. "By the gods."

It was a huge disc-like creature about the size of a small town with an enormous mouth gaping open at its center; rows upon rows of teeth lined the circular opening with a huge tongue that reached out like another arm—a colossal monster clearly designed to hunt and feast creatures much larger than herself.

Tentacles grew out of the body everywhere, making it seem like a horribly disproportionate sand octopus. Each tentacle had strange fin-like appendages that opened and closed, scooping huge piles of sand, and she realized it used those fins to support the sand above itself, and then when it sensed its prey, it would close the fins, creating a huge chasm impossible to escape.

Impossible to escape.

She felt like she was watching in slow motion as the wolf raced down toward the center of the animal. Her breath caught in something between a cry of warning and a gasp of horror.

"Stephania, focus! This is only a distraction. Relax!" The voice continued to plead with her, but she couldn't look away.

The fight was mesmerizing.

She watched as a tentacle with a gaping, ripping mouth, much larger than the ones around her, snapped at the wolf with terrific speed. Her eyes widened as one of the tentacles crashed into the wolf and burned from its magic.

The wolf twisted and with unbelievable agility, chased down the tentacle and sank

317

its own razor-sharp teeth deep into the appendage. Stephania's ears popped as the sand creature screamed in pain when its tentacle was severed. Three more arms reached for the wolf, but it quickly dispatched the first with ease.

Somehow, the wolf managed to get the second two tangled and tearing into each other, leaving a straight shot to the sand creature's gaping mouth.

Stephania cried out in warning and horror, thinking the wolf was going to leap into the creature's throat, but just before it did, the magic surrounding the wolf gathered into a mass that dove into the mouth instead. The wolf barely managed to flee the tentacles that rushed to futilely tear the magic from its throat before the magic exploded. A disturbing amount of blood sprayed the sand and the creature as it screamed in pain. Its arms thrashed, tossing Stephania to the side, suddenly unconcerned with her.

For a moment, as she tried to dodge the arms and stop herself from falling through the sand, she thought the creature was dying, until she realized it was only burying itself again and would bury her with it.

Panic filled her mind, and despite her body succumbing to the creature's poison, she flailed against the waves of sand, crying out to the wolf as it raced toward her.

Moments before it reached her, a wave of sand covered her, and she felt the crushing weight of the desert overtake her.

For a few long moments, she knew only pain and darkness before her lungs began to burn and her consciousness faded.

§

"STEPHANIA? STEPHANIA, IT'S time to wake up. The hatchling awaits you."

Stephania groaned and rolled over, quickly jumping away when the hot sand burned her arm. When she sat up, her eyes locked on the biggest blue eyes she had ever seen.

"What in Susahu ..." She screamed, scrambling to her feet and franticly searching for her weapon when she saw what the eyes belonged to.

It was the wolf, bigger than a draft horse and black as the night with shining blue markings decorating its body. His mouth hung open, revealing deadly canines.

"Do not be afraid."

She stopped her panicked searching and stared at the wolf. *Am I dreaming or did it actually speak to me?*

"I can talk, and I will not harm you. In fact, I just saved your life if you remember."

Stephania rubbed her eyes. They felt a little raw from the sand, but when she opened them, the wolf was still sitting, looming, in front of her, its intelligent, sparkling eyes gazing patiently and expectantly into hers.

"Why isn't your mouth moving?" It was a foolish first question to ask, but she couldn't stop it as it left her mouth.

Something between a growl and a laugh reverberated through the air as the wolf blinked slowly. "I am actually growling softly to you, but you hear words in your language because I am your *Sheseknunosh*, or as you say in the common tongue, Guardian Wolf."

"What in Sushau is that? I've never heard of such a thing." She took a step forward, her wary eyes never leaving the wolf's. She recognized his voice as the one that told her to relax last night, and she faintly remembered feeling fur on the creature that dug her from the sand and pulled her to safety. If he wanted her dead, he wouldn't have saved her from the *Żeufax* and the sand creature, or he would've killed her already. She took another step forward and sensed a certain amount of amusement from him.

"I wouldn't expect you to hear about my Kind. We've been nearly extinct for thousands of years. I believe I might be the last one, or if I am not, few are left."

"Why hasn't Uncle Dalton told me about you? He knows every mythical creature in Rasa."

Another growl of laughter came from the wolf. "Foolish thinking. Not only does he *not* know every creature, but he refuses to believe in some he *does* know. Especially ones that prove the existence of a deity."

"What do you mean?"

"You know your Uncle Dalton is not a religious man?"

She nodded.

"I am the embodiment of a god's will. Here I am, standing in front of you. I exist, I am what I am. You have no choice but to believe in me, your senses prove I am here. And yet, my presence is proof a god exists. If you aren't religious, wouldn't you want to ignore me?"

Stephania frowned. This was too much to think about so soon after waking up and in such blinding light. She sank to the ground, her legs starting to throb where she had been stabbed by the paralyzing barbs. The wolf must've also given her some antidote; or else her body had purged the poison on its own, which she thought was unlikely.

"I suppose I would."

"Then that is why he wouldn't have told you. I am what he doesn't want to acknowledge."

Wait. Where is Uncle Dalton? Her eyes darted around the small camp, but neither Dalton nor the two horses were to be seen. "Where is he?" She jumped back to her feet, despite the stabbing pain. "Did he make it out alive? Where is my horse?"

The wolf's head hung low, and her heart dropped in her stomach.

"No. No. No. He can't be dead."

The wolf quickly took a step toward her, his eyes suddenly worried. "Oh no, your uncle is alive and so is his horse."

"Thank the gods." The sudden rush of adrenaline left her feeling slightly nauseous.

"But your horse, I am afraid, was not so fortunate."

Horror crashed over her again. *Braken is dead.* She covered her mouth with her hand and stifled a sob. *My buckskin. My reminder of Trojan. My horse. Dead.* She bit her lip until she tasted blood and felt the sting of pain. What else would she lose on this cursed journey to Duvarharia?

"I am sorry, Stephania. He was a magnificent horse, a true companion. I'm sorry you had to lose him." He stepped closer, but she turned from him, refusing his comfort.

She didn't have time for grief. If they stayed any longer in this desert, they would run out of supplies. She needed to find Dalton and move on. She had to get to Duvarharia, she had to be done with this journey. "What is your name?" Her voice was cold as she dried her eyes from her tears and started rolling up the thin fabric she had been sleeping on.

"Xavier, servant of the Creator Źuje, Guardian of Stephania Lavoisier." He bowed as well as a wolf could. "And I am here to protect and serve you until you no longer have need of me."

Stephania clenched her fists and nodded. "Where is Uncle Dalton?"

He stood and gestured with his muzzle somewhere into the distance. "He is on his way to the Cavos Hatching Grounds where he will wait for you and where the hatchling waits as well."

"What do you mean, the hatchling?"

"You will know in time. Now, crawl onto my back. I will take you there."

After a moment's hesitation, she threw the small satchel over her shoulder and climbed onto his broad back, wrapping her fingers in his long fur. He stood and gave a small shake of his head; blue sparks like embers fell from his glowing fur as he spoke a few words she couldn't comprehend, then leapt forward.

The air rushed from her lungs, and if it weren't for her firm grip on his fur, she would've been thrown from his back. The dunes rushed past them in a golden-tan blur. Even the sun wasn't hot on her as the air rushed across her skin.

"Warn me if I am going too fast. I am impatient for you to continue your journey."

She couldn't even take enough of a breath to answer.

"Think to me. Direct your thoughts to me, and I will hear them."

It's fine. I just didn't expect it. She wasn't confident he would actually hear her and was surprised when he laughed in response.

"Good. I am pleased. I was able to retrieve two of your packs. One seems to have a few water bottles and your cloak, but the other contains the *Zelauwgugey*."

Her brows shot up as she felt the packs she had haphazardly grabbed before mounting him. Sure enough, the Lyre was still wrapped tightly in one. Unwelcome relief filled her; she had almost been hoping she had lost it and wouldn't have to deal with its curse and the horrible flashbacks it brought, but the connection she had with it still wouldn't let her part with it. *How is he able to see it? I thought it was invisible to everyone but me.*

"It is made of the same sort of magic I am. I have been gifted with seeing the unseen."

She didn't answer, too confused and unnerved that he had listened in to her thoughts to say much.

They rode in silence until the terrain started showing less dunes and more jagged rocks.

"We are nearing the Hatching Grounds. It should only be a few more minutes now."

She nodded, directing her understanding to him, and he grunted in acknowledgement. After weighing whether or not to ask, she finally directed to him a question that had been eating at her.

How did the Źeufax find me?

A solemn silence filled their minds and the air before he answered. "Because Raythuz always knows where you are."

A chill ran down her spine. *How?*

"He is the master of the Corrupt Magic, and it lives inside of you, even when you don't feel it, just the same as the Pure Magic. Unlike Thaddeus, he exists above and beyond this plane and is not restricted by its laws. He does not need spies, or Etas, or petty magic to find and track you. All he needed was for you to let your guard down ever so slightly to infiltrate it, fill it with a vision, and overpower you."

Dread welled up inside her. She couldn't even wrap her mind around how something so evil could know where she was all the time and had access to her mind so easily. It really hadn't been Dalton who had asked for the Lyre. It had been Raythuz and the *Źeufax*.

"But I do not say this to frighten you, Stephania, only to make you aware. More evil lurks in the land than you realize. It is not just Thaddeus and the Etas you have to be aware of. You must understand the enemy is everywhere and can snare you at any time. You must always be diligent."

But will I ever be safe? Will he just appear like that again? How can I trust anything when he can take hold of me like that?

"Some places and people on this world offer protection from him, like the *Gauwu Zelauw* in Trans-Falls, the Dragon Palace in Duvaharia, or Igentis Artigal: anywhere the Pure Magic is strong or barriers of magic have been placed for protection. Though he is not unable to attack those places or people, for he wins by infiltrating the weak and breaking down the individual, it's not as easy for him or likely to happen. But you will not be able to stay in those places or be with those people forever. The Cavos desert is vast and empty. Without strong magical souls around you, you are nothing but a songbird to a lion here. You will find safety in the Hatching Grounds, but someday, you will have to step out into desolate places like this where others can't protect you."

The demon's words echoed in her mind. *In the void where magic doesn't reach, where your calls to the Shushequmok won't be heard, I will be waiting for you. I will be waiting for the Zelauwgugey. You cannot be safe forever.* A cold spread to her limbs and settled in her heart.

How will I ever be able to fight him, then?

"By becoming the same as the places and people he can't easily touch. You must become a creature whose very existence subdues and banishes his power."

Her mind swam with his words. She was terrified and overwhelmed by them. How could she—a Duvarharian without a dragon and who was barely able to make small healing and light magic—become as powerful as the *Gauwu Zelauw* or Artigal? Powerful enough to banish and subdue the *Kijaqumok* instead of succumbing to it?

"We are here."

Pulling herself from her thoughts, she lifted her eyes to the horizon, her breath catching in her throat. The desert gaped open in front of them as if someone had torn a rift in the world itself.

They were standing at the edge of a cliff. Rocks jutted high above the cliff sides, holding the sand back from filling in the canyon. Below them, down tumbling, sharp slopes stretched out a cavernous canyon. Great rock arches decorated the canyon along with huge pillars and oddly shaped monuments. It was weathered by time, and most of it seemed to be swallowed in sand, but its incredible majesty was not lost.

The canyon stretched on for miles and miles. Red clay snaked through the rock pillars, like a natural road. Holes bored into the rocky cliff, and jutting precipices looked almost as if they were remnants of huge, old dwellings, but it was hard to tell from so far away.

Stephania slid from Xavier's back, her feet tingling with the shock, and stepped to the edge of the cliff, hot desert winds blowing through her hair. "By the gods."

Xavier rumbled in approval. "Welcome, Stephania, to the ruins of Yazkuza, the greatest dragon city to ever reside in Ventronovia."

§

IT TOOK A FEW long hours to navigate the treacherous slopes down the Hatching Ground cliffsides. Stephania had insisted on walking most of the way, but when she couldn't find footing, she had been forced to trust Xavier's strength and magic to guide them.

As the slopes leveled out, Stephania stumbled toward a patch of shadowed sand, wishing to collapse in rest, but a cry of distress turned her blood cold. "Did you hear that?" She whirled around to face Xavier.

His solemn, ancient eyes narrowed, and he shook his head. "What did it sound like?"

A frown dipped her lips. "I'm not sure ..." Then she heard it again, this time more clearly. Somehow, she knew exactly what it was, and her eyes widened. "It's a dragon. A young one."

Xavier threw back his head and howled. "Creator be praised! Quickly, Stephania. We must press on. Your destiny awaits you. The shadows await you."

Before she could ask what he meant, he wrapped his huge jaws around her and carefully tossed her onto his back. In her surprise, she barely had time to grab a fistful of his fur before she was thrown off.

The pillars of rock grew bigger the farther in the canyon they traveled, and when the ruins loomed over them as they passed, she realized they were much larger than she had at first thought.

Hard as it was to focus when Xavier was running so fast, she was just able to make out the dug-out portions of rock. A thrill raced through her when her suspicions were confirmed. Many of the holes looked to have been meticulously carved into the rock and some extended into dark chasms bored deep into the monuments, creating huge caverns. Some even had decorative designs, and if the suns hit them just right, she could almost convince herself the designs glowed in different colors as if made from magic.

"Stephania. Look."

Turning her attention to where they were going, Stephania felt her heart stop then slam against her ribs, her blood running cold.

"By the stars."

The cry she had heard pierced the air clearly, echoing eerily across the rock. Her eyes locked on the creature. The world quieted and slowed around her.

It was indeed a young dragonet.

Its form was young and immature, but one characteristic stood out above all others: it was made of shadow. Bits of its body flickered from solid flesh and clean-cut lines to wispy trails of void that melted off its body and faded in the light. It was as if pure darkness had taken the form of a dragon. It screamed again, flapping its powerful wings, throwing sand and rocks at whatever was distressing it.

A horse screamed in fear, and a man shouted.

"Dalton."

Stephania stumbled down from Xavier and stepped out so she could see better.

Dalton was waving his hands at the dragon, trying to frighten it away. The dragonet seemed more interested in eating Austin than it did Dalton, and refused to be scared by the dragon man. It screamed again, its tail lashing out violently. Dalton barely dodged it in time but was rewarded with a face full of sand. A brown shield quickly raised around the terrified horse just as the dragon threw itself at it.

Crying in rage, the dragon stumbled back, and the shield flickered.

"I have to save him. His magic won't last long." She took a step forward and then another, but she couldn't seem to make her body move any more. Her eyes never left the young dragon as it danced through the sand, a hungry, scared craze in its eyes. She could almost feel its heart beating in her chest, feel its hot blood coursing through her veins, feel its hunger in her stomach.

"But how?" She didn't have her sword, and she would never raise a weapon against a young dragon like this. She wasn't confident enough in her magic either.

"Bond with it." Xavier stepped closer to her, his breath hot on her shoulder, an anxious tremor in his voice. "You must bond with it."

Slowly, she shook her head, but just then, the dragon's eyes turned and locked onto hers. A sudden peace fell over her, and determination flooded her as one word raced through her mind.

Mine.

Before she knew what she was doing, she was running down toward Dalton and the dragon, the sharp rocks cutting through her worn boots, the sand slipping dangerously under her.

Skidding to a stop just parallel to Dalton, the dragon between them, she started yelling and waving her arms.

Dalton's eyes widened in shock and elation, and he shouted something along with her name. She wanted to rush over to him and hug him, to tell him of all the crazy things that had happened since the *Zeufax* attacked, but as the dragonet turned to face her, it commanded all her attention.

I am Duvarharian.

The dragonet roared and shook its head and stalked closer to her, moving quickly and slyly like a big cat. Closer and closer it prowled. She could hear Dalton trying to say something to her, but she pushed all thought of him from her mind. She wouldn't back down, not from this. She wouldn't keep running from her problems, from the things that scared her or challenged her.

I am Drox and Andromeda's child.

The dragonet hissed, its pitch-black eyes glinting in the suns' light before it snapped at her. She easily dodged the attack and stepped away.

I am heir to Duvarharia.

A large black wisp streaked out toward her, and she jumped over it, careful to close her eyes. Sand blasted her face but didn't impair her vision, and she was able to duck as the dragon swiped out at her with its razor-sharp claws.

I am heir to Trans-Falls, daughter of Aeron and Frawnden, sister of Trojan and Roan.

With a gust of wind and sand, the dragonet leapt into the air and let out an ear-piercing cry. Stephania's eyes followed it as it looked down at her.

I am Farloon.

It dove down behind her, trying to catch her off guard, but she held up her hand, forming a shield around herself, knocking the dragonet off its feet. It hardly struggled in the sliding sand as it roared in anger and leapt to its feet.

I am Dalton's child.

In a fury of shadow, sand, and blinding sunlight, the dragonet threw itself at her. Using magic and her instincts, she masterfully dodged the attacks, weaving in and out of the thrashing tail, gaping jaws, and slicing claws.

I am the child of the Dragon Prophecy.

Then, in one fluid movement, she stepped past the dragon's reach and up to its chest, her face inches from its, her hand nearly touching its scales.

The whole world stopped around them, and all she could see were those large, slitted eyes staring down into hers. She could feel their hearts beating in time, their breaths ragged in their chests, the sweat dripping down their bodies. She felt the fear and hesitation she shared with the dragon, but more than anything, she felt anticipation.

As she reached her hand farther, the dragonet leaned forward.

I am a Dragon Rider.

Where their skin and scales met, the world began.

Stephania felt her mind fly open, bared to the world. No more barriers or hidden secrets were left. She was known, fully and completely by this creature, and when she reached out past her own mind, she stepped into the dragon's—a world completely unlike anything she had ever known, so foreign and strange, so ancient, powerful, and animalistic, and yet she knew every piece of it, every thought, every hope, dread, and whisper, every memory, every desire.

Suddenly, she felt whole. As if she had only known to walk before, now she felt as if she could run. As if she had been blind before, now she knew she could see. As if she had only heard the loudest sound as a faint whisper, now she could hear the rocks sing. As if she had been dead, now she was alive.

The dragon was Farren, and Farren was Stephania. In body, mind, and soul, they were one.

CHAPTER 30

CAREFUL NOW. WATCH her tail! It's a dance, remember? A dance. Easy!"

Dalton's shouts and words of advice took her back to the days in New-Fars they had spent sparring until the noonday bells.

Left, right, dodge. The same rules, the same advice, the same training applied even now, though it wasn't a man and sword she wrestled with.

Farren's young trumpet echoed off the canyon walls as Stephania dodged a swipe of her tail.

Though their minds were connected, a steady stream of information and feelings flowing from one to the other, their intentions couldn't be further from the other's.

Farren was confused as to why so many strange thoughts not her own were flashing through her mind while also skirting around Dalton as he refused to let her near Austin. Stephania wanted desperately to ride Farren but could hardly get close enough to touch her black, wispy scales, let alone mount her.

Dalton had warned her against riding the young dragonet too soon after bonding since she had grown up in the wild and didn't understand the relationship between a dragon and its rider, but she had been impatient, wanting to feel the wind in her hair and watch the ground fade away beneath her as she had seen in her memories. She knew if she could just show Farren how wonderful it could be, everything would be okay.

While trying to explain to Farren she had no intention of harming her, Stephania found it increasingly difficult to continue dodging the dragonet's fairly clumsy but no less deadly attacks.

"I would give her more time." She faintly heard Dalton call out, and a scowl formed on her face. As the sudden frustration blooming in her mind spilled into Farren's, the Shadow Dragon roared and lashed out her tail.

A flash of fear from Farren blasted Stephania, leaving her mind reeling from the steady connection between her and the dragonet. Not only could they sense each other's emotions and thoughts, but, if they weren't careful, they could also feel everything the other was feeling.

This is so much harder than I could've imagined. The thought made its way to Farren, and for a moment, Stephania felt a sort of peace, as if Farren couldn't agree more. In that split second when they agreed, they stopped fighting and Stephania saw her chance.

Fully knowing she shouldn't overwhelm Farren right away but also determined that if she could just touch the dragonet, she could know they were well and truly bonded, Stephania darted closer. She instinctually knew if she could just feel the realness of dragon scales under her touch, then they both would understand what they were meant to do.

Stephania tossed aside all caution and leapt forward.

A strangled roar left Farren's gaping mouth as Stephania sidestepped a halfhearted swipe of her tail and launched herself onto Farren's back.

For a moment, neither of them moved.

Stephania's heart slammed against her ribs, or perhaps it was Farren's heart, she couldn't tell anymore, and a broad, nervous grin spread across her face as she searched for Dalton's eyes. He was just raising a thumbs up, a boyish grin on his face, when Farren stood up on her back legs and roared.

Stephania had barely enough time to grasp a large spine in front of her before Farren lurched forward, galloping through the sands. She leapt over rocks and dodged under cliffs, sometimes flapping her huge wings as she tried to gain air and buck her rider.

Stephania clenched her eyes shut against the tearing wind and sand, her fingers aching as she clung to the spine. Somewhere behind her she could hear Dalton yelling, but she couldn't tell what he was saying; she could do nothing to get Farren to change her directionless course.

Their minds were in chaos. Stephania couldn't tell if the fear was her own, scared she would fall and bash her head on the rocks; or if it was Farren's, scared that something, *someone*, was riding her. She was sure, however, that her elation was her own. *I'm riding a dragon!* It didn't seem real.

The powerful muscles of the dragonet tensed and released under her as the howling wind tearing through her hair pushed up under Farren's wings, giving them a few feet of flight every so often. Under her legs, she could feel the warm body of the dragon, but the wisps of shadow trailing off in the wind, wrapping around her body and tickling her face, were icy cold, as if she were being touched by the void itself.

Farren jolted and her muscles coiled, her pace quickening in exertion. Stephania looked up to realize they were climbing up a weathered spiral staircase around the outside of a Hatching Ground spire.

Cold fear washed over her.

No, no, no.

The ground stretched out below them as they circled higher and higher. A tearing pain shot through her shoulder, but it wasn't her shoulder; it was Farren's as her wing knocked the side of the rock monument.

Before Stephania could pull herself away from the dragon's mind long enough to realize she wasn't the one injured and that it was only a small scrape on Farren's wing, they had reached the top.

"Oh, gods."

Farren roared, galloping faster toward the sharp edge of rock where only the sky continued.

"We're going to fall."

The edge raced closer and closer, but Stephania's cries to slow down and stop were lost in the screaming wind and Farren's trumpeting.

What if we fall? I don't want to fall!

Everything slowed down. The edge was under them and then behind them as Farren pushed off the cliff, launching herself into the hot desert air.

In that moment, that small breath of time as they soared through the open sky, Stephania felt rather than heard the dragon clearly for the first time.

But what if we flew?

Somewhere between the edge and the abyss before them, Stephania's scream was lost as she closed her eyes and felt the ground pull down on them. But as they fell, tumbling from the sky like eagles too soon from the nest, their minds united, truly united as their intentions aligned, and only one thought could be heard.

Fly!

The sound of rushing air catching against thin flesh filled Stephania's senses as she yelled, pouring every ounce of her strength and energy into the dragon beneath her. The force threatened to tear her from the lithe dragon's body as she twisted in the air, her wings stretched out beside her, tilting, and turning to catch the wind.

With one last push, one last struggle, one last hope, gravity released its grip on them, and with an exhilarating lurch, they were *flying*.

Cautiously, as if she were afraid it would turn out to be a dream if she did, Stephania slowly opened her eyes. The wind was whipping at her face, but for now it wasn't so violent. The steady wing beat just behind her settled into a rhythm, and when she looked ahead, all she saw was the open sky.

A voice rose in her mind. It was both hers and Farren's as they shared their joy. *We're flying. We're really flying!*

Farren roared into the open air as Stephania lifted her arms above her and shouted, whooping and yelling as loud as she could.

At last, she truly was a Dragon Rider.

Shocked, she felt the wind pulling tears off her cheeks, and she quickly brushed them away. *I'm crying, but I couldn't be happier in my life.* She laughed at the irony of it until another voice spoke in her mind, mocking her.

What a cry baby.

For a moment, Stephania didn't say or think anything until she chuckled, shaking her head. *Did you just call me a cry baby?*

Farren cursed something in dragonish before her throat rumbled in what Stephania assumed to be a laugh. A sliver of embarrassment found its way from the dragon's mind into her own as Farren apologized. *I forgot you could hear my thoughts.*

Stephania bit her lip against her laughter as she stroked the black, wispy neck she was astride. Before she could even form the words to say she too forgot but didn't mind and agreed she was a cry baby, Farren rumbled in amusement and agreement.

A lopsided grin spread across Stephania's face. She didn't even have to form her thoughts into words to be understood. Farren understood her completely, more fully than she even knew herself, and for the first time in her life, Stephania didn't feel so alone.

A peace washed over her. It had been a long time since her mind felt so clear and free of the anxiety. It was as if everything were finally in its place. If felt like no matter how difficult life got, no matter what she had to face whether it be her grief from Trojan or fighting Thaddeus himself, she would have the strength she needed.

She turned her attention to the land and gasped when she saw how high they were. She couldn't see Dalton anymore and could barely see the distinct towers of the Hatching Grounds. The Hatching Grounds itself was only a dark, jagged mark against the tan sands of the Cavos.

We're so high!

Farren purred in agreement, and Stephania felt the young dragon had never been this high before.

Why not?

I never had the strength. Not until you gave it to me.

Stephania settled back, unable to fully grasp everything that was happening. When they had been falling and she had urged her energy and strength into Farren, she didn't realize she had actually done so.

We will be able to do incredible things together, I think. More than we could ever do alone.

Stephania nodded, taking a deep breath of the thin, cool air. *I think so too, Farren.* She twined a wisp of shadow around her hand and clenched her fists. A joy she hadn't known before settled in her. *I think so too.*

They flew for a long time, neither of them having to speak. After spending time in silence together, feeling each other's thoughts and letting their minds join, they didn't have to speak; they simply understood.

Farren was able to understand everything Stephania needed her to, especially their bonding. She understood who Stephania was, who she was called to be. She understood the Dragon Prophecy, understood her heartaches. She mourned Trojan as fully as Stephania had and shared in all her hopes and dreams. In turn, Stephania learned everything about this Shadow Dragon: the primal way she was raised, learning to hunt, to speak dragonish, and how to change her body from flesh to shadow, along with the complicated history of the dragons and Yazkuza, the once great dragon city.

In the clear air, as the blue sky turned to red and the moon began to rise across from the setting suns, all was right, and all was well. She wanted to fly, fly until she met the ocean or the mountains and keep flying away from all that scared her or that she didn't understand. She wanted to fly until she learned how to live, truly live, not just survive.

Farren's wings began to cramp, and Stephania felt her own legs cry in pain at the exertion.

Still, they had much to learn. Farren asked more questions than Stephania even began to know the answers to, and the dragonet didn't seem to have an end to her curiosities.

How can you breathe so high in the sky? How do you not fall with no saddle or straps to hold you on? What happens if I turn to shadow while you ride me? Will you fall? Can you really not fly on your own? What do trees and mountains look like? Do you think I am big enough to eat a horse? If you gave me energy to fly, can I give you energy to make magic? If you can channel Ancient Magic, then can I?

Finally, Stephania had to yell over the wind for Farren to quiet her questions and to suggest they land for the night. Dalton was surely worried about them and would have the answers they needed. At least, some of them.

Landing was considerably harder than Stephania would've liked, and though she braced herself, it hadn't been enough, and she found herself thrown from Farren's neck and sprawling into the desert.

Someone pulled her to her feet as she sputtered out sand.

Dalton was laughing and clapping her on the back as she tried to untangle her curls and dust the sand from them.

Through his laughter, Dalton said a quick spell, and she watched in awe as the sand poured off her body like water.

Before she could even thank him, his arms were around her, crushing her to him. "Well done, my child. Congratulations."

The tears streamed down her face again as she laughed with him, hugging him back.

Confusion and fear tugged at the edge of her mind, and she quickly pulled away. "Farren, this is Uncle Dalton."

Farren danced close, her wings held awkwardly as if she was trying to make herself bigger. Stephania quickly thought of her fondest memories with Dalton as a child, and she felt Farren's anxiousness melt away as she crept closer.

Dalton took in a sharp breath, his eyes misting. "Farren, I am Dalton, the once rider of Saorise, and I am honored to meet you."

Stephania's eyes widened as he knelt in the sand, placed two fingers to his lips and bowed his head.

Farren hummed low and stepped forward, placing her head against his.

Stephania cleared her throat and shifted her feet, feeling as if she had been left out of some special information or ritual.

As if on cue, Farren moved back just as Dalton stood.

"What?" Stephania chuckled as she looked from dragon to Dalton.

If a dragon could blush, she was sure Farren would be blushing. The dragonet quickly stepped toward Stephania and nudged her arm, flooding Stephania with the overwhelming feeling that Farren greatly approved of Dalton.

Stephania had to step forward as Farren rubbed up against her, her hand resting on the dragon's snout to steady her as she laughed in confusion. "What was that?"

Dalton winked at Farren before answering. "It's an ancient dragon and rider introduction similar to 'may the suns smile upon your presence.' I'm guessing your dragonet is well versed in her history. It's been a long time since it was used in regular practice, but it used to be the highest respectful greeting one could give a dragon." His eyes moved past her into the distance as a sad smile spread on his face. "Saorise used to love it. Actually, she loved all the dragon formalities. They're a very prestigious race, believe it or not."

Stephania turned to Farren next to her. Staring into eyes red like her own and seeing the few razor-sharp teeth that jutted out from her deadly jaws, it was hard to believe such beasts designed for killing could be partial to manners, but it only continued to prove she didn't know the first thing when it came to dragons and their riders.

I want to learn everything.

A memory from when she had been just a child, before she had even met Dalton, flashed through Stephania's mind.

"Teach me, Artigal."

"And what do you want to learn?"

"Anything I can, Igentis. Anything I can."

A pang of longing shot through her, and her smile faltered. She missed her family, not only the days she had spent with them in Trans-Falls recently, but the days she had spent with them traveling across Ventronovia, the days when she hadn't been so confused as to who she was or where she belonged, the days where she knew she was just as much Centaur as she was Dragon Rider, the days where she knew what she wanted, what she wanted to learn, and who she wanted to be.

She felt Farren's large warm head press into her back, and she closed her eyes, letting her thoughts and emotions flow to her dragon, her soulmate, her other half.

You are whoever you want to be, not who others remember you to be or who they expect you to be.

Stephania jumped at the clear words in her head but didn't let her shock break the sudden, deep connection between her and Farren. She dared not even open her eyes lest this incredible bond be broken.

What do you mean?

Farren rumbled low in her throat.

You don't know who you are because you are the stern Dragon Child, daughter of Drox, and Andromeda. And you are the quiet, little two-legged Centaur, daughter of Aeron and Frawnden. And you are the innocent, bullied, but sensitive girl, niece to Dalton. And you are the Farloon and the heir to Duvarharia and Trans-Falls, and you are sad and broken, but you are determined and ambitious even though you want to give up. But most of all these people, you are Stephania, a creature who feels and cares too much, especially about what others think of you.

Stephania felt the tears run down her cheeks, but she didn't move to brush them away and barely gave them a second thought. Farren was right. She had changed so much over the years, so much that not only could those around her not recognize her, but she couldn't recognize herself.

But you forget one thing, Stephania, little one. Farren paused until Stephania took a deep breath and asked, *What?*

That you don't have to choose. You don't have to choose just one of the many people you are. You are none of them, and you are all of them. You can be determined but want to give up. You can be quiet and thoughtful and also be outspoken and headstrong. You can be innocent and also stain your hands with blood. You can be a leader and still want to crawl into the arms of your parents. You can be an anomaly.

It doesn't matter if it confuses others. Creatures will always want to put you in a box they can understand, whether they mean to or not. You will be constantly misunderstood for who you are and where you came from, and some creatures will want to use you for their own desires and intentions. But as long as you hold on to yourself and understand you don't have to be anyone other than who you want to be, then you will never lose yourself again.

She opened her misty eyes and turned to her dragon. Staring deep into Farren's dark eyes, she placed her hands on either side of her dragon's head and pressed their foreheads together.

Thank you, Farren. Thank you.

Farren purred and pressed her head forward. *But you must never forget one thing.*

Stephania pulled away and searched her dragon's suddenly mischievous gaze. "What's that?"

That you are mine.

Clear laughter filled the air as Stephania nodded, throwing her arms around Farren's neck and squeezing her tightly. "I promise, there's no way I could ever forget that."

§

STEPHANIA'S EYES FLUTTERED open, the expansive, starry sky smiling down on her. The stars were quiet tonight, but if she listened closely enough, she could almost swear she heard them celebrating. A small smile spread across her face as she turned her head to where Farren was curled next to her, sleeping. She had a pretty good idea what the stars were so happy about.

She stroked one of Farren's long claws, staring at the sleeping dragon for a long time, half in denial that she really was bonded with a dragon, and half in sheer awe.

However, something else had woken her up, she was sure. Sitting up, she looked around, but nothing stood out in the sandy shadows and moonlit rocks.

Eyes narrowing suspiciously, she carefully rolled back the warm fur and stood, watching to see if her stirring had woken Farren. The dragon slept on.

Satisfied that Dalton hadn't noticed her either, she tiptoed away from their small camp under an old arch, grateful the sand muted her footsteps.

From under the moonlight, the Hatching Grounds looked much different. During the day it simply looked like desert ruins, nothing too spectacular besides the hints of something much grander in years gone by. But at night, it underwent an incredible transformation.

Instead of the weathering being obvious on the ancient structures, it was hidden in the night shadows, making the ruins look less decayed, and much more mysterious. Without glaring suns to bare every imperfection to the naked eye, the ruins looked more like themselves, like they were still great havens for mighty dragons and had never been anything but.

"So you know who you are."

Stephania startled at the voice but instantly relaxed as the great Guardian Wolf walked out from behind a pillar a few feet ahead.

"I think so."

"Then who are you?"

The words paused in her throat before she threw her shoulders back, met his eyes, and answered with only a slight hesitation. "I am Stephania, rider of Farren the Shadow Dragon. Nothing more and nothing less."

For a long moment, Xavier didn't say anything, didn't shift his weight, or even growl low.

She nervously kicked a rock, feeling the sand shift and drift under her feet, her hands mindlessly playing with a few beads of sand she found in her pocket.

"Hmmm," he growled before sitting, his tail wagging softly like a pup. "Someday, I hope you find you are more than that, but until the Creator Źuje gives you that purpose, I am pleased to hear you know who you are. It will serve you well to endure as yourself, not something anyone else wants you to be."

She nodded and bowed her head, unable to stop the small smile that lifted her cheeks. "Thank you."

"I assume your dragon has given you this peace and understanding?"

She nodded again before meeting his gaze. "Yes, she did."

Something like a smile lifted his lips from his formidable canines. "Good. She will teach you much more, just as you will teach her. Nothing in Rasa is as special and wholesome as the bond between dragon and rider. You are very blessed, Stephania."

"I am."

"Someday, though, you will discover a bond that transcends Rasa, and you will be understood more than your dragon understands you now."

"How?" She frowned quizzically. It didn't seem possible anyone or anything could possibly understand her more than Farren did.

Xavier stood and growled in amusement. "Though I know what I speak of, even I do not understand it. Nevertheless, it is a fact, just as the sand beneath our feet is fact. I challenge you, Stephania, to never stop learning and reaching for things you do not understand or see, even if you are sure nothing is left to learn or find."

"Okay, but I'm not sure I understand." He reminded her of Dalton. *What was with scholars and their riddles?*

"Someday I will help you to see."

"Someday?"

"I am leaving you tonight."

Her heart plummeted as her eyes widened. "What? Why? I thought you were supposed to protect me?"

He shook his mane, sending those strange blue embers floating to the sand below. "I am, but not from the things you think I am to protect you from. Dalton is with you now, but he will not always be with you. You still have much to learn from him, and until his time to teach and nurture has passed, I will not stand in his way."

"When will that be?"

"You ask questions no one but the Creator Źuje has answers to, Stephania. But it is sooner than you think.

"Can you at least stay with us until we leave the desert? What if one of those demons or sand monsters comes back?"

"I am never far from you, but I will not stay with you. The sand creature will not trouble itself with beings as small as yourselves. And as for the *Źeufax*, if you do not travel at night or let your mind wander, you should be able to protect yourself against them using the strength your dragon's mind and soul provides you, but only if you stay focused. You should be safe enough, at least until you finish crossing the danger of the desert."

Stephania's shoulders sagged, and she felt like the joy she had only minutes before had been swallowed up by grief. Did everyone have to leave her? Dalton would too if what Xavier was saying was true. Would Farren have to leave her one day as well? Would she always be alone?

"Stephania ..."

She felt his warm breath on her face and looked up; his glowing blue eyes, reminding her so much of Trojan, stared down tenderly into hers.

"Do not grieve. You will never truly be separated from those you love if you cling to the Creator Źuje. He holds all in the palm of his hand."

"But how can I be sure?"

He pressed his great head to her chest, and she clung to him, tangling her fingers in his silky fur.

"You must trust." Gently, he pulled away and bowed his head low. "Farewell, Dragon Child. I will meet you in Duvarharia." And with one last glance, he was gone, disappearing into the night shadows cast by the great stone pillars.

As she stood after he left, staring at his great paw prints in the sand, she was surprised to find she wasn't as sad as she expected to be. The hope she would see him again in Duvarharia settled in her like a silver lining. She had something to look forward to. Perhaps she wouldn't be so alone in Duvarharia as she thought. Until then, she would have Dalton as well. She hadn't lost anything; she was simply waiting for it to return.

Feeling unusually hopeful, she quickly stepped back to their camp. Taking a long look at Farren, she lifted one of her pitch-black wings, crawled underneath, and rested her head on her leg. It didn't take long before she sank into sleep, and for the first time in too long, the nightmares stayed away.

§

"IT'LL CERTAINLY BE a lot more difficult to travel by day, but I'm sure we can all agree it would be better than facing another one of those *Źeufax*. From what happened to me, and what you told me about your encounter, it seems the demon was able to use the mind-altering state the desert night put us into to slip through our mental defenses, confuse us, and then separate us so it could attack."

Stephania quickly nodded in agreement, thinking back to what Xavier had said about traveling by day and keeping a focused mind. Farren dragged her eyes away from Dalton's horse for a only moment to nod her approval of their new travel strategy.

Poor Austin was standing unnaturally still, his eyes glossed over. Dalton had been forced to use a strong mind-numbing spell on him since he couldn't get used to having Farren nearby. Farren had apologized profusely for trying to eat the horse earlier, but it didn't reverse Austin's trauma, nor did it stop the side-looks Stephania often caught Farren sneaking at Austin when her stomach would growl particularity loudly.

"How long can dragons go without eating?" Stephania questioned with a scolding scowl at Farren's drooling stare.

Dalton laughed when he caught sight of Farren. "A dragon her size and age could usually last up to a week, but only if she maintains self-control."

I have self-control. Farren complained, quickly turning from Austin to lick her claws. *I'm not convinced.*

Farren only snarled, and Stephania shook her head, a smirk on her lips. "We'll be fine until we reach the plains, right?"

Dalton nodded as he drew the map from his satchel and pulled it open. Angling it a few times until he was satisfied he had aligned it with the ground around them, he studied it for a moment before rolling it back up and pointing down the long canyon and just to the north. "According to this map, there should be a path leading out of the canyon not far from here. Of course, you and Farren could just fly your way out."

Stephania winced as Farren trumpeted in protest.

Not today! Not after yesterday. I can hardly walk let alone fly.

Dalton raised his eyebrows as he watched the Shadow Dragon stamp her feet and shake her wings in protest.

It took Stephania a moment to remember Dalton couldn't hear Farren like she could. "Oh, we're both too sore from yesterday."

Dalton rolled his eyes mockingly. "You wouldn't be if you had listened to me to take it easy. Instead, you went and threw yourself off a cliff."

She winced at his tone, but when she met his eyes, she saw nothing but pride.

"So the canyon path it is, then." He only took a few minutes to strap his bedroll to Austin's saddle and mount up before they set off.

Farren was complaining her neck hurt from Stephania clenching it so tightly with her legs and, after a small argument, they determined Stephania would take turns walking and riding.

"How was I able to stay on Farren when I didn't have a saddle or straps? Andromeda had a saddle on Mischievous when they were taking me to you."

Dalton turned to her, the familiar sparkle of excitement in his eyes. "That, my child, is the power of the bond between rider and dragon."

"What do you mean?"

Farren stopped staring at Austin's backside for long enough to incline her head to Dalton, her reptilian eyes focused intently on his. Her curiosity was intoxicating, and it washed over into Stephania.

"Not only is your mind joined with your dragon, but your bodies are as well. In flight, your minds connect so fluently with each other, the bond extends to your bodies, automatically tying you to each other. It's like gravity. You are pulled to Farren just as she is pulled toward you. Riders never fall off their dragons unless their bond is inherently weak or unless someone has attacked their minds and distracted them enough to weaken the bond."

"So why did my mother have a saddle?"

"Because of you, of course. You weren't bonded to Mischievous like she was, and her bond wouldn't have extended to you. The saddle and straps were for you."

Stephania nodded and hummed. "Okay, that makes sense."

Ask him if you would fall if I turned to shadow.

Stephania relayed the question to Dalton and watched as his face lit up in nervous excitement.

"Now, I'm not actually sure, but if you applied the same dragon bond magic from other dragon breeds to the one between a Shadow Dragon and its rider, then it's almost positively safe to say you would also turn into shadow."

Stephania blinked a few times before she shook her head. "I'm sorry. Can you say that again?"

Dalton nodded boyishly and gestured wildly toward Farren. "Dragon bond magic laws declare that every dragon has a unique trait according to its breed or ancestry. For instance, Mischievous was a Poison Dragon. That meant not only could she produce poison, but she was also immune to poison of any kind, possibly even Eta poison. Bond magic ties a dragon to its rider and creates a pathway of shared characteristics. I always taught you that riders will begin to develop tougher skin, pointed ears, and sharper teeth, but the shared characteristics don't stop there.

You will also gain your dragon's unique traits. That means Andromeda was not only immune to her own dragon's poison, but also to all other poisons. It also means, if she tried hard enough, it's possible she could've created poison just as her dragon did. Just the same, Aldwyn was a Combustion dragon and could command fire and was immune to it, Drox being the same way.

If these same laws apply to Shadow Dragons, and there isn't anything to say they don't, then by all the laws of nature and magic, you would be able to share Farren's unique trait to turn into shadow."

Stephania stopped walking, her eyes wide. Farren stopped beside her, her tail swishing excitedly.

Did you hear that? We can change into Shadow together! We would be weightless on the air, absolutely weightless.

Stephania's heart pounded in her chest as she stared down at her hands, then to the wisps trailing from Farren's scales, then back to her hands. *Is that really possible?*

Try it!

Hesitantly, Stephania placed her hand on Farren's shoulder, just next to her wing. She could feel the warmth of solid flesh and her breath as she breathed in and then out, and then she felt ... nothing. A chill spread up her hand, and she could no longer feel solid flesh beneath her hand. In her shock and awe, she stopped thinking about turning herself to shadow.

Look! Your hand is shadow now too.

"By the gods," Dalton breathed in disbelief.

Stephania's eyes widened, and her breath caught in her throat. Sure enough, her hand was as black as night, almost indistinguishable from Farren's wispy scales. She no longer felt the cold, but instead sensed a deep connection with Farren as if she weren't

339

sure where her hand ended and Farren's shoulder began.

She tried to deepen the connection, tried to turn more of her arm into shadow, but as soon as she began to think on it, trying to weed out how it worked, the moment passed, and her hand was once more solid and hovering over shadow, the cold creeping back into her skin.

She didn't even have time to be frustrated as Farren danced enthusiastically and Dalton shouted congratulations.

"With practice, you should be able to master seamlessly changing your form from flesh to shadow, and when used in battle, you will be virtually unstoppable." Dalton's face glowed with pride, and she couldn't help but blush.

"*If* I can master it," she muttered under her breath, still frustrated she hadn't been able to do it perfectly the first time. Dalton didn't hear her degrading comment, but she forgot Farren could hear everything.

Stop it. Just stop it. I will not have your blatant negativity dampen my elation. This is only day one. I plan on spending my whole life with you, learning with you and growing with you. I refuse to let you taint our small victory with your negativity. So no more of that, do you understand?

Stephania's red eyes widened, and she quickly nodded. Her dragon had more sass than she had expected.

Good. Now, we will practice as we walk. We have plenty of time in this vast, empty desert.

So they practiced, both while walking and riding, until Stephania could easily change her arm to shadow while touching Farren and most of her legs to shadow while riding.

"Hey, Uncle Dalton!" Stephania pulled her hand away from Farren, just enough so she wasn't touching the dragon's cold shadow anymore, but not far enough she lost connection to Farren's magic. "I'm doing better!"

Dalton was just turning back, his face lit with pride, when the sand gave out under her, and she fell into a dark abyss.

CHAPTER 31

STEPHANIA FELT THE GROUND crash into her, and for a long while, she couldn't tell if the darkness surrounding her was from a lack of light or if she had been knocked unconscious.

Groaning and holding her throbbing head, she slowly sat up, dizziness washing over her and nausea rising in her throat.

Faintly, she heard Dalton calling out to her from above.

She tried to call back, but her head screamed with pain, rendering her unable to do more than moan. A sharp twist of discomfort shot through her ankles and up her legs when she shifted her weight. She figured if she could still move her toes, she at least hadn't broken her legs. But she must've fallen more than fifty feet, judging by how dark it was and how far away Dalton sounded.

I'm okay. I'm okay. I'm okay. She forced the thought over and over in her mind, trying to push it past her pain toward Farren. Finally, she felt a spark of connection between her and the Shadow Dragon, and she pushed the thought through until their bond grew past her pain and inability to concentrate. She sensed a flash of relief from Farren and felt her trying to somehow communicate to Dalton that she was okay.

Satisfied that Farren would be able to relay her status if only crudely, Stephania focused on gathering her magic to herself, careful not to open the doors leading to the Ancient Magic, and whispered as cautiously as she could the small healing spell Dalton had taught her.

A warm, then cool sensation spread from the top of her head and raced down her neck, shoulders, chest, and all the way to her toes. Though it left an ache in its wake, her head didn't throb as agonizingly as it had, and she was able to put weight on her legs without them buckling under her. When she was able to stand, she turned her attention to the only streak of light in the cavern from where she had fallen.

It had to be at least sixty feet up and was only about four feet in diameter. Shadows from Dalton and Farren cast over it as they peered down.

Again, Dalton called out to her, though he didn't sound as frantic as before. "Are you alright, child?"

She had to lick her lips and try several times before she was able to muster out a shout loud enough to reach him. "I'm alright. Just a little sore!"

"Did you break anything?"

She shook her head but then remembered he probably couldn't see her. "No. But I healed the sprains!"

"Good! Do you see a way out?"

Turning her attention to her surroundings, she realized she couldn't see much of anything at all. Besides the golden sand beneath her feet, lit by the hole above, everything else was pitch black. She couldn't even tell if it was a man-made or natural cavern.

"No, but I'll start looking!"

"Good. Farren and I will see if we can widen this hole in case there isn't another way out!"

"Okay!"

Their shadows disappeared from the opening for a few seconds before she heard them scrapping sand off rock and wood, trying to break their way into the cavern. Fearful they might break rock down on top of her, she quickly ducked into the abyss.

The darkness swallowed her completely. It was unnaturally black, almost as if the room were made from the shadows that trailed off Farren. A silly thought that maybe this was where Shadow Dragons were born flashed through her mind, but then she realized maybe it wasn't so foolish. After all, this was the Cavos Hatching Grounds.

Taking each step slowly and carefully in case of hidden rocks or the floor cutting out abruptly, she made her way, hands stretched out before her, into the abyss.

Once her head stopped aching enough to remember some Ancient phrases, she muttered a few choice words and watched as her Shalnoa started to glow; bits of red light trailed from her arm to her fingertips and then collected like water into an orb that hovered over her hand.

Exhausted from the fall and yesterday's flight, it took more concentration and energy to maintain the light than she would have wanted, but a surge of warmth suddenly pulsed through her; her heart raced faster, and her breath came easier, her head clearing from its fog.

This might help you. Farren's voice rang clearly in her mind, and a smile bloomed on Stephania's face.

It does, thank you.

Anything for you, little one. Now, please find a way out.

Stephania used the new energy coursing through her veins and directed it into the light, willing the red shimmering glow to extend from her hand and out around her.

Further and further she pushed until its light chased back the oppressive shadows and filled the room.

"Gods of all," she breathed as her eyes widened, taking in the cavern.

It was far bigger than she had initially expected, extending hundreds of feet on either side of her. The first thing that caught her attention was a crumbling staircase in the center of the cavern. A shiver ran down her spine when she realized she had somehow perfectly fallen right where it had crumbled away. Ten or so feet to the right or left would've had her tumbling to solid stone without any sand to cushion her fall. Her eyes roamed from the staircase to the hole in the ceiling. From the angle of the stairs and the position of the hole, it made sense she had fallen through rotted material that had once been something like a door to the stairs below; or perhaps someone had used the material to seal off the cavern long ago.

Once again, the notion that this room was a place for Shadow Dragons hit her. Even with her strong red light, the room was unnaturally dark, and wisps of shadows hung in the air where shadows shouldn't have been.

Finally, she turned her attention to the walls of the cavern, and once again, awe stole her breath away.

Though some of the walls looked to be natural, others were polished so fine, she was sure she would be able to see her reflection if she were close enough. Murals of grand intricacy and detail spanned every bare inch of the walls, even onto the ceilings, and they were filled with dragons.

Solemnly, she made her way to one of the walls and pressed her hand to the snout of a painted dragon that seemed real enough to breath its fire onto her. A rider was at the base of its neck, adorned in elaborate riding armor that matched the armor the dragon wore. They were fighting Etas, she was sure, and it seemed the dragons were winning spectacularly; the shape-shifting demons were nothing compared to the might of the Duvarharians.

Walking along the wall, she watched as the murals connected to one another, shifting and changing as if telling a story. She watched the rocky canyon in the Cavos turn from a sandy, barren wasteland into an incredible city of stone, crafted entirely by the dragons themselves. She didn't know dragons could wield magic. She had heard Dalton speak of their traits but never of dragons actually channeling magic the same way riders could. Nevertheless, the murals specifically showed dragons wielding magic just like riders, shaping stone into arches, domes, and sculptures, and effortlessly carving their homes into the desert rocks. She knew the city she was looking at was no mere Hatching Grounds; this was Yazkuza, the greatest dragon city in Ventronovia.

Her study and admiration of the colorful paintings, remarkably preserved in the dry desert heat, brought her to an arching doorway.

She stood before the giant iron doors, her eyes transfixed on their artistic mastery; carved directly into the shining iron were symbols and words she didn't recognize. They weren't Ancient Duvarharian, or Sházuk, nor were they common tongue. Something told her they were far older.

Unsure if she should wander so far from Dalton and Farren but convincing herself she was supposed to be finding a way out, even though she was sure this was *not* the way out, she pressed her palms to the surprisingly cold metal and pushed.

With Farren's dragon strength rushing through her veins, she heaved all her weight against the doors, willing them to open. The old hinges creaked and moaned, protesting the movement after standing so still for so long.

"Come on," she grunted as she shoved. "Just open already."

Her Shalnoa flashed bright red, and before she could even ponder what was happening, streaks of red magic shot from her hands, filling the dips and grooves in the metal, racing through the designs like fire burning a trail of oil.

Baffled and just a little wary, she took a step away from the door, unsure if it was a trap or not. For a breathtaking moment, nothing happened.

Then the magic began to hum and seep into the hinges. With one last moan, the doors swung open.

A dark open maw stretching beyond the doors faced her. For a long time, she could do nothing more than just stand still, staring back, weighing whether or not she should continue.

She found herself moving forward, inch by inch, as if not sure to trust whether the ground wouldn't fall out from under her again. The tips of her boots stuck out over a ledge, and she halted her movement. She could see nothing, not even whether the ledge was a step or the cliff to the center of Rasa.

Calling on her magic, she withdrew it from the room behind her and pushed it before her.

It never stopped expanding.

The ledge at her toes was just a step, but beyond it were thousands more steps, leading down, down, down into the biggest cavern she had ever seen. She couldn't see the end of it either way she looked, nor could she see the bottom of it.

Her red light wrestled with the shadows, tangling with the wisps, dancing with them, almost as if the light and darkness were playing with each other.

Heart racing in anticipation and just a little fear, she stepped down the first step, then another, then another, until she was taking them two at a time. Then she was running down the steps as if she were coming home. Only she had never been here before, had no right to call it home.

The stairs eventually panned out to a long stretch of walkway hundreds of feet wide and stretching on and on into the darkness.

She slowed her pace, but only a little, not stopping as she continued deeper and deeper into this world under the world. A pang of guilt riddled her mind. She was supposed to be finding a way out, not getting herself lost, but she couldn't seem to stop herself.

Just a little bit further. Just a little bit further, she thought to herself, but she wasn't even fully sure they were her own thoughts. In fact, she was more sure it was the shadows speaking, calling her, beckoning her further in.

Stephania, where are you going? Farren's slightly worried voice sounded so distant in her mind, and though she didn't want to answer, she didn't push Farren away.

Deeper, was the only thought she was able to hear as huge columns and arches stretched from either side of her, over her head and lining the walkway she was on. *Deeper into the darkness.* She heard only silence for a few seconds before she whispered quietly, "Come with me."

Something ahead of her caught her eye. She squinted, willing her magic to light it, but a shadowy darkness surrounded it. She crept closer, unsure if the dancing darkness was friendly or not. As the shapes shifted and moved, she thought it looked something like a sarcophagus—a solitary black granite coffin with only a platform under it. Nothing else was around or near it.

Movement just to her right and behind her caught the edge of her attention, but the overwhelming sense of Farren's presence told her it was only her dragon, even if it was hard to tell Farren from the shadows around her.

Do you know what this place is?

A wave of nostalgia from Farren washed over Stephania, but she got the odd sense it wasn't Farren's nostalgia but someone else's. It was the same as the feelings she got from her parents through memories. Was it possible Farren was feeling something from one of her own ancestors?

It is home.

Stephania's heart skipped a beat as she heard the word "home." It felt right, not for her, but because her heart and soul were joined with Farren, she felt it for her dragon, just as she hoped she would feel it for herself one day.

"Have you ever been here before?" Stephania didn't whisper, but the shadows muted her words as they were lost in the dark expanse.

No. The hint of what might have been tears clung to Farren's thoughts. Whispers, in the dragon language Farren spoke before she and Stephania bonded, rose from the shadows, speaking things only the dragonet could understand. *But it is my home.*

As the darkness swirled around Stephania's legs, reaching up her arms, whispering incomprehensible things in her ear and tickling her cheeks, she didn't doubt Farren for a moment.

Together, they moved closer to the strange coffin, and with Farren's breath, the shadows skittered away, hovering nearby as if wary to let the strangers in to what they were guarding but forced to obey the Shadow Dragon.

Stephania ran her hand along the tomb's smooth black granite surface, admiring how the white streaks in its structure looked so much like veins, as if it were alive. A hum raced beneath her fingers, and for a moment, she wondered if it was.

"Who do you think—" Before she could finish her question, the granite lit aflame with burning red magic—*her* magic.

A gasp parted her lips when she tried to pull her hand away but found she couldn't.

Farren growled and stalked to her side, her spines raised and tense.

Stephania's eyes widened as her fear dissolved into awe. Her magic spread across the black granite much as it had the metal doors leading to this shadowy abyss, but this time, it was thick and moved like water.

Like blood. She couldn't tell if it was her thought or Farren's, but it resonated with truth.

The little rivers of blood-like magic mingled with the white veins, covering them and staining them red. Once all the white veins had disappeared under her magic, the granite began to dissolve, falling away like ash in the wind.

She was able to pull her hand away but couldn't force herself to move.

For a moment, she was disturbed they had somehow begun to open this tomb and would find the mummified remains of some creature below, but her fears were instantly laid aside in the wake of confusion as the last of the granite drifted away.

"Armor?"

Farren's confusion mingled with hers as they stared down at the inside of the sarcophagus. No body lay in it, only a magnificent suit of armor, black as the night, and of a design she had never seen the likes of before.

Where is the body?

Stephania could only shake her head, unable to answer Farren.

Her eyes traveled past the gleaming armor to a well-preserved animal skin scroll, rolled up in the gauntlet of the armor's right hand.

Unsure if she even had the right to move the armor and read the scroll but positive a scroll wouldn't have been left if it wasn't meant to be read, she reached over and slipped it out from the armor's cold, unmoving fingers. A spark of energy jumped from the armor and raced up her hand as she jerked it back, her heart pounding in her chest.

The air was thick with apprehension. Even the shadows around them seemed to loom closer.

Her hands shaking more than she would have liked, she gently unwrapped the strip of leather holding the roll of skin closed, draped it on the edge of the coffin, and pulled the scroll open.

It took her a few moments to realize she was reading the first line over and over and not comprehending a single word.

What does it say?

Stephania shook her head and peered at the first word. It looked overwhelmingly familiar, as if she had once been able to read it years ago but had forgotten; try as she did, though, she couldn't understand what it said. It looked somewhat similar to the writing on the metal doors but seemed to have a distinct pattern to it that didn't look so wild.

"I'm not sure. I think it's in a really old—" Before the words had even finished leaving her mouth, the inky symbols on the page began to warp and change, bleeding into each other and separating until the words that stared back at her were very familiar and very legible.

"By the gods." A disbelieving laugh left her lips as she shook her head. "What Uncle Dalton would give to see this."

Once the words were in the common tongue, they didn't fill up nearly as much of the page, and she was shocked to find the message rather short. Realizing Farren couldn't read, she began to relay the words aloud.

"Here lies the last true Shadow of Light. Look not for his body, for he is no longer of this world, having been taken home by Źuje. But to you who reads this, do not walk away. If the magic in your blood has brought this tomb to life, so shall it bring to life the Shadow Armor. So now take it up, and don it. May it be a shield to you against evil, and may the Shadow Blade do the will of the one who sent it. Don it and become a Shadow of Light."

The words echoed loudly through the never-ending halls, leaving a strange energy humming in the air.

Her and Farren's hearts beat together as they listened to the echoing words, feeling the strange throbbing energy through their bodies.

Wordless, Stephania felt an understanding come over both of them.

For some reason, they had been led here, to what Farren instinctively knew to be the spawning grounds of the Shadow Dragons. The magic in Stephania's blood, full of Duvarharian life and the Ancient Magic, and Farren's authority over the shadows had brought the tomb to life.

This is our inheritance.

Without hesitation, Stephania reached for the armor, her breath catching in her throat as the energy tickled her fingers.

As soon as her skin met the cold metal of the armor, her magic rushed over it like a waterfall of blood. It seeped into its every crack and design, soaking it until it glowed with a violent red aura. Then, before their eyes, the armor began to shift and change. No longer was it armor made for a tall, muscular man. Now it had the physique of a petite female, exactly her size and shape.

Hands trembling with anticipation and disbelief, Stephania drew the chestplate from the sarcophagus and held it up before her.

Farren rumbled in excitement as Stephania marveled at the masterful design and how it would perfectly fit her body.

Look!

Stephania turned her attention back to the coffin, her breath catching sharply.

On top of what looked to be metal crafted like dragon scales, lay a sword.

Every inch of it was black: the scabbard, made of a material she had never seen before, the humming gems imbedded in the hilt, and the small bit of blade that peeked from the scabbard.

"The Shadow Blade," she whispered.

As if responding to its name, the blade droned louder, every molecule of it seeming to vibrate with its own life.

Take it, little one.

Stephania slowly shook her head, her hands tightening around the armor she held. "I don't know if I can."

It's calling to you. Don't you hear it?

She did. She heard it plainly, just as she had heard the shadows calling to her from the depths of this cavern.

Something held her back. *What is a Shadow of Light? What does it mean to become one?*

Farren had no answer for her.

The only comfort Stephania drew from the mysterious letter was the name Źuje. Xavier had claimed to be a servant to the Creator Źuje. She couldn't be certain it was the same being, or even if it was real or could be trusted, but she trusted Xavier, whether it was right or not, and she trusted the call of her magic and the call of the shadows.

Before she could change her mind or overthink her decision, she put down the chestplate and reached for the sword.

The moment her hand grasped the hilt, she couldn't let go.

Again, her magic poured like blood into the weapon, sliding down the blade and over the scabbard. With a strange crackling, much like the Etas' shape-shifting, the blade began to change.

"Farren—" she cried, but neither could do more than watch.

Flashing from broadsword to scimitar, to katana, to a bow, to a mace, and then daggers, the blade changed faster and faster. The magic burned Stephania's hand. She tried to wrench her hand free, but the magic bound her to it.

Farren roared, lifting her tail to knock the blade from Stephania's hand, but just before she did, red sparks exploded from the blade, scattering to the ground. Stephania clenched her eyes shut against the bright light but was still blinded by it.

When the pain stopped, Stephania dared to open her eyes. The blade had stopped changing. Instead of holding a broad sword, she was now holding a war scythe. Its five-and-a-half-foot snath curved elegantly into a three-foot blade. It was night black, except for the red veins spreading from her hand and through its surface, weaving through the atoms of its blade, and infusing it with her magic.

"A scythe."

Farren snaked her head around Stephania and pressed her nose to the blade, her black scales lighting up with the red magic within. *It is foreign to you.*

Stephania nodded, turning the weapon over. *Very foreign.* She hadn't heard of scythe fighters before, let alone had the skills to use one. She wasn't even sure Dalton would be able to teach her.

"Why a scythe?" she whispered to the darkness. She received no answer.

Look, little one, on the armor.

Stephania held up the armor. A spark of red magic had formed on the back of the armor, and a hook, one that would be perfect for holding the scythe, molded its way into the metal.

"This armor certainly thinks of everything."

The letter did say it was alive.

Though neither said it, they both felt the same. Should they really claim this armor as their own? It already seemed attached to them, and Stephania felt sure that even if she wanted to leave it, she would never really feel whole without it because her magic now resided in it. It had become a part of her, just the same as the *Zelauwgugey*. Still, she wasn't sure if she was worthy of it. This was armor for a great warrior, a great Dragon Rider. She was neither. Nothing she had done on the battlefield was worthy of recognition in any form. She had done nothing but fail in her fights. She did not deserve armor of this caliber.

The words of the letter, however, rang in her mind. *"But to you who reads this, do not walk away. If the magic in your blood has brought this tomb to life, so shall it bring to life the Shadow Armor. So now, take it up and don it."* When it had said the blade would do the will of the one who sent it, she couldn't help but be reminded of Artigal speaking of the Ancient Magic and how it only obeyed the will of its master.

Your brother, Trojan, did he not have a blade similar to this? One infused with magic and could change to the weapon he desired?

Stephania's eyes widened as she looked at the blade in a new light, turning it over in her hands. "I suppose so." Could this blade be of the same magic as Trojan's Synoliki blade? Only he had been able to wield his blade; would it be the same for her and this scythe?

The more she thought of it, the more confidence flowed in her veins. She had been meant to find this. Why else had she fallen through the roof of that great cavern? Why else had her magic opened a door with runes even she, with all her schooling in myths and legends, didn't recognize? The tomb had come alive with her magic and so had the armor. Farren's ancestors were from this place; it reeked of home and comfort—a place of trust and peace.

Trojan hadn't hesitated when he took up the mantle of Synoliki warrior. She had no one to read a list of demands and expectations for a Shadow of Light, no one to swear her in or bestow magic upon her, but something told her this position was much the same as Synoliki.

"I challenge you, Stephania to never stop learning and reaching for things you do not understand or see, even if you are sure nothing is left to learn or find." Xavier's words from the night before echoed in her mind. This was something she certainly didn't understand. Perhaps it was of the Corrupt Magic, something sent to her from Thaddeus. But nothing about this forgotten cavern, a place of Shadow Dragons and ancient memories, spoke of the purple eyed traitor and his Acid Dragon. Nothing spoke of corruption, only of an old, forgotten power.

If Ancient Magic surrounded her now, it was not malicious or grasping and controlling. If anything, it was comforting and nurturing, as if it were leading her to safety, asking her to trust it. The shadows were sweet and gentle as they swirled around her legs, bleeding into Farren's shape and form.

Her grip on the scythe tightened.

"It is time I make my own choices," she whispered as Farren rumbled in encouragement. "It is time I step out into my own life and choose for myself who I want to be."

The blade glowed red, the blood veins woven through its darkness pulsing with life—with *her* life, with Farren's life.

"And I choose to be a Shadow of Light."

A sudden peace washed over her as her magic lit up the weapon and armor. Across the handle of the scythe, the blade, and the chest piece, markings began to take shape. A hushed breath came over both dragon and rider as they recognized the symbols. They were Stephania's Shalnoa—both Centaur and Duvarharian.

The armor and blade were as much a part of her as Farren, and as she lifted the chest piece over her head and slid it onto her shoulders, feeling its cold metal and warm life against her body, she knew she had made the right choice. With ease, she donned the rest of the armor and hooked the battle scythe on her back, amazed at how impossibly light and flexible it was. Certainly, it was metal, but it acted so unlike metal, she was sure it was something else entirely.

Ah. Now you look like a true Dragon Rider. Farren appreciatively breathed a cloud of shadow over Stephania. *One worthy to rule Duvarharia and Trans-Falls.*

Stephania blushed as she squared her shoulders. "Now for you to look like a dragon worthy of the same." She quickly turned back to the coffin, hoping she had been right about what she assumed the strange dragon scaled metal was.

Sure enough, as she pulled the huge pieces of metal out of the sarcophagus, it was dragon armor.

Farren stood still for a long moment as her eyes searched the magnificent armor decorated with markings and designs matching Stephania's. Hesitantly, as if she were disbelieving what she was seeing, she pressed her snout to a piece of the armor.

A charge of red magic bled over the armor, and just as Stephania's had, the armor shifted and changed, molding itself into the exact shape of Farren's young form.

Farren had no words to describe her emotions, but Stephania easily sensed it all.

With sure hands, she slipped the armor over Farren's neck, chest, and legs. A beautifully crafted leather pad was even attached to the armor.

"No more raw thighs for me," Stephania laughed as Farren snorted.

Saddle pads are for weak riders. You should let your thighs grow callouses. It would be much more practical.

Stephania didn't want to explain all the reasons why she very much *didn't* want callouses on her thighs, so she only shook her head and laughed.

Farren lifted her head high and opened her maw, breathing in a huge shadow that swallowed up all of Stephania's light.

I am Farren, dragon of Stephania, and I am a Shadow of Light.

Markings matching Stephania's appeared on her chest and decorated her shoulders with moons and stars, the same markings on Stephania's neck—the constellations of Trans-Falls.

Always and forever. Farren breathed out the shadows, and the light swelled in the room again as she placed her head on Stephania's chest.

"Always and forever." Stephania wrapped her arms around her dragon's head, tears sparkling in her eyes. Right here, right now, she knew who she was. She knew who she wanted to be. And if she ever forgot, all she would have to do was look at her armor, feel the scythe in her hand, and remember this place—this dark abyss of shadows—and she would know what home felt like and what it felt like to belong.

CHAPTER 32

WE SHOULD GO. Uncle Dalton must be worried about us."
Farren whined sadly, her eyes gazing wistfully into the oppressive
darkness around her.

Sensing her despair and loss, Stephania placed her hand on her dragon, feeling the
new armor beneath her touch. "I know, Farren. But we will return one day. When the
war is over and our enemies' blood waters the earth and all have forgotten the evil, we
will return, and perhaps the Shadow Dragons will too."

Farren nodded, but her heartache and longing were so great, they stood still and
silent for many more minutes lost to the darkness.

I will return, Farren whispered more to the shadows than to Stephania. Without a
second glance back, she began the long walk back to the staircase.

Stephania lingered for a moment more before she reached into the sarcophagus
to find the letter, wanting to take it back to Dalton so he could have another ancient
artifact to add to his collection. To her dismay, she couldn't find it. She wanted to call
to Farren to see if the dragon had it, but she knew she didn't. It had disappeared, and
as she watched the sarcophagus, she realized why.

It was all disappearing.

Just as the lid had faded into ash and shadow, so did the rest of the tomb now.

A certain sadness and horror filled her as she helplessly watched the black granite
coffin dissipate into nothing, leaving only swirling shadows where it had once stood. No
wonder she had never heard of the Shadow Armor or Blade before. It left nothing to
be remembered by.

The armor was truly hers now. She couldn't give it back.

Racing to catch up, a strange unknown feeling settling her stomach as if there was
so much more to all of this than she could even begin to understand, she finally mounted the stairs and drew alongside Farren as they passed through the great metal doors.
She only hoped she would never regret anything she had done today.

As soon as they had stepped through the doors, the metal slammed shut with a resounding *boom* behind them. Jumping at the noise rumbling in her chest, Stephania turned to gaze upon them once more. Her and Farren's hearts sank as they stared at the doors.

Where a crack had slit the two doors, magic now filled it, melding the metal together until they were doors no longer, only a solid wall. The cavern of shadows was sealed.

A deep ache grew inside Farren as she turned away, her wings dragging the ground. Stephania withdrew her mind from her dragon's, fully knowing what it was to feel the crushing weight of losing a home; that was something no one could help with.

Stephania walked back to the door and placed her palm on the cold metal. A spark of her magic jumped from her hand to the designs, but this time it didn't bring the doors to life nor command them to open. Apparently, now that the armor had been taken, the cavern had no reason to remain open. Whatever secrets it still held were meant to remain hidden. For now.

Her fist tight, she pulled away from the door, a resolution sinking inside her. *Somehow, someday, I will learn the mysteries of this place. I will learn of its magic and its purpose, and somehow, I will earn its trust. Then I shall open it again, and Farren will be able to return home.*

With new purpose, she strode after Farren, and they climbed the crumbling stone steps together. However, her determination dimmed as they neared the ceiling of the cavern and the ray of light grew brighter, Dalton's voice growing louder. It would be a long time before she would be able to return. Duvarharia itself posed many new problems, ones she couldn't even begin to fathom. Then of course, she would have to face Thaddeus, Kyrell, and Veltrix.

A throb of pain grew in her lip as she chewed it, her hand finding a spine between Farren's shoulders as they walked together.

You cannot forget to live, little one.

Stephania jumped in surprise at Farren's voice in her thoughts. A nervous laugh parted her lips as she narrowly dodged stepping on a loose rock precariously jutted out over the edge of the stairs.

My apologies for startling you. A hint of worry lined Farren's thoughts as she growled softly.

"Not to worry. I forget someone is always listening to me now."

I could close my mind to you if you want privacy.

"No!" Stephania stopped walking, her heart racing.

Farren turned to look back, her eyes wide as she cocked her head to the side questioningly.

Shaking her head and realizing she had reacted more explosively than she had

354

meant, she took several deep breaths, plastered a smile on her face, and continued walking. "Sorry. I don't want you to feel like you're intruding."

You don't want to feel alone.

Stephania stopped walking again, her gaze lost in the swirling red of her dragon's eyes—eyes that now matched her own. Slowly, she shook her head, heat rising to her cheeks.

Farren snorted black shadow and bobbed her head. *I know because I can feel what you feel. I understand. You don't have to try to hide these things from me.*

With her hand on Farren's leg, Stephania started walking again, nodding. "I know. I know," she whispered. "It'll just take some getting used to. I'm so used to hiding everything."

Farren leaned into Stephania's touch. *Yes. But you will never have to hide again. Not from me.*

Her thoughts and feelings saying more than words ever could, Stephania wrapped her arms around Farren's thick neck and let her tears fall onto the black, wispy scales. They stayed liked that, fully understanding each other's fears and loss, until their hearts had healed somewhat.

"It's getting quite hot out here. I understand having bonding time and all, but could it at least wait until we get to the forest and find some water?" Dalton coughed and cleared his throat. "Surely I'm not the only one who's thirsty or hungry?" Though his words were serious, his voice was full of humor.

At that moment, Farren's stomach grumbled, and she licked her lips.

Grinning, Stephania pulled away from Farren and raced to the edge of the stairs, just under where she had originally fallen in. Dalton was crouched at the edge.

I've been burning in the suns since I was born. I'm sure he can handle it for a few more minutes.

Stephania tried to hide her laughter at Farren's comment but snorted anyway.

"You're not laughing at me, I hope."

Stephania only waved in dismissal.

"It's an inside joke!"

"So I can tell!" His laugh echoed down to them. "I'll get out of your way!" When he stood, he disappeared into the blinding light.

I can fly us through. Farren sounded much more confident than Stephania felt.

The hole was significantly larger than it had been when she had first fallen; Farren must've clawed it out in order to fit through. She wasn't sure it would be big enough to fly out of, considering that Farren's wingspan was much greater than the diameter of the hole, but she trusted her dragon's intuition.

"Ready?"

Farren rumbled, and Stephania quickly mounted, taking a deep breath to calm herself. Soon, she felt warmth, then nothing, then the cold sensation as her legs melted into shadow.

With a heart-lurching drop, Farren threw herself off the staircase and dove down, pulling herself up just before they crashed into the sand. The momentum and shadows under her wings pushed her into the air. Circling around, she started flying toward the hole.

"Farren ..." Stephania gripped the spine in front of her tighter, thankful her legs were part of the darkness that wouldn't let her fall. "Farren, I don't think we're going to fit ..."

Trust me.

Stephania clenched her eyes shut as they raced toward the ceiling, expecting to feel the collision of dragon against rock and then the plummet as they fell to the sands below.

Instead, she felt Farren's wings stop beating as they raced upwards. For a death-defying moment, they hung suspended in the air, gravity yearning to tear them down.

Then she was blinded by light and oppressed by the suffocating heat and sand as they broke out into the desert above, Farren's wings carrying them into the air.

Stephania opened her eyes to see Dalton waving his arms and shouting in excitement. A frown furrowed her brow as she turned back to face Farren's head. The Shadow Dragon began to circle in descent.

"How ...?"

With a roar of pride, Farren shook her head, her neck rippling as flesh changed to shadow and then back to flesh. *A breath before we hit the ceiling, I turned my wings to shadow so they would pass through the ceiling. I made sure you went through the hole, of course, but that's why it felt like we were almost falling.*

A broad grin spread across her face as Farren landed with a jolt. "By the gods. That's amazing."

Smugly, Farren eyed her rider as she dismounted. *I know. But next time, I want to be able to fly right through the ceiling with you. We need to keep practicing.*

"Indeed."

"I see what took you so long. You went on a treasure hunt down there." Dalton's eyes flashed excitedly as he surveyed the armor she and Farren were wearing. He gently took her hand and spun her around; she was reminded of when he would admire her in a new dress he bought her back in New-Fars.

She felt foolish spinning in the dark, almost macabre armor with its spikes, harsh designs, and magic that looked like blood, but the nostalgia warming her heart as she remembered those quieter days back in New-Fars chased her embarrassment away. She didn't have time to ponder that she now thought fondly of New-Fars instead of hatefully, because Dalton was already pelting her with questions about what the armor was made of, why it looked like it was bleeding, where she found it, why it fit her, who it had belonged to, and on and on. The questions made her dizzy, but seeing Dalton's face light up was worth enduring his banter. How long had it been since they had enjoyed time together? A month? Three months? Six? However long it was, she suddenly felt it had been *too* long.

"Hold on, hold on," she laughed as she held up a hand. "I'll tell you everything in just a moment. There's something I have to do first."

He frowned quizzically but didn't press his questions about the armor or what it was she wanted to do.

Her intentions already aligned with Farren's, Stephania nodded to her, and they stood with the cavern entrance between them.

Closing her eyes and drawing on Farren's strength, Stephania whispered the strongest fixing spell she knew, directing her words and magic toward the fallen boards below.

Nothing seemed to happen for a long time, and she began to doubt whether she had the strength to do what she wanted. Sweat beaded on her brow, and while the suns hadn't been too unbearable minutes earlier, now she felt as if they were melting the flesh off her bones. Just as she was about to give up, a rush of new energy filled her. She was surprised to see Dalton standing beside Farren, his hands outstretched, his eyes closed, and his face contorted in concentration.

With renewed effort, she pushed the magic deeper until she felt it begin to heal. The fallen boards raised to the hole, their broken edges and splinters meshing back together. When the magic ebbed away and she opened her eyes, she was pleased to find the hole had been sealed and would be stronger and more impervious to sand and weather than it had been.

Farren bent her snout to the wood, and with a rumbling growl that almost sounded like words, she breathed darkness onto the wood. Sand rushed over the wooden floor, mixing with the darkness until it knit together into black stone with sand colored lightning streaks. It glowed eerily with red magic, and Stephania knew that not only would the cavern be fully protected for eternity now, but she would have no trouble finding it should they ever come back.

As if the act were too holy, too personal to mention, none of them spoke a word about it as they walked away, Dalton mounted on Austin and Stephania on Farren.

She could see how Dalton's shoulders sagged and his eyes drooped. If simple magic like only lighting a fire was exhausting for him, she couldn't imagine how he must feel now. Gratitude swelled inside her. He always gave too much—at New-Fars, when they were traveling, even in Trans-Falls. She didn't know what she was going to do without him; she didn't even know the minimum of what he had done for her through her life. She probably wouldn't know until he was gone.

You are afraid he will not come into Duvarharia with you.

Stephania nodded, thinking of Xavier's words and of the dreadful night she had eavesdropped on her parents and had heard of Dalton's banishment from Duvarharia. *Not that he won't, but that he can't. What if I need him in Duvarharia? If he's banished, he won't be able to come help me if I need it.*

But you will be Lady of the Dragon Palace. Perhaps you could pardon him?

A strange illness settled in her stomach. She could. She would have all the power to. But the question constantly nagging the depths of her mind was dragged from the back and forced to her attention. *Why was he banished?*

She stared at the back of his head as he shakily drew his water skin and took a small sip. What could he have possibly done to deserve banishment? Why had her parents trusted him so much to send their only daughter and the prophecy's fulfillment to him? If they had trusted him so much, why hadn't they pardoned him? Were they the ones who banished him?

Quiet your mind, Stephania. Some things you will never know. He will either come with you to Duvarharia or he won't, and you will find the answers to your questions when you arrive at the Dragon Palace. You won't help anything by worrying about it. You can, however, cherish the time you have left with him. Banished or not, he has done more for you than almost anyone else and loves you more than life. You owe him everything.

Taking a deep breath, she gently urged Farren to walk alongside Dalton.

"Thank you, Uncle Dalton."

He turned to her, looking more tired than she had seen him in a while. His beard was long, almost down to his collar bones, and so was his hair; full of sand and tossed by the desert winds, it hung almost to his shoulders. For the first time, she noticed how grey the roots of his hairs had gotten, how many lines had formed in his skin. Her heart broke as he smiled anyway. "For what?"

"For everything."

His face softened as he slowly nodded. "Of course, Stephania. Anything for you. Anything for my child. You know that."

She nodded and smiled tenderly. "I know. Do you still want to hear about our little adventure?"

His eyes lit up, and some of the exhaustion melted from his features. "Of course. I've been waiting more or less patiently."

Leaving out nothing, she told him everything she could remember from the moment the earth plunged out from under her feet. Somewhere halfway through describing the murals she had seen, he drew out a blank scroll and charcoal stub and furiously sketched everything she described. She only had to correct some details a few times; his ability to listen to what she was saying, pay attention to the smallest details, and then somehow render it exactly as she had seen and described it was incredible.

Perhaps he was an artist before a scholar?

Perhaps.

His questions about what she thought of the doors and symbols, the cavern of shadows, and all the other things she had thought a mystery never ended ... until she mentioned the animal skin note they had found with the armor.

"A Shadow of Light?"

Stephania nodded, a strange dread settling in her as she watched his eyes darken. "What are they?"

He opened his mouth and closed it several times, shaking his head, seemingly unable to find the words, or perhaps he just didn't want to tell her. "They were a sort of cult surrounding the belief that the Great Lord who reigned in Duvarharia's Golden Age wasn't who he said he was, but was actually a god. They also believed some historical events surrounding that time era were false."

"Do you believe in the Great Lord?"

A sudden tenseness washed over him, and when he spoke, his voice was lined with bitterness. "I believe in the historical events of a great lord that took Duvarharia into its Golden Age, but I don't believe he was of a god-like stature some believe he was."

"So, what is so wrong about the Shadows of Light?" Her fist tightened, clothed with one of the Shadow Armor's gauntlets.

"Thaddeus proclaimed to be one."

A chill ran down her spine as her stomach flopped. "He claimed to be a Shadow of Light?" She suddenly wanted to tear this armor off and leave it to rot in the scalding sands.

Dalton nodded. "Yes, but that was nearly eight hundred years ago." He frowned and ran a hand over his beard. "If I remember correctly from the records at the Dragon Palace, something happened to him while he was a Shadow, and he left them. Whether it was because of a personal issue or one he had with their beliefs, I don't know."

"Do you think I should get rid of it?" Her wide eyes met his. She expected him to say yes, but he shook his head.

"I don't think so." He smiled at the shock she knew her face showed. "The armor itself won't corrupt you. Do you feel like it is evil?"

She toyed with the saddle and scrunched her nose. "No. I don't. In fact, it feels more like it's a part of me than anything else."

"You don't feel any of the Corrupt Magic?"

She shook her head.

"You of all creatures should know the difference between evil and good magic. I trust your judgement, as should you. As for being a Shadow of Light, just because the note said you would be, doesn't mean you necessarily are. The Shadows of Light haven't been seen or heard of for hundreds of years. It's likely no one follows their beliefs anymore. And even so, their beliefs weren't harmful, just controversial. Besides, someday you must learn for yourself what you believe in."

She narrowed her eyes skeptically, and he shrugged, turning back to the empty stretch before them. Though he had never pressed any belief or way of life on her as long as he had raised her, she never remembered a time when he had told her she was free to believe in whatever she wanted. It was oddly freeing, as if she hadn't wanted to believe in anything before in fear he would be disappointed, but it also put a new weight on her shoulders, one she wasn't sure what to do with.

Was this his way of respecting Aeron and Frawnden's beliefs and how they had wanted to teach her about the Great Emperor? Did this have anything to do with that last argument they'd had?

"If we sleep tonight and travel all day tomorrow, we should exit the Cavos at about sundown or midnight tomorrow." He gestured to the top of the canyon ahead of them.

She didn't mind him changing the subject. Everything else he had told her was far too much to think about right now, especially when thirst was a constant companion along with the sweltering of the suns.

Tomorrow! Despite her hunger and the obvious glances she kept making to Austin, Farren skipped playfully, her spirits instantly rising. *Tomorrow I shall see the trees and swim in a lake and drink from a waterfall! Perhaps we shall even meet some of the hybrid horses.*

Centaurs, you mean?

Yes, of course.

Stephania rolled her eyes but couldn't stop the elation surging inside her.

When she had first crossed into the barren desert sands, she had been sure the journey would be only hot and uneventful. She could've never imagined the things she had seen and discovered, or the creatures she met. In fact, the whole experience still felt like a strange mirage, as if she would wake up riding Braken and neither Farren,

Xavier, nor the armor she was wearing would be real.

"What's the first thing you're going to do when we get out of the desert?"

Dalton looked startled by her question. She was a little shocked herself. She had never been one to make conversation, but perhaps she would change that; perhaps it was time to start being the person she wanted to be instead of the person she had become.

"Swim, actually. I don't think I'll ever be able to get enough water after seeing all this sand."

She laughed as he turned his waterskin upside down and only a single droplet fell out.

"What about you, Farren?"

Eat! To emphasize her point, she threw back her head and roared, her wings stretched out.

Stephania was just about to translate for Dalton, but he only shook his head in mirth.

"I know that look." He winked at Stephania. "She's hungry."

Farren growled and blinked slowly, her gaze straying to Austin again. The horse shied, and Dalton had to whisper another calming spell.

"What about you, child?"

A small grin decorated her face as she thought of it. "I want to climb a tree again."

"I'm not surprised." He smiled tenderly.

For the rest of the day, they joked about Farren wanting to eat Austin and how she would be the bane of all forest animals until she had eaten her fill. They shared what they were looking forward to most once they left the desert and how good it would feel to rest in a soft bed in Sankyz, even for just one night. However, they didn't talk about Duvarharia, despite the many questions she had of it that were only growing more pressing with each day. She didn't want to bother him with talking of it; she knew how much it pained him. Besides, eventually, she would arrive in Duvarharia, and she would be able to see it all for herself.

CHAPTER 33

I<small>T SHOULDN'T BE TOO</small> much farther from here ..." Stephania turned the map until she felt it was pointing the right way. Up until now, Dalton had always been in charge of their heading. With their water shortage and the exhaustion that clung to him from fixing the cavern ceiling, she had felt a certain responsibility settle over her, so she had taken up the map, trying to learn navigation. On a deeper level, however, she felt the anxious dread that he wouldn't be coming with her to Duvarharia, and not only would she be losing her father figure, she would also be losing her biggest caretaker and advisor. She would have to start doing some things like this on her own instead of always relying on others to do them for her. It wouldn't do for the Lady of the Dragon Palace to not even know how to read a map.

"Stephania? Are you listening?" Dalton's voice broke her from her concentration, and she snapped her head up.

"No, I'm sorry. What were you saying?" She tried wiping the dripping sweat from her forehead but accomplished nothing since her hand was every bit as damp.

"Look!"

Straining her eyes to where he was pointing, Stephania frowned, at first seeing nothing more than the shimmering, waving sands of the desert. "I don't—"

Grass! Farren bound forward, jolting Stephania roughly.

"Are you sure? Or is it just another mirage?" They had seen more mirages in the last day than they had during their first days in the desert, and with a pang of horror, she knew it was due to their dehydration. The only creature that didn't seem affected by their water shortage was Farren, but her hunger was enough to make up for it.

"I'm sure. This time, I am sure." The confidence in his voice and the way his eyes set determinedly on the horizon assured her he was right; if he wasn't, she was positive they would simply die, stranded in the desert after chasing mirages in circles.

See what I see.

With a deep breath, Stephania closed her eyes and reached her mind out to her dragon's, feeling the expanse between them and then touching Farren's mind—an eternity of wonder and power. When she opened her eyes, she wasn't looking through her own but through Farren's. Dragon sight was nothing like what she had expected it would be, though she had never even pondered the possibility of entering the mind of a dragon to see what it saw. Every color was exaggerated, and where she wouldn't have been able to see any farther, Farren's sight went on and on, seemingly forever, before it started to get even a little blurry. Also, dragons could see beyond the spectrum of light Duvarharians could, making them able to track their prey in ways Stephania could've never imagined.

Like a hawk or eagle. Only better.

Incredible.

It had been far easier to focus on learning how to strengthen her and her dragon's bond with the strange numbness dehydration presented; it helped her not to overthink how strange it was to fill another creature's body with her mind or have her own mind invaded by another. Without any trouble, Stephania focused on the distant horizon. Her heart lurched in disbelief and pure joy.

A cry of elation parted her lips as she drew back into her own body and mind. "It is! I can see plains from here and then just after, a forest. We're almost there."

It took all of her and Farren's self-control not to fly straight to it, leaving Dalton behind.

"Finally. Finally, we're going to leave this cursed desert."

A pang of sadness filled her, and it took her a moment to realize it was Farren's emotions. Instantly, she regretted saying "cursed desert". After all, this was Farren's home. She was leaving everything behind, all her memories, everything she knew, to go with Stephania to Duvarharia.

Running a hand over Farren's scales, Stephania pressed a kiss to one of her shadowy spines. *Forgive me, Farren. I don't mean to degrade your home. I know how hard to is to leave something you love behind. I'm sorry for belittling it.*

Thank you, little one. I accept.

Though Farren's offense from Stephania's lack of sensitivity lessened, her sadness did not. Stephania offered the best comfort she could give, but she also knew sometimes no comfort could be given for the pain someone felt inside.

As the waving plains grass grew in sight and the forest behind it visibly rose into small hills and mountains, their spirits inevitably rose with it.

Just over those hills, just through the forest, is Duvarharia. I am finally almost there. I am finally almost ... She stopped herself. Duvarharia was her birthplace, it was her birthright, it was where her family had lived for generations. It was where she belonged. But she had made other places her home, and she had lost them. Would Duvarharia always feel strange and unfamiliar? Or, if she let it feel like home, would she have to leave it one day too?

Quickly, she buried those thoughts and emotions, locking them off from Farren, who was already deep in her own sadness and didn't need Stephania's to also contend with. She would worry about those troubles when she was actually in Duvaharia. Right now, she needed to focus on leaving the Cavos and finding Sankyz so Dalton could rest and recuperate. As much as she wanted to spend the next few days flying nonstop to Duvaharia, her first duty was to him, and he was in no condition to travel all that way.

"You're finally looking your two hundred years, old man."

Dalton grinned wearily, but a sparkle ignited in his eyes. "Oh, I don't know about two hundred. Maybe only one hundred?"

"I can compromise." She smiled, but a bitterness settled in her as his shoulders sank. It felt like New-Fars all over again—her wanting to help him, to talk to him, to shoulder some of the mysterious burden he carried, but him locking it all away, always hiding it from her. *I learned from the best, Uncle Dalton. If you didn't want me to hide my emotions and feelings, then maybe you shouldn't have done so yourself.*

With a ground-rumbling roar, Farren suddenly plunged forward, galloping awkwardly across the uneven sands, the wind catching her wings and lifting them a few feet as she bounded along, leaving Dalton far behind. *I cannot wait any longer!*

"What in Susahu? Farren! Farren slow down!" Stephania yelled, clenching her eyes closed against the spray of sand and biting wind. "Curse the gods, dragon, we can't leave him behind."

Then I shall eat his horse and carry him too! With a loud trumpet, she launched herself into the sky. For a breathtaking moment, Stephania thought they were going to tumble and crash into the sands, but the oncoming breeze caught Farren's wings, and with a mighty push, they soared upwards.

Her stomach dropped as her breath caught in her throat, a surge of adrenaline flooding her veins. *This will never get old,* she thought as she closed her eyes and felt the rush of wind in her hair.

All too soon, Stephania felt Farren start to glide down. She opened her eyes as they landed, this time a bit smoother than their first flight.

Before Farren had even closed her wings, Stephania was down on the grass, rolling in it and laughing.

See. This was the better option. Now, I shall be right back.

"What are you—" Before Stephania could finish asking, Farren had already taken off again, her dark shape a consuming black void against the bright sands and suns.

She couldn't even be upset. With a long sigh, she laid her head back on the ground, feeling the cool grass all along her skin. For the first time, she realized how gritty her clothes were. Taking off her boots, she dumped out two small piles of sand before shaking out her cloak and shirt, wishing she didn't have to put them back on.

A roar from the desert caught her attention.

"By the gods," she laughed, waving her hands at Farren as she glided down. On the dragon's back sat Dalton proudly, his eyes glowing with elation.

"You flew!" Stephania ran up to them as Farren shook her wings and head, slivers of shadow floating to the ground.

A mist rose in Dalton's eyes as he nodded. "I never thought I would again, but yes, child. I flew."

She held out a hand to him to help him down, but he waved it away.

"I never needed your help before, and I won't begin to need it now. You don't need to treat me like an invalid, Stephania. Besides, I have never felt younger."

When she looked up into his face as he dismounted and bowed before Farren, thanking her, Stephania couldn't help but believe him.

"Wait," she slowly turned to Farren, a flash of horror rising over her. "You didn't eat Austin, did you?"

Farren's forked, bloodred tongue passed over her sharp teeth. *I did.*

Stephania's jaw hung open, and her eyes widened, words abandoning her. For a moment, they stood still, Farren's eyes dull and undisturbed, and Stephania's full of horror.

Just kidding. Farren trumpeted mockingly as Stephania lunged after her, a string of playful curses on her lips.

Battered about by the wind from Farren's wings, Stephania chased her until they were rolling in the grass. Stephania laughed until her sides hurt as Farren grunted humorously in a way only dragons could, causing Stephania to laugh harder.

When was the last time I had this much fun? She'd had fun with Trojan, with Ravillian and Lamora, playing by herself in New-Fars or with Dalton, and sometimes before that with Frawnden, but when had she truly been this joyful? This carefree? She had been so solemn as a babe, so stoic and unbelievably uptight, and then as a young girl and teenager, she had been plagued with abandonment and the fears and turmoil the bullying had brought.

Then a shiver raced down her spine as she briefly thought of both the good and horrific events that had transpired so quickly in the last few months in Trans-Falls. But that was all behind her now. It was in the past, and right here, right now, it wasn't chasing her. She thought of how easily she was laughing, tumbling through the grass with her dragon. *Her dragon.* Even that was unbelievable. And she thought of how anything felt possible right now. That she could make the world a better place, maybe not just out of revenge, but maybe because she had a vision for something better.

Shocked by her thoughts, she quickly sat up, her eyes wide.

Farren squirmed from her back onto her side and laid her head next to Stephania, her large eyes staring up at her rider. *What's wrong?*

Have I changed?

It was an oddly simple question, and one she wasn't even sure she could answer right now because she knew her thirst for revenge hadn't gone away. She knew the nightmares would continue to plague her. She knew she would have to face the emptiness Trojan left. Above all, she knew she hated Thaddeus no less than she had. But it was almost as if none of that mattered right now, as if she could be whoever she wanted to be, who she was meant to be if the world hadn't been so cruel—a visionary, a caretaker, a friend, a teacher, a leader, maybe even a lover and mother.

I don't think so, but perhaps you are seeing yourself truly for the first time.

Then I never want to forget her—myself, I mean. This person I should've been.

You won't. I won't let you. I promise.

Thank you, Farren.

Anything for you, little one.

Stephania lay by Farren's head, holding close to her, feeling her warm breath on her face and the cool grass under her. She looked up for a moment and spied Dalton napping not far from them, having made a little bed out of the grass. He looked more alive and rested than she had seen him for over a week, and the cloud over her heart lifted.

She lay back down and mindlessly rubbed Farren's snout as the Shadow Dragon purred.

By the way, whatever did you do with Austin?

Farren snorted, and her eyes blinked slowly. *I entered his mind and told him to run for the forest because I was going to eat him!*

You did not!

I did. Her thoughts were heavy with a smirk.

You could've given him a heart attack.

Perhaps, but he's sturdy. I'm sure he'll be fine. In fact, I think that's him galloping toward us right now.

Sure enough, as Stephania looked to the desert, Austin was galloping toward them, covered in foamy sweat, his eyes white with fear.

Waking up to the noise, Dalton jumped to his feet, and Stephania couldn't help but laugh as he chased down his horse, yelling at him and casting spells on him to assure him he was safe.

That was very cruel of you, you know, Stephania gently chastised.

Farren shrugged, her tongue darting out of her mouth. *Perhaps, but I am a dragon. I am the predator, not the prey, and others would do best to remember that.*

Stephania could only laugh and shake her head.

You would do well to know that Centaurs are galloping toward us as well. From the forest.

For a moment, her words didn't sink in. Finally they did, and Stephania bolted upright, her eyes locking with Dalton's just as he calmed Austin and grabbed his reins.

He was too far to yell at, but his eyes turned to the forest just as the first Centaur broke out from the thicket, sword in hand and his battle cry ringing through the air.

§

"I AM STEPHANIA LAVOISIER, daughter of Aeron and Frawnden of Trans-Falls, of Andromeda and Drox of Duvarharia, and I am Farloon!" Her challenging gaze pierced into the eyes of the Centaur whose axe was aimed at her. The Centaur leader was only a breath away from shouting the command to attack.

They were surrounded by at least twenty Centaur Warriors, each armed to the teeth, their eyes bloodthirsty and almost barbaric.

Red magic swirled from her hands and glowed in her eyes, ready to defend or attack; her scythe was clutched in her left hand, and she tried not to think that if it came to a fight, she had no idea how to use it. She could feel Dalton's eyes on her, and she knew he was thinking the same. "You will drop your weapons, or I will count it an offense against the tribe of Trans-Falls and Duvarharia."

"Your voice holds no authority here unless you have proof." The leader spat on the ground just a few feet in front of Stephania. Her grip tightened on her axe.

"I refuse to bare myself to your Warrior's bloodlust to simply show proof. I have no proof you won't slaughter me and my companions the moment our guard is down. Drop. Your. Weapons." Confidence and authority flooded her voice, the same confidence with which she had spoken to Trans-Falls before they left, though deep down, she only felt fear. Her hands trembled, and her heart raced. Subconsciously, she reached out to find Farren but knew she wasn't with her. The dragonet had taken flight the moment the Centaurs burst from the woods and surrounded Stephania and Dalton.

Red eyes stared down green. Stephania's magic pulsed. The leader's eyes narrowed.

"On the count of three, lower your weapons and magic, and we will do the same."

Stephania nodded.

"One. Two. Three."

For a brief moment, Stephania thought they wouldn't respect their agreement when none dropped their weapons. Letting herself trust and be the better person, she let the scythe slip from her hand. It landed with a dull thud.

Instantly, the plains rang alive with the sound of dropping weapons.

Stephania's gaze narrowed when the leader didn't drop her axe.

"You retain your magic, I retain my axe."

Fair enough. She grudgingly admitted it seemed like the fairest decision. However, though she would never say it out loud, her weak magic wouldn't be an even match against the Centaur's axe.

Slowly, Stephania pulled the clawed gauntlet off her hand and held up the ring of Trans-Falls.

The leader's eyes narrowed, but she said nothing as she waited for more proof.

"The Centaurs of Trans-Falls were supposed to have sent notice of our arrival." Stephania crossed her arms.

"We received such a message." The leader tilted up her head, but before Stephania could say anything else, the Centaur said something she wasn't expecting. "You're not the first creature to arrive claiming to be the Farloon or Savior of the Duvarharian prophecy."

Stephania's eyes widened. "What? Who?" She glanced at Dalton; he was just as shocked as her. *Were Etas trying to disguise themselves as her to infiltrate her allies? Was this another trick of Thaddeus's magic?*

Stephania was pulled back to the present when the leader cleared her throat. "You'll have to do more than flash a little ring to prove your identity."

Clenching her jaw, Stephania pushed her musings out of her mind; she would have to dwell on her imposter later. Next, she pulled the Farloon pendant from where it was tucked close to her heart and held it up. The suns' light caught the gem, scattering rays of humming red light across the plains. A gasp rose from the Centaurs, and they fell to their knees—all except their leader.

"Extraordinary light show, but how do I know it is truly the Farloon pendant?"

Stephania's heart sank in exasperation. If the Farloon pendant didn't make her believe, nothing would.

Enough! With an ear-splitting roar, Farren suddenly dove down into the Centaurs from where she had been gliding overhead. The seasoned Warriors scattered in fear and awe, despite the rallying cries from their leader. Though they were frightened, Stephania watched with surprise as they didn't move for their weapons but instead bowed before the Shadow Dragon in reverence, many of them murmuring things in the Sházuk language that sounded like "high lady" or "holy one".

Farren danced through the cowering Centaurs, roaring and swiping at them with her tail, rage pouring from her.

How dare you accuse my rider of falsities! How dare you slander your ally and Farloon, the very child of the Dragon Prophecy! Of course, no one could hear anything Farren was saying, but her message seemed to be very clear anyway.

"*Guglo-Zshaif,*" the leader whispered as her axe fell from her hands. Slowly, she knelt, placing her hands and forehead on the ground in utmost reverence. "Forgive me, *Zshaif.* Forgive me."

Stephania's eyes widened. She had never seen any Centaur prostrate themselves before, not even for Artigal. The words the Centaur was speaking were foreign to Stephania. She hadn't heard them spoken often, but she remembered something Dalton had read from an old Centaur tome, and the meaning surfaced. *They're calling you Shadow Goddess. They're ... worshiping you?* Centaurs worshiping a dragon? It seemed too strange. All the Centaurs she had grown up around had been fixated on the stars and forest. This seemed uncharacteristic.

Farren stalked toward the leader and bowed her head next to hers, her teeth bared, a low growl rumbling in her throat. Visible terror flashed across the Warrior's face, but she didn't flinch. *Yes, they are. My ancestors were considered gods once, and the Sankyz Centaurs were sworn to praise, protect, and worship them. Though most of the Shadow Dragons faded to myth, they continued to worship my kind, and my lineage stayed in the Cavos to keep their faith alive.* With one last snarl, Farren gently nudged the Warrior leader, motioning for her to stand.

On shaking legs, her eyes sparkling with tears, she stood, her eyes never leaving Farren. Her Warriors followed her lead as she placed her fist over her heart.

"Drylona, at your command, *Guglo-Zshaif.* May the suns smile upon your presence."

Tell her: as do the stars sing upon yours. I am Farren, and this is my rider, Stephania, and her uncle, Dalton the once rider of Saorise, and his beast of burden, which they call Austin. Welcome us into your tribe.

Stephania stepped forward, making herself known. "She says: as do the stars sing upon yours. She is Farren and I am her rider. This is my uncle, Dalton the once rider of Saorise, and his horse Austin, and you will welcome us into your tribe."

Bowing low, her persona radically different than it had been when they first met, Drylona motioned for her warriors to retrieve their weapons and for the Dragon Riders to follow.

"Of course, Farloon. Please forgive me of my rudeness. I was only trying to protect my tribe. Please forgive me."

Stephania looked to Dalton, and he nodded, his eyes clearly telling her to forgive, but the words caught in her throat. She realized she didn't want to forgive; she liked this Centaur Warrior groveling before her, she liked the reverence she was being offered, this stroke of power. Until now, she had been held up as if a porcelain figure of a god—precious and worth dying for but fragile and needing to be sheltered. But now she wasn't helpless. She didn't have power just because others gave or took it, trying to protect her so she could fulfill some destiny or prophecy; she had the power she carved out for herself. She had suffered so much, why shouldn't someone else for once?

"Even so," Artigal's voice echoed in her head, *"take warning that you do not sacrifice them as petty pawns. Even just one of their lives is worth far more than any simple lust of your heart."*

Before she gave in to the small voice inside her demanding control, demanding sacrifice, she blurted out, "I forgive you. We all do."

The relief was immense. Every Centaur released a sigh, and some even laughed nervously. A tear rolled down Drylona's face as she bowed before Stephania.

"Thank you, Farloon. Thank you. I pledge my life to you. I am forever in your debt."

Stephania didn't know what to say and only awkwardly shifted her weight before picking up her scythe and nodding. "Thank you," she managed but was unable to meet Drylona's adoring gaze because of the shame festering inside her.

I am not worthy of this. I am weak.

Farren turned her head to her rider and breathed darkness over her. *No, you are not worthy of it, but someday you shall be.*

"Well done, Stephania." Dalton smiled down at her from Austin. "You have proved yourself a great leader today. With some training, you will make a fine Lady of the Dragon Palace." Pride shone in his eyes.

She didn't feel she would.

"Come, Farloon, *Guglo-Zshaif,* and mentor." Drylona motioned for them to follow as her Warriors formed ranks around them. "Sankyz awaits."

CHAPTER 34

SANKYZ HAD BEEN BEAUTIFUL. The Centaurs were generous when they saw she was Farloon and once Farren introduced herself. It seemed Sankyz still read the stars and believed in Hanluurasa, but they also had an extreme undying devotion to the Shadow Dragons that perplexed Stephania. Farren had been fed so generously by them, Stephania swore she had grown a few feet in just a couple of hours. Spending a night in a soft bed and getting nearly twelve hours of sleep before eating a meal fit for a Chief had been blissful. She wanted to stay one more day, just one, but she knew if she did, she wouldn't ever want to leave again. Especially since she was leaving Dalton behind this time.

Stephania wiped her nose on her sleeve, staring at the dripping mossy rock ceiling above her. *Stop crying. Stop crying. You knew this was going to come. You prepared for this.* But it was happening sooner than she had thought. So much sooner.

"I'm sorry, Stephania." Dalton folded his hands in front of him, unable to meet her gaze any more than she was able to meet his. "I think we both know this is what's best."

"You can't at least come to the border with me?" She hated how much her voice cracked, as if she were six years old again and didn't want to make the long trek to their New-Fars training arena alone.

"I wish I could. I really do. But my magic is wearing thin. It exhausts me to even start fires or read time. Not to mention, Austin isn't in good health from the desert, and the Sankyz don't have any horses to replace him; the few weeks it would take to get to Duvaharia would kill him. Besides, I would only be able to follow you to the Lota woods anyways. I can't travel on foot through its poison swamps. The only way through is by flying over, and Farren can't carry both of us. She can barely carry you. It will take all the extra strength you both have to even carry food and supplies. It's best I stay here in Sankyz."

Angrily, she sniffed and brushed away her tears. "I know. I know that. It's just—" She shook her head, the words catching in her throat. She looked up to Dalton holding his hands out to her. With a sniffle, she stepped into his hug and let him hold her until her tears slowed and her heart stopped pounding. Finally, she found the courage to speak what had been so heavy on her heart. "You were banished."

She felt his breath catch in his throat, his body rigid. Silence stretched between them until he sighed and relaxed. "Yes." His answer was so quiet, she almost didn't hear him. But she did hear the hurt in his voice.

She didn't have the heart to ask him why. If he didn't want to tell her now, she wouldn't press it.

"I'm sorry, my child. I should have told you sooner, I just—"

She shook her head. "No, it's alright. I understand."

A heavy sigh escaped from his lips. After another silence, he spoke again. "When I was banished from Duvarharia, I was relieved. Well, I was angry, and sad, and scared too of course, but I was relieved nonetheless. I thought I was leaving behind everything that had caused me pain, that it would be better if I put it all behind me and started over."

"Even my parents?" She looked up into his face, his beard tickling her cheeks.

He swallowed hard and nodded. "Even your parents. I loved them, but I had done something terrible to them, something I could never take back. And, in turn, they hurt me too."

An ache settled in her heart.

His chest rose with a deep breath. "But now I see I was leaving behind so much more than I could've ever known. I don't want to leave you, Stephania. I've never wanted to leave you. I always wanted to watch you grow up, find a passion, and follow it wherever it took you. I wanted you to move away from New-Fars to some place where you would be accepted. I wanted you to fall in love, maybe have a family. I wanted to see you be successful and happy, not because you had to save the world, but just because you existed, just because you were alive and deserve every happiness the world can give. It was a dream of course, but I wanted it so bad."

His tears dropped onto her neck and shoulder. She couldn't say anything; she didn't even know what to say.

"I never once regretted doing what banished me from Duvarharia. Ever. But now ..." He sniffed and shifted his arms around her. "Now, I couldn't regret it more. I'm sorry, Stephania, that my mistakes have caused pain to you like this. I never wanted this to be the way you left me. I'm sorry."

She tightened her arms around him, barely able to whisper, "It's okay. I'm not mad. It's okay."

But they both knew it wasn't. It had to be okay, but it wasn't. None of this was okay.

She needed to leave. Not tomorrow, not in a week; she needed to leave now.

Everything ahead of her was now the unknown, and this time, she had no one to guide her.

Xavier awaited her in Duvarharia and Farren was with her, but Farren knew nothing about Duvarharia, and Xavier seemed so far away; sometimes she wondered if he had just been a dream or only a desert hallucination.

"I'm scared," she whispered against Dalton's chest, unsure if it was right to admit it.

"I know, child. I know." He kissed the top of her head. "But Farren is with you now. And your home awaits. They will love you, and you will learn quickly. You have changed so much, Stephania. You have grown so much. You're not a child anymore. You know more than you think you do, and you're stronger than you think you are. Duvarharia is lucky to have you; you will make them, your parents, and all those who have loved you and sacrificed for you proud. I know I am. I'm more proud of you than you will ever know."

She nodded, trying to let his words sink in, trying to let reality sink in. This was her goodbye. This was the last time she would be able to spend with just her and Dalton. A drop of water from the small cave's ceiling dripped onto her face and trickled down her cheek, a cold tear mingling with her own. For a moment, she let herself just listen to the roar of the waterfall the little cave they were in snaked behind, like a secret passageway. She let herself wish she could hide here forever, hidden from the world with nothing more to do than listen to the water and watch the moss grow.

Slowly, her eyes dried and fluttered open.

Time would keep moving, just as it always did. She couldn't stop it, and she couldn't make it start. She could only accept what it brought and took.

Everything she wanted was in her grasp—a dragon, magic, power, a new beginning, a chance for revenge. She had to force herself to remember that. Even so, now she had all she had wished for, it all seemed so horrifyingly empty.

"Come with me," she pleaded one last time, fully knowing his answer.

He pulled away and tucked some of her unruly hair behind her ear. "I can't. You know this."

She looked away from his gaze and nodded, whispering, "I know."

"You know I love you, Stephania. No matter what you do, who you become, your failures or victories, what you believe in, I will always love you."

She had to bite back her tears, her teeth digging into her cheek. She was really leaving him, leaving his protection, his support, his love. "I know. And I will always love you too."

His hands on her shoulders, he peered deep into her eyes, his gaze full of nothing but pride. "Good. Now go, Stephania, my child. Go and fulfill your destiny, go make all your dreams come true, go become who you were meant to be." He placed a kiss on her forehead.

As she pulled away, she squeezed his hand one last time before walking to the entrance of the passageway. From here, she could see Farren, decked in her armor, her saddle laden with food supplies, enough for a week. The Centaurs were admiring her, praising her, and lavishing her with gifts she had to refuse because she couldn't carry them.

Duvarharia seemed so far away now, even though it meant Dalton would only be a day or three's flight away. One last time, she turned back, her gaze tender and promising.

"I will come back, Uncle Dalton. I promise I won't forget you."

He smiled through the mist that rose in his eyes as he nodded. "I'm counting on it."

§

IS THIS FOREST ALIVE? *Like the ones in Trans-Falls?*

Stephania's hand strayed to the bundled Lyre, which she had secured to Farren's back. *I don't know. Maybe. It doesn't feel as awake as the forests around Trans-Falls, but maybe that's because it's so far from the* Gauwu Zelauw. *Or maybe because it's only a small sliver of healthy forest between the empty Cavos and the poisoned Lota Woods. Maybe living trees need more space?*

Farren snorted and looked from side to side. *Small sliver or not, it feels like it's watching us.*

A shiver ran down Stephania's back as she followed Farren's gaze. She had to agree, though it didn't feel like the same sort of watching she had always felt in Trans-Falls. It felt like hidden, twisted eyes watched her and Farren. That added with the unnervingly quiet that had settled over the Sankyz forest the moment they woke up that morning made her wish they weren't alone. Although these trees weren't poisoned like in the Lota Woods, it seemed being pressed between a barren desert and poisonous swamp still had its drawbacks, and most of the trees were twisted and bent at awkward unnerving angles, many of which looked disturbingly like arms, hands, or faces.

They had been given the option of an escort. The entirety of the Sankyz army had been far too willing to protect Farren and her rider all the way to the Dragon Palace if need be, even through the Lota Woods, but she had turned them down. The time for escorts and being helpless was over. If she faced Thaddeus now, an army of Centaurs wouldn't be much help anyway, and at this point she knew she was capable enough to fight a few Etas; at least, she hoped she was.

Though she knew Farren had to conserve her strength for when they flew over the Lota Woods, Stephania was already bored of walking. Sometimes she felt like they were traveling in circles; the scenery hadn't changed much for a few unsettling hours.

Stephania ...

The tone of Farren's voice instantly set her on edge.

Look.

She followed her dragon's gaze, and her blood ran cold.

A crow sat on a branch just above them and a little off the path. It was nearly the size of a turkey vulture and had midnight black feathers that shimmered purple and green in the small bits of sunlight that found its way through the thick canopy. Most disturbing was that it had not two, but *four* eyes—eyes glinting red.

It peered down at them intently, tilting its sleek head from side to side, before cawing once then twice and spreading its wings, taking flight.

Stephania, it had four wings. Not two, but four.

Stephania tried to steady her shaking hand as she nodded. *I know. I saw.*

What is it? Do you think it's an Eta?

No ... I don't. But I don't know what it is either.

We shouldn't have anything to worry about, then. Perhaps we're close enough to the Lota Woods that some of these creatures are mutated. The poisonous fumes are said to be extremely strong. Perhaps we should fly?

Stephania didn't answer as her eyes traveled to the trees. "Gods of all."

The forest was full of them.

Everywhere they looked—the trees, the floor, the branches—was full of sitting, four eyed, four winged crows, all of them staring at the dragon and rider.

"Why do you think—?" Before she could finish, Farren jumped forward, stood on her back legs, spread her massive wings and roared as loud as she could.

The branches bent back, and all the crows screeched, instantly taking flight in terror.

Climb on my back, Stephania. I do not think these crows mean no harm. We will fly to Duvarharia. Enough of this walking. I want to be safe. I want this journey to be over. Come on.

Stephania didn't need telling twice. In a moment, she was on Farren's back, and they were galloping through the woods, trying to find a break in the trees big enough to soar through.

They found one just big enough to fit Stephania's body and did the same trick they had to get out of the Shadow Cavern. As soon as they broke through the trees, Stephania felt their hearts skip a beat.

A black cloud hung over the horizon, shifting and molding like a miniature storm cloud driven by a foul wind.

What is—

Stephania saw a flash of red sparks, and her blood ran cold. "Etas."

Farren cursed in her dragon language and shook her head, a low growl in her throat. *Let's fight them. We can stop them. We have to stop them before they reach Sankyz.*

Stephania thought the same, but she shook her head. *We can't. There's too many of them. We'd never make it out alive. We're almost over the Lota woods, and from there, it's only about a few hours flight to the border. Uncle Dalton said there should be enough of the border left to protect us from the Etas if need be. They won't be able to cross most of it, and if they did, we'd have enough time to make it to safety or get help. The Sankyz have been dealing with Etas on their own for a long time. I have to trust they can handle themselves. Uncle Dalton will fight if he has to.*

Then what do we do?

Stephania looked into the sky above them and took a deep breath. *We'll fly over them, and we won't use any more magic than we have to in order to maintain direction. Hopefully, they'll be tracing on the ground, not the sky. With the high altitude and wind, it'll disperse what's left of my magic trace and confuse them. Maybe not for long, but long enough to at least get halfway to the border.*

Without second thought, Farren shifted her wings and beat them harder, propelling them powerfully into the sky. Stephania could feel the strain on her young body, but the Centaurs had fed her well, and new energy coursed through her veins along with adrenaline. Stephania hoped being so high would scramble her trace enough to share her energy, but until then, Farren would have to do it on her own.

Come on, Farren. Stephania gritted her teeth as she peered below them, straining to see the cloud of Etas flying ever closer. She hadn't fought on a dragon before, let alone with her scythe. The possibility of them surviving a fight if it came to it was looking more and more slim by the second. *You've got this, gumewa.*

Farren's rhythm began to slow, and Stephania could feel how labored her breaths had become. *Just a little bit farther. Just a little farther.* She strained toward the line of clouds above them. If they could just make it above the clouds ...

Struggling not to roar or growl in her effort, Farren groaned as she shoved her wings down and they shot through the layer of clouds. As soon as Stephania was sure they were disguised at least a little by the clouds and the air flow was enough to wash away most of her physical scent, she released some of her energy into Farren. Instantly, her lungs filled with fresh breath, and the aches eased out of her wings.

Thank you, little one.

No, thank you.

The Etas below grew closer and closer; through the thin cloud cover, Stephania could make out their individual shapes as the red sparks covered their bodies, turning them into something new. Even if she and Farren passed over them undetected, she knew it would only be a matter of time before they picked up her magic trace and changed trajectory, following them to the Dragon Palace. They had to stay hidden as long as possible.

A dark Shadow Dragon in the world of white, fluffy clouds and bright sunshine was not ideal circumstances for sneaking. They would be easily spotted.

Stephania, I think they're sensing us.

No, no, no. Not yet. Please not yet.

She couldn't do anything to stop it.

With screeching cries, the Etas began to shift and change. A few seemed to have spotted her and were trying to fly higher. They were nearly under Farren and Stephania now.

Just as her eyes locked with one of the Etas, a rush of wind blew a cloud under them, blocking their view.

What in Susahu ...?

It wasn't just one cloud. Clouds were forming out of thin air and positioning themselves directly under Farren and Stephania as they traveled.

I have no idea. Stephania strained to see what was causing the clouds to build and shift like this, but even with Farren's heightened vision, she could see nothing; she felt only the unmistakable sense that once again something was watching her.

Whatever it is, we have to take advantage of it. We'll be able to get farther with this cover, but they'll still pick up on our trace. If this continues for a while, we just might be able to get to the border.

Agreed.

Pouring a steady stream of energy into Farren, Stephania leaned close down to the spines on Farren's neck, feeling the darkness wrap around her, pulling her closer to her dragon. Farren caught a draft and turned her legs and back to shadow, leaving only her wings in the flesh. Without the extra weight, they shot through the air, faster than Stephania had ever thought possible.

Without warning, the clouds stopped forming in front of them. Now Stephania could see down to the woods below. A green haze hung over the forest and horrific screeches of dying or mutated animals rose to meet them along with a poisonous stench.

We're over the Lota Woods now.

Stephania could see the rise of hills and small mountains marking the border of Duvarharia. They were close. So, so close. Her heart raced faster. *We might make it.*

A bloodcurdling roar filled the air behind them, and her hope instantly dissipated. *They found us.*

Though she knew she shouldn't, Stephania turned around. Like a wave of black water, the Etas far behind them rose into the air, changing direction as they caught wind of her magic trace. For an unknown reason, whatever or whoever had been controlling the clouds had given up, and not a single cloud could be seen in the sky. Whoever it was had been generous but only to a point.

Go, Farren!

With a roar, Farren abandoned all hope of stealth and beat her wings faster, diving down to gain momentum before leveling out and rocketing through the air.

Surely, the Etas are no match for a Shadow Dragon. Surely, they can't fly this fast. A boding unease filled her. She didn't think these Etas were acting alone; maybe not with Thaddeus but someone else. Someone else was giving them strength and speed, just as she had been given cover by the clouds. Perhaps it was the same person? Perhaps they were toying with her? She didn't have time to wonder.

Her jaw ground against itself as quiet words in the Ancient language pleading for speed—half-spells and half-prayers—tumbled from her lips.

Soon, a few scout Etas were flying next to them, their screeches filling the air, their bloodthirsty eyes darting from Farren to Stephania as their large noses sniffed and huffed, searching for her magic trace.

Knowing it wouldn't make much of a difference but feeling hopeless, she released a shock of magic that tore through two of the Etas before they could latch on to her trace; their lifeless bodies tumbled from the sky, leaving a spray of black blood behind them. It only bought her a few more seconds, though. When the other scouts found her trace, they let out bloodcurdling screams, enraging the other Etas.

I'm going to have to fight if they get too close, but you have to keep flying, Farren. No matter what happens, you have to make it to the border. We have to trust it will protect us.

Farren was too concentrated to answer, but she didn't have to. Stephania knew she understood.

No matter what.

She placed a hand on her armor, silently thanking it, before drawing the Shadow Blade. The scythe felt awkward and out of place in her hand. *Why did you choose this blade for me? What use do I have for it?* She thought of the countless hours she spent training with the sword after Trojan's death and the countless hours she spent training with the bow before her memories were sealed. She wouldn't be able to put any of it to use. *Typical destiny.* That wasn't counting how awkward it would be to fight with a scythe astride a dragon.

A scream was the only warning alerting her of the Eta before it dove down toward her. She looked up in time to see its panther body angle itself against the wind, its mouth opening into rows of teeth dripping with Eta poison.

Instinct taking over, she lashed out with the scythe, yelling in exertion as the blade tore through the Eta's body, slicing it clean in half and bathing her in its stinking black blood. Half of its body tumbled down Farren's right side, and the other hit her left wing, causing her to falter. As she banked to the left, another Eta whizzed under her wing, right where it would have been seconds before.

She felt Farren wanting to turn and take on the Etas. *No, Farren. You have to focus. Promise me you'll focus.*

Farren snarled and bit through an Eta attacking her head. *I promise I will try.*

Instinct telling her to duck, she lay low on Farren's neck and felt as the edge of an Eta's claws tore through her cloak. Before it could turn to finish the job, she swung the scythe behind her, a satisfying jolt in the snath telling her she had hit her mark.

Now dozens of Etas were flying beside them. They struggled to keep up, and only a few were strong enough to attack while flying, but as their numbers grew, so did their strength.

Spinning the scythe in hand, she watched with immense satisfaction as the shadow blade parted Eta flesh like water. The blade was powerful enough she didn't need much skill to wield it as long as she wasn't fighting more than two or three Etas at a time. Even so, she was surprised how natural it felt despite never having wielded it before. Perhaps the Shadow Blade hadn't made a mistake.

We're almost there. Almost there, Farren kept chanting to herself.

The mountains were rising before them, and Stephania almost swore she could see the shimmering blue of the magic border surrounding Duvarharia. Gritting her teeth, she poured more energy into Farren.

Briefly, she cursed the gems in the Shadow Armor and Blade. With the way they shocked and hummed, she was sure they were full of energy, but she had no idea how to channel it.

With a roaring screech, three Etas divebombed Stephania. One's talons tore through Farren's wings instead, drawing a pained roar from her and a strained cry from Stephania. The second was split in half with Stephania's blade, but the third caught her shoulder, tearing through her skin down her arm, nearly wrenching her from Farren's back.

For a moment, blinding pain overwhelmed her, and flashbacks filled her mind of the Eta that had attacked and poisoned her as a child.

Burning poison poured into her blood, pounded in her mind, muddled the screaming of an Eta as it clawed its way up Farren's shoulder and changed its shape. One of its eight new legs stabbed out at Stephania. She barely had time to dodge it. Its jagged claw slipped on Farren's armor, and for a moment, it nearly lost its footing.

Head reeling and ears ringing, she clutched her shoulder. Her hand came away sticky with red blood and sickly green poison. She leaned her head against Farren's back, her body too heavy to hold up. She could hear Farren roaring at her, trying to wake her from her stupor, but she sounded and felt so far away.

"Trojan?" she whispered, lifting her hand. She could see him, standing over her, as young and alive as he had been that day she was attacked, only his face wasn't worried, not like it had been.

"*Stephania ...*" He reached out to touch her face, but she felt nothing. "*You can't let go yet. Remember what Artigal said? When you wanted to give in to the hate and the darkness? Listen to him. Don't let go just yet. Keep fighting.*"

"Don't leave me again," she cried as his figure faded, replaced by a drooling Eta with the body of a woman but eight spider legs. Its head was wrapped in sparks as it changed from a humanoid head to a horrific toothed worm.

"*Fight the evil within you. Think of your Creator.*" Artigal's voice from all those years ago pierced her mind.

My creator? A single thread of clarity shone like a beacon before her. Had he been speaking of the Creator Źuje whom Xavier had spoken of? Was He even real?

With a screaming roar, the Eta lurched forward when its head finished shape-shifting, its eyeless face locking on hers as it sniffed for her magic trace.

Farren was screaming for her. The Eta dove for her. The world slowed down.

"Save me," she whispered pleadingly. "If you are real, save me, Creator."

In a blinding flash of light, she felt the poison drain from her body. Her limbs filled with life and her mind with clarity. With a roar of determination and new strength, she twirled the scythe upwards, doubting it would even scratch the Eta but suddenly filled with the desperation to live.

A scream parting her lips, she thrust all her momentum into the scythe and felt as it tore through flesh. One of the Eta's legs crashed into her, pulling her farther from Farren's back. Its blood spurted onto her face, temporarily blinding her, but with a strangled croak, it fell from Farren's body, unable to regenerate fast enough before it bled to death.

"Give me the strength I need," she prayed, though she did not believe.

As she dragged herself back up onto the saddle, commanding Farren's darkness to encircle her and her legs to become one with her dragon's body, ensuring she wouldn't fall again, she felt a warmth spread through her from her chest.

Confused, she realized the warmth was coming from the Farloon pendant.

Her eyes widened as the heat grew hotter and she recognized its trace. "Ancient Magic." Before horror and repulsion could set in, she felt her entire body come alive. Energy poured from the pendant into her heart, mind, and soul and from her into Farren.

Roaring, Farren powerfully beat her wings, and they shot ahead of the Etas.

The magic was almost too much to contain. She could hardly take breaths against its power as it surged through her. She would have to channel it if she didn't want to lose control of it like she had back in Trans-Falls. She had to overcome her fear of it.

Struggling past the panic threatening to overcome her, the flashbacks of dead Centaurs with white and black veins under their skin, along with the repulsion that filled her, she reached out to the Ancient Magic and commanded it to obey. Nothing happened. Again, she called for it, demanding it answer to her. Again, no answer.

The Etas were closing in again. This time, she could hardly see through them, their numbers were so great.

Stephania ...

She tried to block Farren's worried voice from her mind.

Stephania, we're not going to make it.

Curse the gods, Stephania cussed, closing her eyes to the doomed reality around her. The magic fought inside her, struggling to take control, wanting to burst forth murderously. *Listen to me. Obey me.*

The Etas grew closer. Red sparks filled the air with their screams. Farren snapped a few out of the sky, but another tore her neck, her red blood stark against her black skin.

Stephania!

With a scream of rage, Stephania opened her eyes and threw out her hands. "In the name of the Creator, I command you to obey me!"

In a heartbeat, the world went still.

Everything was silent, unmoving. Somewhere in the stillness, she heard a small voice—one more powerful than the world.

"As you command, Shadow of Light."

A cry of triumph parted her lips as the magic weaved into her veins, settled itself inside her, calmed its war inside her, and laid itself at her feet.

With a whisper, she commanded it forth. In a raging wave of white, black, and red magic, it poured from her hands, tearing through hundreds of Etas and bathing the sky in their black blood.

Farren breathed in the magic as it raced through her body. Seamlessly, as if it were as easy as breathing, she changed back and forth between flesh and shadow, weaving her way through the Etas, and Stephania changed with her.

The Eta's attacks were useless. Those that escaped the Ancient Magic were either met with Farren's devastating jaws or with Stephania's scythe, the Ancient Magic teaching her the art of scythe fighting and filling her with unrestrained knowledge as it worked flawlessly with the magic inside the Shadow Blade and Armor. Whatever Etas escaped flew harmlessly through Farren and Stephania's bodies, now they could shift from flesh to shadow, their minds and souls as one.

Though the Etas were so thick around them—a seemingly impenetrable cloud of darkness—Stephania and Farren easily cut a path through them, always able to see Duvarharia's shining blue border beckoning them to safety. Etas rained down around them so thick, their carnage stained the tops of the trees black.

Almost. Almost. Almost.

The Etas were closing in. The magic roared deafeningly around them. Stephania could hardly keep track of the Etas as they attacked her, could hardly remember what it was like to feel her body as flesh and not shadow.

She couldn't hold them off for much longer. They needed to cross the border.

Quieting the magic and calling it to her, she let its knowledge fill her, trusting it knew what she wanted it to do and trusting that the Master it served would listen to her pleas.

Take me to Duvarharia, she whispered. *Take me ... home.*

As you command, Shadow of Light.

Instantly, she felt as though they had been torn from the sky by a greater creature. Her stomach plummeted nauseatingly, and it took all her self-control not to throw up. When she opened her eyes, nothing but eternal darkness surrounded her. She could feel Farren under her but couldn't see her. She couldn't breathe. She felt both fully alive and fully dead, as if she were freezing but also burning.

We will be lost. We'll be lost!

Stephania shut out Farren's fear and searched for the Ancient Magic. *Take me to Duvarharia,* she commanded again.

Nothing happened, and she wondered if she had been wrong, if she had resigned herself to the dark powers of the Ancient Magic and they were doomed to be trapped in this in between world forever.

Then they were falling, falling, falling. They were yanked and jerked, being pulled in a thousand different ways, even as the darkness pressed in so hard she was afraid they would explode.

She screamed in agony as Farren roared, and then light was exploding all around them, air filling their lungs, wind stinging their faces, the screams of angry Etas chasing them.

Snapping around, Stephania breathed out a gasp of shock. The border was behind them.

They were in Duvarharia.

The Etas bore onward, but as soon as they flew into the shimmering blue border, their bodies exploded in a mass of twisted flesh and blood, instantly killing them. Hundreds died before the others learned and slowed their attack, hovering just outside the border and screaming angrily.

Somehow, she and Farren had traveled through space, time, and matter to escape the Etas. She had heard of something like this from Dalton's tomes—teleporting through another dimension called *Dasejuba*, the world between worlds.

Slowly, she started chuckling until it grew into loud, clear laughter that rang out through the small mountains, mingling with Farren's elated roar.

"We did it," she breathed unbelievingly as she looked ahead of them to the rolling hills and quiet forests below.

At last, we did. Farren rumbled contently as she glided slowly, letting the wind carry her weary body.

Stephania shook her head, unable to believe anything that had transpired. She had channeled Ancient Magic, killed hundreds of Etas on her own, changed to shadow with her dragon, and made it to Duvarharia.

"We made it to Duvarharia," she whispered as if saying it would somehow make it more real.

She stared into the setting suns, watching them turn the land of dragons to a land of gold and red. Tears filled her eyes as she stroked Farren's neck and wiped sticky Eta blood from her face. "We made it home."

CHAPTER 35

EVERYTHING FELT SO FAMILIAR, so comforting. "I think my
parents flew over these hills when taking me to Uncle Dalton." Stephania
closed her eyes. She could see snippets of the memory, of how the moon
shone through the night air and how the sounds of battle filled the silence.

These exact hills? Or just this hill range?

I'm not sure. Maybe these exact hills.

Stephania opened her eyes as Farren started circling down. Even though they
could make it to the Dragon Palace in just a few hours, possibly even less, the suns
were now quite low over the horizon, and along with feeling utterly exhausted from the
day's events, she was positive she looked a mess and was sure she didn't want that to be
her first impression.

Not that you'll look much better tomorrow without a stream to wash your face in. Farren
smirked.

Rude. But perhaps we'll find a stream later.

Perhaps.

Farren was leaning toward one of the hills, ready to land, when Stephania caught
sight of another. "Can you land there instead?"

Yes, but why? She landed, ruffled her wings, and eased to the ground with a groan.

Stephania slid off, almost falling when her knees buckled. Slowly, she sat down,
feeling the lush grass as it blew in the breeze between her fingers. "Because these *are* the
exact hills my parents flew over. I'm sure of it." She closed her eyes but still saw the hill
they were on, only it was under moonlight instead of sunset. She opened her eyes again,
a small smile spreading on her dirty, blood caked face. "In fact, I think they might have
stopped for a break on this very hill." She pressed her palm to the ground beneath her,
a warmth spreading through her chest.

You want to see them.

Stephania shrugged, but then remembered she couldn't keep anything secret from
her dragon. "Yeah, I do. But I'm scared I don't have the strength left to reach into their

memories." Absently, her hand trailed the Farloon pendant; it still pulsed with warmth from the Ancient Magic, but it was weakening. Now that she knew it contained Ancient Magic, she could easily sense the hum of its energy and knew it was only returning to its dormant state. Perhaps, if she was in need, it would save her again.

Then I will help you. And what little of the Ancient Magic that is left coursing through us will help as well.

"Isn't it kind of selfish to use the Ancient Magic for just wanting to see my parents?"

Since when has being selfish ever stopped you?

Stephania's eyebrows shot up, and she turned to Farren. "Again, that's extremely rude."

Farren yawned, displaying rows of bloodstained teeth, and shrugged before licking her claws. *Perhaps, but am I wrong?*

A knot formed in Stephania's stomach as she was reminded of all the times she had been selfish and what it had cost those around her. Shaking her head in an attempt to dispel the unwelcome memories, she could only shrug. She couldn't deny it.

But even so, I don't think it will harm anything. Come closer to me and touch my face.

Stephania did as she asked, placing her hands on Farren's jaw, and together they closed their eyes. She called on their strength, and quickly, the stagnant image of a hill under the moonlight sprang to life.

§

Suźefrusum, Duvarharia
Night of the Battle of the Prophecy
Nearly 17 Years Ago

THE SOUNDS OF BATTLE *grew dim behind them as they passed over the Suźefrusum–the large forest land in the valley of the Dragon Palace. The moon shone through the treetops of the forest, its light casting flickering patterns on the leafy woodland floor. The stars above twinkled like a thousand eyes, watching and crying their tears of light over the land of dragons.*

Andromeda stared wistfully down into the forest, wondering what lay below and wishing so much of Duvarharia's history and secrets hadn't been lost through war.

She, Stephania, and Mischievous continued to ride in silence. The normally quiet Stephania was even more stony and solemn as she gazed upon the land of her country. She leaned over as far as the straps on her legs and waist would let her, her eyes widening at the view.

"You are heir to all of this, Stephania," Andromeda whispered with a smile. "One day, it will be yours to rule and to care for."

Stephania frowned, looking at the ground, then back up at her mother. "Mine?"

Andromeda laughed. "In a way, yes. It is yours."

Something like a smile lifted the babe's red lips before she focused her attention back on the trees, a little song humming in her throat.

Andromeda continued to glance over her shoulder every now and then to see if her husband and her dragon's mate were behind them.

Nothing but cloud-spotted sky filled her vision.

A heavy sigh fell from her lips as she looked far ahead of her. The small hills and mountains marking the border of Duvarharia were growing ever closer. Soon, they would be at the border itself.

The steady rhythm of Mischievous' wings hummed in the air. The cold, crisp mountain air wafted up to them and smelled of rainfall from only two days ago.

Now, if she looked hard enough, she could see the shimmering blue of the border shield.

The once magnificent, powerful shield was now only a shadow of its former glory. Portions of it were missing, and the remaining parts were either too weak or small to protect against anything stronger than a small Eta army. Andromeda wondered resentfully how many deaths from infiltrating Etas could have been prevented if the border's maintenance hadn't been neglected thousands of years ago.

Drox and Aldwyn are not in sight, *Mischievous informed her, a pang of worry in her voice.*

Let's land and wait for a little while.

The border shimmered and waved gently in the wind not too far away from the small hill they landed on, its protective magic barely visible in the moonlight.

Andromeda shifted uncomfortably in the leather saddle. She would have preferred to not wear a saddle with straps, most riders never used them, but Stephania was with her, and the extra precaution was necessary.

Stephania yawned and snuggled up closer to Andromeda. "Ah we dare 'et?"

The woman chuckled and smoothed Stephania's wild hair. They had been so rushed in the chaos of the ill-timed attack to get ready for their travel, she hadn't been able to brush her daughter's hair. "Not yet, little flame. We still have a long way to go." She gently worked out one knot in the bouncy red curls, then another, and then another.

Stephania sighed heavily and pouted but didn't say anything else. It wasn't long before she drifted off to sleep, catching up on the rest she had been so rudely awoken from.

Thinking of the extraordinarily long journey ahead of them, the Dragon Palace's ruling Lady fingered the bags carefully strapped to Mischievous' saddle. She could feel a great many crystals and orbs inside the bag, and she shook her head before addressing her soul mate.

Do you think we have enough *vuldaheshab*?

The green Poison Dragon scratched at the dark, heavy armor strapped to her chest and legs before grunting. I hope so, because if we want to make it to New-Fars before midnight tomorrow, and especially with all this extra weight, I'm going to need all the energy I can get.

Andromeda nodded and once again ran her fingers subconsciously through her daughter's hair. The trip from the Dragon Palace to New-Fars if on foot or horseback took months. It would be easy enough to fly on a dragon, but doing so in just a little over one night was a stretch. It could only be done with extra energy stored in a vuldahesh—a rare crystal with the ability to absorb and hold energy. It would have been easier, of course, to have teleported several times to cross the distance between here and New-Fars, but with Stephania being so young, even that was too dangerous.

They slowly lapsed back into silence, and Andromeda yawned several times, feeling herself following in her sleeping daughter's footsteps.

After a while, she was jolted awake by Mischievous. Andromeda?

The woman blinked her eyes, struggling to keep them open. "Huh?" *It took her a moment to remember why she was on the back of her dragon and where they were.*

Wake up. We have to leave. It's been long over a half hour, and Drox and Aldwyn haven't arrived.

A pit of dread welled up inside Andromeda. Her husband hadn't come. The worst filled her mind as tears began to cloud her vision.

Stephania raised her head and rubbed her eyes. "'Ere's fatta?"

Andromeda could only shake her head and bite her lip, doing her best not to break down. If Drox was dead, she had to carry on what he had died trying to accomplish. She had to make sure Stephania got to Dalton in New-Fars, and then she had to continue leading her country.

Be strong. The night is not yet over. He could just be delayed. We, however, must hurry.

The woman straightened her back and tried to banish the tears from her eyes and the dread from her mind. "Hold on, Stephania. We're flying again."

Stephania wasn't ready to leave without her father. Throwing a fit, she pouted and scowled. "Where's fatta?"

Andromeda had to forcefully make Stephania sit properly on the dragon and hold onto the straps.

"Father's just a little late."

Stephania huffed, continuing to squirm. "He's ne'er late."

The mother couldn't help but grin at her stubborn, intelligent child. "Well, this time, he is

390

going to be just a little late. Now, hold on to Mischievous, Stephania, so we can leave."

Just to their right, the air exploded in a massive ball of fire.

Mischievous roared in surprise and lunged to the side, violently jerking her riders, before coiling, hissing warningly at the creatures who emerged from the flames, ready to strike.

"Who says I'm going to be late? You know how I abhor tardiness." *A warm, lazy smile spread across Drox's face. He had a large cut running across his arm, and a new wound decorated Aldwyn's back, but other than that, they seemed to be well.*

Andromeda gasped with relief, suddenly feeling ill from the rush of adrenaline. "Joad be praised. It's you."

The fire around Aldwyn disappeared as he stepped closer to Mischievous.

Drox was opening his mouth to say something else when the Poison Dragon lunged unexpectedly at Aldwyn, nearly knocking him to the ground. Mischievous' curses and insults were so loud, even Stephania, who hadn't been taught to speak to the dragons, could hear her clearly.

Curse you, Aldwyn! I thought we were being attacked! What in Rasa made you think you needed to sneak up on us like that? I could have killed both you and Drox!

The shocked Combustion Dragon was skipping away, half-flying and half-running from his mate, his eyes wide and his mind laced with humor. Gods of all. I didn't think you were that easily frightened.

Mischievous roared with rage and threw herself against the larger dragon with abandon.

Two loud cracks betrayed Drox as he quickly teleported from his dragon's neck to the stable ground as Mischievous threw Aldwyn to the grass.

She snapped in Aldwyn's face, hissing and snarling at him. I am not easily frightened! For your information, I was not in the least bit scared. I was ready to attack and kill. I should have just finished the job!

Aldwyn was about to respond with something smug when Drox quickly intervened.

I am very sorry to have caused such alarm, Mischievous. I had put a concealing spell around us so we wouldn't be followed out of the plains. Aldwyn simply had too much energy moving to the magic around us, and when I abruptly released the spell, there was a bit of, uh, extra magic.

Mischievous blew a heavy cloud of harmless poison into Aldwyn's face. Sure, 'a bit'. Seemed more like an unnecessary embellishment on your part, Aldwyn.

Aldwyn's fiery red eyes twinkled. Maybe it was.

Andromeda knew she should have helped break them up, but she was having a hard time containing her laughter at the whole situation, despite she and Stephania being thrown around. Mischievous was about to lay into Aldwyn again, but Drox once again interrupted her.

Oh, for the Great Lord's sake, Mischievous, let it go. You've thrown Andromeda and Stephania around enough. You've probably scared poor Stephania out of her wits.

Stephania, who shocked Andromeda by still being able to hear the telepathic conversation, slapped Mischievous' scales and laughed. "Dat was fun! Again!"

All of them fell into laughter, and for a moment, the ill bearings of the night seemed to lift a little. The moment came too soon when Drox felt they needed to continue.

The riders settled back onto their dragons, and they all took to the skies once again, their steady pace speedily taking them to the shimmering, blue border.

As the dragons flew through the border, the Duvarharians felt the strange sensation of freezing cold water rushing over them before they broke through to the other side.

§

Suźefrusum, Duvarharia
Present Day

WHEN STEPHANIA'S EYES fluttered open, the suns had long set, the moons now casting their light on the land. For a moment, she lay perfectly still, feeling the rising and falling of Farren's chest behind her. If she was still enough, she could almost imagine she was still in the memory, as if time had stopped all those years ago and she was still a babe, her parents still alive, and all of them laughing on the moonlit hills of their homeland.

You will be happy like that too someday.

Stephania rolled over and propped her head against Farren's side. "Do you think so?"

I know so. And when you are, I will be there, and we will be happy together. Farren wrapped her wing and tail around Stephania, and in that moment, she thought maybe she could believe her dragon.

Her eyes grew heavy, and a yawn escaped her lips. Somewhere in the back of her mind, she was thankful the Shadow Armor was so light and flexible because she wasn't sure she would be able to take it off before she fell asleep.

I love you, Farren, she thought quietly as sleep darkened her mind.

I love you too, little one.

§

WITH THE MORNING SUNS rising behind them and the crisp wind across their skin, Stephania felt like nothing could stop them. They were in Duvarharia. After almost a year of hardships and traveling, they finally made it.

"I'm finally home, Farren. I am ... home."

Farren roared, breathing darkness around them to be lost in the wind. *We both are.*

They had woken to find that the Shadow Armor had miraculously cleaned itself of Eta blood and looked as flawless as it had the day they found it in its granite tomb. However, Stephania's hands and Farren's teeth and claws were rank with the foul blood, and they had immediately searched for a stream to wash in. Once the Eta's filth had washed down the clear waters, she finally felt worthy to arrive at the Dragon Palace, though Stephania wasn't sure she would as easily dispel the overwhelming anxiety that had settled in her gut.

They were flying low now, almost low enough for Stephania to reach down and touch the tops of the trees. She could see creatures running through the woods below, but she couldn't quite see what they were. Most of them looked unfamiliar and filled her with the urge to explore and adventure.

Farren beat her wings, carrying them higher as they crested over a rolling mountain.

Stephania. Look!

When Stephania raised her gaze, she felt her heart stop.

As the mountain rolled underneath and behind them, a valley stretched before them. Cradled in rolling, grassy plains, decorated with a river leading to a huge lake from mountain streams, and rising from the massive Stone Plateau was the Dragon Palace.

"Gods of all," she breathed, tears suddenly filling her eyes. She tried to brush them away, frustrated she couldn't see it clearly through her blurred eyes. "It's real." It had felt no more than a myth for so long.

All her nervousness melted away as she stared at the buildings glistening in the morning dew. "Even though—" She choked on emotion as the sunbeams hit the Dragon Palace's dome, causing brilliant rainbows of light to scatter across the rest of the palace and the Stone Plateau. "Even though I've been traveling to it, yearning for it, struggling to get to it, I never really believed or felt like it was real. Not until now. It's not a dream anymore. It's my reality."

And what a beautiful reality at that.

Stephania laughed and brushed her tears away with her still damp cloak. "Indeed."

In awe and mutual inexpressible joy and relief, they glided over the fruitful plains, watching as herds of animals grazed or startled from their morning sleep.

"I want to see what it looked like."

What do you mean?

"I want to see what it looked like before Thaddeus ruined it. I want to see what my homeland should look like and never forget it so when Thaddeus has paid in blood for the pain he has wrought, I will be able to rebuild it just as it was."

How will you do that?

"By using his memories."

Reckless and daring.

A sly smile spread on Stephania's face. "It's a good day for reckless and daring."

Farren rumbled in amusement. *That's my girl.*

Creator, Stephania thought privately, feeling the last bit of warmth from the Farloon pendant. *Help me to see. Help me to see what I am supposed to rebuild and protect. Help me fulfill my destiny.*

Together, they joined their minds, feeling the comfort and strength they gave each other. A surge of strength filled her as the Ancient Magic flowed in her and Farren.

Let us see the beauty that was lost in the face of evil.

When she opened her eyes, it was as if nothing had changed. The Dragon Palace was still only a few grand buildings on the bare Stone Plateau, but as she watched and looked closer, new buildings sprang to life, one on top of the other, each more beautiful and grand than the first, and all built out of magic.

Every kind of dragon flew in the sky. The morning was filled with the sounds of vibrant life, both dragons and their riders.

This was the land of dragons—what it was always meant to be: a place of harmony between riders and dragons and magic and Rasa. This was Duvarharia.

Stephania blinked, and the vision was gone, leaving the small, quiet, shimmering Dragon Palace as it remained now. It wasn't ugly to her. It was beautiful. It was a reminder. She wasn't just taking back what had been stolen from her in the last few years, she was taking back all that should have been hers for hundreds of years.

With clenched fists that changed from flesh to shadow with her dragon, she closed her eyes and focused on Thaddeus, thinking of his flashing purple eyes and of his dragon behind him. This time, though, as she stared into his seductive, misleading gaze, she was no longer afraid, and with Farren with her, neither was she alone.

"I am coming for you, Thaddeus," she hissed softly. "I'm coming for my revenge, and the revenge of Duvarharia."

MEMORIES THAT EMERGE

Eta Stronghold in High Northern Ventronovia

Present Day

S UFFOCATING WHITE AND BLACK magic fought against each other. Screaming split the heavy air. All of it swam in thick red.

Red blood choked his throat.

Red eyes pierced his soul.

He was standing in the clearing—the clearing with the dead Centaurs, the clearing where he would first see Stephania as a babe, when he'd almost taken her from Artigal's grasp.

The screaming stopped. Time stopped.

He looked down. The babe wasn't in his arms. He could no longer hear her young cries or her childish coos.

When he looked up, she was standing before him.

Their eyes met.

She was older. She had grown into her magic. It filled her being, her soul, her mind. It consumed her, and it raged. Dressed in frightening black armor, she was beautiful, terrible—she was everything a Duvarharian should be. Then in the darkness next to her, another shape took form—the shape of a dragon made of shadow.

"Magnificent," he whispered and reached out to touch her, but the earth blackened under him, consumed by shadows, shadows that poured from the dragon at her side.

Then they were standing on the Stone Plateau, but not the barren table it was now. No, this was only a small section of the Plateau, only just the landing pad, the one he had first stepped onto his first day at the Dragon Palace.

Terror filled his veins like ice water. How long had it been since he had seen this? Years. Hundreds of years. So long, he had forgotten what it had looked like.

Absently, he reached out to touch a magic-made marble building next to him, but his hand passed through it like a hallucination. The image wavered as if a mirage, and for a moment, he saw as the building burned and crumbled to the ground, thick purple acid pouring down its walls.

"No, no, no." He tried to step back, tried to run away as the city collapsed and burned around him. All beauty was destroyed. The dragons died by the hundreds along with their riders. Nothing stood in the wake of the acid. Any who resisted were cut down as their home crumbled around them.

"Make it stop." His head throbbed; his heart felt as if it were going to burst from his chest. Blood poured from his skin.

He lifted his eyes to hers—consuming red eyes drowning everything in their suffocating red magic.

"I am coming for you Thaddeus. I am coming for my revenge, and the revenge of Duvarharia."

"No—" He tried to shield himself, but her burning scythe lashed out, tearing into his flesh, spilling his blood.

"No!" Thaddeus sat up, his sheets sticking to him, wet with sweat. His heart throbbed against his ribs, and he quickly used a spell to slow it.

He hadn't seen the Dragon Palace that way for over eight hundred years. He hadn't even thought about anything from eight hundred years ago. That was back when ... He took several deep breaths, trying to block the memories from his mind. He couldn't. They had been stirred. Flashes of the life he had lived before becoming Duvarharia's traitor haunted him when he closed his eyes. He hadn't wanted to recall them. Who wanted to remember their own corruption? He had been so young ... and the memories were so painful.

But something had brought them back.

Slowly, his chuckles grew until he screamed with laughter and jumped from the bed. Abandoning his shirt, which was folded neatly by his bed, he instead wrapped a robe around his slim, muscular shoulders and quickly departed from his chambers.

From deep in the throne hall, he could hear Kyrell shifting in a nightmare.

Slamming the hall doors open with a blast of magic, he strode up to the head of Kyrell and kicked his jaw, yelling at him to wake up.

With an earthshattering roar, Kyrell jerked awaked, his purple eyes bloodshot. *Burning! Burning! Burning!* He roared, thrashing his tail, threatening to tear out the hall's support columns.

"Kyrell!" Thaddeus dodged a snap of his dragon's massive jaws. "Kyrell! It's not real! Nothing is burning! That was years ago!"

Kyrell dug his claws into the rock beneath him as if it were clay and not solid granite. *They want my soul! They want me to pay!*

Thaddeus shoved aside the horrific pain he sensed from his dragon, gathered his magic, and projected into his voice until it was as loud as his dragon's roar. "Kyrell! *Ofi!*"

Kyrell stilled, the fear melting from his eyes as it was replaced with burning anger and hatred. *Stephania.* He snarled, dragging his claws through the rock, the screech echoing in the dark cavern. *She did this. She found our memories.* Shike. *I shall burry her in every pain she has ever lived for a thousand years for this. It will be her soul the abyss screams for.*

Thaddeus placed his hand along his dragon's jaw and his head on his dragon's. "Perhaps someday she will. But with her help, we can make the whole world pay as we remake it. Do not let your thirst for revenge blind you. Then you will only be as weak as Stephania. Remember that."

Kyrell growled but didn't protest.

"Everyone sees us as the evil ones, do they not?" He stroked Kyrell's massive purple scales, admiring their shine and strength.

Fools, but yes.

Thaddeus nodded. "We are the villains. The greatest villains Ventronovia has seen for thousands of years. For us to succeed, for us to make Stephania a villain as well, we must remember what made us."

Kyrell whimpered—a sound Thaddeus rarely heard from the fearless beast. *I do not want to see it again. I do not want to live it again.*

A soft smile spread on Thaddeus's face as the magic hiding his scarred eye fell away. "I know. I know you don't, love. But we can't run from it any longer. We must learn from ourselves how we shall twist her young, pure mind. To do that, we have to go back. We have to remember. We have to remember before she realizes what we're doing to her."

We never sealed those memories. We left them pure and untouched. We have to get to them first and seal them before she can find them and use them against us.

Thaddeus nodded, a sly grin darkening his eyes. "Exactly. We have abandoned those memories for too long, left them in a place too far from us to protect. We have to learn from them and keep them safe. We have to go back together. But when we come back, we will be stronger, and she will never be able find our memories again."

Kyrell snarled and shifted his weight, determination lighting in his eyes. He didn't have to say anything for Thaddeus to know he was ready.

Closing his eyes, Thaddeus settled against Kyrell's head and let their minds merge together, so close they wouldn't lose each other through time.

With a few words from his language, Thaddeus released his magic and dove deep,

deep into the recesses of their minds, to the things they wanted to forget, to the pain, the blood, the burning, the hate. They dove through everything they kept locked up, everything they had learned, everything they had seen. Hundreds of locked, barricaded doors leading to hundreds of years of their lives flashed before them. Lifetimes upon lifetimes, hundreds of thousands of memories, all of them relived and sealed.

Finally, they reached a little door—a little golden door. The door of childhood, of a few years, just a wink in the eye of hundreds.

It was almost too small to fit through and didn't have a single lock, only a door-knob. It had never been relived; it was untouched, unblemished, and unprotected. It led to a world of laughter, light, friends, family, love, joy, and the beginning of all the suffering.

Fear flooded Thaddeus as he looked at it. He would have to relive it all and know every second of it again so he could hide every thought and every memory. Then Stephania would never be able to touch it or disturb it again. He would have to experi-ence it so deeply, he would forget it wasn't reality, he would forget it was only a memo-ry. He wouldn't be able to return to the present until everything had been remembered and sealed away, even if it drove him insane.

Taking a deep breath, he placed his hand on the doorknob. Warmth spread through him, and a beam of golden light spilled through as he cracked the door open. He could almost hear the laughter of children, almost smell a fresh dessert baking.

A small tear fell from his eye, but he brushed it away with a curse. He would have to lock his heart away, would have to push aside the nostalgia, the longing, the hopes for things that might have been but never were. He would have to be stronger than the pull of love.

Without a second hesitation, he thrust the door open and stepped inside—into a world he had long forgotten, a world with a family and a lover, a world of peace where anything was possible.

The golden light melted into sunlight filtering through trees.

He held up his hand against the blinding light. A pang of annoyance filled him when he realized he didn't have Shalnoa on his hand. This was a time before he had bonded with Kyrell, a time before he had even known magic.

A figure appeared in the forest ahead of him. He was running away, and with his now young legs, Thaddeus couldn't keep up.

"Come on, Thaddeus! Last one home is a wingless dragon!" the figure called back.

Thaddeus wanted to turn, to run far away from the figure who called after him, to change the past and avoid all the hurt it brought, but this was memory, not the present, and this had been a time when he had loved his brother.

He could do nothing when he instead shouted and tried to run faster. "Wait up!"

Then a voice rang out, a voice so heavenly, so sweet, so comforting, a voice he had wanted to keep hidden because he knew it had the power to convert him back to love. "Thaddeus! Thanatos! Dinner's ready! Your father will be home soon!"

Tears raced down his cheeks as he called to her, his heart melting. "Coming mother!" Then he was lost to the memory.

In a time before the hurt and the pain, before the betrayal and the revenge, he was young again, running as hard as he could after his brother, to his mother, and running back home, back to everything he had abandoned and betrayed.

Back to love.

§

Peace-Haven, Duvarharia
Year: Rumi 5310 Q.RJ.M (Qużech raż jin mraha– After our Lord)
Time Counted Since the Beginning of the Great Lord's Reign
100 Years After the Dragon Prophecy

BONUS
CONTENT

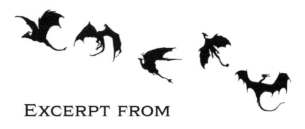

ZUEF GAK HANLUURASA

(TRANS-FALLS'S FUNERAL SONG)

VERSE 1:

Zazelauw, áda fezh kafew?
Da rañ kodaazh koleorau.
Damoñ kagmul ye da fu zeñi,
Moa, gi rañ far da rañ fom.

CHORUS:

Zuef gak Hanluurasa.
Ñádo da fu zufaf,
Kalu da rañ zukodaazh ala,
Zuef gak Hanluurasa.

VERSE 2:

Ofa zuzhágey fáku rok,
Zaiya da fu zufaf.
Sho zuzhágey gak Rasa,
Gak fezh rak zuef.

CHORUS:

Zuef gak Hanluurasa.
Ñádo da fu zufaf,
Kalu da rañ zukodaazh ala,
Zuef gak Hanluurasa.

VERSE 3:

Zhowá zháf ray-gaudak daefa.
Zi fezh zháf ray-ugey,
Zhowu fa zhowu raka,
Zhowu fa zhowu ala.

CHORUS:

Zuef gak Hanluurasa.
Ñádo da fu zufaf,
Kalu da rañ zukodaazh ala,
Zuef gak Hanluurasa.

LAST STANZA:

Fuyushu, Gumewa,
Fuyushu, fom,
Fuyushu kodaazh.
Rañ yá láw lem e.

VERSE 1 TRANSLATION:

Zazelauw, can you hear?
Our Warrior has fallen (fell).
Like wind in your leaves,
Listen as we mourn our brother.

CHORUS TRANSLATION:

Back to Hanluurasa.
Open your rooms,
Welcome our Warriors home,
Back to Hanluurasa.

VERSE 2 TRANSLATION:

Bright stars above us,
Prepare your rooms.
From stars to dust,
To you he returns.

VERSE 3 TRANSLATION:

Now he is gone.
With you he rests,

At last at peace,
At last a home.

Last Stanza Translation:

Farewell, dear friend,
Farewell, brother,
Farewell Warrior.
We will meet once again.

Ventronovia

As seen by Dalton during his travels. — Rumi
1,000 to 6,090 Q.R.J.m.

Legend
★ Cities I've Visited
Desert
Forest
○○○ Country Borders

N
NW NE
W E
SW SE
S

Duvarharia ?

Centaur Territory ?

?

Dragon Palace
Suzzfruzzium
Lota Forest
Sankyz
Hatching Grounds
Dragon Sea
Cavos Desert
Flate
Itans Falls
Hior
Zankie
Zankie Sea ★
New Fars ★
Abasha
Human Domain
Cora Plains
Cidra ★
Glass
Port Crystal ★ Port
Valleta ★ Valleta Isle
Odessa ★
Forgotten Sea
Castle

Pronunciation Guide

&

Glossary

PRONUNCIATION GUIDE

Aeron— ER-un

Artigal— AR-ti-gall

Braken—BRAKE-en

Duvarharia— DU-var-HAR-ee-uh

Elcore— EL-core

Eta— EE-tuh

Farloon— far-LOON

Filate— FI-late

Frawnden— FRAWN-den

Gauwu Zelauw– GAH-wu Ze-LOW ('low' rymes with 'wow')

Gauyuyáwa–GAH-yoo-YAY-wuh

Hanluurasa— han-loo-RA-sah

Igentis— aye-GEN-tis

Kijaqumok— KEE-jah-QUH-mock

Kyrell— KY-rul

Lavoisier— lah-VOI-si-er

New-Fars— new-fairs

Quinlan— QUIN-lan

Raythuz—

Sankyz— San-keez

Saorise— SAY-oh-rise

Sházuk– SHAY-zook

Shushequmok— SHU-sheh-QUH-mock

Sleshqumok— SLESH-quh-mock

Stephania— Steh-FAW-nia

Susahu— Soo-SA-hu

Synoliki— SY-no-li-ky

Syrus— SY-rus (like Cyrus)

Thaddeus— THAY-dee-us

Trans-Falls— trans-falls

Veltrix— VEL-trix

Ventronovia— VEN-troh-NOH-via

Wyerland— WHY-er-land

Wyrider— WHY-rider

Zelauwgugey— ze-LOW-gu-gay ('low' rhymes with 'wow')

GLOSSARY

CENTAUR/FAUN *(Sházuk)*

Da me koyuwuk– My lover

Elu– Idiot

Fazub– Beautiful

Fom– Brother

Fomdaazh– Brothers of war

Fuyushu– Be well (Farewell or goodbye)

Gauwu Zelauw– Forest of Tombs (Also known as the Tomb Forest)

Gauyuyáwa– Tree of our Fathers (or ancestors)

Guglo-Zshaif– Shadow Goddess

Gumewa– Best friend (Intimate Friend)

Kaño daiwzum kiñ zuñi. Daugmoul zuzháf faiwuzh shab da fu zueñi. Yayáfay daiw– Blessed birth, little tree. May the suns shine on your leaves forever (Day of birth celebration song)

Kaogouya– Fabulous, incredible, breath-taking

Kazozh kadu– Mythological beast

Koyuwuk– Love (Used as pet name)

Kuur– Everything

Leño-kofolu– Species of bird, hummingbird-like, native to Ravenwood that hibernates all winter and awakens at the start of spring

Leño-zhego– Species of wildflower native to Ravenwood

Luyuk-daiw– The Centaur spring festival of new birth

Me yuwuk fezh– I love you (to higher authority or with great respect)

Me yuwuk fu muyaa fáfád– You are everything to me.

Medozud– Excuse you (spoken in exclamation ex. hey! Oi!)

Muluk– Warm drink made from steeping herbs, beans, or roots

Ñáfagaræy– Blue, four-eyed, nocturnal rodents native to Ravenwood

Ñáwag-gazu– Species of intelligent mockingbird native to Ravenwood

Raffudafaf– Large feline predators native to Ravenwood

Shafalœ ray zi zoud, Farloon, lear, ray zi rok, Farloon– Emperor be with you, Farloon, and be with us, Farloon

Shábda– Bastard

Synoliki– Elite, honorary Centaur Warrior under the direct command of the Igentis whose dedication is to the protection of all Centaurs

Sházuk– Kin (Native word for Forest Children Kinds. Name of Kind, Name of Centaur Language)

Talfindo–A common exclamation which translates close to "Eureka!"

Uafañoshigo– Tart berry native to Ravenwood, often used to make wine

Uwarñoe– High Medic

Uyuy– Shut up

Wozauñouk– Bitch

Yayáfay daiw– Blessed birth (happy birthday)

Yeazh– Extremely vulgar Centaur expletive

Yu'jac– A popular, Centaur strategy game

Zháf wafu zhœk zi mazh– She will be safe with me

Zhego-leláfa– Blossomvine

Zuru– Damn

Zuru fuñofufe– Damn this

Zuru zhor– Damn him/her/it

Zelauw-fafu– Large bear-like predator native to Ravenwood

Zelauwgugey– Forest Essence. Lyre of the Fauns

DUVARHARIAN *(Ražugub)*

Dasejuba– World between worlds, the path between all realms, time, space, and matter

Hanluurasa– Sky realm

Kijaqumok– Corrupt Magic

Kvažajo– Helper of the prophecy

Mraha– Lord

Qužech raž jin mraha– After our Lord

Ražugub– Chosen People (Native word for Duvarharians, or Dragon Riders. Name of Kind)

Rumi– About/Around

Shalnoa– Permanent markings made from unique to each creature like fingerprints, similar to tattoos

Sheseknunosh– Guardian Wolf (Name of Kind)

Shushequmok– Pure Magic

Sleshqumok– Ancient Magic

Sukunhale– Curse lift

Suluj– Damn

Susokxoch– Commander

Susahu– The realm of darkness. Hell

Sużefrusum– Peaceful Forest

Vuldahesh(ab)– Energy crystal(s)

Yazkuza– Once the largest, most sophisticated dragon city in Ventronovia. Located in the Cavos Desert

Żeufax– Demon of Susahu. Warrior of Raythuz

WYRIDER *(Džoxsenä)*

Džoxsenä– People of New Birth (Natives of Wyerland. Name of Kind)

Ñekol– Bastard

Ofi– Wake up

Shike– Bitch

Siv– Damn

Tägäsutyä señekol– Worthless Bastard

ACKNOWLEDGEMENTS

T O KICK OFF THE acknowledgements where we now find ourselves, I would like to thank Elohim, my inspiration, my motivation, my provider, and my God. Ultimately these books are for Him, and they couldn't be possible without his provision, inspiration, and patience.

Of course, this wouldn't be an Effie Joe Stock acknowledgement section without mentioning my incredible parents. For the last year, I have been on night shift at my job which means I don't get home until very late. Without fail, I always have a million book and publishing related things to bombarded them with and somehow without fail, they do such a splendid job of tolerating me despite my keeping them up way past their bedtime. They're literal superheroes and while also being such incredible, supportive, inspirational role models, they still help make sure I get to book signings on times with all my necessary rubbish, along with remind me of basic necessities like eating and breathing which I tend to forget most of the time while I'm floating in the clouds. I don't know how I'll ever pay you guys back for what you do for me.

Great big, huge acknowledgement for H.A. Pruitt my editor. She always sees the best potential for my books and does whatever it takes to make them the best they can be. It's always such a pleasure working with her seeing as she knows exactly how to bring up huge suggestions that somehow don't feel like the end of the world, even if I am super sensitive when it comes to my book babies. I will never not rain praises down on her, especially now that she has her own little baby bean to contend with (love you little Eldun!) and still manages to be a top-notch editor and author. You're such an inspiration to me!

I have such an outstanding team of writer friends from whom I have stolen hours of their lives away with ranting about all the things I want to do with my series, explaining worldbuilding that will most likely never get used, whining about how hard writing and publishing is, and sharing writing memes, or book art. Just a few of these incredible people are Katie Marie, Cerynn McCain, Bethany Meyer, and Abby. The patience and support you guys have is over the moon. I love you all to death.

Huge thanks to GC Annison who has done a splendid job of proofreading Heir of Two Kingdoms and the re-publication of Child of the Dragon Prophecy. Your help couldn't come at a better time. You're a lifesaver!

Special thanks to Andy, my chef friend who's also lost an ungodly amount of his life listening to me talk on and on about my books and other ridiculous rants I randomly decided to dedicate my week to. I don't think I would've survived starvation had he not been there to feed me. Thanks for always giving me good food, something to laugh about, and making my days at work that much better.

I have to give a special shoutout to my brother Zach for always being so supportive and for staying up late just to be goofy with me, listen to me rant about books, or play video games. Thank you for being my best friend.

Special thanks to Bookish, an Indie Shop for Folks Who Read, and its owner Sarah who's done so much to build a supportive reading and writing community in our hometown. I'm so proud to have my books at Bookish and excited to see where this community takes us.

Docuprint once again was an integral part of getting this book published. From printing art prints, to bookmarks, to flyers, business cards, and copies of this book I sent to my editor, they always put out such beautiful, high-quality works and have done so much to help me cut costs of production which has let me do more than I could without them.

Last but never the least, thank you, reader, for loving my world so much, you came back for round two. I apologize for the death in this book, but I'm also kind of not sorry. I suppose that's just what being an author is all about. I hope you laughed a little, cried a little, and maybe let this book sit somewhere special in your heart and soul. I was thrilled to bring this second installment of the series to you, and I am just as excited for book three as I hope you are. You make everything worthwhile and possible.

May the suns smile upon your presence.

—Effie Joe Stock

About the author:

EFFIE JOE STOCK

Effie Joe Stock is the author of The Shadows of Light series, creator of the world Rasa, publisher of the Aphotic Love Anthology, and head of Dragon Bone Publishing. When she's not waitressing at a local café in Arkansas, you can usually find her in front of her computer, hacking away at her never-ending list of projects. She also enjoys playing music, studying psychology, theology, or philosophy, playing fantasy RPG video games, riding motorcycles, or hanging out with her farm animals. Her publishing journey only just beginning, she hopes to release her first children's book soon along with another Dragon Bone Publishing Anthology.

Instagram: @effie.joe.stock.author
Facebook: Effie Joe Stock Author
Website: www.effiejoestock.com

For more books like *Heir of Two Kingdoms,* visit:
www.dragonbonepublishing.com

COMING SOON:
BOOK THREE OF THE SHADOWS OF LIGHT

SON OF THE PROPHET

TWO BROTHERS.

ONE PROPHECY.

THE FALL OF DUVARHARIA BEGINS.

Follow Effie Joe Stock and Dragon Bone Publishing online for updates on the third installment of The Shadows of Light Series.

Ingram Content Group UK Ltd.
Milton Keynes UK
UKHW041658250423
420401UK00034B/247/J